"When I came ba ~~to myself~~ that I wouldn't lean on **to myself that I wouldn't lean on anyone else. I would stand on my own two feet."**

"Nothing wrong with that," Daniel said, "except that it's not the Amish way. We help one another, as you know very well. You wouldn't hesitate to help me if I needed it."

Rebecca's arguments were being cut from under her, and she struggled to find a solution they both could accept.

Daniel crossed the distance between them and stood smiling at her. "What's wrong? Can't find anything else to say?" His voice teased her gently.

"Suppose we do this. You let me help. Surely there are things I can do. And you don't turn down other jobs to work for me."

"Deal," Daniel said. He grinned at her. "See, that wasn't so hard, was it?"

She'd tell him it was, but he wouldn't understand. None of them would, because they didn't know what her life had been like with James.

She had to walk away from the past. She had to accept Daniel's help to do so. He held the door open to her new life, but she had to pass through, and she would.

A lifetime spent in rural Pennsylvania and her Pennsylvania Dutch heritage led **Marta Perry** to write about the Plain People, who add so much richness to her home state. Marta has seen nearly sixty of her books published, with over six million books in print. She and her husband live in a centuries-old farmhouse in a central-Pennsylvania valley. When she's not writing, she's reading, traveling, baking or enjoying her six beautiful grandchildren.

Carrie Lighte lives in Massachusetts, where her neighbors include several Mennonite farming families. She loves traveling and first learned about Amish culture when she visited Lancaster County, Pennsylvania, as a young girl. When she isn't writing or reading, she enjoys baking bread, playing word games and hiking, but her all-time favorite activity is bodyboarding with her loved ones when the surf's up at Coast Guard Beach on Cape Cod.

MARTA PERRY

The Wedding Quilt Bride

&

CARRIE LIGHTE

Anna's Forgotten Fiancé

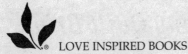

LOVE INSPIRED BOOKS

ISBN-13: 978-1-335-47010-2

The Wedding Quilt Bride and Anna's Forgotten Fiancé

Copyright © 2019 by Harlequin Books S.A.

The publisher acknowledges the copyright holders of the individual works as follows:

The Wedding Quilt Bride
Copyright © 2018 by Martha Johnson

Anna's Forgotten Fiancé
Copyright © 2018 by Carrie Lighte

www.Harlequin.com

Printed in U.S.A.

CONTENTS

THE WEDDING QUILT BRIDE

Marta Perry

This story is dedicated to my husband, Brian, with much love.

Trust in the Lord with all thine heart; and lean not unto thine own understanding. In all thy ways acknowledge him, and he shall direct thy paths.

—*Proverbs* 3:5–6

Chapter One

Two days after Rebecca Mast's return to her childhood home in Lost Creek, she walked down the lane of the family farm toward her future. Her black widow's dress contrasted starkly with the pale greens and bright yellows of a sunny spring day in the Pennsylvania countryside. Her son, six-year-old Elijah, trudged next to her, holding tight to her hand rather than skipping and hopping ahead down the lane like one of his cousins would.

It was early yet, she assured herself. Surely soon he'd forget the darkness of the past few years and be like any other Amish child his age. That was the heartfelt prayer of her heart for her son. As for her…well, the return to normal would take longer, if it ever happened.

But at least she was home, with her family around her, and today she would take the first step toward a new life for her son and herself. That alone was something to make her heart thankful.

The two-story frame house came into view ahead of them, standing at the point where the farm lane met the country road. When her mammi had written that old Mr. Evans had gone to live with his daughter and put the house up for sale, she'd known exactly what she wanted to do with the money she'd receive for selling the farm she and James had owned in Ohio.

The down payment James's brother, John, had given her had been enough to cover the cost of the house. John's continuing monthly payments would pay to remodel the old place into a secure, peaceful home for her and Elijah, and the quilt shop she'd have in the downstairs rooms would support them. That was the extent of her dreams for the future, and it was enough.

Daniel King stood, waiting by the back porch, leaning against one of the posts as if he could wait there all day for her, if need be. As they came closer, her stomach tightened as she searched the tall, broad figure for a glimpse of the neighbor boy who'd been her childhood playmate. She didn't find him, nor did she see the gangly teenager who'd told her all about his crushes on the girls in their rumspringa group.

Daniel had grown into a strong, sturdy-looking man. It was her own uncertainty that made her long to find something in him that was familiar. The rich, glossy brown of his hair was a bit darker now, and the fact that he didn't have the traditional Amish beard allowed her to see his stubborn jaw.

He'd always had that stubbornness. His golden-brown eyes had a glint of kindness that she felt sure reflected his kind heart, and his lips curled in a familiar grin. Her tension evaporated, and she smiled.

"Rebecca!" He came forward now to greet them, taking her hands in both of his for a momentary squeeze. "It's wonderful gut to see you again." His face sobered. "I'm sorry for your loss."

She nodded. She had a stock of reasonable comments to use when someone commented on her widowhood, but they didn't seem appropriate for Daniel, who'd known her so well.

Daniel didn't seem to notice. He'd focused on Lige, who was hiding behind her skirt, and he squatted down to eye level.

"You must be Elijah. I've heard about you from your grossmammi. She told me you just turned six. Is that right?"

Lige, clutching the fold of Rebecca's skirt, gave the smallest of nods. Fortunately, Daniel didn't seem to expect more.

"I'm Daniel," he said. "I live over there." He pointed across the field to the neighboring farm. "When your mammi and I were your age, we used to play together every day."

Still no response. She tried to think of something to say to pull his attention from Lige, but Daniel was already rising, his smile intact. "Ach, it's hard to get to know a lot of new folks at once, ain't so?"

"Yah, it is," she said, grateful for his understanding. "Sam tells me that your carpentry business is a wonderful success these days." Sam, Rebecca's older brother, had been best friends with Daniel's older brother, Caleb. It had seemed natural for her and Daniel to pair up, as well.

"Ach, I wouldn't say great, but it's doing okay. It doesn't give me much time to help Caleb with the dairy farm, but I do what I can. And he's got Onkel Zeb and young Thomas Stoltz to work with him, too."

"I'm sure he needs it, running such a big dairy operation." Daad had told her how Caleb had increased his herd until it was one of the larger ones in the valley. "I'd be most happy if you have time to take on this job for me."

She glanced at the house, trying to picture it the way it was in her dreams. With Daniel's help, that dream could be a reality.

"Let's go in and have a look at what you want done," Daniel suggested. He held out a hand as she reached the three steps up to the back porch. "Mind the treads, now. There's a loose board there I'll fix right off."

She nodded, turning to help Lige up to the porch. "It's a little bit run-down now," she told him. "But Daniel will help us turn it into a gut home for us."

Lige darted a cautious sideways glance at Daniel, but he still didn't speak. She tried to suppress a sigh. If she'd realized earlier the harm James's behavior was doing to Elijah…but what choice did she have? James had been his father, and there was no getting away from that.

The back door opened into the kitchen, and they stepped inside.

"The cabinets need some repair," Daniel said, swinging a door open and closed. "But they're good solid wood—none of those thin layers they use sometimes now."

Rebecca was busy picturing the kitchen with the cabinets freshly painted white and seedlings growing in pots on the wide, sunny windowsills. "The gas range is perfect," she said. "But I'll have to replace the electric refrigerator with a gas one."

"I don't know much about the electrics, but there's a man I worked with on a few Englisch houses who does that kind of work. He could take out all the electrics for you."

"Wonderful gut." Surely the fact that things were falling into place meant that her plans were in accord with the gut Lord's will. "Our table will fit in this space, won't it, Lige?"

He nodded but hadn't yet let go of her skirt.

"When do your things arrive?" Daniel pulled himself out from behind the refrigerator, a cobweb clinging to his straw hat.

"In a few days." Smiling, she reached up to lift the cobweb away, inadvertently brushing his cheek. She withdrew her hand quickly, trying to ignore the way it tingled from the brief contact. "The family will store everything for us until we can move in here."

The back of the house held the kitchen, a pantry and two smaller rooms. One would be their living room and the other a storeroom or workroom. Swinging the door open, Rebecca stepped into the room at the front of the house. Her breath caught.

The room extended across the whole front of the house, and sunshine poured in through the windows to lie across the wide-plank floors. The back wall would be perfect for shelves, and she could have a display area of quilts on one side and stocks of fabrics and notions on the other.

"You look happy," Daniel said, his brown eyes warm. "Is this going to be your living room?"

"No." She swung in a slow circle, taking it all in. "This will be what I've been dreaming of. This will be my quilt shop."

She knew her happiness had to be shining in her face. And when she looked at Daniel, she saw her anticipation reflected in his eyes, crinkling as they shared her feeling. There, at last, was her old friend.

Daniel stood still for a moment, transfixed by the sheer joy on Rebecca's face. He couldn't help but share it. Obviously, this quilt shop was important to her, but why? So far as he knew, she hadn't had a shop in the past.

He didn't doubt that she was a wonderful quilter. Rebecca's sister-in-law, Leah, had shown off the baby quilts Rebecca had made and sent for each of her young ones. Rebecca's mother had a gift for designing patterns, and she must have inherited it.

"Can you make this ready first?" She swung toward him, all eagerness. "I need to open the shop as soon as possible."

Need? That was a funny way of putting it. He'd heard that Rebecca sold the farm she and her husband had owned in Ohio. He'd think that would have given her enough that she wouldn't have to rush into business for herself.

Still, it might be that she felt she had to have something to occupy her mind and heart. Her husband had died less than six months ago, and grieving was hard—he knew that as well as anyone.

"I have plenty of time for your job," he said. And if he didn't, he'd make time to accommodate her, especially if it kept her looking the way she did now.

He couldn't deny that he'd been shocked when he first saw her, so thin and pale, with an almost-haunted look darkening the blue of her eyes. Rebecca had always been as bright as a ray of sunshine with her golden hair, rosy cheeks and the sparkle in her clear blue eyes. He nearly hadn't recognized his friend, and that had set a distance between them.

Already she was withdrawing into herself again, her face becoming strained. But at least now he'd seen the old Rebecca, if just for a moment.

"So, you'll tell me what you want done in here, and I'll do the measurements and work out a plan." He glanced toward the front door that led directly into the room. "We'd best check out the front entrance as well, if your customers are going to come in that way."

Rebecca nodded, looking around the room as if seeing it looking very different. "I'll want tables to hold bolts of fabric on this side," she said, gesturing. "And then some open space where I can have a bed to show how a quilt will look and a counter near the door for checking out."

Daniel made notes on his pad that no one would ever understand but him. "What about the walls?"

"They'll need to have several different-sized racks to hold quilts, crib quilts, wall hangings and table runners." She unfolded a sheet of paper, and they both bent their heads over it. "See, here are the kinds and sizes I need and where I thought maybe they could go."

She'd printed it all up for him with sketches. "So neat," he said. "Just like your schoolwork used to be." He glanced at the boy, standing quiet and solemn next to his mammi. Did he ever laugh? "When we were in school together, your mammi had the best printing of anyone in the school. Whenever a sign had to be made, we'd get her to do it."

Lige nodded, as if he didn't doubt it, but still he didn't smile or speak. Well, he'd get a smile out of the boy even if he had to stand on his head to do it.

He turned to Rebecca. It wouldn't be bad to get another smile from her, as well. "Do you want to make decisions about the rest of the house today, or just focus on the shop for now?"

"Just the shop today," she said quickly. "It's more important than getting moved in right away."

"If I know your mamm and daad, they'd be happy to have you stay with them in the grossdaadi house for always, ain't so?"

Her lips curved a bit, but her blue eyes were still dark and serious. "That's what they say, but we shouldn't impose on them."

Now all he could do was stare at her shuttered face. "Impose? Since when is it imposing to have you home again? Your folks have been so happy since they knew you were coming that they're acting ten years younger. Sam and Leah and their young ones have been marking the days off on a calendar because they're so eager. You're not imposing."

Rebecca stiffened, seeming to put some distance between them. "It's better that I stand on my own feet. I'm not a girl any longer." She looked as if she might want to add that it wasn't his business.

No, it wasn't. And she certain sure wasn't the girl he remembered. His Rebecca, so open and trusting, would never have doubted her welcome. Grief alone didn't seem enough to account for the changes in her. Had there been some other problem, something he didn't know about in her time away or in her marriage?

He'd best mind his tongue and keep his thoughts on business, he told himself. He was the last person to know anything about marriage, and that was the way he wanted it. Or if not wanted, he corrected himself honestly, at least the way it had to be.

"I guess we should get busy measuring for all these things, so I'll know what I'm buying when I go to the mill." Pulling out his steel measure, he focused on the boy. "Mind helping me by holding one end of this, Lige?"

The boy hesitated for a moment, studying him as if looking at the question from all angles. Then he nodded, taking a few steps toward Daniel, who couldn't help feeling a little spurt of triumph.

Carefully, not wanting to spook Lige, Daniel held out an end of the tape. "If you'll hold this end right here on the corner, I'll measure the whole wall. Then we can see how many racks we'll be able to put up."

Rebecca, who had taken a step forward as if to interfere, stopped and nodded at her son. "That's right. You can help with getting our shop ready."

Daniel measured, checking a second time before writing the figures down in his notebook. His gaze slid toward Lige again. It wondered him how the boy came to be so quiet and solemn. He certain sure wasn't like his mammi had been when she was young. Could be he was still having trouble adjusting to his daadi's dying, he supposed.

"Okay, gut. Now, you let the end go, and I'll show you how it pops back to me. Ready?" Lige put his end on the floor and took a cautious step away, as if not sure what to expect.

"Now." Daniel pushed the button, and the steel measure came zooming back, rerolling itself. "There. Did you ever use one of these before?"

Lige shook his head and hurried over to Daniel without hesitation. "Can we do it some more?"

"Sure thing. Let's measure how wide the window is, because we wouldn't want a quilt to cover it, would we?"

Without being told, Lige pulled the end out so that they could measure the width of the windowsill. When they'd finished, Daniel held out the tape measure to the boy. "Do you want to roll it up this time?"

Lige came eagerly, his shyness of Daniel forgotten. Daniel put his large hand over the boy's small one, showing him the button. "Now, push."

Lige did, and the tape measure performed its vanishing trick again. He looked up at Daniel, and the sight Daniel had been looking for appeared. It was tentative and a little stiff, but it was a genuine smile.

"Did you see, Mammi? I did it all by myself."

"Yah, I saw." Some of the color had come back into Rebecca's pale cheeks, and she met Daniel's gaze with one that was so filled with fierce maternal love that it startled him. "Denke, Daniel."

He shrugged. "It's nothing."

Somehow that simple incident seemed to dissolve much of the strangeness between them. They worked their way around the room, measuring and talking about what she wanted in the shop, until finally Daniel squatted down and put his notebook on his knee to figure out an estimate.

He stole a covert glance at Rebecca, who was saying something to her son. He hadn't missed the slight apprehension in her face when he'd talked about the supplies they'd need. Was the money a problem?

It shouldn't be, not if she'd just sold a thriving farm, but how did he know? He'd do the work gladly for nothing in the name of their old friendship, but he knew Rebecca wouldn't hear of it. That steely independence of hers was new, and he wasn't sure how to handle it.

Finally he had an approximate materials cost worked out. He stood, catching that trace of apprehension in her eyes.

"How much will it cost to do what I want?"

In answer, he held out the notebook page. "That's an approximate guess as to the cost of the materials. Unless the mill has upped its prices for a board foot," he said. "Just joking," he added quickly, not sure she was in the mood for humor.

"But that's not including your work," she said. "I should give you the whole amount…"

"Not up front," he said, interrupting her. "You pay for the initial materials, so I can start. Then you can pay my labor when the job is finished." Seeing the objection rising in her face, he added firmly, "That's how it's always done, Rebecca. If that outlay for materials is more than you can manage at one time, we can always break the job into smaller units."

"No, no, that's okay." She opened a small bag and began counting out the money into his hand.

He didn't miss the fact that there was very little left in the bag when she was done, and it troubled him. But when she looked up at him with the smile he remembered, it chased other thoughts away.

"I'll go to the mill first thing tomorrow, and then I can start work in the afternoon." He glanced at Lige. "You'll bring my helper back, ain't so?"

The boy's smile rewarded him. "Can I, Mammi?" He tugged on her apron.

"Yah, as long as you listen to Daniel and do just as he says."

"I will. I promise."

"Sehr gut," Daniel said. "Tomorrow then." Shouldering his tool bag, he headed out.

Rebecca and her son followed him to the porch and stood there, watching him go. As he cut across the field toward home, he took a quick look back and again was assailed by that sense of something he didn't understand. The two of them looked oddly lonely, standing there on the porch of that decrepit house.

Rebecca was home, but he sensed she had brought some troubles with her. As for him…well, he didn't have answers. He just had a lot of questions.

Supper in Leah's kitchen was a lively time, with the long table surrounded by cheerful faces—Leah, Sam, their children, her mamm and daad, and now her and

Lige. Lige, sitting next to her, had been engrossed in looking from one to another during the meal, his small face gradually relaxing as he realized all the chatter was normal and accepted.

It had been normal when she was growing up, as well. It never would have occurred to any of her siblings that their contributions wouldn't be welcome. But life with James, especially after his accident, had been another story entirely.

At least Lige was beginning to lose the tension that told her so clearly he was waiting for an explosion. He actually laughed at something one of his cousins said, and she breathed a silent prayer of thanks.

With the last crumb of apple crisp consumed and the silent prayer at the end of the meal said, the boys began getting up from the table to do their chores. Sam, who'd been saying something to Daad, glanced up as they headed out the door.

"Joshua." He raised his voice to call his eldest back.

And Lige cringed, wincing back in his chair, his face strained and fearful.

No one moved. Rebecca could hear their indrawn breaths, could see the comprehension dawning on the faces of the adults. Rebecca bent over Lige, speaking softly.

"Hush now. It's all right. Onkel Sam just wants to tell Joshua something."

Leah seemed to get a grip on herself first. "Yah, he wants to tell Joshua to take Lige out with him and let him help. Ain't so, Sam?"

"For sure," Sam said.

Kindhearted Joshua came and squatted down by Lige's seat. "Want to komm help me feed the buggy horses? You can measure the oats, yah?" He spoke softly, holding out his hand to Lige.

Lige looked up at her, as if asking for guidance.

"You'll like that," she said, flashing a glance of thanks to her nephew. "Go along with Joshua and the other boys now."

Lige slid off his chair, probably glad to get out of the kitchen. He took Joshua's hand, and they went off together.

At a look from Leah, Sam and Daad went out, too.

"You girls make a start on the dishes now," she said. "I want to show your aunt Rebecca some of my quilts."

"Yah, you go on," Mamm added. "I'll look after things here."

Mamm was obviously trying hard to erase the shock from her face. Maybe she needed time as much as Rebecca did just now.

Leah ushered Rebecca into the sewing room and opened a trunk to reveal the quilts inside. "You don't have to look at these now," she said. "I just thought you might want a reason to be by yourself for a minute."

"Denke," she murmured, feeling the blood mounting to her cheeks. "It must wonder you why…"

Leah touched her hand. "You don't need to explain anything. But when you do want to talk, I'm here and ready to listen." Leah put her arms around her for a quick, strong embrace. "I'm your sister now, ain't so?" she murmured.

It was a struggle to hold back tears. Maybe it would

be a relief to talk, but not now, not when the emotions were still raw, even after months.

"I'll check on the girls," Leah said, seeming to understand. "You take as long as you want." She slipped out quickly.

Alone, Rebecca slid down on the floor next to the trunk, her hand resting on the Sunshine and Shadows quilt that lay on top. Sunshine and Shadows, she repeated silently. There had been mostly shadows for so long. She longed to believe the sunshine was coming back to their lives.

As for talking about it…how could she tell anyone? Mamm and Daadi hadn't wanted her to marry James so quickly, to go so far away with someone they barely knew. But she'd been captivated by James's charm and his lively, daring personality.

She didn't know then about the quick temper that seemed to be a part of him. It had flared rarely in the first years of their marriage, and each time it did, she'd made excuses for him.

And then had come the accident. James's daring had led him a little too far, determined to climb to the top of the windmill to repair it, unwilling to wait for someone to come help him. And annoyed with her when she tried to stop him.

So she'd stood, watching, wondering what made him so eager to take risks. Then… Her memory winced away from the image of him falling, falling…

Everyone, even the doctors, said he was fortunate to be alive. That his injuries would heal, and he'd be himself again.

But he wasn't. After the injury to his head, James seemed to lose all control. His rages were terrifying. If she dared try to calm him, he'd turn on her. Lige had become a little mouse, always afraid, trying so hard not to do anything to bring on the anger. And she hadn't been much better.

Until the day he'd almost struck Lige with his fist. Then she had found the courage to fight back. When his family seemed unable to help, she'd dared to go to the bishop.

Bishop Paul had been everything that was kind. He'd insisted that James go for treatment, making all the arrangements himself. For a time, the treatment helped. The rages became a thing of the past, and it had seemed a blessing to be able to hope again.

Then it had all fallen apart. James had lost his temper with a half-trained horse, determined to force it to obey. The animal had reared, striking out, and in a moment, James was gone.

Rebecca pressed her fingers to her eyes, willing the images away. James was gone, but the damage he'd done lived on after him, it seemed.

No. She forced herself to stand, to wipe the tears from her face. That was the past. It was over and done with. She and Lige had a new start here, and they would make the best of it. But she would never again make the mistake of trusting a man with their lives.

Chapter Two

When Daniel turned into the lane and drew the horse to a halt at the back door of Rebecca's new house, the troubling thoughts about her returned in full force. Onkel Zeb, sitting next to him on the wagon seat, started to get down and then looked at him.

"Was ist letz? Is something wrong?"

"No, no." He secured the lines and scolded himself for daydreaming. "It's nothing. I can unload myself, if you have something else to do." He'd appreciated the company on the trip to the hardware store and lumberyard for the materials he'd need for Rebecca's job, but he didn't want to keep his uncle working all day.

Onkel Zeb, as lean and tough as he always was, hopped down nimbly. "Nothing as interesting as this," he said, heading for the back of the wagon. "I want to see what you and Rebecca are going to do to this place. Mason Evans let it go those last few years, that's certain sure."

"He didn't seem to have much energy for it after his

wife passed, did he? But we'll get it fixed up fine." He slid a couple of two-by-fours off the wagon and balanced them on his shoulder. "If you'll get the door, I'll take the bigger pieces in. Rebecca said she'd leave it unlocked for us."

Nodding, Zeb stepped up to the porch and swung the door open. "I was hoping Rebecca would be here when we got back. I haven't seen her yet. How is she looking?"

Daniel moved past him to start a stack of the lumber inside while he considered how to answer that question. "All right, I guess," he muttered.

His uncle propped the door open before turning to give him a probing look. "Seems to me you're not so sure about that, ain't so?"

He should have known there was no getting away with evasions where Onkel Zeb was concerned. He'd been like a father to all three boys, especially after their mother left and their own daad just seemed to fall apart at the loss.

Don't go down that road, he told himself. *This is about Rebecca, not you.*

"Truth to tell, I'm not sure." He pulled another couple of posts out and hesitated. "She's so thin and pale I almost didn't know her. It's not so long since her husband died, so I guess that's natural, but…"

"But what?" Onkel Zeb leaned against the buggy, ready to listen as always.

Daniel frowned absently at the boards. "Seemed like her whole personality has changed from what she was. She was all tense and keyed up, and the boy… He seemed almost scared."

"Of you?"

Daniel shrugged. "Maybe. Or maybe of everything. Just didn't seem right." He eyed his uncle thoughtfully. "You and Josiah Fisher are pretty close. He say anything to you about Rebecca?"

Onkel Zeb hesitated so long Daniel thought he wasn't going to answer. Finally he spoke. "Josiah and Ida have been worried about Rebecca for a while now, her being so far away that they couldn't help as much as they wanted when she had all this trouble."

That wasn't really an answer, and they both knew it. "So why did they start worrying to begin with?"

"What do you remember about when Rebecca got married?" Onkel Zeb answered the question with a question.

Daniel cast his mind back. "I remember she went away that summer—out to Ohio to help a cousin of hers who was moving. She stayed quite a time, and then we heard she'd met someone and was going to marry him." He rubbed the back of his neck. "Funny. We'd always been such gut friends, but she didn't write to me about him at all."

"That was the summer you were chasing after Betty Ann Stoltzfus," Onkel Zeb put in. "Maybe you were too busy to pay much attention to what Rebecca was up to."

Daniel had a moment's gratitude for the fact that he'd broken it off with Betty Ann when he did. They wouldn't have suited anyway, and it was not long afterward that his little brother, Aaron, took off for the Englisch world, tearing up his heart.

Onkel Zeb made a sound that expressed his general disapproval of Betty Ann. "Anyway, Josiah and Ida didn't want her to get married so quick, especially to someone they hardly knew, who lived so far away. But she was determined, so they accepted the best they could."

"Rebecca being the only daughter, I guess it's natural they'd want her to stay close." He picked up another armload of planks. It had begun to sound as if Onkel Zeb was doing a good bit of talking around the subject, maybe not wanting to repeat anything Josiah said about his daughter in confidence.

"Yah." Zeb slid out some of the smaller pieces and a box of nails and followed him to the house. "Natural, like you say. They always thought maybe you and Rebecca would make a match of it, as close as you were."

That startled him. He'd never imagined anyone could be thinking that. "We were friends, that's all," he said quickly. "Neither of us ever thought of anything else."

There was a skeptical expression on Onkel Zeb's lean, lined face, but he didn't argue. Instead, he turned back toward the door. "I'll bring the rest of the small stuff in."

He'd need the sawhorses and his tools, but for a moment, Daniel stood where he was, processing that idea. All he could think now was that it had been fortunate he and Rebecca hadn't been more than friends. He wouldn't have wanted to let her down.

It wouldn't have to be that way. The small voice of hope spoke in his head, but he squashed it. Maybe it didn't have to be, but it was. After all, it had happened before. When Mamm left…

He'd been the closest to their mother of the three boys. So close he'd always thought he even knew what she was thinking. But he hadn't. She must have been unhappy for a long time to run away to the Englisch world and leave them behind. And he'd never seen it. If he had, he might have made a difference.

Logic might say that a ten-year-old couldn't influence what a grown woman did, but somehow Daniel didn't believe in logic when he thought about running upstairs to Mammi's bedroom to tell her about the good grade he'd got on his spelling test, only to discover that the room was empty of everything that belonged to her. Everything except the letter that lay on the pillow, addressed to Daad. Nothing for him, her favorite.

There had been times when he'd nearly run off to try to find her. And worse times when he didn't know whether it was worth it to go on living. Daad, shattered himself, hadn't been any help. They'd never have got through it without Onkel Zeb.

And then, just when Daniel had begun thinking that losing Mamm that way hadn't tainted him forever, Aaron had left. Little Aaron, the baby brother he'd always looked after, taken care of, defended. He'd told himself taking care of Aaron was his job—maybe he'd even taken pride in how close they were.

But he'd failed Aaron, too. He hadn't known that the forces of rebellion were growing so fiercely in Aaron that he'd pack up and leave. Like Mammi, except that Aaron hadn't even left a note.

Daniel had understood then. He couldn't be trusted not to fail the people he loved. So he certain sure couldn't take the risk of letting a wife and children depend on him.

Onkel Zeb clattered back in with another armload. "You want to help me with the sawhorses?"

"Yah, sorry. I'll get them." Daniel shook off his mood. No sense reliving the past. This was now, and there was work to be done.

But when they pulled the last few things off the wagon, it was Onkel Zeb who paused, his thoughts clearly far away.

"You know something more about Rebecca," Daniel said, knowing it was so. He waited. Was he going to hear what it was?

"I can't tell you all of it," his uncle said, continuing the conversation that was on both their minds. "Parts I don't know, and parts Josiah most likely wouldn't want repeated." His solemn gaze met Daniel's. "But I do know that Rebecca has seen more trouble than most folks twice her age. And right now, what she needs most is a friend." He paused, and Daniel thought for a moment that he was praying. "You can be that friend she needs, Daniel. If you will."

"Yah, for sure." He didn't need to know any details to promise that, but his heart was chilled, nonetheless. "I've always been Rebecca's friend, and I always will be."

By the next day, Rebecca had begun to feel that, aside from a few bumps in the road, Lige was doing better each day. And if he was, that meant she could be happier, as well. She and Leah were doing the breakfast dishes together after the younger children had left for school, and Leah's sunny kitchen seemed to hold the echo of the kinder's chatter and laughter.

"Come September, your Lige will be joining the other scholars on their way to school," Leah commented. "He'll like it, I'm sure. Teacher Esther is wonderful gut with the kinder."

"It's hard to believe my little one is that old. I'll miss him." Rebecca's smile was tinged with a little regret. In a normal Amish family, Lige would have been joined by a couple of younger siblings by now.

"You won't miss him as much as you think." Leah's tone was practical. "By then, your quilt shop will be thriving, and you'll have plenty to keep you busy."

"I hope so." Rebecca breathed a silent prayer.

"I was thinking about the shop," Leah said. "How would it be if I asked some of the other women to bring in quilts on consignment? I know several fine quilters who would like a regular store to sell their goods, instead of relying on mud sales and the like."

Rebecca blinked. It seemed Leah was thinking ahead even more than she had. "That's a grand idea, for sure. I'd love it. Do you really think they would? I've been away so long that they probably feel they hardly know me by now."

"Ach, that doesn't make a bit of difference. Folks remember you. You'd be doing a gut thing for them. And then there are some women like Martha Miller. She doesn't get around much now, but she'd love to do more sewing for folks. You could get her some work by letting customers know that she does hand quilting."

"Yah, I could." Excitement began to bubble. "I could have a bulletin board, maybe, where I could post things like that for customers to see. Denke, Leah. You…" Her throat tightened. "I'm sehr glad Sam had enough sense to marry you. I couldn't ask for a better sister."

Leah clasped Rebecca's hand with her soapy one. "Ach, it's nothing. We're wonderful glad you've come home."

The back screen door closed softly, and Rebecca turned to smile at her son. It had to be Lige, because any of the others would have let the door bang.

"Mammi, can't we go yet? Daniel is counting on me to help."

"In a few minutes, Lige. I'll be out as soon as I'm ready."

He looked disappointed, but he didn't argue. Sometimes she almost wished he would. Instead, he slipped quietly out again.

A silence fell between her and Leah, making her wonder if Leah was thinking the same thing.

"That Daniel," Leah said. "The kinder are all crazy about him. It's a shame he doesn't have a passel of little ones of his own by this time."

"I've thought that, too," Rebecca admitted. "I kept expecting to hear he'd been married, but it didn't happen."

"No." Leah shook her head. "I hope he wasn't listening to that foolish talk that went around after Caleb's first wife left him. Folks saying that history was repeating itself, and that the King men couldn't find happiness in marriage."

"That's not just foolish, it's downright wrong. Just because of their mother, and then Caleb's wife…" Rebecca was too indignant to find the right words. "Anyway, with Caleb happily married now, surely that shows they were wrong."

"Yah, you'd think so, wouldn't you?" Leah dumped the dishwater and dried her hands. "But it's hard to know what Daniel is thinking sometimes. He took it awful hard when Aaron jumped the fence."

"He would," Rebecca said, her heart aching for Daniel's little brother, out there in the Englisch world somewhere. "Daniel always felt responsible for Aaron, especially after their mother left. He…"

Whatever she might have said was lost in the noise as a large truck came down the lane. Leah craned her neck to see out the window.

"It's the moving truck," she exclaimed. "Your things are here!"

Together they hurried outside, and Rebecca felt her heart beat a little faster. Her belongings—the furniture she'd wanted to bring, Lige's toys, her collection of quilts—they were finally here. Now she could start to feel at home.

When they reached the rear of the truck, the driver was opening the door and letting down the ramp. Almost before he'd finished, the rest of the family had arrived—her mother and father from the grossdaadi house, Sam and the older boys from the barn and the eldest girl from the chicken coop. She even spotted Daniel hastening down the lane toward them.

Mamm put her arm around Rebecca's waist. "Now you'll start to feel settled, ain't so? You're really home." Her eyes clouded over with tears, making Rebecca wonder how much Mamm had been worrying about her.

"I'll need to sort things…" she began, and Daad interrupted before she could head into the van.

"All you have to do is say where each thing goes as we bring it off. Someone will carry it there." Daad's voice didn't allow an argument.

But still she felt vaguely guilty, drawing them all away from the things they'd been doing.

"Furniture in our basement for now," Leah said. "It's all cleaned and ready. Just pick out what you want in the grossdaadi house. You won't want anything to go in your new place yet, ain't so?"

Rebecca shook her head. "It would just be in Daniel's way."

"That's right," Daniel said, tapping Lige's straw hat. "We men need to have room to work, ain't so, Lige?"

Her son nodded, his smile chasing any tension from his face.

The next few minutes were a scramble, as things started coming out of the van so fast that it was all she could do to keep up. Lige showed a tendency to want to open boxes to see what was inside, until Daniel showed him how they were marked.

Sam marshaled his young ones into a line. He picked up each item in turn, checked with Rebecca what she wanted done with it and then gave it to one of the kinder to hurry off with. Daniel came out balancing several large boxes and headed for her.

"My quilts!" Her heart seemed to lurch with excitement. There they were, all packed up, the things that would allow her to support herself and her son.

Daniel's grin said he understood, at least a little, what this meant to her. "Should we toss these in the chicken coop?" he said, teasing her the way he'd teased the girl she used to be.

"Into my sewing room," Leah said firmly. "I don't need the space just now, and they'll be handy for you there."

Joshua, Leah's eldest, seized the boxes from Daniel. "I've got it, Mammi." He strode toward the back door, Lige scurrying ahead to hold the door open for him.

They'd left Rebecca nothing to do but watch as the van emptied and Leah produced coffee and crullers for the driver. "I hate to put everyone to so much trouble," Rebecca murmured. "I shouldn't…"

"Ach, don't be foolish." Daniel gave her a friendly nudge. "Look at them. See how happy they are? It would be wrong to take away their joy in doing something for you."

All of her arguments about standing on her own feet and taking care of herself and her son seemed useless against Daniel's perceptive comment. She glanced at him. He was right, and his smile said he knew it.

Maybe she should argue, but she was too happy just now to care.

Chapter Three

Rebecca walked into the shop the next morning to hear the sound of a saw. Obviously, Daniel was already at work, and that gave a boost to her already-optimistic frame of mind. She hadn't realized how much it would mean to have her own belongings here with her and Lige.

Maybe every mother had these strong instincts to create a nest for her family. With their own things surrounding them, she and Lige could feel at home. And how much better it would be when this place was finished. She looked around the kitchen, seeing it not as it was, but as it would be, with the gas appliances, the pie cabinet she'd inherited from her grandmother, her dishes on the shelves and pots of herbs growing on the windowsills.

But there was work to be done, and dreaming wouldn't get it accomplished. Rebecca headed into the front room.

Daniel looked up from the sawhorses with a warm smile. "You're here, but where is my helper?"

"He'll be along in a minute. He's been begging to be allowed to bring the mail from the box, so I said he could today." She could see him now through the front window, skirting along the edge of the road toward the box.

"Lige will be fine," Daniel said, apparently reading her thoughts. "He's growing a little every day. Like you did at that age." He grinned. "That was when you started wearing your braids pinned up under your kapp, remember?"

"I remember thinking it was a gut idea, because then you and the other boys couldn't pull my braids," she said with mock tartness. "You were a bunch of little monsters at that age."

"Were not," he said quickly, just as he would have all those years ago. Then he turned back to his work, measuring a board he'd laid out. "Funny thing," he said.

"What's funny?" She bent to pick up the pencil he'd dropped just as he reached for it.

"I'm just thinking that with gut friends, you can pick up just where you left off, no matter how many years it's been in between."

Rebecca was speechless for a moment. Sometimes it seemed she was looking at Daniel with new eyes, seeing things she hadn't noticed before. "Yah, that's true, I think. When did you get so wise? You didn't show any signs of that when you were little."

"What kid does?" he asked. "It takes a bit of living to find some qualities in yourself. And maybe some folks never find them."

Could he be right? If so, then she might have had the

seeds within her the whole time to bear the burden of James's injury and the effect it had had on their marriage. It wasn't anything she'd ever expected.

She shook herself out of her momentary absorption, not wanting Daniel to think he'd made her sorrowful. "I certain sure never showed much sign of wisdom myself. Like the time I tried to prove that I could climb higher in the willow tree than Sam, and got stuck there. And all Sam could do was stand there and say he'd told me not to do it."

"Sam was the one who wasn't smart," he said, grinning. "We knew how strong-willed you were. Telling you not to was the surest way to get you to do it."

"I can still remember how small he was when I looked down at him from above. It would have been a triumph if I hadn't outsmarted myself by going too far to get down."

"You did get back to the ground, though. And you managed it without falling on your head." He marked the board with care.

"Only because you talked me through it, climbing up to me and showing me exactly where to put my hands and feet so I could get safely down."

"That was my strength," he said, his grin smug. "I could talk you into things. Did I ever tell you I was scared stiff you were going to fall and Onkel Zeb would blame me? I had a lot to lose if I didn't get you down."

"I should have known there was something in it for you. Just like the day you talked me into sneaking one of Mammi's cherry pies. I'll never forget how you looked when Mammi caught us with cherry all over our faces."

They were both laughing at the image when Lige came in, the mail clutched against his chest with both hands. He looked from one to the other, his eyes wide. Most likely, he didn't expect grown-ups to behave that way.

Rebecca swallowed her laughter. "Ach, Lige must think we're crazy." She smiled at her son. "It's a funny story about something we did when we were little. I'll tell you about it later," she said. "You can go ahead and run the mail to Aunt Leah, and then come back and help."

"There is one for you, Mammi." Lige extracted it carefully from the bunch. "I'm delivering it first. Now I'll take the rest, and then I'll come back and help Daniel, yah?"

She had to smile at his solemn attitude toward his new responsibilities. "Sehr gut. Denke, Lige."

With a quick smile for Daniel, he hurried off with the mail, his shoulders squared with responsibility.

When he'd gone, Rebecca turned her attention to the envelope in her hand. It was from John, James's brother, so it must mean that he'd sent the amount of his first monthly payment. Relief washed through her. Thank the good Lord it was here. She'd been running low on cash, and she wouldn't feel right asking her parents for help. They'd done enough for her already.

Ripping it open, she looked for the pale blue check that was sure to be enclosed. But it wasn't. There was just a letter from John, brief and to the point. He couldn't pay her now. No excuses, no reason. Just a short statement.

She stared at the page, her body rigid while her mind raced. What was she going to do? How could John do this to them?

Daniel, watching her, saw the color drain from Rebecca's face as she stared at the letter she'd received. His stomach clenched into a knot. She looked worse now than she had on the first day after she'd come back.

He dropped the tape measure. "Rebecca, was ist letz? Is it bad news you got?"

As if suddenly aware of his presence, Rebecca spun away from him, turning her back. Shutting him out. He had a brief flare of totally inappropriate anger.

Her hand, still holding the paper, was trembling, and sympathy washed away the anger in an instant.

"I can see it's bad news." He kept his voice gentle. "Won't you tell me what it is?"

"It's…it's nothing," she said, but her voice and her body gave the lie to the words.

"It's something," he said, propelled by the need to help close the distance between them, but not quite daring to touch her. "Trouble shared is trouble halved, ain't so?"

Rebecca turned to face him. For an instant, he thought she'd burst out with it, but then he saw that her lips were folded tightly together.

His jaw tightened in response as he took in that refusal. "Remember what I was saying about friendship never changing? It looks as if I was wrong, yah?"

For an instant, she glared at him, and he thought she was going to walk out. Then she sucked in a deep breath. "I... I'm sorry if it seemed that way. This affects you, so I guess you'll have to know anyway."

He wanted to reach out and touch her, but instinct told him it wouldn't be welcome. Instead, he waited, sure now that she'd tell him, whatever it was.

Rebecca gave a sidelong look at the letter, almost as if she needed to avoid it. "The note is from my brother-in-law, John. The one who is buying the farm in Ohio from me."

She seemed to have difficulty getting the words out, and he tried to help her along. "Yah, I know. You mentioned that you'd used his down payment to buy this house."

"I did. And his monthly payments were intended to cover the costs of remodeling and getting my business started. The first one should have come by today." The hand holding the letter trembled again before she saw and seemed to force it to steady. "But he says he can't make the payment this month. He'll send it later."

Daniel frowned, trying to make sense of it. "But... does he say why?"

"No. No explanation. But then, John's not one to explain himself." She rubbed her arms, almost as if she was cold.

He was beginning to form a picture in his mind of the brother-in-law, and it wasn't a very complimentary one. What was the man about, to fail in his duty to his dead brother's widow and child?

"Did you have a written contract with him?" It wasn't his business, but he hoped now that she was talking, she'd keep going.

"Yah. I maybe wouldn't have thought of it, but Daad was there at the time, and he insisted a written contract was proper. I think James's family was a little offended by his attitude, but Daadi wouldn't let it go." She might have seen his surprise that she'd even let her father handle the negotiations, because she made a small movement with her hands, as if pushing something away. "Daad and Mammi gave us money to help buy the farm to begin with, so it only seemed right for him to have a say in what happened."

Thank the good Lord that Josiah had such a business-like attitude toward it. Folks didn't usually get the better of a hardheaded Pennsylvania Dutchman easily.

"Seems like it was smart you listened to him. At least you have it in writing." He hesitated and then said what was in his mind. "Maybe you should remind John of that contract he signed." He was probably going too far, but Rebecca seemed to need bolstering up where her in-laws were concerned.

He wasn't sure she took in what he said, but finally she shook her head. "No. There's nothing I can do. I don't want to start a hassle with James's family."

"Seems to me John is the one who started it."

She just looked at him, and he knew what she was thinking. Finally he shrugged, his palms up. "Yah, all right, I know. It's not my business. I just don't like to see him take advantage of you."

"I'll handle it." Rebecca retreated into herself. Clearly, she had nothing else to say.

He had a few more arguments he'd like to express, but he restrained himself. Turning back to his work, he had to start again with the measurements, having totally forgotten what he'd come up with. It didn't help that he watched Rebecca covertly all the time he was doing it.

She might not be talking, but her body language was clear enough, with that stiff back and tight face. Why was she so determined to handle everything on her own? It wasn't natural in an Amish family, where helping each other was considered God's plan, and that sort of independence drew very near to pride, about the worst thing for an Amish person. But if he said *that* to her, she'd probably never speak to him again.

Finally Rebecca seemed to pull herself out of her worried thoughts. She moved toward him, so he looked up from his work, and his heart twisted. Rebecca looked as if she were picking up a burden that was too heavy for her.

"You'll have to stop work." She blurted the words out and then sucked in a breath. "I'm sorry. This isn't fair to you, but…"

"We talked about this." His voice might be calm, but his thoughts were spinning rapidly, trying to come up with a way to change her mind. "You have already paid for the materials, and you don't owe me anything until the job is finished. Surely by then your brother-in-law will have paid what he owes you."

Rebecca's hands clung to each other until the knuckles were white. "That would not be fair. I can't accept your work when I don't know when or if I'll have the money to pay you."

"Ach, Rebecca, I would do the work for nothing for an old friend. The money doesn't matter."

"It matters to me," she snapped. "I won't accept charity."

"Charity?" He straightened, his own temper finally flaring, although he wasn't sure whom he was angrier at, Rebecca or that brother-in-law of hers. "Who's talking about charity? The Fishers and the Kings have been doing things for each other for a hundred years. Seems to me your time away from here has made you forget a lot of things. It's made you prideful."

He shouldn't have said that, but he could be just as determined as she could. Rebecca might have been able to push him into a mud puddle once and not have him shove back, but she wasn't going to push him around now.

Rebecca's face had tightened into a mask that bore little resemblance to the girl she'd been. "Prideful or not, this is my decision. And my house. Please put down your tools and stop. Now."

"And when Lige comes back ready to help me? How are you going to explain that to him?"

"Lige is my son. I'll tell him what he needs to hear."

Daniel stared at her for a long minute, trying to make sense of her attitude. He couldn't.

"If you reject my help, Rebecca, you are rejecting our friendship."

He knew he shouldn't have said it the instant the words were out, but it was too late. Rebecca took a step away from him. She crossed her arms.

"Please go, Daniel."

There was nothing for it but to pick up his tool bag

and leave, berating himself the whole time for handling her so badly. And yet, what else could he have done?

The trouble was that he kept thinking he knew her, and maybe he was wrong. Maybe he didn't know Rebecca at all.

Rebecca didn't look forward to telling Lige that the project was off and he wouldn't be working with Daniel for now. She waited until they were walking back to the farmhouse, thinking it would be easier away from the place he connected with Daniel. It would hurt, but she assumed he'd take it as silently as he did everything else.

But in this, she was wrong. To her astonishment, her quiet little son started to argue with her. Lige, who never spoke up for himself, was actually disagreeing.

"But, Mammi, you can't do that. Daniel wants to work on the shop with me. You can't!" He tugged on her apron, as if that would make her see reason.

She stared at him, trying to gather her wits. "I'm sorry, Lige. I know you're disappointed, but that's how it is right now. When I can afford to pay Daniel, he'll come back. You'll see."

"But I want to work with him now." It was almost a wail. "Won't he come back now if you ask him?"

Rebecca bit her tongue to keep from saying something that would put the blame on Daniel. She couldn't be that unjust to him, even if it were easier on her. "Daniel is willing, but it wouldn't be fair. Carpentry is how he makes his living. He has to be free to accept jobs for people who can pay."

Lige's lower lip came out in a decided pout. "He'd rather work for us. I know. We make him smile."

"Daniel is friendly. He smiles at everyone."

"Not like that. Please, Mammi. Please, please, please."

Her father came around the house in time to hear Lige's words, and his face crinkled. "It sounds as if this boy really wants something. What is it, Lige? A cookie?"

Lige shook his head. "Mammi says Daniel can't work for us anymore because we don't have money to pay him. But Daniel would, wouldn't he? You tell her, Grossdaadi."

Her father's gaze studied her face, and she longed to turn away but couldn't. Daadi touched Lige's cheek lightly. "I'll tell you what. You go and help Grossmammi with the cookies she's making, and I'll talk to your mamm."

"Snickerdoodles?" Lige asked hopefully. At his grandfather's nod, he darted off, leaving Rebecca to face what would probably be a lecture.

"Let's sit down on the steps."

She wanted to argue, but she couldn't. Daadi led her to the porch steps and waited while she took a seat.

"I know what you're going to say, but I don't want you to pay Daniel. I need to do this by myself. Don't you see?"

"No. I don't." Her father didn't scold. Instead, he seemed disappointed. "Did John Mast not send the money he owes?"

She shook her head. "He wrote and said he couldn't

right now. The point is that I can't let Daniel keep working if I can't pay him. It wouldn't be right."

"What did Daniel say to that?"

"He offered to keep on working." She evaded his steady gaze.

"How did you convince him to stop, then?"

She'd never doubted her father's wisdom. He could go straight to the heart of what his children weren't saying to him. "I… I said something that hurt his feelings. But it wasn't all my fault. He was the one who…"

Rebecca let that trail off, because it was starting to sound like her explanations of the quarrels she'd had with her brothers when they were small.

Daadi gave her a disappointed look. "He is your friend, Rebecca. I shouldn't have to tell you what you must do when you've hurt a friend."

She wanted to argue, but she couldn't think of a thing to say. Daniel shouldn't have pushed her into that position. But she certain sure should have found a way of dealing with him that didn't involve causing him pain.

Sitting there debating with herself wasn't getting her anywhere. She didn't have to let Daniel continue to work for her, but she did have to ask his forgiveness for her anger. She pushed herself to her feet.

"You will find Daniel in his workshop," Daadi said calmly. "I saw him go in a few minutes ago."

Rebecca headed reluctantly toward the King place. She should have hired someone she didn't know to do the work for her, she thought rebelliously. Then she wouldn't have been put in this position.

Daniel's shop was a square-frame building situated

at a little distance from the barns. Daad had told her that he'd built up quite a business for himself in the past couple of years, even doing some kitchen remodeling for a few Englisch families. Daniel was a hard worker who deserved success, and that wouldn't come if he spent his time on work he wasn't paid to do.

The sound of a saw reached her even before she opened the shop door. A motorized saw, as it turned out. Daniel had apparently found it worthwhile to install a generator for his business, much as dairy farmers like Sam and Daniel's brother had to do for their milking equipment.

She stopped inside the door, trying to find the right words while she waited. Daniel must have seen the movement when she entered, but he finished what he was cutting before he stopped the saw and stood, pulling off the safety goggles he wore.

"Rebecca. I didn't think I'd see you over here." His voice didn't express anything—not anger, not apology, nothing.

Unable to find the right words, she looked around the shop. "This is a fine setup you have here. Daad says that you've been doing a lot of remodeling jobs. It looks as if you could handle most anything with all this equipment."

"I don't think you came here to admire my shop, Rebecca."

He wasn't going to make it easier for her, in other words. Rebellion flared. He was the one who'd equated their friendship with letting him work without pay, after all.

Unfortunately, she also knew full well that if she hadn't been totally caught up in her problems, she could have handled it better, without the need for this breach between them.

She sucked in a deep breath, knowing what she had to say. "I came to tell you I'm sorry. Getting that news was a blow, but I had no right to take it out on you. Please forgive me."

His eyes were very dark in the muted light of the shop, and she couldn't tell what he was thinking. If she'd broken their friendship entirely... Panic flashed like lightning, showing her what that would mean.

"I'll forgive you on one condition." Now his smile was back, and her heart lifted. "You let me keep working on the shop."

"Maybe I didn't explain it very well." She struggled to hold on to her emotions. "When I came back, I made a promise to myself that I wouldn't lean on anyone else." The way she'd leaned on James. "I would stand on my own two feet."

"Nothing wrong with that," he said, "except that it's not the Amish way. We help one another, as you know very well. You wouldn't hesitate to help me if I needed it. Like Sam, over here every day to help do our milking, as well as his own, when Caleb was laid up. That's what we do."

Her arguments were being cut from under her, and she struggled to find a solution they both could accept.

Daniel crossed the distance between them and stood, smiling at her. "What's wrong? Can't find anything else to say?" His voice teased her gently.

"Nothing that wouldn't necessitate another apology," she said tartly. "Suppose we do this. You let me help. Surely there are things I can do. And you don't turn down other jobs to work for me."

"Deal," Daniel said. He grinned at her. "See, that wasn't so hard, was it?"

She'd tell him it was, but he wouldn't understand. None of them would, because they didn't know what her life had been like with James.

It hadn't been his fault, she told herself once again. *The injury was to blame.*

Whether that was true or not, she had to walk away from the past. She had to accept Daniel's help to do so. He held the door open to her new life, but she had to pass through, and she would.

Chapter Four

By Saturday, Daniel had begun to feel confident that Rebecca wasn't going to back out of their agreement. She showed up every day, determined to help, sometimes with Lige, sometimes by herself.

He had to admit, the work went more quickly with another pair of hands, even unskilled ones. He took a step back, assessing the shelf he'd just installed on the back wall. Rebecca wouldn't come today, he felt sure, since the Fisher family was hosting worship the next day. Everyone would be busy cleaning and cooking to prepare for the church's once-a-year visit.

So it was with considerable surprise that he heard the back door open and the now-familiar sound of Rebecca's footsteps. He lifted his eyebrows in a question when she appeared in the doorway.

"I thought you'd be completely occupied with getting ready for worship. Don't tell me your mamm let you out of the kitchen."

Her smile came more easily now than it had at first.

"I tried to help, but what with Mamm and Leah and the girls, we were starting to get in each other's way. Mamm thought I'd be more use here."

"What about my little helper?" He picked up the next shelf, and she hurried to grasp the end of it.

"Lige went off with Daad and Jacob to pick up some extra peanut butter for the sandwich spread. You know my mother—she never thinks there's going to be enough food."

He nodded. It was a common enough description of most Amish mothers. "Gut that Lige is getting to know his cousin Jacob. Having a cousin just a little older will ease the path for him, especially when he starts school in the fall."

"Yah." Rebecca paused, and he suspected she was comparing steady, calm Jacob with her small son, always so shy and fearful. Then she brightened, as if she'd shoved the unwelcome thoughts away. "Lige needs to have friends to count on, like Sam and I counted on you and Caleb."

"Counted on us to keep you out of mischief, that's for sure." Keeping the talk on happy subjects was best, he thought.

"I remember it the other way around." She glanced up at him, her eyes alight, and she looked suddenly years younger. "Caleb was usually the instigator, but I remember one time when you dared Sam to jump from the hayloft. Remember? He landed right on the bags of fertilizer and broke them open. He was covered with the stuff."

He grinned. "Mostly, I remember how Sam looked,

and when you started sloshing water over him, that made the mess even worse."

"And your Onkel Zeb walked in on us. He just stood there, looking at us until you felt guilty enough to confess."

"That's Onkel Zeb, all right. I've never figured out how he does it." Daniel's smile lingered as he thought of all the times his uncle's solemn look was sufficient to get the truth.

"He put us all to work cleaning up the mess, and I didn't have anything to do with it." She gave him a playful swat and he ducked, laughing.

Laughing…and then the laughter was arrested suddenly, by his awareness of her. Rebecca, so close to him, wasn't any longer just his friend and playmate. She was a woman who seemed to draw him closer with just her smile.

Daniel drew in a shaky breath and hoped his expression hadn't changed. Ach, that wasn't right. He shouldn't be looking at Rebecca that way, or feeling the longing to find out if her lips were really as soft as they looked.

Fortunately, Rebecca didn't seem to have noticed anything, maybe because her thoughts had turned back to her son. He could read it so clearly in her expression.

"Sometimes I wish…" She let that trail off, shaking her head.

"What do you wish, Rebecca?" He kept his voice calm, interested, just the voice of a friend.

"I guess I'd like to see Lige get into a little mischief once in a while. It's natural enough for a boy that age."

He wasn't sure what to say. There were too many things he didn't understand. "It's natural enough that he's still grieving his daadi. He was probably fine before that shock, ain't so?"

For a moment, he thought she wasn't going to respond, but then she shook her head. "James had an earlier serious accident, nearly two years before he passed. I'm afraid Lige doesn't remember much of his daadi from before that."

"I didn't realize." Maybe this was what Onkel Zeb had meant when he'd spoken of the hardships she'd gone through. His heart swelled with sympathy. "I'm sorry for your trouble."

"It's…"

Her words were cut off by the front door banging open. Barry Carter, the electrician Daniel sometimes worked with, made his usual noisy entrance. "Hey, there you are!" he shouted.

Any reply vanished from Daniel's mind when he saw Rebecca's face—saw her flinch, saw her eyes fill with panic for just a brief instant before she regained control.

His wits started working again, and he stepped in front of Rebecca, screening her from view. "Barry, it's gut to see you, but do you have to come in like a tornado? You made me forget what I was measuring." His only thought was to keep talking until Rebecca had a chance to collect herself. "You got my message, yah?"

"Yep, finally listened to my answering machine. I've been that busy this spring—you wouldn't believe. You looking to move in here?" He was looking around as he spoke. Big and burly, with hands like a couple of hams, Barry had a heart as soft as butter, Daniel knew. He'd be horrified to think he'd frightened Rebecca.

Frightened. But why?

He pushed the question aside. He'd have to consider that later. "It's going to be a quilt shop for our neighbor, Rebecca Mast." A quick glance told him that Rebecca looked as if nothing ever disturbed her. "Rebecca, this is Barry Carter. He's the man to take out the electrics for you."

Recognizing the meaning of her warning glance, he added quickly, "It'll take him some time to fit you in, but this way he can check out what needs done."

"Nice to meet you, Mrs. Mast." Barry touched the bill of his ball cap in greeting. "I ought to be able to get to it by the end of the month, if there's no hurry."

"No, none at all." Rebecca sounded perfectly calm and in control. "I'm sure Daniel can show you what needs done better than I can."

Daniel nodded. "Come through to the kitchen. That's the main thing."

He led the way, with Barry following, and started explaining what needed to be done. Barry had converted Englisch houses to Amish ones before, so it didn't take all that much explaining on his part.

Which was good, because his thoughts were in a crazy jumble. Rebecca's reaction, Lige's timid behavior… He could think of one obvious reason for that, and he found his hands curling into fists at the thought.

Horrified, he forced them to relax. James Mast was dead now, and whatever his faults, he'd face a more competent judge of his life than Daniel King.

A passage came into his mind and clung there. It looked to him as if the wrong men did, as well as the good, live on after them.

* * *

Rebecca dunked her mop into the pail of sudsy water. Cleaning the cellar floor in preparation for worship tomorrow was just the sort of hard work she needed to keep her mind off what had happened.

She'd given herself away to Daniel. She'd never intended it, but the man bursting in had taken her completely by surprise. Pretending Daniel hadn't noticed was useless. He'd shielded her, stepping between her and the man and engaging him in conversation to give her time to recover.

Keeping the truth about her marriage private was becoming increasingly difficult. And Daniel seemed to know her too well.

Impulsively, she turned to Leah, working alongside her, with a question.

"Do you think we can know everything about another person if we've been close enough?"

Leah seemed to take the query seriously, as if they'd been talking about that very thing. "I guess it depends on exactly the kind of thing you're talking about. I mean, I'd say I know how Sam will react in every situation, but sometimes he proves me wrong."

She smiled, halting the rhythmic movement of the mop. "I remember one time he had an offer from a different dairy to buy our milk at a much better price. We'd been a bit short after putting in the new milk tank, and I thought he'd jump at the offer."

"He didn't?" Milk tanks and dairies didn't seem the point, but since she'd asked the question, she'd best show an interest in the answer.

"He turned them down flat. When I asked him why, he said he'd heard talk the man was trying to undercut the other dairy and had even spread rumors about the quality of their milk. Well, when I heard that, I understood. See, I might not have known that he'd turn it down, but I do know that Sam would never be associated with anyone who wasn't straight about their business. So I guess I did know him, after all."

"I'd say so." Rebecca smiled. "And that's Sam, all right. His honesty is a part of him."

"Yah, that's what I meant. If you know somebody well, you know what they're like right at the core. Who they are inside doesn't change." She shot a bright glance at Rebecca. "Even if we haven't seen them in a long time."

"I didn't…" She started to protest, and then she had to laugh at Leah's expression. "All right, I did mean Daniel."

"That's what I figured." Leah's voice was demure, but her eyes were full of mischief. "He hasn't changed all that much, ain't so?"

"That's what wonders me. He looks so different that, at first, I wasn't sure. But the more I'm around him, the more I see flashes of the boy he was. When we talk about different things that happened, it's as if no time at all has gone by."

Leah leaned on her mop, prepared to talk. "So, what was he like as a boy? I didn't know him all that well, you know."

Rebecca considered, trying to isolate the qualities Daniel had shown even as a boy. "He was steady, you know? Always calm, not easily excited. Your little Jacob reminds me of him in a way."

She nodded. "A man of few words, that's our Jacob. He's a gut peacemaker."

"Yah, exactly. That's what Daniel was, too. And…" She sought the word. "Steadfast, I guess. You could count on him to stick by you."

"Sounds to me as if Daniel isn't much different as an adult than he was as a boy, then. A gut person to have as your friend."

Leah's eyes were twinkling again, and Rebecca knew she had to protest.

"A friend, that's all. I don't want any other kind of relationship."

"You feel that now, with your husband so recently gone. But maybe, in a time, it will be different." Leah clasped her hand warmly. "You'll see. No one thought Caleb could love again after he lost his wife, but now he's happy as can be with Jessie."

"It's different for me. I…just know that marriage is not for me." Leah didn't know, couldn't know, all the reasons why it was impossible.

Leah shrugged, turning back to her mopping. "Seems to me that's Daniel's attitude, too. He acts like he's sworn off marriage. So maybe the two of you make a gut pair."

Leah didn't understand. She couldn't. But if it was true that Daniel didn't intend ever to marry, in a way, that made things easier for her. Their friendship would be less of a risk that way, and she wouldn't have to worry about either of them being hurt.

* * *

It was the first worship Sunday since she'd returned, and Rebecca was filled with happiness. Being part of worship with those who had known her since childhood made her feel that she was really home. It was a joyful step in her new life.

The usual greetings and chatter were still going on when they lined up to go in—women on one side, men on the other. Rebecca took her place in the group of young married women with Leah. Small girls were joining their mothers, while the boys joined the line of men.

Lige, though, was clinging to her skirt. She detached his hands gently. "It's time for you to go in with Grossdaadi. Remember, we talked about it."

She'd tried to rehearse everything that would happen today to make Lige feel at ease...not that it was very different from worship out in Ohio. But no matter how prepared he was, Lige seemed to be intimidated by the large group of people, all of whom knew each other.

"Komm, now." She clasped his hand to keep him from grabbing onto her again. "Do you want me to walk over with you?"

"Ach, Lige doesn't need that." Daniel squatted down beside Lige and held out his hand. "What about it? We'll go find your grossdaadi, yah?"

Lige hesitated. Then the slightest smile crossed his face, and he put his small hand into Daniel's large one. They walked off together, and Rebecca found her throat was tight.

"I never saw a bachelor so gut with the kinder as Daniel is." The woman ahead of her smiled, turning to face her. "I'm Jessie, Caleb's wife. I've been wanting to meet you, but I thought you might be too busy getting settled to want to bother with company."

"We're never too busy for you, Jessie," Leah said. "You'll come and have coffee one day this week, ain't so?"

"Do, please," Rebecca added. She'd been wanting to meet the woman Caleb had so suddenly married. It didn't take more than a glance to persuade her that they were happy. Jessie's face glowed, and Caleb's little girl pressed close against her.

"I'd like that." Jessie touched the little girl's cheek. "Becky, this is our new neighbor. She has the same name as you. Rebecca."

The child gave her a friendly stare. "Does anyone ever call you Becky?"

"No, I've always been Rebecca. A gut thing, ain't so? Or they might be mixing us up."

Becky grinned at the idea, and Rebecca smiled back.

The smile lingered on her face when she looked up, but in an instant, it vanished. One of the older women was staring at her. Lydia Schultz, it was. Rebecca remembered her, but she couldn't imagine why she was staring... It was almost as if she wanted to say something to her.

The line started moving just then, so there was no opportunity. She'd make a point of greeting Lydia afterward, she told herself.

From the moment the song leader sang the first notes of the hymn, Rebecca was giving herself up to the joy and beauty of worshipping together, hearing much-loved voices raised in praise.

When he began to speak, Bishop Thomas Braun seemed to be talking directly to her. The Scripture was the story of the Good Shepherd. Bishop Thomas spoke lovingly of Jesus carrying the lost sheep home on his shoulders, and she felt tears sting her eyes. There had been so many times in the past few years when she'd felt lost and alone. And yet she always had the sense that God was there, holding her up.

It wasn't until one of the other ministers rose to speak that she sent a cautious glance across the room. Lige was leaning against Daadi, with his grandfather's arm around him protectively. Someone else was watching Lige, she realized. Daniel, a few benches away, let his gaze rest on her son.

Daniel's expression caught at her heart. It almost seemed he was looking at something he longed for but could never have.

The service moved on, carrying her with it, reassuring her with the familiarity of long usage. When it ended she sat still for another moment, holding on to the peace.

But there were things to be done, and she should be helping. She rose and headed for the kitchen.

In all the flurry of getting the meal on after the service ended, Rebecca didn't have time to talk with anyone except to exchange a few hurried words with Leah. She noted with amusement that even Leah's usual calm had deserted her at that point.

Lunch after worship was basically the same each time, and of course no one would admit to taking pride in how well they did it. But that didn't stop every woman from wanting lunch to go perfectly when she was in charge. Leah had everyone scurrying to follow orders, and Rebecca caught more than one long-suffering expression from her kinder.

Finally everyone had been fed, and the kitchen crew could sit down at the tables to finish. Since the weather had turned warm, the tables had been set up outside, and it was pleasant to relax and enjoy the scene.

Some of the older girls had organized a baseball game with a plastic bat and ball for the younger children, while the babies had been rounded up on blankets in the care of older siblings and cousins. Rebecca scanned the group for Lige, spotting him at last on the fringe of the game. He wasn't alone—Daniel was with him. He was patiently showing her son how to swing at the ball.

Rebecca started toward them, torn between her desire not to bother Daniel and her delight in her son's obvious happiness. She was still a few paces away when Lige finally connected with the ball. He was so startled he dropped the bat. Then a huge grin split his face.

"Gut job," Daniel said. "I think you're ready to play with the others. Just remember to keep looking at the ball, whether you're catching or hitting it."

"I will. Denke, Daniel." Lige hesitated, and for an instant she thought he was going to hug Daniel. He stopped short of that, and Daniel, maybe understanding more than she'd thought, patted him lightly on the shoulder.

When Lige had run off to join the other children, Rebecca approached Daniel. "Denke, from me, too, Daniel. That was wonderful kind of you."

"Ach, it was my pleasure. He's a gut lad, that boy of

yours." He hesitated, and she could see a question in his eyes. "I wondered... Well, Lige said that his daadi didn't ever play ball with him."

"No." The sadness gripped her for what might have been. "James was never himself again after that first accident. I don't think Lige even remembers him from before that."

"James had brothers, yah? A father?"

She nodded. It was so hard to explain what it had been like to someone who hadn't lived through it. "His daad tried, but it seemed to upset James to see someone else interfering. People just started leaving us alone rather than upset him."

"I'm sorry. It sounds like it was hard on everyone."

"That's so." Rebecca was relieved to have brushed through the subject without more difficulty. "I'd best go and let Leah put me to work again." She walked away quickly.

Leah was cleaning one of the tables, so Rebecca joined her, filling up a tray with as much as she could carry. As they walked together toward the kitchen with their loads, Leah scanned the group scattered around the yard.

"Don't tell me you're trying to press your kinder into service again," Rebecca said, a laugh in her voice.

"Just making sure they're not skimping on the work." Leah glanced at her and smiled. "I know, I know, they all think I fuss too much when we have worship here."

"Wait until they have homes of their own. Then they'll understand. We were probably the same way."

"I suppose so, but don't let my kinder hear you say

that." Leah stepped cautiously up onto the porch, wary of the heavy tray. "You're happy, ain't so?"

"Yah, I guess I am. Seems as if being back in worship with everyone was gut for me." She frowned, wanting to explain and not sure she could. "Not that I didn't love worship in Ohio. But with everyone knowing about James's injury and…well, everything else. I felt like people were either feeling sorry for me or blaming me."

"Blaming you?" Leah's eyebrows rose. "Surely no one would think it was your fault that James was the way he was."

Rebecca shrugged, trying to hold the screen door with her elbow. "You can never tell what folks will think. Anyway, I'm just as glad to leave it behind."

They stepped inside. Only a few women were left in the kitchen, but they weren't cleaning up. Instead, they were gathered around Lydia Schultz. At the sight of Rebecca, several of the women averted their eyes and abruptly became busy. Lydia didn't. She stared at Rebecca, as she'd done in worship, while a flood of color swept over her face.

Rebecca stood where she was, clutching the tray, unable for the moment to move. She knew only too well what that reaction meant. They had been talking about her.

It seemed she wasn't able to leave the past behind, even here.

Chapter Five

Daniel got to the house earlier than usual on Monday, intent on unloading his wagon before Rebecca showed up. If she realized he'd brought some extra materials, she'd be intent on either paying for them or stopping work if she couldn't. So the best thing was not to tell her, it seemed to him.

Picking up several planks, he headed in through the back door, stepping over the broken board automatically. He'd got inside the kitchen when he realized he hadn't had to use the key Rebecca had given him. At almost the same moment, a footstep from the shop area froze him in his tracks.

The door to the shop swung open, and Daniel relaxed. Not Rebecca, thank the gut Lord.

He grinned at Sam. "It's just you, Sam."

Sam's eyebrows lifted. "What do you mean, just me? Who were you worried about?"

"Rebecca." He moved past Sam to deposit the planks on the stack of them against the wall.

Sam planted himself between Daniel and the door. "Komm on, spill it. Why don't you want to see Rebecca?"

"I do want to," he protested. "I don't want her to see me with this load of supplies, or she'll try to either pay me for them or insist on stopping work if she can't."

"So you thought you'd go around her." Sam's expression was disapproving for an instant, and then he grinned. "What are you waiting for? Let's get the rest of it in."

Together they carried the remaining supplies in. Sam took a step back and assessed the stack of planks and the box of brackets. "Aren't you afraid she'll notice it's different?"

Daniel considered. "I don't think so." He shoved the box under a tarp with his foot. "Would Leah?"

"Probably not. Now, if it was a question of something she worked with, she'd be on it in a second, but not this." He frowned for a moment, sketching a movement as if to pull out money. "Let me take care of this."

"Forget it."

"I ought to cover it," Sam protested. "She's my sister, not yours."

"She's my friend, and it's my job. Now, forget about it. I warn you, I'm going to lose my temper if you persist."

"Hah! You never do. At least, not since you were about ten. Then I seem to recall a certain episode where I ended up in the pond because I was teasing your little brother."

"I didn't really push you," Daniel said, remembering that hot August day. "We were all looking for an excuse to get wet anyhow."

"Not pushed, maybe. You just managed to stick your big foot out, so when Caleb jostled me, I tripped and landed in the pond."

"At least we all joined you." The water had felt so good after a couple of hours spent working in the sun.

"Yah." Sam grinned. "I could probably be stricter with my own kinder if I didn't have such a memory of doing the same things when I was their age."

"I'd best unhitch Molly before I start to work." Daniel headed back outside, Sam following. They worked together to unhitch the placid buggy horse, and Sam led her into the fenced-in paddock behind the house.

"So, what are you going to tell Rebecca when she sees you brought a horse and wagon with you this time?" Sam asked.

"That I had planned a stop in town today, before I came. That's true enough, and she won't ask what I went for." He'd thought it out, knowing he couldn't give Rebecca the slightest hint that he'd paid for those supplies, unless he wanted an argument.

He and Sam stood, watching the mare for a moment, arms resting on the fence rail. Sam had something more to say. Daniel could read his face too well not to know that. So he waited.

Finally Sam shook his head. "I wish I knew what was going on with Rebecca. She's my kid sister. Wouldn't you think she'd confide in me? We all know..." He seemed to change his mind about the direction that sentence was going. "We all want to help her, but she keeps shutting us out. Makes me want to shake her."

He'd have to be careful about this, Daniel decided. He didn't know everything, but he did have a little insight into why Rebecca was so determined to stand on her own.

"I don't think shaking is a gut idea," he said.

"No. But I have to do something." Sam pounded his fist against the railing in a sudden gesture. "If she were your little sister, you'd want to help her. You'd do anything..."

His words cut short, and embarrassment flooded his face. "Sorry, Dan. I didn't mean to make you think about Aaron."

"I know." The ache that always lurked in his heart made itself felt. "If I knew where Aaron was, I'd do anything to bring him home safe again, but I don't."

"Yah, I know." Sam buffeted his shoulder awkwardly. "We all pray for him."

Daniel could only nod. He swallowed the lump in his throat and forced himself to concentrate on Rebecca. "Maybe the best thing for Rebecca is to let her tell you what's going on when she's ready."

"That's what Leah says," Sam admitted. "I want a little more action."

He could understand. That fierce need to do something...anything...to help the one you felt responsible for—that was what he felt constantly. But that didn't mean it was the best choice.

"Leah's a wise woman." It was all he could think

to say. "Rebecca seems like she's been through a lot. Maybe she just needs time."

"If only she'd let us give her the money she needs." Sam's steady gaze focused on his face. "You know I'd give you the money for this job in a minute."

"Not unless you want to end up in the pond again."

"I'd like to see you try." The concern in Sam's face dissolved in a smile.

Daniel turned back toward the house. "Well, this isn't getting any work done. I figure that's all I can do for Rebecca right now—get her shop ready to open. She'll maybe start feeling better about herself once she knows she has money coming in."

"I guess you're right. Suppose I give you a hand until she comes and kicks me out. Okay?"

Daniel nodded. He understood Sam's frustration, because he felt it himself. But nobody was going to be able to take care of Rebecca until she decided to let them, and he didn't know if that would be ever.

Rebecca straightened her back and stretched when she and Daniel finished attaching the counter to the floor.

"I never realized how hard carpenters work. I'll be more grateful in the future."

Grinning, Daniel rose easily to his feet. He seemed able to work steadily no matter how difficult the circumstance. "It's really coming along, isn't it?"

Rebecca's breath caught as she looked around the room—her shop. It shouldn't come as a surprise to her, since she'd helped with just about every inch of it, but still, the change from an empty room into an actual shop astonished her. Had it really come about so quickly?

"I'm wonderful glad. And thankful." She glanced at him to be sure he knew it was him she was thanking, as well as the gut Lord. "I can actually start planning where to put things. How long, do you think, until I can clean and start arranging stock?"

Daniel seemed to be counting up the time to accomplish what was left. "Not long. Maybe by tomorrow afternoon, we can get on to the cleaning."

"We?" She shook her head. "That's not part of your job."

"Now that's where you're wrong," Daniel said. "I always do a thorough cleanup when I finish a job. I tell my customers that, when I leave, it'll be ready for them to use. And I mean it." He smiled at her expression. "Don't start arguing with me, now. It's part of my satisfaction in a job well-done."

It was hard to argue with that, and she suspected that was why he'd said it. He went on quickly, before she could pursue the subject.

"Do you have enough to put everything on display? And what about the racks? Is anything else needed?"

Rebecca tabulated display areas. "I think this is all that's needed. I was thinking that a cradle would be nice to show off the baby quilts, but I can find one somewhere, I'm sure. And I won't have enough fabric bolts to begin with, but once I have money coming in, I'll be able to order more."

She could almost feel the sympathy in his look. "Nothing from your brother-in-law yet?"

"I'm sure it will come any day now." Rebecca hoped she sounded more optimistic than she felt. "As for the number of quilts, I was worried at first, but Leah has brought in several that people want to sell on consignment."

"That's great, ain't so? So why do you look concerned about it?"

How could he tell? That was the problem in dealing with a childhood friend. They knew you too well.

"I'm not concerned about the stock. It's just that ever since Leah got the idea of bringing things in on consignment, she's been working on that like crazy. I don't want…"

"What?" Daniel gave her an exasperated look. "To accept her help? Knowing Leah, I'd guess she's having the time of her life."

She had to smile. "You know, she is. I wish I had half her energy and determination. But she has her own work to do, and I shouldn't monopolize her time."

"If that's all that's worrying you, I'd say to forget it. As far as I can tell, it's giving her a lot of fun. Probably she enjoys the idea of being a part of your business."

"But…"

"And if it's the fact that she's doing something for you, why don't you offer her part of the commission on the sales she brings in?"

Daniel seemed content to let that sink in, leaning against the counter, studying her face.

Amusement bubbled in her. "You're looking very self-satisfied," she said. "You think you have me figured out."

"Don't I?" The twinkle in his eyes became evident. "You haven't changed all that much over the years. And I think Leah would be pleased to have something other than the kinder to spend her energy on."

"I hadn't thought of it that way," she admitted, turning the idea over in her mind. It was very tempting to consider sharing even a portion of the burden with someone else. "Maybe I'll mention it to her."

"You'll soon have your chance," he said, looking past her out the front window. "Looks as if Leah has been to the mailbox and is stopping here."

Rebecca turned and watched her sister-in-law approach. Was it too much to hope that, in her bundle of mail, there was a check from John?

The door swung open. Leah stopped just inside, looking around. "My goodness, just look at this place. How much you've got done in the last few days! You'll be ready to open soon, ain't so?"

"I guess so." Rebecca's stomach fluttered at the thought. "I suppose there's a lot I should do to get the word out to folks."

"Yah, signs up on bulletin boards all over town, a big sign out front... Ach, Rebecca, I almost envy you. I've always thought I'd be good at running a business, but I've been so busy with the family, I haven't had time to think about it. Anyway, what could I do?"

Daniel evidently took that as a signal, because he nudged her.

She ignored him. What if she asked and Leah only agreed out of pity for her? If she...

"Funny thing," Daniel said, "we were just talking

about you." Ignoring her glare, he went on. "Rebecca wondered if you'd be interested in taking on the consignment side of things. For a share of the profit, of course."

"Only if…" Rebecca began, and then she stopped. The answer was written all over Leah's face. It lit up like the sun coming out on a cloudy day.

"You mean it?" She acted as if they'd offered her a wonderful gift. "I'd love to. You wouldn't have to give me anything…"

"I couldn't do that," Rebecca said quickly. "It wouldn't be right. Our arrangement would have to be business. A percentage of the sales. What do you think?"

"Ach, you can tell, can't you?" Leah seized her hands and squeezed them. "It would make me wonderful happy to be a part of the shop." Dropping her hands, Leah moved a few steps away, seeming to picture the place filled with quilts and quilting supplies. "I have so many ideas. I can't wait to get started. I must make a list of all the people I want to contact."

Daniel spoke in Rebecca's ear. "I hope we haven't unleashed something you can't control."

A gurgle of laughter welled up in her as she turned to face him. "I'm glad there's not a creek nearby. You're so ready to push that you'd probably push me into that as well, the way you did Sam."

"Only if I knew you really wanted to go in," he said, his face solemn but his eyes dancing.

Rebecca started to say something tart about his habit of thinking he knew best. But her gaze met his laughing eyes, and the words got all tangled up in her head.

Her breath caught, and her heart seemed to swell. Heat rushed to her face, shocking her.

She ought to look away. She ought to say something light to hide the feelings.

But emotions were bubbling inside of her and flooding her senses. She wanted…

Reality hit with a crash. She could not be feeling this… She didn't want to give it a name. She couldn't very well deny it. But even so, she couldn't have felt anything for Daniel except friendship. That was all. Friendship.

Daniel moved a couple of careful steps away from Rebecca, reading only too clearly the play of emotions on her face and knowing they were echoed on his own. Where had that flare of man-and-woman attraction come from? If he'd felt it earlier for Rebecca, he'd denied it, but he couldn't deny this, not when both of them felt it.

It was impossible. That was what he kept telling himself. He couldn't risk marrying and then letting down someone he loved again. And yet… Caleb must have felt some of the same guilt he had, and Caleb had moved on, finding happiness with Jessie. Was it too much to think it could happen for him?

Rebecca seemed to have conquered whatever she'd felt very quickly. She and Leah were chattering away a mile a minute about the shop, and he could watch her without her noticing.

Leah was good for her—he could see it. Leah had such a positive, upbeat attitude that it was infectious.

Rebecca had been like that once, too. He had a fairly good idea what had changed her, but she persisted in trying to hide it.

Maybe, if she wouldn't confide in him, she'd confide in Leah. Perhaps she'd feel more comfortable talking to another woman, and Leah was safe. He knew instinctively Rebecca wouldn't burden her mother with the knowledge, knowing what pain it would cause.

Both of them turned in his direction, and he tried to look as if he were intent on his work. Fortunately they weren't, as it turned out, paying attention to him.

"I'd best get back to the house and see how much mess Mary Ann has created making snickerdoodles with the little ones." Leah's smile denied any expectation she had of finding a mess. Mary Ann, her eldest daughter, seemed to love nothing better than tending the little ones.

"Isn't she in school today? Or did you keep her home just to bake cookies?" he teased.

"Her cold seemed a bit worse this morning, so I thought she'd best stay in. But she seems to be getting her pep back now."

"We should relieve her," Rebecca said. "I can imagine what Lige and your little Miriam are doing with the cookie dough." She was smiling and acting normally now, as if she'd forgotten any emotional upset already.

"I'll handle it," Leah said, scooting out the door. "You get on with your work. Your daad wants to have Lige do some planting with him, so he'll be well occupied."

Rebecca nodded and let her go, and he thought she showed a little constraint when she turned back to him.

"It'll be sehr gut for Lige to work alongside his gross-daadi, so they can get to know each other better."

"They haven't had much time together." He asked the question that wondered him, "Why didn't you visit more often when you were out in Ohio?"

Rebecca seemed to draw into herself. "James couldn't get away from the farm."

He guessed she wanted him to accept that, but he felt compelled to push a bit harder. Surely a friend had that right.

"You and Lige could have visited without him," he pointed out.

For an instant, he thought she'd snap at him, but she didn't. "James didn't like to be left alone." She turned away, signaling that the conversation was over.

She was hugging her pain to herself, and that hurt him.

"Ach, Rebecca, you can trust me with the whole story. Don't you know that?"

Rebecca looked up, startled at his tone, her eyes wide, her face softening. If she would only speak…

The sound of someone on the porch had her retreating. Frustrated, he frowned at the door, wishing the intruder well away from them.

The door opened, and he was surprised to see Eli Gaus coming in. Eli, a couple of years younger than him, was partners in the sawmill with his father and brother.

"Eli." He tried to sound welcoming. "If you're here to try and sell me another batch of two-by-fours, I have plenty."

Eli's serious expression sat oddly on his youthful, freckled face. "Your brother said you were working over here, so I figured I'd drop by." He seemed ill at ease, and he glanced at Rebecca. "Could I have a word? In private, I mean." He gave Rebecca an apologetic smile.

"Of course. I'll be measuring the back windows for shades if you want me," she said.

Daniel waited until she'd gone and then looked at Eli, frowning a little. "What's happening?"

If anything, Eli's awkwardness increased. "I... Well, the thing is, it's about your brother. About Aaron."

The name hit him like a blow. People so seldom mentioned Aaron, who had jumped the fence years ago, that it was odd to hear it. Not that he ever stopped thinking of him or stopped wondering.

"What about Aaron? Not...not bad news?"

"Ach, no, not exactly. Sorry." Eli's fair skin reddened. "I didn't mean you to think that. You see, I saw him."

"You saw him?" He repeated the words, only half believing. It had been so long since they'd had any word at all. "Where?"

"I was out in Indiana for a wedding." Now that he'd got started, Eli seemed to find it easier. "One of the cousins took me for a ride past the racetrack where they sometimes get buggy horses. Aaron was working there."

"How is he? Did you speak to him?" *Did he say anything about us?* That was really what he wanted to ask.

"He looked all right, I guess. Seemed funny to see him there, but he always was one for the horses, ain't so?"

Daniel managed a smile, thinking of a small Aaron walking right up to a mammoth Percheron and lifting its hoof to remove a stone. "Yah, he was. So he's working with the horses there at the racetrack?"

"He's a trainer, he said." Eli hesitated. "The other guys around were a pretty rough bunch, I thought. Not like the horse people we're used to."

He understood, he guessed. Most Amish in farm country had a relationship with the Englisch horse people around, building barns, serving as farriers to Englisch and Amish alike, going to the same livestock auctions.

"Did he seem happy?" He couldn't make his brother come back and be one of them, but he still wished him happiness.

Eli considered the question. "He seemed like he fitted in with them, I guess. But happy? I don't know. One thing, though. You can't let him know I told you. I agreed I wouldn't, but when my Elizabeth heard about it, she scolded me up one side and down the other. Said his family at least had the right to know he's alive."

He was looking at Daniel pleadingly, obviously caught between loyalty to his childhood friend and his wife's firm belief in what was right.

Daniel nodded, the fact sinking in. Aaron was alive and apparently well. But he couldn't reach out to him, and no matter how he looked at it, he'd still failed his little brother.

It was a lesson to him. He'd begun to think he might let Rebecca depend on him, but he couldn't. He didn't dare.

Chapter Six

Rebecca knelt at the overgrown flower bed along the side of the house, cleaning away the dead leaves that had blown there over the winter. How much was left of the colorful plantings she remembered, the ones old Mrs. Evans had tended so lovingly?

She'd heard Daniel's visitor leave a good half hour ago, but Daniel hadn't called to her to come and help him, so she'd left him alone. There had been something in his face when he'd walked out to the porch with Eli that had warned her off. She didn't know what they'd been talking about, but it must have been something serious.

Eli Gaus had been younger than they were, but she remembered him as a freckle-faced child, inclined to mischief. He'd been a good friend of Aaron's, as she recalled. All grown-up now, like all of those children she'd once shared a schoolroom with.

Yes, his visit had had something to do with Daniel's brother Aaron—she'd caught the name before the door closed and she'd moved away. She'd been married before Aaron jumped the fence, but Mamm had passed on the news in her weekly letter. It had hit his family hard, Mamm had said, as was natural. Daniel had always looked after his little brother, so he'd have had trouble coming to terms with it.

If Eli had come to discuss something about Aaron… well, she wouldn't pry. If Daniel wanted to confide in her, he would.

Brushing aside the last of the leaves, Rebecca found the fresh green spears of tulips. Her heart lifted at the sight. The clump of daffodils at the corner was already blooming, and they'd look much better once everything was cleared around them. Nothing said spring quite as well as tulips and daffodils.

If only she could have the flower beds looking their best before her opening…but she could only do what she had time for. It was more important to have some money coming in right now than to make things perfect.

"Finding some treasures?" Daniel had come up behind her so softly she hadn't heard him on the fresh grass.

She looked up at him and shielded her eyes. With the sun behind him, he looked enormous. Brushing dirt from her hands, she rose to her feet.

"Mrs. Evans had flowers all along this side of the house. I'd like to see it looking that way again."

"It's been neglected for a time, but it'll come back." He squatted to clear some dead branches away from a small shrub. "This is a miniature lilac." He cradled a tiny bud in his hand. "It'll bloom this year. Just needs a little loving care." Now he looked up at her. "About what happened before, when Eli came… I'm sorry for asking you to go out of your own place."

"That's all right." She spoke quickly, trying to hide her desire to know what had set that frown in his eyes. She'd seen it there from the moment he came out. Eli had left him with a problem for sure. She longed to know what it was.

"I… I heard him say it was something about Aaron. I hope he's all right."

"Fine." Daniel snapped out the word as he stood. "It wasn't important."

In other words, he had no intention of sharing his problem with her. She nodded, unable to think of any answer that wouldn't sound like prying.

"Maybe we should get back to work." She started to move toward the door, but he stopped her with a gesture.

"Sorry." He seemed to be fighting a battle within himself, but finally he gave a rueful smile. "I'm not practicing what I preach, am I? I wanted you to talk to me about your troubles, but I slam the door in your face when you expect the same."

"It's not so easy, is it? Some things… They're just too hard to talk about."

He grimaced, shaking his head. "I'll have to talk about this. To tell Onkel Zeb and Caleb, anyway. Maybe I should practice on you." Daniel's chest moved as he drew in a deep breath. "Eli saw Aaron when he was out in Indiana recently. Talked to him in fact."

So that was it. He was hurting at the reminder that Aaron was out there in the Englisch world and hadn't cared enough to let his family know where he was.

"Is he well?" she asked, aware of the need to tread carefully.

"So Eli said." Daniel's voice was tight with pain. "He didn't send any word to us. Doesn't want us bothering him, I guess."

"Oh, Daniel, I'm sure it's not that." She struggled for another explanation. "Maybe he's afraid you'll make him feel bad about going away."

She'd like to have Aaron here right now. She'd give him a good shake for letting people who loved him worry this way.

"I guess I'd feel less guilty if I knew he was happy enough with his decision that he could still have a relationship with his family. You know what I mean. Lots of families have someone who jumped the fence, but they still get along all right."

She nodded, but she was fixed on the one word. *Guilty?* She knew, only too well, how responsible Daniel had felt for his little brother, especially after his mother left. So of course he felt guilty for losing him—as if he'd lost his grip on his brother's hand in the crowd at an auction.

"He's a grown man, Daniel." She kept her words gentle, not wanting him to shut her out again. "We can't keep people from following their own paths, no matter how much we love them."

Her thoughts spiraled off into the past, to James's mother turning on her after his fall, saying she should have stopped him from doing anything so dangerous. They'd both known at the time that nothing stopped James when he was determined, but maybe it made his mamm feel better to blame someone else.

Daniel didn't look convinced or comforted by her words. Naturally not. She was trying to do what she'd just said was impossible—to keep Daniel from the path of blaming himself. He wouldn't stop. He couldn't. And if he could... She faced the stark reality. If he could, he wouldn't be the man he was.

It wasn't until milking time that Daniel was able to get Caleb and Onkel Zeb alone together. Caleb would probably tell Jessie about Aaron of course, but he wouldn't want to do it in front of the children.

The usual milking routine ran along smoothly, and they could work and talk at the same time, often laughing together over the events of the day. But not this time. Not when Daniel had told them about Eli finding Aaron.

For a moment, no one spoke, and the only sound was the steady murmur of the milking machine.

"We must go after him," Caleb said, his jaw setting in the way it did when he was determined. "We must see him and persuade him to return home where he belongs."

Daniel had known that was what he'd say. "But what about Eli? You know what friends they were. He doesn't want Aaron to know that he gave him away."

"This is too important for childish promises. His wife saw that, even if Eli didn't. Eli is a grown man, and so is Aaron. It's time Aaron came home. He belongs here." Caleb was looking and sounding like the head of the family.

Daniel knew his love for his little brother was real, but he also knew that Caleb had never had much patience with Aaron. Caleb had grown out of that impatience in time, and he was a gentle and patient father to his young ones. But then… Well, neither of them had been old enough for the responsibilities thrust on them when their family fell apart.

"What if Aaron doesn't want to return?" Daniel tried to shrug away the tension that rode him. "I'd do anything to have Aaron home, but it wouldn't be much use if he didn't want to be here."

He turned to Onkel Zeb before Caleb could answer. "You haven't said anything yet, Onkel Zeb. What do you think?"

His uncle's lean, weathered face was taut, his faded blue eyes pained. His grief over their missing one had never been so obvious, and it hurt to look at. A quick glance at Caleb told him that his older brother was similarly affected.

"Yah," Caleb said, his voice husky. "What should we do?"

"Nothing," he said at last, and the word seemed to carry a heavy weight. "It would be wrong to break Eli's trust, but even if it were not so, I'd say the same."

"But Onkel Zeb…" Caleb began.

"Ach, Caleb, do you think I don't understand? But you reminded us that Aaron is a grown man now. He's not the little boy who sat on my knee."

"We can't forget him." Daniel's heart hurt. "We have to do something, but what?"

"Wait. Have patience." Onkel Zeb put a hand on his shoulder and reached out to Caleb with the other. They stood there in silence for a moment, linked. "And pray that God will show him the way home."

Rebecca's words echoed in his mind. *We can't keep people from following their own paths, no matter how much we love them.*

He wanted to argue. He was responsible for Aaron. He always had been. He was his brother's keeper.

Rebecca stood, holding the door of the shop open, marveling at what had been accomplished in a couple of days. The carpentry work was complete, and the entire place spotless. And here came a wave of people bringing the merchandise to stock the store for its opening tomorrow.

Her stomach gave a little flip at the thought. Tomorrow! After all the work and heartache, her dream was about to come true.

She stepped back, letting a line of nieces and nephews carrying boxes get past, and then hurried to show them where each should be placed. When she started to open a box, Mary Ann—Sam and Leah's oldest girl—took it from her.

"I'll see that all the fabric gets out on the tables," she said. "I know just how you want them. The young ones will help," she added, from the superiority of her twelve years.

Rebecca gave way. She'd pictured herself doing all the unpacking and arranging, but she could no more stop the flow of determined people than she could stop Lost Creek in its course. All of her family was there of course, and all of Daniel's kin as well, along with several of the women who'd brought quilts for consignment. Their happy chatter filled the air.

Leah and Jessie, Caleb's wife, were following Mamm's directions as they started hanging display items, and she hurried to help them.

"What do you think?" Leah held out her arms, a quilt draped over each. "The Sunshine and Shadows next to the Broken Star? Or should it be the Log Cabin?"

She'd made the Broken Star pattern when she was expecting Lige, and it was dear to her for that reason. But the other two seemed a better match to go side by side. "Let's put these two next to each other, and then that pretty heart applique one. I want a mix of the consignment quilts with mine, and I like the way the colors go."

"Wonderful gut," Jessie said. "The colors flow into one another. It will look like a rainbow once they're all up." She lifted one of the quilts, and the curve of her belly spoke of the new baby who'd soon arrive, not that anyone would mention it with the men and boys around.

Silly, she supposed, but that was the custom. No one would talk about the forthcoming baby in mixed company until it was safe in its crib. She gave Jessie the knowing smile that one mother would give to another. Caleb was truly blessed in his second wife—a wonderful mammi to his two kinder and now a new baby to fill their house with joy.

Mamm was unpacking a box with smaller items, like wall hangings and place mats. "I put in some of my quilted pot holders," she said. "Some folks will come tomorrow just to see what's what. They maybe won't be ready to buy a quilt, but they'll want to spend money on something, and the pot holders will be gut for them."

Rebecca felt joy bubbling up inside her. To be here,

her goal within reach and her family supporting her—what more could she ask?

"You're a wise woman, Mammi." Rebecca helped her put them on the small stand Daniel had cleverly contrived. "I'm certain sure you're right about it." She paused with a pot holder made of a folded star in her hand. "This is too pretty ever to pick up a hot kettle with."

"So someone can use it to set the teapot on," Mamm said. "No reason why something can't be pretty as well as useful."

Jessie was nodding in agreement. "I heard an Englischer say a quilted piece was a work of art, and I thought that was a funny way to look at it. But maybe she was right. We don't think of it as art when we're stitching, but if it brings folks joy, what difference does it make what you call it?"

Leah chuckled. "Mostly I'm thinking it's a gut reason to sit for a time and sew something more interesting than the holes the boys make in their knees."

"Better for kinder to wear out their clothes than their sheets," Mamm said, repeating the old saying as if it were new today.

"For sure," Rebecca replied. Any mother would a hundred times rather be sick herself than have her child sick.

"Look." Leah touched her arm, nodding toward the door. "Your daad and Zeb have a surprise for you."

Rebecca swung around and froze, hardly able to believe her eyes. Daadi and Daniel's onkel Zeb stood there, holding a sign between them, both of them grinning self-consciously.

And what a sign—the lettering was so clear and neat

it looked as if it had been done by a professional. It said Rebecca's Quilts, and below it was a painted representation of a quilted square, its colors bright.

"Daad, Zeb…" She rushed toward them, blinking back tears. "It's so beautiful. You made it for me?"

"I did the design and Zeb did the painting," Daadi said, beaming. "He's a wonderful gut hand with a brush, that's certain sure."

"I can't believe it." She ran her hand lightly over the painted surface. "Denke. How can I ever thank you enough?"

"Ach, it's nothing," Zeb said. "We had a gut time with it. And Daniel put in the posts and hardware, so we can hang it outside."

"Your customers have to know where to find you, ain't so?" Daad said. "You keep on with your work, and we'll get it put up."

She couldn't help watching them as they carefully carried it out to where Sam waited next to a pair of posts that seemed to have appeared when she wasn't looking. Daniel's doing, of course. Where had he got to? She had to thank him.

Glancing around at the busy figures in the shop, she saw everyone, it seemed, except Daniel. Silly to feel the loss when he wasn't there. He had other work to do, that was certain.

Joshua, her oldest nephew, maneuvered a stepladder past her and set it up beside the door. She looked at him with a question in her face.

Joshua blushed a little, showing her the object he was carrying—a small bell. "Lots of shops have a bell on the door, so I thought you should, too. That way, if you're busy in the back, you'll know when a customer comes in."

She wanted to give him an enormous hug but restrained herself. Boys his age were unaccountable, and it might embarrass him. She contented herself with a warm smile.

"That is so very thoughtful of you, Joshua. And you're right—it's just what I need. Denke."

His color deepened, and he ducked his head. "I'll get it fastened up right away," he said and scurried up the stepladder.

Rebecca stood smiling, looking around the shop. It was taking shape beautifully. But she shouldn't stand and watch while other people were working for her. She joined Mary Ann, who was directing her young crew in arranging the bolts of fabric.

"This is the way you want it, ain't so?" Her niece looked a little anxious, eager to get it right. "All the prints together, and all the solid colors together right across from them."

"That's right." She patted Mary Ann's shoulder. "You're doing a wonderful gut job. You even got Lige and Jessie's little ones doing something useful."

"We didn't want them running around underfoot." Mary Ann was as practical as her mother. "And they really do want to help. Lige especially."

"Yah." Rebecca watched her son, pleased. "It's important that he know he's contributing his share."

Mary Ann tilted her head, as if turning that over in her mind. "I didn't think of it that way, but I see what you mean. Grossmammi says that in a family, everyone works for all."

"That's what she always taught us." The impact of her mother's oft-repeated phrase stuck in her mind. They were family, and it was important that she let them help for their sakes, not just hers. She'd lost sight of that in her need to stand on her own feet.

Mary Ann straightened a bolt, stroking the fabric. "I wondered... Well, maybe, if you like... I could help you in the store sometimes."

Rebecca bit back a quick response that she could handle it. What had she just been telling herself?

"That would be a big help, Mary Ann. After all, I'll want to take a break sometimes, and I'll need someone I can trust."

Mary Ann's wide smile was all the response she needed.

Mamm, coming up behind her, slipped her arm around Rebecca's waist. "Mary Ann is that, all right. Now, come and tell me which of the table runners you want displayed."

They were deep into a discussion on what to display where when she heard the back door open and close. Not surprising on this busy day, but everyone seemed to have fallen silent at the moment. She turned to look.

Daniel had just come in, and he carried a large maple cradle in his arms.

"The cradle. Ach, that's perfect for showing off the baby quilts," Leah said. "Isn't it perfect, Rebecca?"

"It's just exactly right." Rebecca blinked back a quick tear. Everyone was being so kind...and not just kind but thoughtful. "How did you know I wanted a cradle?" She helped Daniel put it into position.

"You mentioned it one day, and I remembered when I went to an auction, so I bid on it." He grinned. "You should have heard the men making fun of me, but I made them promise they wouldn't mention it. I wanted it to be a surprise."

"You succeeded." She stroked the curve of the maple, marveling at the condition of the cradle. "You must have refinished it to have it looking so good."

He nodded, reaching past her to show her the underside of the cradle. "The legs and the rockers just needed some work, that was the main thing. I didn't dare try to take the one that's in the attic. Caleb wouldn't let me out of the house with it."

"I can imagine."

Daniel righted the cradle, and his hand brushed hers. Rebecca tried to ignore the warm tingle that spread up her arm at his touch. His fingers moved slightly against her skin, almost as if he were stroking it the way she had stroked the cradle.

For an instant, he didn't pull away, but then he straightened, looking around the shop as if nothing had happened. "It's almost ready."

"Yah, thanks to everyone's help."

"Helping has made them happy," he said softly, just for her ears.

Her gaze tangled with his. "I know," she said. "I understand now. Doing it together is gut for all of us."

Chapter Seven

Rebecca found it impossible to eat breakfast the next morning. Her stomach was filled with so many butterflies that she couldn't possibly put any food in it. Instead, she busied herself helping Mamm and Leah in packing up the food they insisted on bringing to the shop opening.

She took a tin of snickerdoodles from her mother. "Mammi, I don't think any customers we have are expecting to be fed just because they come to the opening."

"You're just not thinking then," Mamm replied tartly. "Most likely half the church, at least, will stop by sometime today to wish you well. The least we can do is have some coffee and snacks for them."

Leah nudged her. "No point in arguing. If you have food, someone will eat it. If it's not used up, the kinder will finish it off in no time."

Mary Ann hurried into the kitchen from outside. "I have the pony cart all ready to take the coffeepots and cookies to the shop. Shall I start loading?"

"Yah, for sure." Leah handed her a basket and a large tin. "Get the young ones to help you."

Rebecca, realizing no one was paying any attention to her protests, picked up a box containing a couple of coffeepots and headed out. Clearly the decision was out of her hands. When Mamm, who was always so soft-spoken, gave instructions in that voice, they had to be obeyed, no matter how old you were.

It was pleasant to be walking up the lane with Leah in the wake of the pony cart, each of them carrying a few things there hadn't been room for. The weather had cooperated, and surely the spring warmth and sunshine would encourage people to come out.

"It's a gut day for a new venture," Leah said. "Look, there's a whole patch of lilies of the valley blooming where Mrs. Evans used to have her bench. She always said how sweet they smelled when she sat there."

"I hadn't even noticed them before Sam and Joshua cleared out some of the overgrown brush." Rebecca shook her head. "I told Sam they had enough to do, but he didn't listen."

"Sam's gut at not hearing what he doesn't want to," Leah said, her eyes twinkling.

Rebecca chuckled. "He always was, as I remember."

"We'll set up in the kitchen," Leah said, going up the porch steps. "Mary Ann will help. Then we can just carry trays into the front as we need to refill them. I was thinking to use that table in the corner of the shop for the coffee and cookies, yah?"

"That sounds fine, except that there's so much lumber stored in the kitchen..." But as they went in, she discovered that was no longer the case. Even now, Daniel was carrying the last few things toward the living room.

"Almost done," he said. "I wiped down the counters, too."

"You didn't need…" she began.

Daniel shook his head at her. "Leah told me to. I didn't want to get on her bad side when I heard she was making whoopie pies."

Leah laughed. "Daniel is easy to manage. He responds to food like most men."

Mary Ann, leading her group of small helpers, began bringing things in and putting them on the counter, and for a few minutes, Rebecca was too busy to talk. But soon Leah was sweeping the younger ones out on the porch, promising that she'd bring them cookies in a few minutes if they stayed there.

Lige detoured on his way to the porch to tug on Rebecca's apron. "Did we do a gut job, Mammi?"

"You did a wonderful gut job," she said, hugging him. Grinning, he ran out to join his cousins. She watched, her heart swelling. Lige was turning into a typical little boy—more so every day. This life was what he'd needed. He finally felt secure.

When she turned her attention back to the others, she found Daniel gesturing to the few existing cabinets. "I'd like to extend the cabinets all along this wall, and we talked about putting a few more on the end wall, as well." He grinned. "You should hear the Englisch ladies talk about the cabinet space when I work on their kitchens. Everything has to be pullouts and turntables and such. But Rebecca just wants regular cabinets, only more of them."

"Yah, and you could put one tall one in to store brooms and mops and such. That's what I've been wanting, and Sam keeps promising."

It was time she interrupted before they had her whole kitchen mapped out for her. "I'm not going on with it right away, remember, Daniel?" She gave him a warning look. He'd better not say anything about her money problems.

"Just doing a little planning, that's all," he said in that easygoing way of his. "We don't have to start right away, but planning is half the work of the project. Makes it a lot easier once I actually start work."

Rebecca had a feeling he was manipulating her, but there didn't seem to be anything she could say. She couldn't stop him from thinking about the job, could she?

"Ach, I hear a buggy already," Leah exclaimed. "And me with the coffee not on yet. Here, Mary Ann, take that tray out. Rebecca, you'd best get the door unlocked. You have customers."

Her stomach fluttering, Rebecca rushed to the front door, unlocking it and setting it ajar before the first visitors had time to get to it. Ready or not, the quilt shop was open.

What was she thinking? Of course she was ready. This was what she'd been working toward, after all. Now the time was here.

As usual, her mother had been right. The steady flow of friends, neighbors, people from the church district…

It seemed they'd all planned to stop by early, just to meet and greet and to wish her well. They headed gratefully toward the coffee and treats, and she was thankful to see that mothers steered their young ones out onto the front porch with their treats. The last thing she'd want was sticky fingerprints on the new fabrics.

Somewhat to her surprise, one of the early visitors was Lydia Schultz, who had clearly been talking about her that Sunday after worship. She'd managed to avoid the woman since then, but inevitably they'd run across each other in their small community. It was too bad she hadn't remembered earlier that Lydia had a cousin who'd belonged to a neighboring church district to theirs out west.

Not that it would have made a difference if she had. If folks were inclined to gossip, they would do it, whether they had a reason to or not. Pinning a smile on her face, she went to greet Lydia.

"How nice of you to stop by our opening, Lydia. Will you have some coffee?"

Lydia, looking uneasy, shook her head. "I just thought I'd stop by and pick up some batting for the crib quilt I'm making. You do have it, don't you?"

"Yah, of course. Let me show you…"

"I'll do it, Aunt Rebecca," Mary Ann said quickly, appearing at her elbow. "I know just where it is." Showing a surprising amount of poise, she led Lydia off.

Rebecca turned to Leah, who was making an effort to appear busy. "Did you set that up?" she said in an undertone.

"Maybe," Leah admitted. Then her smile broke

through. "No sense in giving Lydia a chance to pump you. Whatever you said would be twisted out of recognition by the time she repeated it, ain't so?"

"I gather Lydia has a reputation." Her momentary queasiness at seeing the woman had vanished. If folks wanted to talk, she couldn't stop them.

"Ach, she's the worst blabbermaul in the county," Leah said. She shot a glance around to make sure no one had heard. "I guess I'm just as bad if I talk about her, ain't so?"

"Maybe not quite," Rebecca said, teasing.

Grateful as she was for the support of the church, by midmorning Rebecca was starting to feel a little overwhelmed and maybe a bit embarrassed.

"Why is Edith Stoltzfus buying pot holders from us when everyone knows she makes them herself?" she murmured to Leah after one sale.

Leah didn't seem troubled in the least. "So what if folks are buying things they maybe don't need? They'll give them as gifts, and that's gut advertisement for the shop, ain't so?"

When Rebecca still looked troubled, Leah patted her. "You're getting hungry—that's what's wrong with you. You go back to the kitchen and have yourself a snack before you keel over. Your mamm and I will look after things here."

Rebecca couldn't deny that the butterflies in her stomach seemed to have been replaced by a chasm. She didn't think food had anything to do with her feelings, but she hadn't been able to eat much breakfast, so it wasn't a bad idea.

When she reached the kitchen, she found Daniel leaning against the counter, drinking a cup of coffee and eating a whoopie pie. She chuckled at the cream filling that decorated his chin.

"You look like you have a white beard. What are you doing still here?"

"Eating," he said, wiping the cream away with a napkin. "And sorting the boards and such that are left over from the work on the shop. I don't like it when I buy too much, but sometimes it's hard to estimate."

"I wouldn't worry. You can always use it up, can't you?" She poured herself a cup of coffee and cut a generous wedge of shoofly pie. "I couldn't eat at breakfast this morning," she said in explanation.

"Too excited, ain't so? It certain sure sounds like it's a big success with all those women chattering at once." He nodded toward the shop. The sound was a little muted here, but it came through. "Sort of like the henhouse when the feed goes in."

"Women from the church," she said in explanation. She frowned down at her coffee. "They're all buying things…even things I'm sure they don't need. I wish…"

"What?" Daniel said. He gave her a gentle smile. "You're in business now, Rebecca. You're supposed to be happy when folks buy what you're selling."

"I am. I just don't want them to feel they have to." Couldn't he understand that?

Daniel set his cup down and focused on her. "Look at it this way. When you go to a mud sale, you buy something even if maybe you don't need it right at the moment."

"That's different. A mud sale benefits the school, or the fire company."

"It benefits the community," he said, patient as always. "Your shop is part of the community. Folks want to see it succeed. The more businesses there are, even just on this road, the more people will come down here and maybe stop at Stoltzfus's farm for berries or Edna Byler's place for homemade fudge or my sister-in-law Jessie's for baked goods. We're all in this together, ain't so?"

"I guess, when you put it that way, I understand. But I still think some of them are coming just because they want to help me."

"Nothing wrong with that. You came to my business in place of someone else's, ain't so? We all help each other."

She was forced to smile. "You always have an answer for everything, don't you? I don't remember you being so smart when we were kinder."

"Wisdom comes with age," he said. "Now, you get back to work and sell something."

Her doubts allayed, Rebecca headed back into the shop.

"It's going well, ain't so?" Leah straightened the display of quilted pot holders on the counter.

"Yah." Rebecca hesitated. "It's wonderful kind of the Leit to show up like this, but we need some Englisch customers to make a go of the shop."

"They'll be here. Just wait." Leah seemed confident. And of course it didn't really matter whether Englisch customers came today or another day, as long as they came. But still...

However, it seemed Leah was right. By late morning, several cars had pulled into the improvised parking area behind the shop, and clusters of Englischers buzzed happily around the shop. Rebecca, Leah, Mamm and even Mary Ann were all kept busy answering questions.

Rebecca chanced to overhear Mary Ann explaining the pattern of a Tumbling Blocks quilt to two of the women. Her young niece had more poise than she did, it seemed, and she chattered away quite at ease.

"You see?" Leah took a moment away from the counter. "I told you we'd get Englisch customers. In the summer it will be even busier, because travelers will stop, too."

"That's right." A young woman with a baby in a carrier against her chest entered the conversation. "You should be sure your shop is listed in that little booklet the county puts out for visitors. We moved here just a month ago, and I've used that to find all kinds of things."

"That's a gut idea," Leah said. "We didn't think of that. I'm Leah," she added, "and this is Rebecca Mast. She owns the shop."

"I'm Shannon Wilbur." She leaned against the counter, looking a little tired. She was a slim, tiny young woman, and Rebecca didn't doubt that the weight of the sleeping baby was dragging on her shoulders. "I've seen your name on some of the quilts, haven't I?"

Rebecca nodded. "I made many of them, but other Amish women from the area made some, too."

"They're lovely." Shannon hoisted the baby a little, probably to relieve the pressure of the straps. "We have more room in our new house, and my husband suggested getting a locally made quilt, so we'll have something to remember if we move."

"You're thinking of moving already? Don't you like it here?" Leah sounded a little shocked.

Shannon's effort at a smile seemed a bit forced. "It's my husband's job," she explained. "He has to travel a lot, and the company transfers him where it needs him. I never used to mind moving, but with the baby…" She let that trail off, but Rebecca understood.

She tried to imagine what it must be like in a strange town with a small baby and a husband who traveled, but she couldn't quite manage it. When Lige was born, a day didn't pass without some relative stopping by to help out.

Leah, with a gesture, summoned Mary Ann to her side. "This is my oldest girl, Mary Ann. Why don't you let her mind the baby while you're looking around? She loves babies, and she has lots of experience."

"That's right," Rebecca chimed in. "Have some coffee and a snack and enjoy yourself. Your little girl will be fine."

"Betsy." Shannon smiled down at the sleeping baby. "If you're sure…" She looked at Mary Ann, who was already holding out her arms. "All right. Thanks." She handed the sleeping child into Mary Ann's arms, watching for a moment to see how Mary Ann handled her. Then, apparently reassured, she walked toward the refreshment table with a light step.

"That's a kind thought." Rebecca was about to say more when her mother approached with an older woman—an Englischer with a warm, friendly air.

"Here is my daughter, Rebecca. This is Mrs. Allen. She loves to quilt."

"Glenda, please." She smiled from Mamm to Rebecca. "Your mother and I met last year at the spring mud sale. Your shop is just what we needed here. Now I won't have to drive twenty miles every time I run out of thread or batting."

"I'm glad. If you think of any other supplies you'd like me to carry, be sure you let me know."

"Oh, I will." The woman chuckled. "Everyone knows how outspoken I am. But you have a nice selection. I'm sure you'll do very well."

Shannon had come back up to them in time to hear her, a cup of coffee in one hand and a cruller in the other. "I think so, too. I hope you'll consider having a quilting group that meets here. I belonged to one where I lived before, and it was such fun to sit and sew with others who were interested. And then we'd have a quilting whenever one of us had a project ready." Her face was alive with enthusiasm for the idea.

"That's a wonderful idea," Glenda broke in. "My goodness, yes. I'd join in a minute. And I know a few other women who'd be interested. Now, let me see. When would be the best time to meet?"

Rebecca opened her mouth to speak and then closed it again at a look from her mother. The two women were chattering away happily, discussing days and times as if it were all settled. She glanced at Leah, who was smiling.

"Let them do it," she said softly. "Glenda Allen will do all the organizing for you, and it will bring more people into the shop, ain't so?"

Rebecca had to nod. Of course it was just what the shop needed. She should have come up with the idea herself. "I might need a little help."

"You have that without asking." Leah clasped her hand warmly. "Your mamm looks eager to volunteer, and I'll help, too. Maybe we should have Mary Ann here to watch any babies who come with their mothers. She'd love it."

Rebecca nodded, thankful. Of course they would help. Her mother was nodding and smiling as Glenda consulted her about the idea, and Mary Ann's face was blissful as she cradled the sleeping baby.

Rebecca looked around the shop, mentally seeing it as it had been that first day when she and Daniel had begun planning. Now it buzzed with color and movement and the happy sound of women's chatter. Her shop was just as she'd dreamed it.

Daniel squatted down by the back porch of the shop to have a closer look at the steps. He'd waited until after closing time, not wanting to be in the way when folks were leaving. But he had a bad feeling about those steps, even though he'd replaced one rotten board.

The back door opened, startling him, and he thought Rebecca was equally surprised to see him.

"What are you doing still here?" She stood above

him at the top of the steps, looking down with a little apprehension.

"I was going to say the same to you." He chuckled. "We certain sure surprised each other. I thought you'd left with the others."

A faint flush touched her cheeks. "I know they thought I was silly, but I wanted to be there by myself for a little bit."

With the pink in her cheeks, Rebecca looked more like the rosy-cheeked girl he remembered. "Just to be sure it's real, ain't so?"

"You understand." She sounded surprised.

He nodded, rising to his feet. "I felt the same when I opened my carpentry business." He hesitated, wondering whether she wanted to talk or to be on her way. "It was a gut day, yah?"

"It was. I know every day won't be busy, but today made for a fine start." She looked down at the steps. "You didn't tell me what you're doing. You already fixed the step that was broken."

"Yah, but I don't like the looks of the uprights underneath. They're starting to give, and I wouldn't want someone to get hurt."

"I can't afford…" she began, but he shook his head.

"You already have the materials needed, left over from the shop. It won't be much work either. I have to go out tomorrow morning to give an estimate on a job, but I can do it in the afternoon."

She still looked uncertain, and he squatted by the steps to gesture. "Just take a look under here, and you'll see what I mean."

Rebecca took a quick stride down, bending. Her foot hit a stone, making her stumble, and he grabbed her arm to steady her.

In an instant, it seemed as though time had stopped. Rebecca winced away from his grasp as if he'd struck her, her blue eyes darkening with fear.

"Rebecca." He said her name softly, hardly trusting himself to say more. He eased back from her, giving her space.

She turned away from him, her breathing rapid, and wrapped both arms around herself. "I'm sorry. I don't know what…" She let that trail off, probably seeing that the reason for her reaction was only too obvious.

Daniel had control of himself now. He wouldn't let the fury he felt toward James show. James was gone beyond the reach of anything humans could do, and God would have the judging of him. It wasn't for a fallible man like him to judge.

But Rebecca… She couldn't go on like this, trying to hold on to her secret when it kept leaking out of her and hurting her all over again.

"Komm." *Gently, gently.* He didn't dare touch her, even to help her up. "Sit here with me on the step. It'll hold a bit longer." He couldn't quite manage to say the words as lightly as he intended.

"It's all right." She stood, still avoiding his gaze. "I should go home."

"James hurt you," he said flatly. "Do you think I can't see that? Did he hurt Lige, too?"

"No!" Her breath caught. "Not…not physically. But Lige was hurt, anyway, by his father's anger and the way he acted. I don't think I realized how much it affected him until I came home and saw him with Sam and Leah's kinder."

At least she wasn't pretending. "Do they know? Did you talk to them, to your parents?"

Rebecca put her hand to her forehead, shielding her face. "They guessed because of Lige. But I didn't... I don't want to tell them. It would hurt them."

"Ach, Rebecca, don't you think they would be imagining even worse. Just knowing he hurt you—"

"People hurt each other in all kinds of ways." She seemed suddenly weary. "And it wasn't James's fault."

Daniel struggled to control himself. "How could it not be his fault? He was a grown man, not a child."

"In a way, he wasn't. Grown, I mean." She rubbed her temple. "You have to know about it to understand. James... Well, he was always a bit quick-tempered. And daring, almost as if he enjoyed taking chances. But that was all, until the accident he had injured his head. Afterward, it was like he couldn't control himself. The doctors explained it to me. They said the injury had affected his impulse control. He'd flare up at the least little thing."

"And hit you." That was what he couldn't get past. He clenched his hands into fists despite his effort not to react.

"Not really hit." She pushed the word away, still trying to defend him. "He'd just grab me, push me...sometimes I'd fall." She shook her head. "I tried to get him to go back to the doctor. His parents tried. But he wouldn't listen. He didn't think there was anything wrong with him. It was everybody else who was at fault."

"If you'd left…" he began, knowing it was foolish even before he got the words out.

"He was my husband." There was dignity in Rebecca's answer, and he saw her draw on some inner strength.

"I know. You wanted to help him." Could she have had any love left for him by that time? Or had he killed it by then?

"Finally I went to the bishop. That seemed the only answer. And Bishop Paul was wonderful kind. He made all the arrangements for James to go into the hospital, to have the medication and counseling. He didn't give James a choice about getting it. And it seemed to help."

"So, you know you did the right thing in going to the bishop." He suspected there were a few people who'd call that disloyal. "It was the only thing you could do to help him recover."

Rebecca shrugged, seeming to find it easier to talk now that the worst was told. "Everyone didn't think so, but I had no choice but to act, for Lige's sake, as well as for James." She hesitated, her eyes darkening.

"What happened?" He longed to clasp her hand, but he controlled himself. "Something went wrong."

She nodded. "Maybe I counted on it too much. Maybe… Ach, I don't know. But one day, it all seemed to fall apart. He flew into a rage over a half-trained buggy horse, trying to force it into the harness. It reared up, hit him…" She pressed her lips together, but she didn't need to finish. He could see the outcome in her face.

"So that's how he was killed." He'd wondered, and now he knew.

Rebecca was silent, maybe even spent with the effort of telling her story. He wanted so much to put his arms around her and hold her close. To tell her...

What? There was little he could say or do. When she'd fallen as a child, he'd comforted her, but there was nothing he could do about this pain.

You can be her friend. His thoughts went back to Onkel Zeb's advice. That was what Rebecca needed right now. Not a new love, not someone to tell her what to do. Just a friend—a friend she could trust.

"It's over now." He picked his words carefully. "Lige is getting better, and you have a new life ahead of you."

"You won't tell anyone..."

Maybe she was regretting telling him already. "No, I won't tell anyone, though I think you should tell your mamm and daad the whole story. But it's up to you." He hesitated, praying he was finding the right words. "I'm your friend, Rebecca. I won't speak unless you tell me to. You can always trust me."

Chapter Eight

Rebecca was just as glad not to see Daniel on Sunday. Maybe it was natural to feel regret and embarrassment after having told someone else something so personal.

But no, she didn't really regret it. The story had been ready to pour out of her, and Daniel was safe. She could trust him, and he wouldn't be as hurt by it as her mamm and daad would be. So the thing was done, but still, a break before she came face-to-face with Daniel was for the best.

Since it was an off Sunday for worship, the family had welcomed Aunt Ruth and Onkel Thomas and their children and grandchildren for the afternoon. Sam had cooked chicken on the grill; Mamm had baked, and she and Leah had prepared food for a whole host of folks. Naturally, Aunt Ruth and her daughters and daughters-in-law had insisted on bringing dishes, as well. The day had been filled with talk and laughter, and Lige had played with so many new cousins he'd lost count of them.

Now it was Monday, and Rebecca found the quiet shop a fine place to be, even though she'd only had one customer all morning. She still had some clearing up to do after the opening on Saturday, and she was engaged in planning how she would set up for the quilting group. The front corner of the shop would be ideal for that purpose, and she could set up a circle of chairs and a round table for folks to lay out fabric.

As she worked, she listened to the sound of voices filtering in from the back porch. Daniel had started work on the porch steps, and Lige had run eagerly to help him. Daniel's slow, deep voice contrasted with Lige's excited chatter, and both their voices were punctuated by the periodic sound of the hammer.

When had she heard Lige chattering like that to anyone but her? The thought seemed to touch her heart and resonate there. He was normally as silent as a little mouse, and though he'd begun to come out of his shell, he still didn't talk that freely to any adult except her. And now Daniel.

What a blessing it was to have come home again. James's parents hadn't wanted her to take Lige so far away, of course. That was only natural. But she thought they had understood, even though they didn't talk about it, how much Lige had been affected by his father's troubles. Perhaps this summer they'd come for a visit. She wasn't ready to take Lige back there yet, but eventually, maybe even that would be possible.

Busying herself with getting out books of quilt patterns for the group to see, she lost track of time, but eventually she realized that she wasn't hearing the voices from the back porch any longer, although the hammer still tapped. A vague uneasiness touched her, and she put down the book of quilt patterns and went back through the kitchen. No harm in leaving the shop unattended for a few minutes—she'd hear if a car or buggy pulled in.

Daniel still knelt by the steps, fitting a board into place, but Lige had wandered off into the yard. He knelt in the grass, seeming to concentrate on something.

Daniel finished what he was doing and looked up with a smile. "Are you taking a break?"

His relaxed expression bridged the faint awkwardness of the moment, and she was grateful. "Just a short one. You seem to have lost your helper."

"He'll be back. We noticed how many violets are blooming, and he decided to pick some for you. Hush, it's a secret."

"I promise to be surprised." She watched him return to his work, appreciating the skilled way he fitted each plank into place. He never hurried—each one had to be right before he moved on.

That reminded her of the appointment he'd been out on this morning. "How did your meeting go with the people who want their kitchen done? Did you get the job?"

"I don't know yet." He grinned. "The truth is the two of them haven't agreed yet on what they want. Everything I suggested, either the wife agreed and the husband didn't, or it went the other way around. I finally had to tell them I couldn't give an estimate if I didn't know what the job entailed."

"Usually it's the wife who has the final say about a kitchen," she said. "After all, she's the one who'll be working in it."

"Not with these two. It seems the husband prides himself on being a chef, and he wants everything organized just so. And his wife seemed more interested in having the latest style. Somehow I don't think it's going to end up being the right job for me."

That didn't seem to bother Daniel. "If she's so concerned about fashion, it wonders me that they'd call in an Amish carpenter to begin with, in that case," she said. "You'd think an Englisch company would be more to her taste."

"Oh, but the woman said having an Amish-built kitchen is all the rage now. Good workmanship and all that."

"That's true enough." It was just what she'd been thinking about him. "They couldn't do better than to hire you."

Daniel stopped working, sitting back on his heels. "The truth is that I'm not all that eager for the job. I have enough work to go on with, and I don't need something that might be a constant hassle." His smile was back, crinkling his eyes. "I don't want to be an umpire."

She laughed. "I don't blame you." For a moment they were silent, smiling at each other, and then Rebecca gave herself a mental shake. "I'd better get back to my work and let you get back to yours."

Escaping to the kitchen, she reminded herself that Daniel was a friend. Just a friend. That was all he wanted and all she wanted, as well.

She took a step toward the shop, and as she did, she heard Daniel shout loud enough to make her wince.

"Lige! Stop!"

Heart pounding, she ran back to the porch, jumped over the steps and raced toward her son. Lige stood by a pile of old boards lying next to the shed, seeming frozen to the spot, his small face white with fear.

Reaching him, Rebecca knelt to wrap her arms around him and hold him close. "It's all right," she crooned. "Nothing is wrong. You're safe."

She glared at Daniel, who'd come up beside them with a hoe in his hand. "How could you?" The words tumbled out, angry and unforgiving. "You know how he feels. I trusted you, and then you…you behaved just like James."

Daniel's face didn't change at the battering of her words. He took a step toward the pile of rotten wood and raised the hoe. The sun glittered for a moment off the blade as it flashed down.

Daniel struck again. Then, using the hoe, he lifted something from the woodpile and dropped it on the grass, safely distant from them. It was a copperhead.

Cold settled into Rebecca's heart. What had she done? She had to speak, to tell Daniel she was sorry…

But he ignored her, not even looking at her. He knelt next to her son and spoke softly.

"I'm sorry if I scared you, Lige. I didn't want to yell, but I had to. I was afraid that if you moved any closer, the copperhead might be startled." He touched Lige's back with a gentle hand. "Did you ever see a copperhead up close?"

Somehow the soft voice seemed to break through Lige's fear. He let go of Rebecca's skirt, looked at Daniel and then shook his head.

"Do you want to?" he asked. "It can't hurt you. It's dead now." He held out his hand. "Komm. Have a look."

Rebecca wanted to grasp her son and hold him back, but she knew instinctively that would be the wrong thing to do. He was responding to Daniel, and there was a lesson to be learned right now. She couldn't interfere.

Lige hesitated. He looked up at her, and she managed to give him a nod and a smile. "Go ahead."

Her son reached out, and Daniel's large hand wrapped around his securely. Together they approached the snake. Daniel began showing Lige the markings, describing the hourglass pattern. She tried to watch, but tears stung her eyes.

She couldn't stand here any longer. She had to leave before they saw her cry. With a murmured excuse, Rebecca fled for the shop.

But even there, she couldn't be alone. Mamm was there waiting for her.

"Mammi." Rebecca turned away, trying to hide her tears. Her mother's arms went around her, and her mother's hands wiped her tears away.

"Hush, now, hush. It will be all right. Mammi's here."

The words calmed her as nothing else could. They were the words her mother had used when she was a small child—the same words she used when Lige was hurting.

Rebecca straightened, blinking back the last of her

tears. "How...how did you get here? Why didn't I see you?"

Mammi took a step back, but her faded blue eyes still watched Rebecca with tender care. "You and Daniel seemed to be having words. I didn't want to interrupt, so I slipped in through the front."

"Maybe it would have been better if I had been interrupted." She managed a shaky laugh. "I made such a fool of myself. Worse, I hurt Daniel—hurt him terribly. I don't know if he'll ever forgive me."

"There's nothing so bad it can't be forgiven," Mamm said. "You know that, and I'm sure Daniel does, as well." She hesitated. "Do you want to tell me about it?"

Rebecca's heart hurt that her mother felt she had to be so careful around her. What had she and Daad been imagining? They couldn't help but see that something had been wrong with her marriage...the marriage they hadn't wanted her to hurry into. Had they, even then, had doubts about James?

Rubbing her forehead, she tried to focus. Her head was aching from the thoughts and regrets that spun around her. She had to tell Mamm something.

"I heard Daniel yell at Lige. I didn't realize what was happening...just jumped into thinking it was like...like James all over again. I'm not even sure what I said to him, but I know I hurt him. And here, all along, he was just trying to protect Lige."

Her throat seemed to close at the thought.

Mamm touched her arm. "What did Lige need protecting from? Is he all right?"

"Yah, he's safe. It was a copperhead in that pile of old lumber by the shed. Daniel killed it. There's no danger."

"Ach, I told your daad that he and Sam should clean up back there." Mamm's voice took on a scolding tone, and Rebecca thought she was relieved to concentrate on something she could fix. "Well, they're going to do it before they're much older, I'll tell you that."

"Don't scold them too much." Her smile came more easily now. "We've all had so much to do, and I… I haven't exactly been acting as if help is wilkom."

Mamm patted her. "We're family. We help each other. You just got a little…a little shortsighted for a bit."

Rebecca wasn't sure *shortsighted* was a strong enough word for it. She seemed to be seeing herself through her mother's eyes, and she didn't like what she saw.

She had let what happened with James change her deep inside herself. She'd turned into someone afraid to trust, afraid to open up even to those who loved her.

It wasn't a pretty picture, was it? Worse, she wasn't even sure she could change. It was one thing to recognize her fault, but another entirely to become again the woman she should be.

But at least she could begin to mend fences with her family easily enough, just by letting them help when they wanted to. Daniel was going to be more difficult.

"I have to tell Daniel how sorry I am. I have to ask his forgiveness."

"Yah, you do." Mamm glanced toward the back, where the duet of male voices could be heard again. "Wait a bit, maybe. Let him and Lige have some time together. Then you can talk to Daniel. He won't be building up a grudge, and you'll know when it's the right time."

Rebecca let her mother's words sink in, trying to believe she'd know when the time was right. And praying that, when it was, she'd be able to find the words.

Daniel forced himself to focus on Lige, blocking off the memory of Rebecca's angry words. Right now he couldn't do anything about Rebecca, but he could reassure Lige and bring him back to where they'd been before the incident.

His calm explanations seemed to bear fruit. Together they had taken the snake and tossed it into the deep weeds at the edge of the mowed yard.

Lige stood, staring at the spot. "Should we dig a hole and put it in?"

"We can do that." Would that reassure the boy? He was in over his head now, never having been a father and trying to think what Caleb would do in these circumstances. "But if we leave it there, it will scare mice and moles away from the yard. Mammi wouldn't like mice in her shop, would she?"

"Mammi doesn't like mice at all." Lige's small, serious face relaxed into a smile. "So that's a gut plan." He seemed satisfied, so Daniel let it go, hoping the boy wasn't in for a nightmare about snakes.

"I'd better get back to work on the steps. Do you want to help me?"

Lige nodded. "I'll hold the boards for you. Then I can tell Grossdaadi that I'm learning about making steps."

He skipped on ahead to the steps and then circled back. "Grossdaadi is gut at teaching me how to do things. But so are you."

It was a generous compliment, Daniel decided. "Denke. Let's see if we can get finished."

Returning to the steps, they worked without saying much for a few minutes. Then Lige gave him a solemn look. "My daadi got kicked by a horse, and he died. If I got bit by a snake, would I die?"

Once again, Daniel was in way over his head. But the boy had asked him, and a question deserved an answer. "No, you wouldn't die. I'm right here, and I'd get the doctor to give you some medicine to make you better. You might feel sick for a while, though."

"Oh." He pondered Daniel's words. "I don't like medicine. But Mammi says sometimes we have to take it anyway."

"That's right." He tapped the final step into place. "I never could figure out why it has to taste so bad, though. What about you?"

Lige actually giggled. "Me, too. Mammi always gives me a drink afterward to take the taste away."

"Gut idea." His heart had warmed at the sound of that giggle. Lige would be all right.

As for Rebecca...who could say if or when she'd be all right? Her explosion at him had hurt him, not just because of what she'd said, but because it showed how far she had to go in recovering. The girl he'd known was gone, and he wasn't sure how to help the person she'd become.

He and Lige finished and packed up his tools. "Denke. I was wonderful glad to have your help."

"Me, too." Lige jumped off the new step. "I'm going to ask Mammi if I can go find Grossdaadi." He scrambled back up the steps and darted into the house.

Daniel hesitated. Should he leave? Or should he wait around, on the chance he could have a word with Rebecca? Not that he knew what he'd say if it happened.

He was still there when Lige ran back out, waved and trotted down the lane. Rebecca came out of the house, crossed the porch and walked slowly down the steps, looking everywhere but at him.

At the bottom, she stopped. "You made a wonderful gut job of the new steps."

"Lige and I," he amended. "I couldn't have done it without him."

"Ach, Daniel, you are so kind to him." She looked at him, her eyes filled with misery. "And, in return, I said such terrible things to you. Please, can you forgive me? There's no excuse. I just…"

She seemed to run out of words, but he knew what she was thinking. "You just felt as if you and Lige were back in the past. I understand."

"Do you?" Rebecca's expression was rueful. "I don't see how you can. You would never be so thoughtless and mean as I was."

"Rebecca, it was not such a terrible thing as you are making it." He almost took her hand but stopped himself.

"I hurt you." Her lips trembled on the words, and she pressed them together.

"Yah, I was hurt." He couldn't very well deny it. "But I knew what was happening. I understand."

Tears glistened in her eyes, but she smiled. "You always do understand. That's what makes you such a wonderful gut friend."

Friend, he reminded himself. All he could be to her was a friend, but that was what she needed. He had to keep telling himself that, so he wouldn't give in to the longing to put his arms around her.

"If you need to hear me say it, I forgive you," he said, keeping his tone light and teasing.

"Denke." She hesitated, and the worry came back into her face. "Now I have to explain it to Lige. I don't know what he must think."

Daniel thought of the child's questions and comments. "Lige may understand more than you might guess." He touched her hand, very lightly, pleased when she didn't pull away. "It will be all right. He'll understand that you were frightened for him. And that you love him."

"I hope so." She turned her hand, clasping his for a brief instant before turning away. "Denke, Daniel."

He stood, watching her as she walked away toward the farmhouse. His hand was still warm where she'd touched it, and he was smiling for no reason at all.

Chapter Nine

By the next morning, Rebecca had decided that she should take a step forward in conquering her fear of letting people in. Standing where she was didn't seem to be an option, and she'd seen the proof of Daniel's advice in the pleasure the family had taken in helping with the shop's opening.

At the moment, they were cleaning up the kitchen after breakfast, and the men and younger kinder had scattered to their chores. She brought a platter to the sink, where Mary Ann was washing dishes and Leah was drying.

"I was thinking about the quilting group coming this afternoon. You did say that you'd like to help, Leah. Do you think you have time today to sit in on it? I'm not sure how experienced any of them are, other than Mamm's friend."

Leah's face lit with a smile. "Ach, I was planning to get in on the group today. I'm looking forward to it. I can bring a table runner I'm working on, just so I have some reason for being a part of it."

"Why would you need a reason? You're working with me on the shop, remember?" It was easy to see that Leah was genuinely pleased and not just pretending in order to be helpful.

"Can't I do something, Aunt Rebecca?" Mary Ann turned, her hands full of soapsuds. "I can help any customers who come in while you're busy. And if the lady with the boppli is there, I could watch the little one for her."

She glanced at Leah for her approval, and Leah nodded.

"Denke, Mary Ann. I'm pretty sure she's coming, so that would be helpful."

"Shannon doesn't seem to have any close friends or family here in the valley," Leah said. "That's a shame. It's not easy to manage everything, especially with a first baby." She smiled and flicked her dish towel at her daughter. "That wasn't you, you know. I made all my mistakes on your brother."

"I'll tell him so the next time he starts bossing me." Mary Ann's eyes twinkled, making her look very like her mother.

"You'll never break a big brother of that," Rebecca said. "Your daadi was my big brother, and he still thinks I need his help and advice, just because he claims he held my hand when I was learning to walk."

Leah shook her head in mock sorrow. "Poor Sam. We'd best not tell him we were talking about him."

Rebecca nodded, but the light words made her wonder if she'd hurt her brother's feelings when she didn't seem to need him. There seemed to be no end to the possible wrong steps she could take with those who loved her.

"How many women do you think will be there this afternoon?" Leah dried her hands and hung up the towel. Together they finished putting dishes back in the cabinet.

"I wish I knew. Probably at least three, but from what Mamm's friend said, she intended to tell others about it."

"Glenda Allen," Leah said, supplying the name. "Glenda likes to organize things, that's certain sure. I guess they'll bring their own supplies, but it wouldn't hurt to have a few extra needles and such ready."

"I'll get some out once I open the shop this morning."

Leah stood with her hand on the cabinet door, as if she had something on her mind. Finally she turned to Rebecca with her quick smile.

"I'm wonderful glad you asked me to be a part of the shop. I know you've said you wanted to stand on your own feet since James's death, and I didn't think I should push. But I wanted to, like I always do." She gave a little laugh, as if admitting a fault she wasn't really sorry for.

"I'm glad, as well." She clasped Leah's hand in an impulsive movement. "I've been a little silly about that. Anyway, that's what Daniel says."

"So you'll take advice from Daniel, will you?" Leah's tone was teasing. "I might have known. Sam says the two of you were always telling each other your secrets when you were small."

"We did." She frowned a little. Was that still appropriate, to be so close when they were grown?

"Now, don't start worrying about it," Leah said, seeming to read her thoughts. "Daniel is a friend." She darted a quick, teasing glance at her. "Maybe someday he'll be more."

Before Rebecca could deny it, Leah had whisked out the back door, calling to one of the children.

Rebecca stood where she was, seeing what had been hidden from her until this moment. Daniel had moved from being her childhood friend to being someone whose presence and support was necessary to her happiness.

That frightened her, because she'd promised herself she'd never lean on a man again. And more important, because Daniel had never given a sign that he wanted anything more than friendship from her.

It was nearly time for the quilting group to gather, and Rebecca was a bundle of nerves. Could she really pull this off? Leah, who must have been interpreting her expressions, gave her a quick hug.

"You'll do fine. Everyone is coming to quilt, not to judge."

"You're right. I'm being foolish, I suppose, but..." She stopped when the bell over the door jingled, surprised because she hadn't heard a car.

It was Jessie, Daniel's sister-in-law, and she carried a workbasket. "This is the right time, yah? Leah told me about the quilting group, and I'd like to join."

She looked a little uncertain, and Rebecca hurried to make her welcome. "I'd sehr be glad for you to join us. I don't know how much the Englisch ladies know about quilting, though."

"That's fine." Jessie set down her basket in order to remove her bonnet and pat her hair into place.

She was about Rebecca's age, Rebecca thought, with a serene, pleasant face and that glow women had when they were expecting a baby. For just an instant, Rebecca envied that joy. Would she ever experience it again?

Leah had mentioned once that Caleb's first wife, Jessie's cousin, had been a beauty. No one would say that about Jessie, she supposed, but Jessie radiated kindness in a way that drew people to her.

"Caleb thinks I need to get out and do things with other women. He's always worrying I'll feel out of place so far from my family. I tell him it's nonsense, but he worries." A slight shadow crossed her face, and Rebecca wondered if she were thinking about her cousin.

"Caleb loves you, that's all." Leah said, smiling. "I'm glad he thinks of things like that, especially if it means you'll join us."

A car sounded on the gravel outside, and in a moment, another one. In a few minutes, the shop was filled with the sound of women's voices.

Shannon had been the first one there, and she willingly surrendered little Betsy to Mary Ann. "Thanks so much. There's a bottle in the diaper bag if she seems hungry. And you can always hand her back to me if she's fussy."

"We'll be fine." Mary Ann bounced the baby adeptly. "Betsy remembers me. Don't you, Betsy?"

The baby cooed up at her, for all the world, as if she were agreeing, and the other women laughed.

"Relax," Glenda said. "Amish girls seem to be born

knowing how to handle babies. Every young mother needs a respite now and then. I still remember how my back would ache from walking the floor with a fussy baby."

The friend she'd brought with her—a woman about her age that she'd introduced as Alice—shook her head. "Being with my babies was the happiest time of my life. I wouldn't have traded a second of it."

Shannon, hearing her, looked a little abashed, as if she'd been a bad mother for handing her baby over to someone else, even for a moment.

Then the third Englischer, Debby, a woman with a dark, lively face and a wealth of dark curls, gave a chuckle. "Alice, you know perfectly well you're looking back at those days through rose-colored glasses now that your children are all grown and gone. Believe me, I have three school-age boys, and sometimes I'd give a million bucks just for a little peace and quiet."

"Shut yourself in the bathroom," Glenda said and looked surprised when everyone laughed. "I'm serious. When my kids were little, that was the only place I could go that they wouldn't come looking for me."

Somehow that frank admission seemed to break the ice, and Rebecca was able to get everyone settled in the area she'd set up for them. In a few minutes, each of the women had brought out a project and started comparing notes about quilting techniques.

Listening carefully, as she nodded and smiled, Rebecca realized that Glenda was probably the only advanced quilter in the group. She and Leah would need to spend a little time showing techniques as they went along.

Shannon took out a fairly simple Log Cabin square that was, she said, intended for a table runner. "I took a class the last place we lived, and that's where I started it. But then we had to move, and I didn't get to finish the project."

"Well, you can do it now," Leah said. "If there's anything that you don't understand, just speak up. Someone will have an answer."

Glenda nodded in agreement. "It must have been hard moving when your baby was so small."

Shannon shrugged. "It's Rick's job," she said. "He's a sales representative, and the company keeps transferring him where they need him. It wasn't so bad at first… kind of exciting, really, to see new places. But now…"

"Things are different when you have a baby," Rebecca finished for her when she seemed reluctant to say the words. "I remember when my Elijah was small, and we lived out in Ohio. My husband's family was kind and helpful, but I longed for my mother and my cousins, even so."

The other women began sharing their own experiences, and soon they were chattering as if they were old friends, while their needles flashed through the fabric. It was like an Amish quilting frolic, Rebecca realized.

Maybe the point was that women were women, no matter whether they were Englisch or Amish. If they'd had or were going to have babies, they had a common bond that brought them together.

Glenda spread out the crib quilt she was working

on—a lovely applique pattern in pastel colors, with teddy bears and puppies. "This is for the new grandbaby we expect to see in September."

They all oohed and aahed about it, and it just confirmed Rebecca's opinion that Glenda was an excellent quilter. So good, in fact, that it wondered her why Glenda had been eager to belong to a group. But maybe she, like Shannon, enjoyed the companionship.

"This will be ready for quilting by next week." Glenda looked from Leah to Rebecca. "Do you want to have everyone participate in the quilting?"

"That would be fun," Debby exclaimed. "Could we?"

"For sure. If everyone agrees, I'll have a quilting frame set up." Rebecca glanced around the room. She'd have to move a few things to fit her quilting frame in so they could all sit around it. "I'll get everything ready for next week."

Jessie was looking at the available space, as well. "If you want, you can use my portable quilting frame. It would be plenty big enough for a crib quilt, and easier to bring in, I think."

"That would be wonderful, if you're sure you won't need it yourself."

Jessie shook her head. "I don't have anything nearly ready for quilting."

"It's all set then."

Glenda obviously enjoyed having things settled. She smoothed the crib quilt with her palm.

"I have a crib quilt that was made for me by my grandmother. Now I'm making one for my expected grandchild. That's nice, isn't it? To think how women's handiwork passes on from one generation to the next."

They all nodded, touched, but it was Shannon who spoke. "I have one, as well. That was really what got me started in quilting. My grandmother said she sewed love into every stitch."

Rebecca felt tears sting her eyes. The two Englischers, between them, had said exactly what she felt about quilting, women and love.

Daniel ran his hand along the curve of the back piece for the rocking chair he was making. Jessie, he felt sure, would love it even if there were flaws, but he wanted the gift to be perfect—or at least as near perfection as he could make it. No craftsman could ever claim that something he'd made was perfect.

The door to his workshop opened, and he looked up, startled to see Rebecca linger on the step, as if not certain of her welcome. But surely they'd put the discomfort of her explosion behind them.

"Rebecca, komm in. What brings you here?" He sent a quick look around the room, wishing it looked a little neater. But it was a workshop, not a parlor, after all.

"Jessie said…" She stopped, smiling a little. "I'm starting backward, I guess. Jessie came to the quilting group today, and she mentioned a portable quilting rack I could borrow. To use in the group, you see. I'm sure I could have carried it, but she said you could bring it when you come over the next time."

"I'd be glad to bring it. Jessie probably wants to make sure it's spotless before it goes over to your shop."

"Maybe so." She moved a bit closer. "What are you working on? A new kitchen job?"

"Ach, no, not now." Daniel stepped out of the way so she could see the half-finished rocker. "It's for Jessie. What do you think?"

"She's going to love it." Rebecca smoothed her hand along the back, much as he had done. "I didn't realize you made furniture as well as doing remodeling."

"A little bit of everything, I guess," he admitted. "I haven't made a rocker before, but Onkel Zeb helped me with shaping the rockers. That's the only thing that was tricky."

"You wouldn't want it to creak and wobble when she's rocking in it."

Rebecca's smile was sweet as she looked at it, as if she were remembering rocking her own little one, and it touched his heart. Of course, they both knew Jessie needed the rocker because she was going to have a baby, but custom insisted that babies weren't talked about in mixed company, until they were safely in their cradles.

She would leave in a moment, her message delivered, and he found he didn't want her to go.

"How did the quilting group go this afternoon? Were you pleased with it?"

"Oh, yah, so happy." Rebecca smiled, shaking her head a little. "I don't know what I was worried about. Englisch or Amish, women are interested in the same things. We chattered away as if it were an Amish quilting frolic."

"See? I knew it would work out. And having the group will draw people to the shop."

"That's what Leah said. Quilters will hear about us and want to buy their supplies at our shop. I'm thinking we could do just as much business with fabrics and notions as with the quilts and such."

"More business maybe, but not more money. Some people will drive miles to find a handmade quilt, so I've heard. I was thinking about that—you need to get listed in that little booklet about things to see and do in the county."

"Actually, Shannon, the one who has the baby, mentioned that on the day I opened the shop, and reminded me again when she was leaving the quilting group. One of the others said she'd take a picture of the shop and send it in for me on her computer. Wasn't that kind?"

He nodded, thinking other people besides him found Rebecca an easy person to be kind to. "It wouldn't be a bad idea to put up some signs, too. Pretty soon you'll have as much business as you can handle."

"I don't know about that, but I'm wonderful happy to think that I'll be able to support my son with my business. And besides, it's just what I've always wanted to do."

"To be able to work at something you love is a gift," he said soberly, thinking of the times when he'd thought himself destined to spend all his life working the dairy farm, until Caleb's son was old enough to help more.

"I can't tell you how much I appreciate what you've done." Rebecca reached out impulsively but stopped short of touching him. "I'd never have done it without your help."

"You would have. You've turned into a strong woman, Rebecca."

It was true. He didn't know why he should be surprised at that. Despite all the unhappiness she'd endured in recent years, she'd come through it with her inner self still strong. Maybe she didn't recognize it entirely herself yet, but she would, in time.

Rebecca didn't seem to know what to do with his words. After a moment, she shook her head just slightly. "Denke, Daniel. I'm not so sure about it myself, but I'm grateful I've been able to count on you."

Her words seemed to hit him right in the heart. Could anyone really count on him? "I wish…" he began and then let the words fade away.

"You're thinking of Aaron, ain't so?" Rebecca's eyes filled with sympathy.

"How did you know?" he asked, somewhat reluctantly, not sure he wanted to talk about his brother.

"There's a look on your face when you think of him— love and hurt mixed up together." She hesitated before going on, maybe wondering if she was going too far. "Have you heard anything more of him?"

"No. Onkel Zeb says we just have to wait and pray that Aaron will decide to return to us. I guess we can't make the decision for him. But it's awful hard to do nothing now that I know where he is."

Rebecca was silent for a moment, frowning a little. "I wouldn't want to argue with Zeb, but…" She paused again. "You know, after James died, I got sort of stuck. I couldn't make up my mind which way to turn, and everyone else was telling me what to do. And then Mamm and Daad came. They didn't try to decide for me. They just let me know that a home was waiting for me and Lige here. I think maybe I needed to hear that from them."

Daniel let her words sink in, and they resonated in his heart. Could it be true? Was it possible that Aaron needed to hear that his home was waiting for him?

If so, they had to tell him.

Chapter Ten

Rebecca moved around the shop, putting away things she'd got out for the quilting group the previous day. She now had the portable quilting rack against one wall, and she didn't want the shop to start looking cluttered.

Daniel had shown up early with the quilting frame, but then he'd left, saying he had some things to do. That was just as well. If she found him working on her house again, she'd have to tell him to stop. She couldn't let him continue working without pay.

There might have been another reason for Daniel's quick disappearance this morning. Had he been disturbed by what she'd said when he'd talked about Aaron? It was certainly possible. She'd tried not to give advice, but to stick to what had helped her when she was far from home. But maybe, even that was unwarranted interference. Daniel was very sensitive about what he saw as his failure with his little brother. She certainly hadn't wanted to make him feel even worse.

And now that she considered the circumstances, it

had probably wondered him why she was in his workshop at all. There hadn't been any very good reason for it. Jessie could have passed the word along herself.

The truth was that Jessie was matchmaking, she feared, just as Leah was. Oh, they were being careful. They probably thought they'd been very subtle, but she'd seen through them quickly. They thought she and Daniel would make a good pair.

Maybe they would have at a different time, but not now. Not when Daniel was tied in knots over his perceived failure with people he'd loved, and not when she felt it impossible to trust her future and Lige's to another man. If only...

A futile line of thought was broken when a car pulled in by the shop. Rebecca gave a quick brush to her apron and pretended to be busy sorting the thread rack.

The bell jingled, and a tall well-dressed Englisch woman came in. Not just well-dressed, but maybe a bit over-dressed for the country. She'd look more at home on a city street, Rebecca considered. Not local, that was certain.

She smiled and moved toward the woman. "Wilkom. May I show you something?"

The woman looked around, frowning a little, before speaking. "I'm interested in full-size quilts. What do you have in stock?"

"This way." Rebecca led her to the bed she'd set up to display some of the full-size quilts. They were spread out on the bed, one on top of the other, so the customer could see how each one looked. "Were you interested in any particular color or pattern?"

"No, not really." She stared at the classic Nine-Patch quilt that was on top, running her hand along it, leaning close to examine the stitching, examining the back and then flipping up the tag on the corner that listed the price and the maker.

Then she jotted a couple of notes in a small notebook she took from her handbag. "The price is a little high for a simple nine-patch, don't you think?" Without waiting for an answer, she went on. "Let's see the next one."

Rebecca carefully folded back the top quilt to reveal the one underneath. This quilt, one that she'd made herself, rather than one of those on consignment, was a Tumbling Blocks quilt done in rather bold colors. She'd felt a qualm or two about the colors herself, but she thought it was something that might appeal to an Englischer.

"Hmm." The woman obviously wasn't one to commit herself, but the sound seemed favorable. She went through the whole process again, just as she had with the first one, and jotted down information in that small notebook. Again, she frowned at the price.

"I might be interested, but the price is far too high," she said crisply. "Consider cutting it in half, and I'd think about it."

Rebecca was speechless for a moment. She'd told herself to expect rudeness at times from customers, but didn't the woman realize that what she'd suggested meant that Rebecca would receive pennies an hour for the work that had gone into the quilt?

Perhaps not. Or maybe she was just accustomed to bargaining for everything she bought.

"I couldn't do that," she said, trying to keep her voice firm. With a quick movement, she turned back the Tumbling Blocks quilt to reveal the Log Cabin quilt in shades of blue and yellow that one of Leah's friends had made.

The woman made a gesture, as if she'd pull the other quilt back, but she checked it. Instead, she studied the one in front of her with that same careful assessment.

Rebecca couldn't quite figure it out. She'd watched people buying quilts often enough, but they usually had a color scheme in mind and were looking for the perfect quilt to fit into it. They didn't usually jot down so many notes either, maybe just asking the prices on some they were interested in.

This woman was certainly a meticulous shopper. They went through the whole process with every quilt, and by the time they'd finished, Rebecca figured she'd probably filled up her entire notebook.

At last, frowning at what she'd written, she spoke abruptly. "Let me see the Tumbling Blocks quilt again."

Rebecca turned back, reminding herself that patience was a necessary requirement for a shopkeeper. "The Tumbling Blocks pattern depends upon the colors the quilter chooses to give the impression of movement in the design."

"Yes, I know. Did you make it?"

Rebecca nodded.

"Good, then you can negotiate the price," the woman said briskly. "I'll give you two hundred and fifty for it. Cash." She actually opened her purse and took out a roll of bills.

"I'm sorry." Rebecca resolutely turned her gaze away from the money and declined to think about what she could do with the money. This was a business, not a private matter. "I couldn't possibly."

"Come on now. You can't possibly get the price you have marked. You don't exactly have people lined up to buy your quilts. Isn't it worth it to you to make a sale and have some ready cash?" She began counting out the sum.

Somehow, the gesture was the last straw. It was rude in any culture. Rebecca wouldn't allow herself to become angry, but she suspected her cheeks were flushed.

"No. I couldn't think of it. The quilt is worth every penny of the price."

"It's only worth what someone is willing to pay for it," the woman replied.

True enough, but she wasn't going to give away the work of her hands that easily.

"I couldn't." A wave of annoyance swept through Rebecca. The Englischer looked ready to stand there and argue all day. "I might consider discounting the price a little, but I would have to discuss it with my partner first."

"I thought this was your shop." The woman's tone was sharp.

"It is, but I have a partner, and she's not here today." Leah was only as far away as the farmhouse, but there was no reason why she needed to know that. "If you'd care to come back another day, we can talk about it."

It took several repetitions of that statement, but finally she seemed to get through. The woman shoved her notebook into her bag, snapped the bag closed on notes and money and stalked out.

No sooner had she gone than Leah came rushing in the back door, flushed and breathless. "That woman," she gasped. "You didn't let her talk you into anything, did you?"

"Of course not." Rebecca pushed away the thought of how tempting that cash had been. "She offered me a ridiculous price for the Tumbling Blocks quilt, and I turned her down. Why?" Obviously there was something going on that she didn't understand.

Leah leaned against the counter, getting her breath and laughing a little. "Oh, dear. How silly I must have looked, running down the lane like a loose pony. I recognized the car, you see."

"No, I don't see," she said, smiling at Leah's amusement. "Leah, what are you talking about?"

"That woman," Leah said. "I recognized the car, because I happened to see it at Elsie Schutz's house one day. Elsie said the woman is a dealer. She drives around the county buying up quilts as low as she can get them, and then offers them for three or four times that at a shop in the city. Elsie said I should warn you, but in all the fuss of getting open, it slipped my mind."

"Ach, so that's it." Rebecca leaned against the counter next to her, giggling a little and feeling weak in the knees at the same time. "I should have guessed, but I never thought of it. I figured she was just looking for a bargain. And maybe thinking she could get the better of a dumb Amish woman."

"So long as you didn't give in. That's the important

thing. I was kicking myself when I realized I hadn't warned you and there she was already. Ach, I'm sehr sorry, Rebecca."

"Nothing to be sorry about." Rebecca patted her arm. "It ended fine. I didn't let her take advantage of me."

She repeated those words to herself. No, she hadn't let the woman take advantage of her. Maybe she was regaining a little of the spunk she used to have after all.

Daniel had no sooner started removing one of the old cabinets from the kitchen wall than Rebecca erupted into the room from the shop.

"Daniel, what are you doing? I thought you understood we couldn't go on with the work until…" She glanced at Lige, looking at her with wide blue eyes, and seemed to change her mind about the end of that sentence. "Until later."

From his perch on the step stool, Daniel gestured to Lige. "That one," he said. "The biggest screwdriver."

Lige handed it up to him, eager to help.

"Please stop."

She sounded determined, and he suspected he was in for a battle. That was one reason he'd stopped at the farmhouse and picked up Lige. The other was that he just plain enjoyed being with the boy.

"All I'm doing is prep work right now," he said, attacking the old screws that were rusted into place. "I want to see what condition the wall is in behind this cabinet. Then I can be more realistic about the work I'm going to do."

"But you should be taking other jobs. I'm sure there

are people who want your services. People who can…
Who are in a position to…" Rebecca stopped, obviously
not wanting to mention her lack of money in front of
her son.

He couldn't help smiling, and she saw it. "I suppose
you know there are things I can't say with little pitch-
ers around."

Daniel's smile grew into a grin. "That's why I brought
this one."

He moved on to the next screw. Given the shape they
were in, this was going to take a while. He could just
break up the cabinet, but it went against the grain to do
that needlessly. A craftsman didn't just discard materials. If he could get it off in one piece, it might work in
the cellar for Rebecca to store her canned goods.

Rebecca seemed to have stopped arguing, but her
expression was somber as she watched him. Finally
he sighed and climbed down from the stepladder. He
turned to face her squarely. It looked as if they'd best
have this out.

"Listen, here's the way it is. I really don't have any
big jobs on hand right now. Just a few little things I can
fit in here and there. I was meant to be starting work on
a project this month, but it's been delayed, and nobody
knows for how long. So I can't really start anything else
big, because I have to be available when they need me."

"I see, but…"

"So you'd be doing me a favor by letting me fit this
in now."

"It seems to me it's the other way around when it
comes to favors," she said, her voice tart as a lemon.

"Ach, don't be foolish, Rebecca. I can wait to be paid later. What I can't do is two things at once. So let me get on with this while I'm free. And while I've got Lige to help me."

He tapped the top of Lige's straw hat, and Lige grinned.

"Yah, Mammi. Come September, I'll be in school, and I won't be here to help Daniel."

For a moment longer, she held out against him. Daniel saw the exact instant she gave in—when a tiny smile started in her eyes.

"All right, all right. I guess I can't argue with the two of you. But mind, if you get a chance to work on something else, you take it."

He nodded, feeling triumphant. Rebecca was never going to know whether he turned down another job to work on her house. He'd see to that.

Lige seemed to be losing interest in the adult conversation. He poked at the cardboard box Daniel had carried in with him.

"What's this, Daniel? It looks like plants."

"That's what it is, and I almost forgot to tell your Mammi about it. I'd be in trouble then." He bent and lifted the box to show Rebecca. "This is from Jessie. She saw that you were cleaning up the flower bed alongside the house, so she sent you starts from some of her plants."

"How kind of her." Rebecca came at once to peek into the box. "What did she send?"

Daniel had to shake his head. "To tell you the truth, I don't really remember. I'm not much of a hand for flowers. I just know they're pretty and they smell nice."

"Would they interest you more if they were made of wood?" She was burrowing through the box, and she didn't seem to have any trouble identifying them, just from the young shoots. "That's coreopsis, I'm sure. And coneflowers. And this looks like some type of daisy."

"Can we plant them, Mammi?" Lige bounced up and down at the thought of digging in the dirt. "Please?"

"Why don't we all do it?" Daniel said. "We'll come back to this later, yah? The plants should go in while they're fresh and green. And I see that Jessie even put some trowels in for us to use."

Lige grabbed his mother's hand, but Daniel thought she didn't really need much urging.

"I'll see the car or buggy if anyone comes, so I guess it's all right to leave the shop." She laughed as Lige tugged her along. "Okay, I'm coming."

The three of them trooped outside, with Daniel carrying the box. Planting flowers wasn't exactly part of his job, but he liked seeing the boy's excitement and Rebecca's obvious pleasure. If it were that easy to make her happy, he'd bring plants every day.

Lige, of course, wanted to plunge right in to putting something in the ground.

"Wait, now." Kneeling, Rebecca put out her hand to stop him. "We don't want to get too close to some things that are already here. See those yellow tulips? We'll go over a little more to put in these coneflowers."

"Why is it a coneflower, Mammi?" Lige seemed full of questions these days. Maybe that was a sign he'd started to feel safe here.

"That's a gut question." Daniel echoed, "Why is it a coneflower?"

"You think I don't know, don't you?" Her eyes laughed at him, and it was like old times. "It's because the seed heads in the middle of the blossom get so big they look like cones. The butterflies and birds love them."

Lige poked him. "See? Mammi knows everything about flowers."

That made them both laugh. "Maybe not everything," Rebecca said. "But I do know the coneflowers will spread out, so we have to give them space."

Lige began digging enthusiastically in the spot she indicated, and Daniel leaned across to help him. The soil was rich and friable, since the previous owners had planted there for years. "We'll watch the birds eating the seeds in late summer, ain't so?"

"Yah, we will." Lige's face clouded suddenly. "But what about next year? Will we see them then?"

"For sure." Rebecca was so quick to reassure him that Daniel realized she wanted him to know that this was their permanent home. "These flowers are perennials. That means they come back again, every single summer."

"Gut." Lige gave a little nod, the cloud disappearing from his face.

Daniel exchanged glances with Rebecca, and they shared a moment of understanding about her son. If only... He let that thought drift away. They were both satisfied with things the way they were between them. Why go looking for trouble?

They worked their way along the side of the house. Rebecca seemed able to visualize just where she wanted each plant, and what it would look like when it was in place. She had an eye for shape and color, he guessed. It came through in her quilts, and maybe it also applied to her flowers.

When they reached the end of the planting, Rebecca sent Lige to the outside spigot to rinse off the trowels. "We want to send them back to Jessie nice and clean, ain't so?" she added when he looked as if he'd balk at the chore.

Lige nodded, grabbing the trowels, and ran off happily enough. Rebecca continued to kneel, staring at the plants in front of her, clenching her hands in her lap. Finally she looked up at him.

"I'm thinking I should apologize for what I said yesterday. About your little brother, I mean. It wasn't any of my business, and I shouldn't…"

"Ach, stop." Impulsively he put his hand over hers. In the instant he had to be sorry he'd touched her unexpectedly, he realized Rebecca didn't wince or pull away. He breathed a little easier. "Of course it's your business. We're friends. I know you care about Aaron."

Her hand relaxed under his.

"I certain sure care about him." Her lips curved in a reminiscent smile. "I still see him as the little bruder who tagged along after us, teasing and wanting to do everything you did. And I care about you. I… I hate to see you hurting and blaming yourself for what Aaron did. But maybe your onkel Zeb is right."

"Maybe so. Yah, of course he is right that Aaron has

to make the decision. But what if you were right, too? What if, like you, Aaron is waiting for someone to assure him that he still has a place here? That could be true, ain't so?"

"I guess so." Her gaze searched his face. "You've decided to do something. What is it?"

He had to laugh a little. "You always could read me like a book. Yah, I can't rest until I've done something. So I found out the name of that place where Eli Gaus said he was working. And this morning, I went to the library and used their computer to get the address."

"You're going to write to Aaron." Rebecca's blue eyes shone. "Daniel, I'm wonderful glad."

He found he loved having her look at him that way, with her face alight and her eyes shining. He couldn't get enough of that expression.

Slowly it began to fade, and a troubled one took its place. "But if he doesn't answer, you'll be hurt all over again. I don't want that to happen." She was actually holding his hand between both of hers, pressing it close between her palms, and he could hardly breathe for fear she'd realize what she was doing and pull away.

"It will still be better than knowing I didn't try when I could have." He looked down at their clasped hands, feeling as if he drew courage from her touch. "After you said what you did yesterday, I began to wonder. What if God was telling me something?"

She shook her head slightly. "What if it was just me saying too much?"

"No." The more he thought of it, the surer he was. "First there was Eli running into Aaron, and then his wife insisting he tell us, so we know where Aaron is. And then you saying that about needing to know you'd be wilkom if you came back home again. How could I ignore it if that was God's leading?"

"You couldn't. I see that now."

Her eyes met his. Emotions seemed to ripple between them—hope, joy, sorrow, longing—all mixed together. It was like a living thing stretched between them, linking them, stretching into both the past and the future.

His breath caught, his fingers tightening on hers. That was what life was, wasn't it? All those feelings and experiences coming at a person, good and bad mixed together. And if you were very fortunate, you had someone who cared, someone who felt them with you, sharing them.

He leaned toward Rebecca, irresistibly drawn. Her lips parted, the blue of her eyes seeming to darken. If only...

Then Lige came running back to them, the trowels clattering in his hand. Rebecca swung toward her son, and the moment was gone.

But it had happened, Daniel thought, watching the two of them chattering together. It had happened, and what were they going to do about it?

Chapter Eleven

Daniel hadn't found any answer to his question during a mostly sleepless night. Nothing had changed between him and Rebecca, and yet everything had changed.

How could it be? His love for her had changed from that of childhood playmates to the love between a man and a woman. It seemed sudden, and yet it must have been growing steadily, out of sight, but it burst forth like a plant breaking through the blanketing soil.

He'd eaten breakfast automatically, giving the wrong answers when anyone asked him anything and making his niece and nephew giggle when he nearly put sugar on his eggs. He had to get hold of himself. Onkel Zeb was already watching him with a question in his wise old eyes, and he'd see the truth too easily.

When they'd finished, Daniel made a quick escape and hurried to the workshop to gather any materials he might need today. Last chance, he told himself. This would never work, for reasons he knew only too well.

He'd failed too many people that he loved. He couldn't possibly add Rebecca and Lige to the count.

Besides, Rebecca had problems of her own. After what she'd told him about her marriage, it didn't take much imagination to see what her response would be to the idea of marrying again. She'd never trust her and Lige's happiness to another person. She was probably already denying that anything had happened between them yesterday.

He was right back to where he'd been before. Rebecca and Lige needed a friend, nothing more. He was that friend, so he'd better get himself to work before they wondered where he was. But it wasn't going to be easy to be around Rebecca and behave normally.

As it turned out, he didn't have to be around her all that much. She was heading into the storeroom when he arrived, but she turned back for a moment.

"There, Lige, I told you Daniel would be here." She gave her son a little pat on the shoulder and glanced at Daniel, then away again. "He's ready to work. And I want to rearrange the storeroom, so I'll be back there. I don't expect anyone to come in the shop this early."

Daniel nodded. Was she a little wary of being with him this morning? Maybe, but if so, she seemed to be coping. "Okay, Lige. What say we get the rest of the old cabinets out today?"

"I'm ready." Lige tried to flex his muscles. "When are we putting up new ones?"

"I've been working on the new ones in my workshop, and they'll soon be ready. We might need to do some repair work on the walls before they go in."

"Let's get to work, then," he said, sounding so much like his uncle that it made Daniel smile in spite of his distraction.

The rest of the cabinets seemed to come off more easily than the first one had. Lige, in a talkative mood, chattered about this and that, and Daniel could work and listen in amusement without difficulty. It sounded as if Lige was longing to be like his year-older cousin and go to school, but that would happen soon enough.

"Come September, and you'll be going off with the other scholars first thing every morning. What will I do for a helper then?"

Lige's small face grew serious. "I could help when I come home from school. And when I'm old enough, I could be your apprentice." He beamed, as if delighted with the thought.

Daniel was unaccountably touched, even knowing that Lige was at the age to have completely different plans tomorrow. "I'll save a place for you," he said. He frowned, lifting his head. "I thought I heard a car, but I guess not. Here, can you put this on the floor?" He handed down a cabinet door, gripping it until he was sure Lige could manage.

Funny. He thought he heard something again, but it must be Rebecca in the storeroom. Once or twice, he'd heard her humming, so she must be feeling happy. Well, why not? She was getting what she wanted. And it was all she wanted.

He was climbing down the ladder when he heard something again, and this time there was no doubt what it was. A baby was crying in the shop. Someone had come in, and apparently neither they nor Rebecca had realized it.

Since he was near the door, he stepped through it, intent on telling the customer that Rebecca would be right in. But there wasn't a customer. Just the sound of crying coming from the cradle he'd refurbished, and tiny hands waved in the air, setting it swaying.

Daniel covered the floor in a few long strides, reached the cradle and came to an abrupt halt. He wasn't imagining things. There was a baby in the cradle—a girl, to judge by the pink bonnet and the blanket she'd kicked off. Apparently she didn't want to be there, because she was crying lustily, and her small face was bright red.

"Daniel, what…" Rebecca's footsteps sounded as she crossed the floor quickly behind him.

"It's a baby," he said, knowing he sounded idiotic.

"Obviously it's a baby." Rebecca bent over the cradle and picked up the squalling bundle. "Hush, now, hush. Everything will be all right."

Holding the baby close against her, she patted it. Apparently that was the right thing to do. After a few more cries, the infant snuggled against her shoulder.

"Where's the mother?" Daniel pointed out the thing that was far more shocking than a baby in a display cradle. He looked around, but the shop was empty except for them and Lige, who was staring, his eyes huge. And the baby. "We don't even know whose she is."

"Don't be silly," Rebecca said. "I know perfectly well whose she is. This is little Betsy, Shannon's baby. You know, the young Englisch woman from the quilting circle."

Daniel tried to focus, amazed that Rebecca was taking this so easily. He vaguely remembered the young woman. Mary Ann had been walking around with a baby during the quilting group—this baby, he supposed.

"I'm glad you know that much. But what is she doing here without her mammi?"

Rebecca glanced out the front window. "Maybe Shannon went back to her car for something."

Sounded reasonable, but he didn't think so. He walked out onto the porch, looked around and came back in, a bad feeling settling in the pit of his stomach.

"She's not out there, Rebecca. It looks as if she put her baby in the cradle and then just…left." His mind grappled with the problem that presented.

"There has to be a reason." Again, Rebecca sounded perfectly calm in these extraordinary circumstances. "Look in the cradle. Is there anything else?"

He stooped, moving a couple of baby quilts out of the way. "A diaper bag." He hefted it. "Filled up with stuff, by the weight of it. And there's a note." He picked up the folded paper, started to open it and then realized that it was marked with Rebecca's name. He handed it to her, watching her with a worried frown.

Rebecca flipped the paper open and began to read, her brows drawing together. "Shannon doesn't say much. 'Please watch Betsy for me. I can't do it. I can't manage…' It just trails off then." She shook her head. "Poor thing."

He wasn't sure if she was referring to the mother or the baby. "Rebecca, you must call the police. This is for them to handle."

Rebecca stared at him. "Call the police? For what? Shannon asked me to watch the baby for her. People don't call the police for that."

"She didn't exactly ask you. She left the baby with a note. People might say she deserted her baby."

"No one will say that unless the police are called." Rebecca sounded as if she knew exactly what she was going to do. "That poor girl was alone most of the time with a young baby and no one to help her. She was just overwhelmed, that's all. Every young mother feels that way sometimes."

"But..."

"No buts about it. I'm not going to report her for feeling the way plenty of perfectly fine mothers do. They might take her baby away if I did that. I'm going to do just as she asked and watch Betsy for her."

"Rebecca, stop and think." He couldn't help being afraid for her. "Maybe lots of mammis feel that way, but most of them don't run away."

"I know." For an instant, worry darkened her eyes, and then she looked at the infant in her arms and cradled it close to her. "I understand what you're saying, Daniel. But try to understand how I feel. Shannon felt desperate, with no one to help her. As soon as she comes to her senses, she'll return. I have to give her that chance."

He opened his mouth to protest again, saw that it wasn't going to do any good and closed it again. He looked at the child and saw trouble. But obviously Rebecca looked at her and saw a baby to love and a mother to help.

The little one started to fuss again, chewing on her fist this time.

"I think she wants something to eat," Lige said.

"I think you're right." Rebecca smiled at him. "I'd better warm up a bottle for her. Here." Without warning, she plopped the baby into Daniel's arms, and they automatically curved to receive her. "You amuse her while I do that."

"I'm no good with a boppli," he protested. "Maybe you should call Leah…"

"Don't be silly." She was already nearly out of the room. "Just bounce her a little." She disappeared into the kitchen with the diaper bag.

Left alone, he looked helplessly at Lige, as if a six-year-old would be able to rescue him.

"You could sit in the rocking chair and rock her," Lige said. "That's what Mammi does when I'm sick. And I can talk to her. I like babies."

Since he didn't have a plan of his own, that sounded reasonable. Balancing the child carefully, he went to the rocking chair and sat, holding her against his body the way Rebecca had. Lige leaned over the arm of the chair and made cooing sounds.

Apparently that worked, because she stopped fussing. Her arms waved as if she tried to reach Lige's face.

Daniel was glad little Betsy was happy, but he certain sure wasn't happy himself. He didn't know where this situation would end, but he didn't like the idea of Rebecca getting involved. Why had the Englisch woman picked her?

The answer was obvious when he put it like that.

She'd picked Rebecca because Rebecca was kind, gentle and loving. He just hoped those qualities weren't going to land her in a peck of trouble.

Rebecca dwelled on what Daniel had said while she warmed the bottle in a pan on the stove. Daniel wanted what was best for her of course. She didn't doubt that. She knew he feared her getting entangled with the Englisch world in a way that might hurt her.

But he didn't know Shannon, and he probably couldn't understand what she and Leah had seen instantly about the young woman—the loneliness and the sense of being overwhelmed. And how she'd changed when she'd felt the understanding and acceptance of the women in the quilting group. It had been like watching a flower opening.

Only another mother could understand how complicated a woman's feelings were with a first child. Surely every mother had, at some time or other, feared that she was a terrible mother, that she couldn't do this, that, if she couldn't relax for a few minutes, she'd fly apart. They'd talked about it the day of the quilting group.

Guilt nibbled at Rebecca's heart as she tested the bottle. She'd understood, but she hadn't done anything. Caught up in her own problems, she'd ignored a neighbor in need. She could have stopped in town to check on Shannon one day, but she hadn't. All the more reason why she had to do what she could now.

Shannon would be back. She was perfectly sure of that. Probably, as soon as she'd managed to get some rest, she'd wake up, realize what she'd done and return.

How could Rebecca possibly run the risk that Shannon would find herself in the police's hands when she did come back?

Rebecca stood for a moment, the bottle in her hand, a prey to apprehension. No matter what she'd said to Daniel, she had to admit that she was a little afraid of what tomorrow would bring.

A saying of her grandmother's slipped into her mind so clearly that Grossmammi might be standing there beside her. *Don't worry about tomorrow. Just do what God puts in front of you right now and leave the rest to Him.*

Grossmammi had been a wise woman, and Rebecca would do her best to follow that advice. Carrying the bottle, she went through the door to the shop. There she stopped, her heart seized by the sight before her.

Daniel sat in the rocking chair, cuddling the baby. He was crooning to her in Pennsylvania Dutch, his voice soft and soothing, while Lige hung on the arm of the rocker, totally entranced.

Oh, Daniel. Watching him made her heart ache. He deserved to have a wife who loved him and children to love. If only he could get past his conviction that he was to blame for the decisions other people had made.

He glanced up and saw her, giving her a smile. "It's working. She's stopped crying."

"She'll be even happier once her little tummy is full." Coming to them, she handed him the bottle.

"Wait—shouldn't you do this? What if I get it wrong?"

The panicked look on his face made her laugh.

"There's no wrong about it. Just put the nipple in her mouth. She'll know what to do with it."

Sure enough, Betsy was already waving her hands toward the bottle, trying to grab it. Daniel barely got the nipple within reach of her mouth when she was sucking noisily, her face pink with effort.

"She really likes it, doesn't she?" Lige hung over her in fascination. "She likes us, too. Can we keep her, Mammi?"

"No, no, we can't keep her. She's not ours." She was going to explain further, but Lige wasn't finished.

"She could be ours," he insisted. "You could be the mammi, and Daniel could be the daadi, and I could be the big bruder. I'd be a gut big bruder."

Rebecca couldn't look at Daniel, and she knew her cheeks were as pink as the baby's. "I'm sure you'd be a fine big bruder, Lige. But Betsy is Shannon's baby. She's a lady in my quilting group. We're just babysitting her for a while."

She wished she could say how long, but she couldn't.

The sound of a horse's hooves and buggy wheels drew Rebecca's attention to the front window, and she watched in dismay as Lydia Schultz climbed down. She glanced at Daniel, but he was totally occupied with the baby.

She could hardly ask him to go and hide with the baby. Somehow, she'd just have to handle Lydia's nosiness for herself.

Lydia came in, and of course her eyes went instantly to Daniel and the baby. Then they shifted to Rebecca, and she saw too clearly the rampant curiosity raging in them.

"I didn't know you had an infant, Rebecca."

She certain sure knew Rebecca didn't have any such thing, but it wouldn't help to point that out. Rebecca tried to produce a natural-sounding laugh.

"Lige is wishing I did," she said. "No, I'm just watching her for a friend. What can I help you with today, Lydia?" She took an inviting step toward the fabrics, but Lydia didn't follow the hint.

"It looks like Daniel is the one who's babysitting, ain't so?" Her head poked toward Daniel with the question.

Rebecca remembered Sam saying that the reason Lydia's nose was so pointed was because she kept poking it into other people's business. That had earned him a reproof from Leah, but Leah thought it true nonetheless.

"I had my hands full for a moment, so Daniel stepped in," she said. "Lige, would you go and see if your cousin Mary Ann or Aunt Leah can help me for a bit? We should let Daniel get back to his own work."

Lige tore himself away from the baby and spurted out the back door. Daniel probably wished he could go with him. But he was smiling pleasantly at Lydia.

"Go on and take care of whatever Lydia needs," he said, giving Lydia a bland smile. "The cabinets will wait a few more minutes."

"Denke," she murmured, grateful that he was taking it so well. She turned back to Lydia again. "What was it you said you needed?"

Maybe sensing there was no more to be gained from Daniel, Lydia moved toward the rows of fabric bolts. "I need some backing material, but I haven't decided what color yet. I brought some samples from the pieced top."

Rebecca nodded, taking in the color scheme of the swatches Lydia held. "Something in the yellow or rust colors, maybe?" She led the way to the solid colors.

"Whose baby did you say that was?" Lydia was obviously not done probing.

"An *Englisch* friend of mine," she said and tried to emulate Daniel's cool smile. She pulled out a few bolts of suitable colors. "Perhaps one of these would do."

Maybe the smile worked, because Lydia got down to business and concentrated on the fabrics. Of course, she still wasn't easy to please. She had to pull every bolt out twice, at least, before she decided what she wanted, and she had one bolt carried to the cutting table before deciding on a different one.

Finally she was gone, but before Rebecca could say anything to Daniel, she heard Lige coming back. It sounded as if he had both Leah and Mary Ann with him, and they all came into the shop together.

Mary Ann headed straight for the baby. "I'll take her, Daniel. Did you burp her yet?"

He shook his head. "Nobody's taught me burping." He grinned at her. "I'm sure you're just fine at it." He rose, smiling down at the little one in his arms before transferring her carefully to Mary Ann. "Goodbye for now, little one. Lige, I guess we're not needed here, so we'll get back to work."

Once they'd gone, Leah caught Rebecca's arm and

drew her a little away. "How did you get Daniel to do that? I've never seen him with a baby before."

"I just plopped her in his arms. He had to either take her or drop her." She smiled, remembering his tenderness with the baby. "He got to like it once he did."

Leah nodded, smiling. "He needs a family, that's certain sure. But what about Shannon?"

"I didn't see her. If I had, maybe I could have helped." She drew out the note Shannon had left and gave it to Leah, who read it quickly.

"Ach, poor child. I don't know which one I feel worse for, but the boppli won't remember anything of it. Poor Shannon. She came right out and said how lonely she was. Why didn't I go to see her?"

"That's just what I feel myself." It relieved her considerably to hear Leah echo her own thoughts. "Daniel thought at first I should go to the police, but I can't do that. Think what it would do to that little family."

Leah considered it, her face solemn. "Yah, I see. No, we can't go to the police. Not unless she doesn't come back in a few days."

"She will," Rebecca said, squashing any doubts she might have. "She'll come to herself and realize what she's done. You know how it is with a first baby, and her without any family or friends to help her, and her husband away, as well."

"Taking care of the boppli is no problem," Leah said. "We'll all help, and be glad of a chance to do something gut for the young woman. Beyond that, it's in the hands of the gut Lord."

Rebecca nodded, sending up a silent prayer for Shannon, wherever she was. Perhaps she'd call her husband, and he'd be able to help.

"That's all we can do." Rebecca smiled at the sight of Mary Ann in the rocking chair with the baby, but her wayward imagination kept showing her an image of Daniel sitting there, cradling the infant.

Lige's innocent words came back to her, and she could feel herself blushing just thinking of it. She'd have to say something to Daniel—something light, just making a joke of it. But she couldn't think how she was going to manage it.

Chapter Twelve

Rebecca had forgotten what it was like to be roused from sleep by the cry of a hungry baby. By the time she'd warmed the bottle, it seemed forever, until Betsy was contentedly sucking away.

Rebecca settled back in a comfortable position against the headboard of the bed. As far as she could tell, Lige hadn't stirred from his bed in the next room, and she hadn't roused anyone else.

No, she'd been wrong, she realized as the door opened softly. Mamm slipped in. Rebecca smiled at her. With her graying blond hair in the loose plaits she wore at night, Mamm looked even younger than she did normally, her face round and rosy with sleep.

She came and settled down on the bed, reaching across to give the baby a pat.

"Betsy woke you," Rebecca said softly. "I'm sorry."

Mamm just smiled. "No mother ever loses her reaction to a baby's cry." She studied Betsy for a moment.

"She'll be giving up that middle-of-the-night feed soon, I'd think. Lige had by this age, ain't so?"

"Mostly," Rebecca said. "But if he did wake, it certain sure was easier, since I wasn't fooling with bottles."

"Maybe the strange place troubled her, poor little mite," Mamm said. "Think how upset her mammi must have been to leave her here."

Rebecca had thought of little else. "I guess we were the first people who took an interest in Shannon since she moved here. It sounded as if she'd been holed up in her house, alone with the baby, except for coming to quilting."

Mamm nodded. "It's not easy to make friends in a new place, I guess. Still, most folks are kind, if you give them a chance."

"I had a chance to do more, and I didn't." Her guilt pushed the words out. "I knew she was lonely and overwhelmed. I could have gone to see her."

"So could any of us," Mamm said. "We get caught up in our own lives and don't see our neighbor in need. This will be a gut lesson for us, I think."

Both Leah and Mamm had expressed the same guilt she felt. That didn't make it less, but as Mamm said, God was teaching them a lesson they needed.

"She reminds me of when Lige was this size. Hard to believe that now, when he's starting to outgrow my lap." She stroked the fuzz of fine hair on the baby's head.

"The years slip away fast," Mamm said. "The boppli becomes a child, then a girl, then a woman with a family of her own, all in the twinkling of an eye." She was silent for a moment, maybe remembering the time when her own young ones were babies. "It's wonderful gut to have you back here, my Rebecca. Mind, I love Leah like a daughter, but still, it's not the same. A woman wants the comfort of a daughter nearby as she gets old."

"You're not old," Rebecca protested.

"Maybe, but it's a different stage of life when it's your grandchildren clustered around instead of your kinder. Having you and Lige here is such a blessing I hadn't expected ever to have."

Rebecca looked down at the baby in her arms, wishing... What? She couldn't change what she'd already done, and at least she had Lige. He was worth any hardship she had to endure. And even though there had been times when God had been silent, she'd always known He was holding her up.

"It means so much for me to be here. Just to know that my home was here, waiting for me, after..." She let that trail off, not wanting to get into the subject of her marriage.

Her mother leaned toward her, her face filled with love and pain. "Ach, Rebecca, you don't need to tell me anything. I already guessed a lot about your marriage to James, and what we didn't guess, his daad told yours."

"He did?" She'd thought she was finished being surprised by the Mast family. "I never thought he would say anything."

They'd always tried to protect James. She'd understood that, but it hadn't really helped any of them.

"It's in the past now." Mamm patted her. "Hard as it is to forget, you must forgive."

"I have," she protested. "At least, I've tried. I want so much to just…get on with our lives, mine and Lige's."

"Yah, I know." She smiled a little. "Lige says he wants a baby sister or bruder."

"I know." She didn't want to talk about something that was so unlikely, nor to try to explain why she felt that way.

"Rebecca." Her mother's voice was serious, and she reached toward Rebecca as if she had something important to say. "What happened with James doesn't mean that you must live alone the rest of your life. Surely God will give you a man to love in your future, a good man who is all the things James wasn't."

Rebecca was swept by the longing to express her doubts and fears. She tried to suppress it. "I… I can't. I can't risk it. How can I trust myself and Lige to someone else?"

"Ach, Rebecca, you were eighteen when you met James and fell in love. You only knew him for a month before you decided to marry him."

True enough. "I was young and foolish."

"You're not young and foolish now," Mamm pointed out. "You're home, surrounded by people you've known all your life. You can take time and let love and trust grow." Before Rebecca could protest, Mamm stood up. "I won't push. Just think on it," she said. "Good night."

The door closed behind her before Rebecca could find a response. Betsy lolled in her arms, limp and drowsy. As she tended to the baby and tucked her up in the crib Sam had moved into the room, Rebecca searched her heart for an answer.

Had Mamm been thinking of Daniel? True, he wasn't far from her own thoughts these days. Strange, that just when she was thinking it might someday be possible for her to love him, that Daniel, in his preoccupation with his brother, should seem to move further away from her.

Daniel, packing up what he'd need for the day of work, looked up when the workshop door opened.

"Onkel Zeb. What brings you out here? Is there something Caleb wants me to do?"

"No, no, only to get on with your own work." Zeb glanced over the contents of the workbench. "You're going over to Rebecca's place, ain't so?"

He nodded. "I'd like to finish the prep work in the kitchen. She'll need to have the electric refrigerator taken out, so I'd like everything ready for the new one."

"Gut." He spoke absently, and Daniel realized something was on his mind—something other than the work Daniel proposed to do that day.

"So, what is it?" Daniel snapped his toolbox closed. "I can tell when you're deciding whether or not to speak, you know."

His uncle smiled, but his faded blue eyes were grave. "Guess I'd better just spit it out, ain't so? When I was in town, I heard rumors. Gossip, that is."

"About what?" Zeb's seriousness alarmed him. "Something about Aaron?"

"Ach, no. Not Aaron. It was about Rebecca, and the baby that's turned up at her place all of a sudden." He met Daniel's gaze. "And about you being involved somehow."

"Lydia." He clenched his fists on the edge of the workbench. "I know it."

"Lydia?" Onkel Zeb looked confused, as well he might. "Is that the name of the boppli?"

"Lydia Schultz. The little one's name is Betsy." Seeing that Onkel Zeb looked confused, he went on, choosing his words. "You know what a blabbermaul Lydia is. She came in the quilt shop yesterday and saw me holding the baby. Of course she'd have to make a big story of it."

Zeb shook his head, but at least he was smiling now. "Whose baby?"

"Rebecca is watching the daughter of an Englisch friend of hers while the woman's away. You know what a kind person she is. She'd never say no when someone needs her."

"So that's it. Leave it to Lydia to make a big story out of something simple."

"That's certain sure."

He was relieved that his uncle accepted it so easily, but he reminded himself he wasn't out of the woods with this story. He'd have to tell Rebecca what was going on. She'd be upset, but it would be worse if she heard it from someone else.

"I'd best be on my way." He clapped his uncle on the shoulder. "Denke. I'd rather hear it now than have folks talking and not know it."

"I think I'll make an excuse for another trip to the hardware store," Zeb said. "That'll give me a chance to set the story straight." He grinned, as if he looked forward to it. He always said the men did as much gossiping in the hardware store as the women did anywhere else.

Raising his hand in farewell, Daniel strode out of the workshop and off toward Rebecca's place. The sooner she knew what was going on, the better.

Maybe he should speak to her again about talking to the police. How long was she willing to wait for Shannon to come back? This couldn't go on for long, especially with people already talking.

All was quiet when he went in the back door of the shop. Maybe she had left the baby back at the farmhouse, out of sight of any customers. Or maybe Shannon had returned.

But when he pushed open the door, he realized he'd been wrong on both counts. Rebecca sat in the rocking chair, moving slowly forward and backward, the baby in her arms. A tiny hand waved, brushing her cheek, and she kissed it lightly.

Daniel couldn't move. All he could do was stand and stare at her, while his imagination gave him a picture of Rebecca looking lovingly at their baby. He could see it, could even imagine what their boppli would look like, with Rebecca's clear blue eyes and a little fluff of blond hair on its head.

No. The reaction hit him hard. He couldn't let himself think that way. Bad enough when he'd entertained those thoughts about Rebecca and Lige, but what about other children they might have if he let himself love her? How could he let them rely on him, when he'd already failed the two people he'd loved most?

Even as he thought he'd back out without disturbing her, Rebecca looked up and saw him. She smiled, and that sweet smile nearly did him in.

"It's all right," she said. "I'm not trying to put her to sleep. Just enjoying her company until Mary Ann gets here to watch her. Komm. I know Betsy would like to see you."

Daniel walked toward her, struggling to compose himself. "I don't think Betsy even knows who I am." But he bent over her obediently, unable to resist smiling when the baby's eyes focused on his face. "How are you this morning? Did you keep everyone up?"

"Not at all. Well, she did get me up for one feeding in the night, and Mamm came in and kept me company, but Lige and Daadi slept right through it."

"They would." He grinned. "I probably would, too." He'd have his chance to find out when Caleb and Jessie's baby was right there in the room across the hall from him.

"Mammi says that a mother never loses the ability to wake up at the cry of a baby." She smiled down at the little one. "I hated to disturb her sleep, but it was gut to sit and talk in the quiet."

Was he imagining it, or did Rebecca's cheeks flush slightly when she said the words? It made him wonder what women talked about in the middle of the night.

Much as he hated to upset the peace between them, he had to ask the question that was in his mind. "Have you heard anything from the baby's mother?"

"Not yet. But soon, I'm sure." There might be the faintest trace of doubt in her voice.

"Maybe…"

"No," she said. "I know what you're thinking, but

I'm not going to go to the police and say that Shannon deserted her baby."

"You wouldn't have to say it that way," he protested. "After all, you might be worried about her safety, since you haven't heard from her. It would be logical to ask the police for help in case she's sick or had an accident."

"And how would I answer all the questions they'd be sure to ask me?" She shook her head. "I can't. I know you mean well, Daniel, but I just can't."

He'd argue, but he knew it wouldn't do any good. Besides, the door opened and Lige rushed in, followed more quietly by Mary Ann.

"Daniel. Did you see the baby? What's she doing?"

"Nothing much." He grinned as he watched Lige lean over her, staring in fascination. "Babies that age don't do much."

But Lige wasn't paying attention. He tugged at his mother's sleeve. "Mary Ann says I can help her watch Betsy. Can I, Mammi?"

Rebecca glanced from his face to Daniel. "I thought you were going to help Daniel today."

"Oh." Lige stared at him in consternation. "I forgot."

"It's all right," Daniel said, giving in to the obviously strong attraction of the baby. "Why don't you babysit until the little one falls asleep and then come help me?"

Lige nodded eagerly. "All right, Mammi?"

Rebecca seemed silently to consult with Mary Ann before she nodded. "Be sure you listen to Mary Ann, though."

"I will."

Rebecca stood, shifting the baby to Mary Ann's

arms, and Lige bounced along beside his cousin as they headed out the back.

In a way, it was a relief to Daniel when they'd gone. Somehow he had to bring up the subject of the gossip Onkel Zeb had heard, and he was afraid it would hurt her.

Maybe the only way was to just come out with it.

"There is something I must talk with you about, Rebecca."

Her gaze was slightly impatient. "I thought we'd already discussed the impossibility of talking to the police."

"We have. I'm not sure I agree with you, but I respect your right to make that decision. You must know that, Rebecca."

"I'm sorry." Her expression was rueful. "I wish I weren't in this position, but I am, so I must make the best of it."

He couldn't expect that Rebecca's loving heart would allow her to follow any other path. In fact, he wouldn't want her to. Did she even realize how much she'd changed since she'd come home? He suspected she was becoming the woman she'd have been if she hadn't ever met James.

"Onkel Zeb was at the hardware store when he heard something that troubled him." He paused, trying to come up with the right words, and then pushed on. "He says there's some mixed-up gossip going around about you and the baby. He came to me about it, because apparently my name figured into it."

They looked at each other, and he could see the understanding dawn in her face. "Lydia," she said.

"I'm certain sure that's the source. Who else could it be?" He shook his head. "I'm trying hard not to judge a sister in the church, but it's not easy. I hope…well, that you're not too upset by it."

Rebecca had the air of one picking up a burden. "I can't say I'm surprised. Especially since…"

"What? Is there some reason Lydia would do such a thing?" It seemed important to him to get to the bottom of it. Surely Rebecca, after all her griefs, shouldn't have to put up with gossip in her own community.

"Lydia has a cousin in the area where we lived in Ohio." Rebecca seemed to study the display of quilt bindings on the rack next to her. "When everything was going on with James, I'm afraid there was a lot of talk. Some folks thought it was disloyal of me to go to the bishop about him."

"That's ridiculous." The very idea made him hot with protective anger. "James was not a well man. Surely the Leit could understand that you were trying to help him. Especially when the bishop himself intervened."

"Most people did, I think." She pressed her fingers against her temples, as if her head had begun to ache. "But there were those who questioned."

It didn't take all that much imagination to see the reasons. "If he had had a broken leg or a heart condition, they'd understand that you had to push him to see the right doctors to help him."

"Exactly." Rebecca gave him a quick glance, but it was long enough for him to see the way memory darkened her eyes. "It was his brain that was hurt, and that's harder for anyone to understand. Maybe that made it more natural for folks to question and wonder."

"So you think Lydia heard some of this from her cousin." He could see that easily. Cousins stayed in touch, and most likely, there were regular letters exchanged.

"If not at first, then certainly when it became known that I was coming here to live. She'd have written, probably rehashing the old rumors." A tiny smile flickered and was gone. "It won't surprise you to hear that Lydia's cousin had her own reputation as a blabbermaul."

"It must run in the family." He dared to touch Rebecca's arm lightly. "I'm sorry for it. I explained to Onkel Zeb that you were watching the baby for an Englisch friend, that's all. Not that he'd believe anything else." He made a disgusted sound. "Anyone with any sense would realize that the baby wasn't yours. How could it be?"

"I don't think sense is a necessary quality for people who like to tell tales." Her tone was mild, and he realized she was getting over the initial shock. "Please tell your uncle that I appreciate his letting me know."

He managed to smile. "Don't think Onkel Zeb is stopping there. He was looking forward to heading right back down to the hardware store and setting folks straight." His initial enjoyment of Zeb's attitude slipped away. "The only thing is that he doesn't know everything. I didn't tell him about Shannon just leaving the baby here without asking."

"No, we can't let that get around." She rubbed her

temples again. "I wish I could see what was for the best. If I don't hear from her by tomorrow..."

Daniel struggled to see a path forward that would be best for everyone. "If you're right that she'd come to her senses soon, I'd think surely you would hear by then." He hesitated, not wanting to suggest something that would offend her. "Is there anyone among the Englisch women in the quilting group that you could talk to? Someone you could trust to understand and maybe give you advice?"

Rebecca was silent for so long that he started to think she wouldn't answer. At last she looked at him, her face troubled. "I hate the idea of telling anyone what she's done. But there is someone who might understand."

"Who?" He'd give a lot to have this burden lifted from Rebecca. Or at least to have someone to share it.

"There's Glenda Allen. She's the older woman that Mamm knows. She seemed to have sympathy for Shannon, and she might understand."

"She'd look at it from an Englisch woman's point of view," he said carefully. "That might be a help."

He could see the struggle going on in Rebecca's heart. Finally she nodded. "If I haven't heard from Shannon by the time the quilters come tomorrow, I'll think about telling Glenda the whole thing. I just hope I'm not making a mistake."

Everything in him yearned to reassure her, even to take the burden from her shoulders. Her eyes met his, and it seemed she knew exactly what he was thinking.

"I don't think you can make a mistake when you're acting out of love." Daniel lifted his hand to touch the soft curve of her cheek. It felt like down under his fingertips, and warmth spread through him, making his skin tingle. Even that light touch was enough to make him long for more.

Rebecca didn't draw away from his touch, and her eyes darkened as they met his gaze. Her lips parted on an indrawn breath. For an instant, he couldn't breathe. They were so close. A step would bring her into his arms.

And then he remembered all the reasons why he couldn't do this. He couldn't risk hurting her. She was too precious for that. But stepping away from the hope in her face was the hardest thing he'd ever done.

Chapter Thirteen

Rebecca felt the day dragging on and tried to dismiss Daniel from her thoughts. She couldn't change him. Only God could do that, and even their loving God could act only if Daniel made himself open to realizing what he was doing to himself.

Those moments when he had touched her face came surging into her thoughts too frequently to be ignored. She put her palm against her cheek. It seemed to be still warm from his hand. They'd looked at each other, and she'd seen the barriers between them crumble. She was a different person now from the frightened, embittered woman she'd been such a short time ago. In another moment, they would have kissed. But Daniel… Daniel had drawn away.

Rebecca found herself looking up at every sound, hoping and praying that it would be Shannon. But although several cars pulled in, none of them contained the person she wanted to see.

And invariably, after each customer had left and the shop was quiet, her thoughts returned to Daniel.

"I am being wonderful foolish, ain't so, little one?" She smiled down at Betsy, ensconced in a basket Leah had brought over.

Betsy waved her arms as if in agreement. Then she seemed to lose interest, having caught sight of her foot in the air. She became engrossed in trying to catch it with her hands and, once she succeeded, brought it to her mouth.

Rebecca couldn't help but laugh. "Now, that's a big accomplishment, Betsy."

The back door swung open. "Did you say something, Rebecca?" Daniel stood in the doorway.

Praying he hadn't heard all of it, she managed to smile in what she hoped was a normal way. "I was just talking to the baby. I sent Mary Ann and Lige back to the house to have their lunch."

He took a couple of steps forward and then stopped, as if determined to leave a good big space between them. For safety's sake, she supposed.

"I wanted to tell you that I'll have to be away for a couple of days later in the week or maybe over the weekend."

Was he so panic-stricken at what had nearly happened between them that he felt the need to run away from her?

"I see. That's fine." She wanted to ask where he was going, but she couldn't.

Daniel stood for a moment, irresolute, and she could

see him struggle to say something. If he intended to talk about what had happened between them, she'd be mortified.

"You know that letter I said I was going to write to Aaron?"

Her thoughts had been so occupied by what was happening between them that it took Rebecca a moment to refocus. "What about it? Did you write it?"

He made a rueful face. "I wrote it about ten times before I gave up. I couldn't find the right words, not in a letter."

"I'm sorry." It was all she could find to say. What a pity if he gave up so quickly on approaching Aaron. But perhaps it was for the best. Who was she to judge?

"So I've decided. I'm going to see him." He sounded determined.

She stared at Daniel's face, hardly able to believe the words. No such thought had been in his head when they'd talked about Aaron. She'd have known, if so.

"Are you sure that's the right thing to do?"

It would be hurtful enough if he wrote a letter at her suggestion and then Aaron didn't answer. How much worse would it be if he saw Aaron in person and Aaron rejected him? Was she setting him up for more pain? She should have stayed out of it.

"Yah, I'm sure. I feel it. Don't worry." He smiled at her, seeming to look right into her scrambled thoughts. "This is my decision, just like coming home is Aaron's. If I end up getting hurt, it's still better than not seeing him and telling him we still love and want him."

His words stilled any objection she might have made.

"I understand. I'll be praying for you and for Aaron. When do you leave?"

"Not until after this business with the baby is settled. I couldn't go before then. I've made arrangements with Dave Smith to drive me, and we'll go out one day. I'll see Aaron, and we'll come back the next. He doesn't mind all the driving, and I don't want to be away longer than that."

"If it's better for you to go now, you should do it." She tried not to show how bereft she'd feel if he took her up on that. "You don't need to stay here for my benefit, and there's really nothing anyone can do."

"No." He looked a little disconcerted at her words. "I suppose not, but still, I'll feel better if I'm around. Just in case you need me." He forced a smile. "After all, I was the one who found Betsy first, remember?"

"Only by a hair," she responded, smiling a little.

But she didn't press the idea, because if she were honest with herself, she wanted him here. She had family supporting her, but as Daniel said, he'd been in on this from the beginning. And Daniel...well, he was Daniel, her rock.

He was frowning a little as he watched the baby. "Are you still thinking you'll talk to your mamm's friend about Shannon and the baby if she's not back tomorrow?"

Rebecca nodded. "I'll ask her to come a little early so we can talk privately. I feel as if I know her better than the others, and Mamm thinks highly of her."

"You're worried," he said, taking a step closer.

"For sure. I've been worried from the beginning. If

only Shannon would come back on her own. I wish I knew how to get in touch with her husband."

"Surely she wouldn't let him return from his trip and find her gone." But Daniel's tone said he could imagine that too easily. After all, it was what his own mother had done.

There was nothing she could say about that, clearly. "Glenda may have some idea about how to reach him. Or even a cell phone number for Shannon." She looked down at the baby, deeply engrossed in sucking on her foot. "I can't believe she won't come back by tomorrow."

"I pray you're right." He hesitated. "Whether she does or not, I won't be leaving as long as you might need me. That's what friends are for, ain't so?"

She forced herself to nod, to smile. And to pretend that her heart wasn't aching. Daniel was her friend, and he'd made it clear that was all he'd ever be.

Glenda came early the next afternoon, as Rebecca had asked. By that time, Rebecca's nerves were stretched to the limit, and the questions kept ricocheting around in her mind. Was she doing the right thing? What if something had happened to Shannon? What if she didn't come back?

In fact, she was so shaken she no longer had any doubts about sharing the burden. She had to confide in Glenda. So she poured out the whole story, holding Betsy in her arms and bouncing her gently to comfort her.

"Did I do the right thing? What should I do now?"

She didn't intend to sound quite so panicky, but that was how she felt.

The lines around Glenda's eyes and mouth had deepened as she listened, but she immediately reached out to pat Rebecca's shoulder. "I don't see how you could do anything else," she said. "After all, Shannon did ask you to watch the baby, so it's not as if she'd abandoned her."

"But she hasn't been in touch. I thought surely I'd hear something by today." But her tension had eased at the reassuring words.

Glenda nodded slowly, her eyes on the baby. "Betsy is doing all right?"

"She's fine." Rebecca smiled down at her and touched the baby's rosy cheek. "At her age, she doesn't know what's going on, poor little mite."

Glenda was smiling, too. "Shannon knew what she was about when she picked you to care for her baby. Now...if only I had got a cell phone number for her." She shook her head, frustrated. "I have her house phone number, but that won't do us any good."

"Do you know where she lives?" It was embarrassing that she hadn't even found out that much.

"Yes, I did ask her that. I had thought, at the time, that I'd drop in on her. It was obvious that she was lonely. Then I got busy...but that's no excuse. I should have made it a priority."

"That's what I've been telling myself, too. And Leah and Mamm. We all feel so guilty that we did nothing." Rebecca patted the baby's back, feeling the little body relaxing into slumber. "If we could reach her husband... But I don't know if that's the right thing to do or not."

"He has a right to be told, I suppose, but I wish I had some feel for how he'd react. I wouldn't want to cause trouble between them. And anyway, I have no idea how to contact him." Glenda frowned, as if scouring her mind for an answer. "There might be something in her house that would tell us, but that would mean bringing the police into it. I wouldn't want to do that unless I had to."

"Yah, that's what I am thinking, too."

They looked at each other, and it wondered Rebecca how much risk they were taking by doing nothing. Was that what Glenda feared, too?

Finally Glenda shook her head. "I keep coming back to the thought that Shannon asked you to watch the baby. She must have been overwhelmed even to think of going away, but she behaved responsibly in that, packing the diaper bag and providing the bottles and formula. Still, if we don't hear from her today, we may have to ask for help to find her."

Leah and Mamm came through from the kitchen with Jessie, and Mamm glanced from Rebecca to Glenda. "You have told her then."

She nodded, and Glenda smiled. "I should have known you two would be involved in this. Don't worry too much. We'll sort it out together."

A car pulled up just then. Rebecca's heart leaped, but it was just the other women arriving for quilting.

Another problem loomed in Rebecca's mind. "What should I say to them? I don't know if it's wise to tell anyone else."

Glenda considered. "I think you could trust them.

But maybe it's best to keep it between us. Let's just say you're watching the baby for Shannon. I guess there's no need to bring others into it unless we have to."

Rebecca was so relieved to hear her say "we" that she could actually feel her heart lighten. She bent over the cradle, laying Betsy down and pushing it lightly with her knee to make it swing.

Alice and Debby came in, their chattering lowered when they saw the baby. Debby dropped her workbag and came to bend over the cradle. "What a little sweetheart! They grow so fast at that age."

Alice followed her, smiling almost involuntarily at the sight of the baby. She glanced around. "Where's her mother?"

"Shannon had to be away today," Glenda said before Rebecca could speak. "Rebecca is babysitting."

"What fun." Debby shook her head. "What am I saying? If I spent any amount of time around a little one that age, I'd start wanting another baby myself, just when I've got mine in school all day."

"I loved it when my children were still at home." Alice was just a bit disapproving, which didn't seem to bother Debby in the least.

"That's because you don't remember how wonderful it is to have several hours to yourself." Debby grinned, taking any sting out of the words.

From what Rebecca could see, these two knew each other well despite the obvious difference in their ages. Debby seemed to treat the older woman more like a big sister than anything else.

Debby must have seen her watching them, because

she laughed. "Don't worry, Rebecca. Alice doesn't mind me. Despite her attitude, when my kids were babies, she used to come to my house when I was feeling overwhelmed and chase me out for an hour or two. She always said I'd be a better mother if I had some time to myself."

"Nonsense," Alice said, but her cheeks flushed and Rebecca could see the affection in her eyes. Maybe it wouldn't be a bad thing to confide in them.

A car pulled up outside with a shriek of brakes, gravel scattering. For an instant, Rebecca's heart nearly stopped, and then she saw—it was Shannon.

Breathing a silent prayer of thanksgiving that God had heard her pleas, she hurried to open the door. Shannon rushed in, her face white, her eyes huge.

"My baby—"

Smiling, even as she blinked back tears, Rebecca gestured to the cradle. Shannon flew to it, dropping on her knees as she scooped the baby up in her arms.

"I'm here. Mommy's here. I love you…" The words came out in a rush of sound. "You're all right."

"Of course she's all right," Glenda said. She knelt next to Shannon and put her arms around both of them. "Rebecca was taking care of her."

Galvanized by her response, Rebecca joined them, putting a comforting arm around Shannon's shoulders. "Everything's fine now. You're here, and it's all right."

Shannon looked up, tears staining her cheeks. "I was so ashamed. I just drove and drove until I was so tired I couldn't keep going. I pulled into a park and just fell asleep in my car. When I woke up, I realized what I'd done…how long I'd been gone."

"Komm, now." Rebecca patted her. "You did exactly what I thought. As soon as you had some sleep, you came back. I knew you would."

From the corner of her eye, she saw Alice open her mouth, but a look from Glenda silenced her.

"It seemed to take forever to come back. I ran out of gas, and I was frantic by the time someone stopped and helped me. I thought I'd never get here, and all I could do was pray." She stroked the baby's head and showered it with kisses. "How could I have done such a thing? I'm not fit to be a mother."

"Now, stop that. You were all alone, and you most likely have postpartum depression, as well." Alice came closer, touching Shannon gently. "I did. It was so bad I can't talk about it even now. But I got help, and you will, too."

Rebecca could only stare at Alice, seeing the tears in her eyes. In spite of the things she'd said, she did understand. More, she did something about it.

"That's right," Debby said. "You just need to have family to help you. Since they're far away, we'll fill in. We'll be your family." She joined them, so that they were surrounding Shannon and the baby, touching each other, united.

Surrounded by love, Rebecca thought, her heart full. They were good people, and they knew what it was to be a new mother. They wouldn't let Shannon down. Shannon would have their help for as long as she needed it, and one day she might have a chance to help another young mother, and she would remember.

Daniel, coming toward the shop, late that afternoon, paused and watched as the women from Rebecca's quilting group came out. They were clustered around the younger woman, Shannon, who held little Betsy close in her arms.

He felt a momentary pang at realizing the baby was leaving. She'd grabbed hold of his heart with her small hand in the time she'd been here. Still, he'd no doubt see her again when the quilting group met.

So things had worked out just as Rebecca hoped. She stood, watching as the cars pulled out one after the other, lifting her hand in a wave. Leah and Mamm headed for the farmhouse, and Jessie started toward home, giving him a quick wave.

He waited for a moment until they'd all got on their ways. Then he propped the plywood he'd been carrying against the porch railing and went to join her.

"So you were right," he said. "Shannon did come back."

Rebecca turned the full force of her joy on him, and it rocked his heart. "Ach, it was wonderful fine to see. As soon as she came to her senses, she turned around and started back. And the other women—they were so loving with her. They won't let her down."

"No. And you won't either, I'd guess."

"I should have acted before," she said, starting back into the shop and seeming to take it for granted that he would come. "Thank the good Lord I had a second chance."

A second chance. He repeated the words thoughtfully. Was that what he was looking for? A second chance to do the right thing?

They'd reached the shop, and Rebecca stood for a moment, looking at the circle of chairs she'd put out. Her lips curved in amusement. "No one got much quilting done today, I'm afraid. But there will be plenty more chances."

"About Shannon…" He began, thinking there was more to be said.

"She'll be all right. They're all rallying around her. We'll make sure someone goes to see her every day when her husband isn't there."

"Do you think Shannon will tell him? Her husband, I mean?"

Rebecca hesitated. "I don't know. I haven't met him, so how can I tell what kind of man he is? If she can trust him to understand, that would be the best thing for that little family, ain't so?"

"Yah." There it was again. Trust. Each time she mentioned it was like a little dart in his soul.

Bending, Rebecca pulled the sheet from the cradle pad. "I guess you never thought what use the cradle would be put to when you brought it to me." She seemed just a little sad as she rearranged baby quilts on the cradle.

"No, but I'm glad it was here. Glad it could be used the way it was intended." He helped her fold one of the quilts. "You're sorry not to have the baby around, ain't so?"

"I guess I am. But happy for Shannon, for sure." She glanced at him and then looked down again at the yellow and white crib quilt in her hands. "Shannon needed a family desperately and didn't have one. And I... I had a family loving me and longing to help, and I kept trying to push them away."

"Maybe so. But you're different now."

A smile touched her lips again. "Yah, thanks to all of you. I remembered what it feels like to love and trust."

Daniel's heart was so full in that moment that it seemed words would pour from him. He couldn't let it happen. Much as he cared about Rebecca, fear still held him back—fear of himself.

Silence fell between them, and he didn't know how to break it. At last Rebecca did. Giving the quilt a last twitch in place, she turned away from him.

"At least now that things are settled with Shannon, you don't have to worry about me. You can go and look for Aaron."

"Yah, I can." The sooner the better, it seemed. He was doing no good, standing here, looking at her and longing for her.

"I'll set it up to leave tomorrow morning."

Maybe if he could repair the damage done to Aaron, well, maybe then he'd be free of the guilt that crippled him.

Chapter Fourteen

Once Lige was settled in bed that night, Rebecca gathered her writing materials and settled down at the kitchen table in the grossdaadi haus. Mamm and Daad were in the living room, and she could hear their soft tones without distinguishing their words.

A comforting sound, she decided. She remembered drifting off to sleep in the farmhouse as a child, hearing the low murmur of voices from downstairs. She'd always felt so safe when she heard it, knowing that Mamm and Daadi were near at hand. It had been her image of what marriage was, that quiet communication between two people who loved and cared for each other and their children.

Perhaps Lige was beginning to feel that, as well. She hoped so. He needed that sense of safety and stability in his life, and she was finally able to provide it.

For a time, she'd almost begun to believe that Daniel might be a part of that stability for Lige and for her. She'd done everything short of saying it outright today, and he hadn't responded. So that was a brief dream better forgotten.

Smoothing the tablet of writing paper in front of her, she tried to think how to begin. The words eluded her.

She heard a step behind her and turned to find Daadi there, watching her.

"What has put that frown on your face, Rebecca?" He rested his hand on her shoulder. "Is something amiss?"

"No, nothing." She closed the tablet, her first instinct to deny it and insist everything was fine.

Then she saw her father's face. He knew. Daadi always knew when one of his children was troubled. And it wasn't just the knowledge that stirred her. It was the hurt she saw there. Daadi was hurt because she was shutting him out.

The words she'd said to Daniel earlier seemed to mock her. She'd talked about learning to love again. To trust again. But she wasn't acting as if she'd learned that lesson very well, was she?

She let out a long breath and then pulled out the chair next to her as a silent invitation. Her father sat down, rested his elbows on the table and waited.

"It's John Mast," she said finally. "I still haven't heard from him. I haven't had a payment." She shook her head. "It seems silly, but I hadn't thought until today about how long it's been."

"Too long," Daadi said so promptly that he must have been thinking about it himself. "The money was due the week you arrived here. It was all very well to say he couldn't send it immediately, but how long does he expect you to wait?"

"I don't know." She toyed with the pen and writing pad in front of her. "I thought maybe I should write again and remind him, but it's hard to do that when it's family. I don't want to cause hard feelings."

Daad's reply was prompt. "Yah, it is difficult." He patted her hand. "But John Mast entered into a contract with you. It's not the action of an honest man to refuse to send his payment."

"I suppose he feels that since he's James's brother, I should give him whatever time he needs." She was surprised to find herself excusing him. "If he's had unexpected expenses this month…"

"Is that what he said in his letter?" Daadi interrupted her, which was a sign he'd been building up something he wanted to say.

"No," she admitted. The tone of that letter had been curt. "He didn't give any reason. Just said he'd send it when he could."

Daadi put his hand over hers, making her look at him. "That's not right, Rebecca, and you know it. If he were paying a mortgage to a bank, would he do that?"

"No, but when it's family…" Why she was defending John, she couldn't imagine. But she was anxious to be fair.

"All the more reason to meet his obligations," her father said firmly. "I think you know better, Rebecca. Would any Amish man see his brother's widow and child go without, even if there wasn't a matter of a contract? John is not behaving as he should."

The sternness in his face eased a little as he studied her face. "Ach, Rebecca, you are bending over to excuse John Mast because he is James's brother, but that isn't right. More, it's not gut for him. Your lenience is allowing him to move along a road that will harm him in the end."

She smiled involuntarily. "That's the way you raised us, ain't so? Knowing that our spiritual and moral growth depended on being taught to do right."

"And the way you are raising Lige, as well. John doesn't seem to have learned the importance of keeping his word. It would be wrong not to call him to account."

"That's what's been going through my mind today. Once I knew that Shannon was back and the baby safe, I felt…" She struggled to find the words, but they escaped her.

"You stood up for what you knew you should do, and you were proved right." He patted her hand. "Now you must do the same with John. You've already decided that in your own heart, ain't so?"

"I guess so." She picked up the pen. "Even if it causes hard feelings in the family, I must remind John of his responsibility."

Daadi smiled. "Remind him as well, that he signed a written contract. No need to threaten. Just a reminder will do."

"Thanks to you, we have a contract. He kept saying it was in the family and there was no need to put it in writing. I might have given in if you hadn't insisted."

"Maybe then you would have, when you were worn down by everything that had happened. But not now. Now you have your strength back." He pushed his chair back. "I'll leave you to get on with it."

She hesitated, and then she knew what she wanted. And what would please him.

"When I've written it, will you take a look at it before I send it?"

Daadi's smile warmed his lean face. "I would be wonderful glad to, Rebecca." He went back to Mamm, looking as if she had given him a present.

She opened the pad and began to write, feeling the support of her family behind her with every word she put down. This was the way it should be in a family— all of them giving and receiving help and love in equal measure.

"The stables should be just ahead." Dave Smith, Daniel's driver, leaned forward to peer at a road sign. The retired truck driver seemed as fresh as could be after all those hours behind the wheel.

Daniel decided Dave must be used to it. He couldn't say the same for himself, though. His muscles were stiff with the inactivity, and he'd begun to feel that if he couldn't get away from the radio Dave played constantly, his head might explode. How did people stand having that artificial noise constantly in their ears?

A long, low stable appeared on their left, and Daniel's stomach lurched. That was the place. Now, if only his brother were working today...

A nightmarish thought rushed into his mind. What if Aaron had left? What if he were on vacation or away on business or even having the day off?

Then he'd wait. Or he'd follow Aaron, wherever he'd gone. He hadn't come all this way to be balked at now.

Dave pulled up next to the stable, and Daniel saw now that another row of stalls lay beyond this one. All around were paddocks and training grounds, and the oval of a track showed between the buildings.

"Big operation," Dave muttered, looking around before giving Daniel a sideways glance. "I hope you find him."

Nodding his thanks, Daniel got out slowly. He stretched, not hurrying, just thinking it over in his mind. He'd had plenty of time to figure out what he was going to say to his brother. In fact, in the middle of the night, he'd been very eloquent.

Now his mind was numb and his tongue felt paralyzed. He'd be fortunate if he could say anything at all once he came face to face with Aaron. He started walking toward the nearest door. *This is a mistake. He'll be angry. It will backfire, and he'll never want to speak to you again.*

Rebecca's concerned face appeared in his mind, chasing away the dark thoughts. He tried to repeat her words, as best he could remember them. She'd needed to know that home was still waiting for her. That people still loved her there. That was the gist of it, if not the exact words.

Maybe that was something Aaron needed to hear, as well. He hadn't found a way to say it in a letter, so he'd have to try it in person. Surely, just to see his brother's face again would make the trip worthwhile, even if that were all he had.

An older man in jeans and a flannel shirt was shoveling a stall just inside the door. He gave Daniel an incurious glance and then looked again, taking in the black pants and the straw hat he wore.

He leaned on the stall door. "Help you?"

Daniel took a deep breath. "I'm looking for Aaron King. I heard he worked here."

The man studied him for a moment longer and then shrugged. "Through that door at the end. He's got a two-year-old out in the paddock."

"Thank you." He kept himself carefully to Englisch, suspecting the man wouldn't know anything else.

He walked on, wondering. It hadn't occurred to him to think that Aaron might not want his friends here to know he was Amish. But it was possible. He knew that some young men who left tried hard to forget everything about being Amish. Seemed like the further away they got, the better, as far as they were concerned.

Funny how that worked. Some folks right in his own church district had kin that had jumped the fence, but they still had good relationships with them. Like Sarah and Luke Bitler, whose Englisch grandchildren came to spend every summer with them.

But it seemed Aaron hadn't been one of those. When he'd left, he'd cut off all ties. Thinking of the years when they hadn't known if he was dead or alive, Daniel felt a wave of bitterness and regret. They couldn't go back to that at least. Now they did know he was alive.

And working with horses—always his first love. There he was, working a young horse at the end of a long line, snapping a buggy whip in the air to signal the animal. Daniel moved closer, content to feast his eyes on his little brother at last.

Not so little, that was certain. Aaron was taller than he was, with a lean, rugged strength that handled both the line and the whip effortlessly. His hair had darkened, but it was still a lighter brown than either his or Caleb's. He wore jeans and a flannel shirt, like the other man, with brown leather boots that made Daniel think of a cowboy.

Aaron, turning in a circle as he worked the animal, caught sight of Daniel. His face expressed nothing—not welcome or anger. Just…nothing but a tightness so hard he might have been carved from stone.

Daniel's heart caught. What made him look so hard? It couldn't just be the sight of his brother. He'd already worn that expression before he even noticed Daniel.

Ignoring him, Aaron focused on the horse, slowing him down from a trot to a walk, shortening the rope until the animal came to a halt in front of him. Holding the halter, Aaron crossed the paddock to him, stopping a couple of feet away and looping the rope over the fence.

"So," he said at last. "I should have known Eli would talk. He never could keep anything to himself."

"Don't blame him." Daniel kept his tone easy with an effort, sensing he had to be as gentle with his brother as Aaron would be with an untrained colt. "His wife made him do it."

Something that might have been a smile tugged at Aaron's mouth. "Guess that would happen. Who'd he marry?"

"Esther Stoltzfus. You remember her from school?"

Aaron nodded. "Bossy."

There was nothing much to say to that, since it was a fine description of Esther.

Aaron picked up a towel from an equipment caddy that sat on the ground by the fence. "I've got to get back to work. What do you want, Daniel?"

Daniel ducked between the rails and picked up another cloth, starting to wipe down the other side of the horse. The two-year-old rolled his eyes toward Daniel and then seemed to decide not to protest.

"Wanted to see how my little brother is doing," he said. "Not so little anymore, yah?"

He'd switched to Pennsylvania Dutch without thinking of it when he'd seen Aaron, and his brother had answered him in dialect, too. So at least he hadn't forgotten the language of his family.

"Bigger than you anyway." He seemed to focus on the horse, but finally he glanced at Daniel and then away. "How's the family?"

Daniel breathed a silent prayer of mingled gratitude and longing. "Caleb is fine. Broke his leg pretty badly a while back, but it's healed okay, so he's back to running the dairy farm. That gives me time to devote to my carpentry business. He's married again now. Jessie's a fine woman and wonderful gut with the kinder. And they're growing like weeds."

"And Onkel Zeb?"

Was that anxiety in his voice? Would he be grieving if something had happened to the old man since he'd been gone?

"Zeb's the same as ever. He gets up before dawn for

the milking, and he puts in a full day of work. Some-times we have to trick him to get him to take a rest."

Aaron didn't respond, but Daniel thought his expres-sion eased a bit. "You're not married, I see."

Daniel brushed a hand along his beardless face, try-ing not to think of Rebecca. "I run too fast," he said lightly.

Silence again, and he sought for something to say to keep Aaron talking.

"Looks like quite an operation here. You doing the training, are you?"

Aaron gave a short nod. "It's sulky racing mostly around here. The boss breeds them and sometimes picks up likely youngsters at the auctions. I go along to help out with that."

"You were always gut at judging horseflesh."

Aaron shrugged, not volunteering anything else.

"Are you satisfied here?" He didn't ask if Aaron was happy. It certain sure wasn't happiness that had given him a face like a stone.

"It's okay. As long as I can work with the horses, that's good enough."

"Plenty of horses to work with back in Lost Creek," he ventured.

Aaron's body become taut, as if every muscle stilled. Then he tossed the curry brush in the caddy. He grasped the horse's halter, untying the rope. "I'd better get back to work." He didn't look at Daniel as he opened the gate and led the horse through.

Daniel followed, feeling his chances slipping away. On impulse, he reached out to grasp his brother's shoulder. The muscles felt like iron under his hand, but Aaron didn't pull away.

"Now that we've found you, we don't want to lose touch. Just let us know you're well from time to time. Please."

"I've got a new life now." He muttered the words, not looking at Daniel. Then he stepped away, so that Daniel's hand fell from his shoulder.

"Yah, we know. We respect that." He hesitated, but he had to say it. It was what he'd come to say. "But the farm is always home for you, if you ever want it. We will always love you and want you."

For an instant, he thought Aaron would fling away from him. Instead, he stood, his face working as if he struggled to contain it.

Finally he spoke. "Denke." His voice was gruff. "Goodbye, Daniel."

Daniel waited for a moment, hoping for more. For Aaron, ramrod straight, walked away.

Daniel looked down at the hand that had touched his brother after all this time. For a moment, they had been connected. He had longed to grab Aaron—to pull him into his arms.

But it would have been a mistake. If Aaron came back, it had to be because he wanted to, not because Daniel had pushed and manipulated him.

His thoughts lifted in a silent prayer for his brother as he walked slowly toward the car. He might have little to show for this visit, but he would never regret it.

Chapter Fifteen

Rebecca, getting ready to leave for the shop on Monday morning, was trying not to wonder what happened with Daniel and Aaron. Unfortunately, trying didn't seem to be enough to keep the subject from her mind. *When would she know?*

Leah glanced at her from the counter where she was kneading bread dough. "I saw Daniel got back from his trip last night. I hope things went well with Aaron."

Everyone seemed to know the purpose of Daniel's trip. That was inevitable in the close-knit Amish community. Some folks probably thought it a foolish errand, but most would have prayed for him. And for Aaron.

No member of the Leit wanted to lose one of their own, and since Aaron hadn't been baptized into the church, he could still return, confess and slip into his place, as if he'd never been gone. The church would close around him, and the community would be whole again.

"Yah, I hope so, too." What else could she say? The

weight of the part she'd played in his decision pressed on her.

"Have you heard how it went?" Apparently not satisfied, Leah resorted to a direct question.

Rebecca managed a smile at her tactics. "If I knew, I would tell you, but I haven't talked to him yet. And even when I see him, I don't know that he'll want to talk about it."

"As close as you are, surely he'll confide in you." Leah gave the smooth mound of dough a pat, as if she were patting a baby, and turned around, wiping her hands on a towel. "You and he were always close, ain't so?"

"That was a long time ago." She tried to speak lightly, but it was difficult when her heart was yearning to help Daniel.

"Not so long." She fell silent and then shook her head slightly. "Ach, I can't do it. Sam would tell me to keep silent, but I can't, not when I see you hurting so much. I want to see you and Daniel as happy as Sam and I are. You two belong together. You always have."

Rebecca would like to believe that, but she couldn't. "Maybe, once, it would have worked out. But when I went away, Daniel still looked on me as a friend, nothing more."

"Daniel was as foolish as most boys were at that age," Leah said tartly. "He'd have grown out of chasing after other girls in time. He'd have realized that his true friend was also his true love."

"We'll never know, ain't so? I didn't wait. I rushed into marrying, and now it's too late." Her marriage to James would have ended any chance for her and Daniel, even if Daniel's stubborn insistence on bearing guilt that was not his own had not existed. But she had Lige, and she could never regret the choices that had given him to her.

Leah looked as if she'd like to argue. Then, pressing her lips together, she came to Rebecca and hugged her. "You deserve your happiness," she said softly. "And so does Daniel."

Rebecca hugged her back, comforted. "Perhaps. But we must be satisfied with what the Lord sends us."

She pulled away, gathering up what she'd need for the day. She would stop thinking about being anything else to Daniel and focus on being his friend. Whatever had happened with Aaron, he needed a friend now.

To Rebecca's surprise, when she reached the shop, Daniel was already there. The kitchen looked like a construction zone, with the old cabinets gone and one of the new ones Daniel had been making set up on a pair of sawhorses.

"I didn't expect you—" she began and then stopped, startled. "What happened to the refrigerator?"

Daniel looked surprised, as well. "Didn't you know? Your daad came in first thing this morning. He traded it in for a gas one. He said the store was bringing a new gas refrigerator to the daadi haus and moving that one in here."

"But he didn't say a word to me about it." She couldn't decide whether she was upset or thankful. Maybe a little of both. "I wish he wouldn't do things like that. I'm sure Mamm didn't think she needed a new one. It's just an excuse to get one put in for me."

Daniel didn't go so far as to chuckle, but there was laughter in his eyes. "I don't think you're ever going to outfox him. And I bet, if you ask her, your mamm will say she loves her new refrigerator."

"She'll agree with him, that's certain sure. I just don't want him spending money on me."

"I thought you were going to let him help you. Isn't that what you were telling me?"

"I know." She felt herself flush. "But even so...well, if John comes through with the money he owes, I can pay him back."

"I doubt you can get him to take it." Daniel seemed to be clearing a path to the spot for the new refrigerator. "Have you some reason to think your brother-in-law has come to his senses?"

She probably shouldn't let him talk that way about John, but the trouble was that she thought the same. "Not yet, but I wrote to him a few days ago." She still got a little queasy feeling in her stomach when she thought about it. "Daad and I agreed that he needed a reminder of the contract he signed. I hope that's all he needs. It was hard enough to make myself go that far."

"But you did." He was studying her with what seemed to be approval. "I'm glad to see you're getting your spunk back."

"I don't know about that." She smiled at the word. "But I guess everything that's happened has given me some courage—opening the shop, dealing with that business over Shannon. I feel like I can cope with things now."

"You can," Daniel said, his voice firm. "You always

could. Your confidence just got a little dented there for a while."

She ducked her head, not sure what to say. Then it struck her that Daniel might well be keeping the talk on her because he didn't want to tell her about Aaron.

If so, shouldn't she respect that? Or was it the part of a friend to encourage him to open up about what happened?

In the momentary pause, Daniel bent to pick up a hammer. Then he just stood there, staring at it, as if he didn't remember what he'd intended to do with it.

"You...you had a long drive." A hopeless way to start, but all that came out of her mouth.

"Yah." He was still studying the hammer. Finally he put it down and looked at her. "I guess you want to know what happened."

"Only if you want to tell me." She took a step closer, wishing she knew how to make this easier.

"Well, I saw him." He gave her a fleeting smile. "My little bruder is all grown-up."

"I guess he would be," she said, trying not to sound too eager. "How did he look?"

"Okay, I guess. Englisch." He grimaced slightly, making her long to comfort him.

"That would be hard." How would she feel if Sam had left, or one of her other brothers? How would it be to see him after all that time, looking like a stranger?

"It's funny, but it wasn't as odd as it seems. I knew he'd have changed, but when I saw him working with a young horse, it was just like watching the old Aaron. You know how he was with the horses."

She nodded, remembering. "I remember Daadi saying that Aaron was born able to talk to the horses. It's a gift, ain't so?"

"Yah. And at least that hasn't changed. He acted like he was satisfied with his job there."

It seemed to Rebecca that Daniel was making an effort to talk about it without letting his emotions run free. Maybe he was afraid of what he'd say if he let go.

"Was he...was he happy being Englisch? Does he have friends? People he can count on?"

Daniel shrugged. "How can I say? We only talked for a few minutes. By his choice, not mine."

He sounded annoyed, and it was probably better to let him take his frustration out on her than on himself. If she knew him, he was already blaming himself still more.

"I'm sorry. I wish you could have had more time with him."

"No, I'm the one to be sorry." He gave her a sideways, sheepish look. "It's not your fault. I wish that, as well."

"You were disappointed."

"No, not exactly. At least I saw him. I did ask him to let us know from time to time that he's all right." He seemed to turn that over in his mind. "You know, now that I go back over it, I think he was almost surprised to hear that we still think of him and want him back."

"I'd say that if you succeeded in doing that, you've done a lot for one short visit, ain't so?" She held her breath. Was he going to explode at that idea?

Instead, he looked as if he were actually considering her words. "You might be right. If you'd asked me what I expected from the visit beforehand, I'd have said I'd be content just to see he was all right." He gave a wry smile. "We're always expecting more from the Father, aren't we? Thinking that He will give us what we want in exchange for very little effort on our part."

She turned that over in her mind. Had she sometimes expected that result from her prayers? Thinking that God might swoop in and solve her problems? Probably so.

"Are you disappointed then?" She held her breath for the answer, fearing the increased pain he'd feel if he thought he'd failed his brother again.

For an instant, Daniel looked surprised. "No, I guess I'm not," he said slowly, as if he were thinking it through. "At least I saw Aaron. I told him what I wanted him to hear—that we loved and missed him and wanted him back. But Onkel Zeb was right, too. Aaron is a grown man now. He has to decide for himself what he wants."

Rebecca felt able to breathe again. He was taking this better, more sensibly, than she'd have dared hope. "You did all you could," she said.

Daniel nodded, and his face wore an expression of peace she'd never seen before when he talked about his brother. "I opened the door. I will pray he walks through it, but that he has to do on his own."

Once they had separated, each going to work on the day's project, Rebecca lifted her heart in prayers of thanksgiving. God had given Daniel release from some of the grief and regret that bound him. She could only hope and dream that he would move the rest of the way to healing.

Rebecca busied herself by cutting the five-inch squares of quilting fabrics several of her customers had asked for. Apparently, a lot of quilters found it made more sense to buy the squares already cut than to buy fabric by the yard and perhaps waste some.

Not that she'd ever found it a waste. The leftover material could always be used for something, she'd found. Still, she was in business to provide what her customers wanted, and if they were willing to pay a little more for precut squares, she was happy to oblige them.

One of the Englisch women who'd come to the shop had even said she'd bought precut squares through the internet. It seemed strange to Rebecca to buy fabric when you couldn't see it or feel it in your hands, but apparently it was so.

The work kept her hands occupied and left her mind free to wander. It went, as it so often did recently, to the changes she saw in herself since she'd returned to Lost Creek. What a pitiful creature she'd been—tied up in knots and blaming herself, afraid even to trust and rely on those who loved her best. Being here had healed her.

Or rather, the good Lord had healed her, working through those around her. Even someone like Lydia Schultz, with her gossipy tongue, had contributed, showing Rebecca that she was becoming strong again.

Most of all, always there, so necessary to her happiness, there was Daniel. For so long, she hadn't even recognized that she was learning to love him in a new way. She hadn't seen it until it was too late to prevent it. She couldn't stop loving him, even if he never made a move toward her.

Those moments when Daniel had responded to her… she hadn't imagined them. He had feelings for her. She was sure of it. But if he never allowed himself to recognize those feelings…

Footsteps sounded on the porch, and even as she looked up, the door opened, bell jingling wildly. A man strode in. Not just any man. John Mast, James's brother.

The scissors dropped from her suddenly nerveless fingers as she struggled for control. That letter. He must have come in response to her letter.

"John." She forced herself to sound cordial, forced her stiff lips to smile. "I wasn't expecting you. Wilkom."

His face was set in lines so harsh they seemed engraved into his skin. He stalked to the counter, and his expression had her taking an involuntary step back.

No. She would not be that person again. Just because John looked like James in one of his rages, she could not let herself cower. She was over that.

But her throat was dry, and her stomach had clenched into a knot.

John slammed something down on the counter. Her letter.

"I came because of that." His voice was loud, like his brother's when he was angry.

Rebecca grasped the edge of the counter, trying to quell the trembling inside her, and sent a silent plea flying in prayer. *Please, Lord. Help me.*

Finding himself at a momentary standstill in the kitchen until the new refrigerator arrived, Daniel had gone upstairs to check out what was needed there. The room at the front of the house, over the shop, was the largest, plainly intended to be a master bedroom. It actually had an adjoining bathroom, which the last owners had installed.

The wooden planks of the floor were in pretty good condition, but they'd need to be either refinished or painted. He took a step and found one that creaked and gave under his foot. Frowning, he knelt to check it out.

He was kneeling there when he heard the slam of the shop door. His eyebrows lifted. The ladies who came to the quilt shop were not usually quite so noisy. Motionless, he listened for any sound from below.

A few minutes later he could have heard clearly without any need for kneeling. The voice of the man who'd entered the shop carried clearly. It didn't take much thinking to realize this was Rebecca's brother-in-law. She had written to him to remind him to pay, and it sounded as if he'd come to deliver his response in person.

The loud, bullying tones set his teeth on edge, and his hands curled involuntarily into fists. Daniel forced them to relax. That wasn't the Amish way of solving problems, but if anyone deserved to be forcibly reminded of his manners, it must surely be John Mast.

A human being could only take so much. Daniel surged to his feel and went quickly out of the room and down the stairs, his thoughts forced on Rebecca. How was she coping?

A second later, that thought fled, because of what he saw. Lige was at the foot of the stairs. He'd curled his small body into a ball, so that Daniel couldn't see his face. But he could see the way he was trembling, his hands clamped to his ears.

Focused on the boy, he reached the bottom of the

steps and spoke softly. "Lige, it's all right. It's Daniel. Can you look at me?"

There was no movement at first, and he feared the boy had retreated beyond his reach. But finally Lige raised his head enough for Daniel to see his white tearstained face. Daniel's heart wrenched as if a fist had grabbed it.

"It's all right," he said again. He opened his arms, and Lige bolted into them. The boy wrapped his arms around Daniel's neck and buried his face in Daniel's shoulder.

Daniel scooped him up and carried him quickly to the back porch. It hurt to walk away from Rebecca, but it sounded as if she was holding her own. Lige needed help now.

Setting the boy down, he knelt beside him, tipping his face up gently. "It scared you, ain't so? Hearing your onkel that way."

Lige nodded. "It…it sounded like Daadi," he whispered, lowering his face again.

Daniel's heart winced. "It's not, but we can't let him talk that way to your mammi. So I'm going to go in there, and I want you to run to the farmhouse and tell Grossdaadi what's happening. Can you do that?"

The small face suddenly looked up at Daniel's. "But Mammi…" he whispered.

"I'll take care of Mammi. I need you to be brave now and run as fast as you can. Okay?"

Lige hesitated, his huge blue eyes fixated on Daniel's face. Finally he nodded. He turned and spurted off the porch as if he'd been shot from a gun, running toward the farmhouse with all his might.

Lige had trusted him. The thought overwhelmed him. Lige trusted him to know what was right and do it.

Daniel walked quickly through the house, toward the shop. Rebecca might not feel the same way Lige did. She'd expressed, again and again, her need to handle things on her own. She'd probably be ready to tear a strip off him for interfering.

But no matter how angry it made her, he couldn't stop. The people who loved her had the right to stand beside her in times of trouble. He did.

There was no time to analyze that thought. He pushed the door open and went into the shop.

Rebecca and her brother-in-law stood facing each other on either side of the counter, at the front of the shop. Mast seemed to loom over Rebecca, and it sounded as if he was hectoring her to change the terms of the contract.

As for Rebecca…her pallor smote his heart, but in spite of that, she stood erect, her shoulders back. Her voice was so soft in comparison to the man's that he couldn't quite make out her words.

Forcing down his anger, he went to them, his movement drawing Mast's attention. He glowered as Daniel moved to stand behind Rebecca. She didn't speak or turn, but she took a half step closer to him, and he could almost feel her gratitude reaching out to him.

Mast glared at him. "This is a private conversation."

"Daniel is my friend." Rebecca spoke firmly, her voice sounding louder, more certain. "I have no objection to his being here. What I have to say is simple. You signed a contract, and you will have to honor it."

Mast's face darkened. "It's not right. That property

belonged to my brother. He'd have wanted me to farm it. You had no right to sell it away from the family."

"I didn't. I sold it to you." She put a faint stress on the word sold.

Mast glanced from Rebecca to Daniel and seemed to make an effort to switch his ground. "You'll get your money. Just because I happened to be a little short this month is no reason for you to make a fuss."

For a moment, Daniel feared Rebecca would waver. She'd stood up against anger, but an appeal was something different. He prayed she wasn't going to let her soft heart betray her. He probably shouldn't speak, but the words were out before he could stop them.

"Your brother's son shouldn't have to suffer for your financial problems. You signed an agreement."

Rebecca shot him a look, but he didn't have time to reassure her. Obviously, he'd infuriated Mast.

"It's not your business." He glared at Daniel and then shifted back to Rebecca. "I'll pay when I'm ready and not before. You're not going to sue your own brother-in-law, and there's nothing else you can do, contract or no contract."

Silence greeted his ultimatum. Maybe he'd guessed correctly. Rebecca would be reluctant to go that far, and his hands were tied.

"If you refuse to pay what is owed, I will help my daughter take you to court."

Rebecca's father came toward them, with Sam right behind him. The old man's face was stern and calm, but Sam looked as if he were having difficulty containing himself. Behind them, Lige slid in, moving like a shadow to Daniel's side.

Daniel put his hand on the boy's shoulder, and they stood together.

Mast hesitated, his confidence seeming to dip for the first time. "You wouldn't do that. Amish don't sue other Amish."

"I would rather not, but I don't really think that will be necessary." All of Rebecca's strength must have come back now, and she seemed to know just what to say. "I will speak to your parents first. I don't think they want to see their grandson cheated of what is his. And if that doesn't work, I'll speak to the bishop. You will meet your obligations, John."

Daniel nearly smiled at the baffled expression on the man's face. He'd clearly expected to have no difficulty in cowing Rebecca into agreeing with him, and he didn't know what to do with the Rebecca who faced him down. She was a different person from the one he'd known in Ohio.

With a sudden movement, he slapped a wad of cash down on the counter. Without a word, he turned and lumbered out of the shop.

For a long moment, there was silence. Maybe they were all waiting to hear the driver who'd brought John leaving. When the sound of the car turning out onto the road came, Rebecca took a deep breath.

She turned and looked from one to another of them. "Denke," she said softly. "Thank you for standing with me."

Chapter Sixteen

Daniel felt oddly flat that evening after his happiness at the successful conclusion of Rebecca's business with her brother-in-law. *Why?* He frowned at the cabinet he was making for Rebecca's kitchen, but it had no answers.

What was he regretting? Rebecca had obviously not held it against him that he'd intervened and that he'd sent for her father. He should be happy. Her response had told all of them that she'd regained what she'd lost in her marriage to James. She was not the girl she'd been, but she was the woman she'd been intended to become.

Onkel Zeb came in, interrupting his musing, and he attempted to look busy. Zeb, next to him, ran his hand along the curve of the cabinet door.

"Fine piece of work. It's for Rebecca's kitchen, ain't so?"

He nodded, smiling a little. "It's a surprise, so don't say anything. It'll fit right into that corner by the refrigerator, and it's just deep enough to store some of her canned goods, nice and handy."

"Special built, just for her kitchen." Onkel Zeb studied his face. "A gift of love, you might say."

He supposed it was, but he certain sure didn't want to be that obvious. "I saw one like it in an Englisch kitchen, that's all. Thought it was a gut idea, and Rebecca should have one. Maybe I'll put them in all the kitchens I do."

"Maybe," his uncle agreed. "But only this one is what I said—a gift of love."

"Onkel Zeb..." he began, but he didn't get any further.

"Ach, don't bother denying it. Not to me. Do you think I don't know you any better than that after being around your whole life? You love Rebecca. So why aren't you doing something about it instead of hiding in your shop?"

"I'm not hiding," he was momentarily indignant. "I'm doing my job."

"Hiding," Zeb said firmly.

Daniel frowned at him, but Zeb's wise old eyes merely looked amused.

"All right," he said, capitulating. "Yah, if you must know, I... I have feelings for Rebecca."

"The whole county knows that. But have you told her so?" His uncle was clearly not letting this go.

The answer to that was evident, he supposed. "It's too soon. It hasn't been that long since her husband passed."

"And small loss to anyone, if half what I've heard is true. That's no reason for not telling her what you feel. Even if it is too soon to expect her to marry you all in a rush. Still, from what I can remember, no woman objects to being told she's loved."

Daniel glared at his uncle, who was unperturbed. "There's Lige to consider, too. I don't want to rush either of them. Is that all right with you?"

"Ach, Daniel, I've seen you with the boy. It's clear that he loves you and trusts you. He relies on you, and so does Rebecca. Can't you see that the two of you were made for each other? Everyone else can."

His uncle was awfully good at disposing of his reasons, but there was one he couldn't deny.

"Our family hasn't had much success with women. Maybe I…"

Zeb put a hand on his shoulder, giving him a light shake. "Don't talk that way. Your mamm hurt all of you when she left, but that's no reason to hide from love. Look how happy Caleb and Jessie are. And my Mary— even though we had just two short years, she made me happier than anyone else could in a lifetime."

His throat tightened. "I'm sorry. I didn't mean anything about you. It's me. What if… I make promises to them, and then I let them down?"

The hand on his shoulder squeezed tight for an instant. "Daniel, Daniel. Always so conscientious. Always blaming yourself when things go wrong. But that's foolishness. We can't control everything that happens in life, even for those we love the most. We can only love them, do our best and trust the Lord for everything else."

The message wasn't new, but the way his heart responded when he heard it was. He thought it would leap out of his chest. Onkel Zeb was right. Why was he wasting time when he had a chance at a love like Rebecca?

Onkel Zeb must have sensed the change in him, because he smiled. He gave Daniel a gentle push toward the door. "Go on. Go to Rebecca. Right now."

Daniel's first few steps were tentative, dragged at by doubts. And then they fell away, and he was running across the field. He looked like a madman, and he didn't care. He had to see Rebecca.

Rebecca was sitting in the living room of the farmhouse with Leah and Mamm that evening, and they were all focused on a basketful of mending. Daadi was in the daadi haus with Lige, and as Mamm said, mending was more enjoyable when they made a work frolic out of it. Their conversation flowed easily as they worked, with the companionship of women who knew each other so well that words weren't always needed.

She heard the back door close, and in a moment, Sam appeared in the doorway, a smile teasing the corners of his mouth.

"Somebody to see you, Rebecca. Out on the back porch."

Putting her needle in the patch she was sewing, she rose. Surely John hadn't returned for another try. But no, Sam would hardly look amused at that. "Who is it?"

He gave her a gentle push. "It's Daniel. Seems to be something important, by the looks of him."

Rebecca eyed her brother suspiciously. "If you're trying to play a joke on me, it's not funny."

"It's no joke." Putting his arm around her waist, he

propelled her across the room. "Go and put the poor man out of his misery."

She pulled herself free and frowned at him, but her heart had begun thudding in her chest. "I suppose you think you're funny. Go find something to do with yourself."

Her knees showed a sudden tendency to shake, but she forced herself to walk steadily out to the porch. Daniel spun toward her at the movement of the door.

"Rebecca." For a moment, it seemed all he wanted was to look at her. Then he held out his hand. "Will you take a walk with me?"

She nodded, hardly daring to hope. They walked in silence along the lane and past the barn. When they reached the drooping branches of the old weeping willow by the pond, Daniel paused.

"Do you remember when you had a hideout under the branches of the willow?" He smiled down at her, but his eyes were dark and serious.

"I remember. I went there when I wanted to get away from Sam's teasing."

"It might still be a fine place to get away from anyone watching."

"Is someone watching?" He was facing toward the house, but she wasn't, and she wouldn't give anyone the satisfaction of looking.

His smile widened. "There's a face at every window."

Rebecca parted the long fronds of the willow stems, inviting him with a glance. They stepped inside, and the drooping branches fell back into place, enclosing them in a leafy green cave, with just enough light from the setting sun to see each other.

She waited. It was Daniel who'd come to her, so he had to speak first.

He seemed to have trouble getting started, clearing his throat a couple of times. "I… I hope you're not angry with me for sending for your father earlier."

Rebecca had a sense that he had intended to say something different. She had to pause, adjusting her thoughts. Of course he might feel she'd be upset about his interference, since she'd so loudly proclaimed her ability to stand on her own feet.

"You do know I've got past that feeling, don't you? Especially when you've helped me with it so much." *And confided in me. And let me confide in you. That means something, doesn't it?*

"That's…that's gut. You have your confidence back. You can do anything."

"Not anything." She suspected she'd have to help him, or he'd never get to what he wanted to say. "I can't start a new family. Not by myself."

His lips twitched a little. "Rebecca, are you asking me?"

"No, I'm trying to encourage you to do the asking."

Daniel reached out and touched her face. Such a light, gentle touch, but it seemed to go straight to her heart.

"I have longed so much to tell you what I feel." His gaze held hers, drawing her closer and closer. "I've been afraid—afraid of letting you down, afraid of hurting Lige, maybe even afraid of myself."

Sure now, she put her hand over his, pressing his palm against her cheek. "So foolish," she murmured. "You don't have it in you to hurt either of us."

"No. I knew that when I heard John berating you today. When I went and stood with you. I didn't even think. I just did it because that was where I belonged. Because love means standing together at times like that." There was a light in his eyes, like a tiny flame flickering with his love for her.

"I know. I felt you there, and I wasn't afraid."

"My Rebecca. We belong together. Will you be my wife?"

Rebecca lifted her face to his. "I will."

She pronounced the words solemnly. It was a vow, a solemn promise before God. A recognition that the past was gone and a new future lay ahead for both of them.

Daniel leaned closer. His hand slid from her cheek to the back of her neck, spreading warmth everywhere he touched. He tilted her head so that their faces were very close—close enough that she could smell the honest male scent of him, close enough that his breath caressed her skin, making her tingle.

With a little sigh, she moved into his embrace. Daniel's lips met hers, sweet and gentle and filled with love. Rebecca knew, with his kiss, that the last faint vestige of pain was gone from her heart. Her arms slid around him, feeling the strong, flat muscles of his back, and she gave herself to his embrace.

Through all the dizziness and joy, Rebecca felt the truth that filled her heart. God was giving both of them a second chance to make the right choices. A chance to have a lifetime of happiness, a life that grew from two children playing together to a man and a woman who belong to each other, no matter what life brings.

Her heart overflowed with joy. They were both where they belonged at last.

* * * * *

ANNA'S FORGOTTEN FIANCÉ

Carrie Lighte

For anyone who has ever suffered a bumped head
or a bruised heart, as well as for those who have
experienced the healing power of love.
With special thanks to my agent, Pam Hopkins,
and my editor, Shana Asaro.

Trust in the Lord with all thine heart; and lean not unto thine own understanding. In all thy ways acknowledge him, and he shall direct thy paths.
—*Proverbs* 3:5–6

Chapter One

Anna Weaver slowly opened her eyes. Sunlight played off the white sheets and she quickly lowered her lids again, groaning. Her mind was swirling with questions but her mouth was too dry to form any words.

"Have a drink of water," a female voice beside her offered. "Little sips. Don't gulp it."

The young woman supported Anna's head until she'd swallowed her fill and then eased her back against the pillow. Anna squinted toward the figure.

"You've had an accident," she explained, as if sensing Anna's confusion. "You're at home recovering. It's your second day out of the hospital. How do you feel?"

"Like a horse kicked me in the head," Anna answered in a raspy voice. She blinked several times, trying to focus.

"You recognize me, don't you?" the woman asked. "I'm Melinda Roth, your cousin."

Technically, the woman wasn't Anna's cousin; she was her stepmother's niece. *I doubt I could ever forget the person who captured my boyfriend's heart*, Anna thought. Aloud she replied, "Of course I recognize you. Why wouldn't I?"

"The *Englisch* doctors said you still might have trouble with your memory, but apparently you don't," Melinda answered, appearing more disappointed than relieved.

Anna felt a pang of compassion. It was obvious Melinda felt guilty for what had transpired between her and Aaron. Anna had forgiven them both, but forgetting what happened was a little more difficult, especially since she had to live under the same roof—and share the same bedroom—with Melinda. Each time Melinda tiptoed into the room after her curfew, Anna was made acutely aware of how much her cousin was enjoying being courted by Aaron.

"The only trouble I have is that I'm a bit chilled," Anna said.

Melinda placed a hand on Anna's forehead. "You don't have a fever, thank the Lord. The doctor warned us to watch for that. I'll ask Eli to bring more wood inside for the stove."

"The woodstove in August?" Anna marveled. "That would be a first. Please don't trouble Eli on my account. I'm certain once I get up and move around, I'll be toasty warm."

"Lappich maedel!" Melinda tittered as she referred to Anna as a silly girl. "It isn't August. It's the first week in March."

Anna propped herself up on her elbows. Although she figured Melinda probably meant to be funny, her head was throbbing and she was in no mood for such foolishness. She knit her brows together and questioned, "You're teasing, right?"

Melinda shook her head and gestured toward the maple tree outside the window. "See? It doesn't have its leaves yet."

"How could that be?" A tear slid down Anna's cheek.

"Uh-oh, I've said too much." Melinda jumped to her feet and unfolded a second quilt over Anna's legs. "That should keep you warm."

Anna stared at her cousin, trying to make sense of the scenario. Then she began to giggle. "Oh, I understand! I'm dreaming!"

"Neh, neh," Melinda contradicted, giving Anna's skin a small pinch. "Feel that?"

Completely befuddled, Anna bent her arm across her face. First, she'd lost her boyfriend, then she'd lost her father, and now she feared she was losing her mind. It was simply too much to take in and she began to weep fully.

"You mustn't cry," Melinda cautioned. "The doctor said it wasn't *gut* for you to become upset. We don't want to have to take you back to the hospital."

Melinda's warning was enough to silence Anna's weeping. "I don't understand how two seasons could have passed without my knowing." She sniffed.

"The doctors said it's the nature of a head injury like yours. You may remember things from long ago, but not more recently. You've also been on strong medications for your headache and for hurting your backside when you fell, so even your hospital stay might be fuzzy."

"It is," Anna acknowledged. "And I don't recall injuring myself. How did it happen?"

"You appear to have slipped on the bank by the creek, hitting your head on a rock," Melinda replied. "Do you know what you may have been doing there? Or where you were going? It was early Tuesday morning."

Anna tried to remember but her mind was as blank as the ceiling above. She shook her head and then grimaced from the motion.

"That's okay," Melinda said cheerfully. "How about telling me some of the more important events that you *do* remember?"

"My *daed*'s funeral," Anna responded. "It was raining—a deluge of water—and then the rain turned to sleet and then to ice."

She remembered because at the time she felt as if the unseasonably cold weather mirrored her emotions; a torrent of tears followed by a stark, frozen numbness that even the brightest sunshine couldn't thaw.

"*Jah*, your *daed* died a year ago. Last March. What do you remember after that?"

Anna thought hard. The days, weeks and months after her dad's sudden death from a heart attack were a blur to her even before her head injury. "I remember… your birthday party," she said brightly.

"My eighteenth. *Gut*. That was in late August. Do you remember when I got baptized last fall?"

It felt wrong to admit she couldn't recall Melinda making such an important commitment, but Anna said, "*Neh*. I'm sorry."

"That's alright. The doctor said your memory loss

probably wouldn't last long, especially if you're at home, surrounded by familiar faces."

"Well then, if that's what it takes to cure me, I should get dressed and join the boys for breakfast," Anna stated, although she would have preferred a few more moments of rest before joining her four stepbrothers downstairs. She slowly swung her legs over the edge of the bed.

"They'll be glad to know you're well enough to rise," Melinda remarked. "But it's nearly time for supper, not breakfast. And the one who is most anxious to see you is your fiancé. He'll stop in after work again, no doubt."

"My fiancé?" Anna snorted. "But I broke up with Aaron after I caught you and him—I mean, Aaron is walking out with you now, isn't he?"

"Jah, jah," Melinda confirmed. Her cheeks were so red it appeared she was the one who had a fever. "You and Aaron broke up over a year ago. Last February, in fact." She hung her head as if ashamed, before looking Anna in the eye again and clarifying, "I was referring to your new suitor. That is, to your fiancé, Fletcher. Fletcher Chupp, Aaron's cousin from Ohio."

"Fletcher?" Anna sputtered incredulously. "I'm quite certain I'm not acquainted with—much less *engaged to*—anyone by that name."

Fletcher stooped to pick up a cordless drywall screw gun and a handful of screws that had fallen to the floor.

"Don't forget to gather all of your tools before leaving the work site for the evening," he reminded Roy and Raymond Keim, Anna's stepbrothers.

"We won't," Roy responded. "But those aren't ours—they're Aaron's. We didn't know if he was coming back or not, so we didn't dare to put them away."

"Where has he gone?" Fletcher inquired.

"Probably buying a soft drink at the fast-food place down the street," answered Raymond as he folded a ladder and leaned it carefully on its side along the wall.

Fletcher wished Aaron would set a better example of work habits for Raymond and Roy. He worried what their *Englisch* clients would think if they saw him taking numerous breaks or leaving early. Aaron's habits reflected on all of them. Although their projects had been plentiful over the winter due to an October tornado damaging many of the office buildings in their little town of Willow Creek, there was no guarantee that future contracts would be awarded to them, especially if their reputation suffered. Fletcher would need all the work he could get when he became a married man with a family to support. *That's* if *I become a married man*, he mentally corrected himself.

Nothing about his future with Anna was as certain as it had seemed when their wedding intentions were "published," or announced, in church on Sunday. Only two days later, on Tuesday morning, Raymond delivered a sealed note to him from Anna. *Fletcher,* it read, *I have a serious concern regarding A. that I must discuss privately with you before the wedding preparations go any further. Please visit me tonight after work. —Anna.*

The message was so unexpected and disturbing that if he hadn't been responsible for supervising Raymond and Roy, Fletcher would have left work immediately to speak with Anna. By the time he finally reached her home that evening, he was shocked to be greeted by a neighbor bearing additional alarming news: that morning Anna suffered a fall and was in the hospital. Although he loathed knowing she'd been hurt, he was simultaneously informed the doctors said she was going to be just fine. But it tormented him that he had no such assurance about the future of his relationship with her.

Each time he visited Anna, she was resting or couldn't be disturbed. Now, it was Friday and he still hadn't spoken to her. Ever since receiving her note, he'd felt as if he'd swallowed a handful of nails, and he'd barely eaten or slept all week. *Please, Lord, give me patience and peace, even as You provide Anna rest and recovery*, he prayed for the umpteenth time that day.

"I suppose Aaron's allowed to take breaks whenever he wants since he's the business owner's son," Roy commented, interrupting Fletcher's thoughts.

Although Fletcher agreed with the boy's observation, he chided, "Enough of that talk. My *onkel* Isaiah showed you special favor yourself in allowing me to apprentice you here, because your *mamm* was married to Anna's *daed* and he was such a skilled carpenter. Isaiah has been a *gut* employer to me, too. Regardless of how anyone else performs their work, *Gott* requires each of us to work heartily in whatever we do."

The boys finished tidying the site before stepping out into the nippy early-evening air. They wove through the rows of *Englisch* vehicles to the makeshift hitching post at the far end of the parking lot. Aaron's sleek courting buggy was nowhere to be seen as Fletcher, Raymond and Roy climbed into Fletcher's boxy carriage, given to him by his *groossdaadi*, or grandfather.

"Go ahead and take the reins," Fletcher said to Roy, the younger of the two teens. "It's important for you to learn to handle the horse during what the *Englisch* call 'rush hour' traffic."

As Roy cautiously navigated his way through the western, commercialized section of Willow Creek, Fletcher gave him instructive hints. He knew what it was like to lose your dad at a young age—and these boys had essentially lost *two* fathers; first, their own dad and then Anna's. He figured they needed all the guidance and support they could get.

"*Gut* job," he remarked when Roy finally made it through the maze of busy streets and down the main stretch of highway. From there, they exited onto the meandering country back roads that eventually led to the house Anna shared with her stepmother, Naomi, and Naomi's four sons, Raymond, Roy, Eli and Evan.

"Fletcher!" seven-year-old Evan whooped, sprinting across the yard when he spotted them coming down the lane. He tore alongside the buggy shouting, "Anna's awake!"

"*Bobblemoul*," eight-year-old Eli taunted, referring to his brother as a blabbermouth. He leaped down the porch steps after him. "You weren't supposed to tell. She said she isn't ready to see him yet."

"She said what?" Fletcher asked, hopping from the buggy after Roy brought it to a halt.

"Now who's repeating something they shouldn't?" Evan retorted to Eli.

"Roy, please hitch the horse for me," Fletcher requested and strode toward the porch, his heart hammering his ribs.

Naomi greeted him at the door with a wooden spoon in one hand and a bowl in the other. "*Kumme* in," she invited.

"Hello, Naomi. How are you?" he inquired politely before asking the question that was burning on his tongue.

"I'm *gut*," she said. "I see you're teaching Roy how to handle the horse in *Englisch* traffic? *Denki*—I worry about him around all those cars. He needs the practice."

"He's improving already," Fletcher remarked and then cut to the chase. "Is it true? Is Anna awake?"

"She is," Naomi replied. "But there's something you need to know."

"I've heard," Fletcher acknowledged. "Eli said she isn't ready to see me yet. I realize she probably needs a few minutes to get dressed and find her bearings. I can wait."

"Oh, dear," sighed Naomi. She sat down at the kitchen table and tapped a chair to indicate Fletcher should sit, as well. "I'm afraid that's not what she means by not being ready to see you. Do you recall the doctor said her memory might be impaired after the fall?"

Fletcher moved toward the table but he didn't sit, despite the heaviness in the core of his gut. He braced himself for another distressing disclosure. "*Jah*, I remember."

"Then you recall he instructed us it most likely would only be temporary, so there's no cause for alarm,"

Naomi continued cautiously. "However, before you see her, you should be aware she's having difficulty remembering anything at all that happened after late August or early September."

Fletcher gulped when he realized what Naomi was getting at. "I moved to Willow Creek in early September."

"Jah," confirmed Naomi, answering Fletcher's unasked question. "But the doctor said putting a face with a name may help her recollection. It's possible as soon as she sees you she will remember who you are. However, she might not. At least, not right away."

"Please, will you tell her I'd just like to see her?" he pleaded. "I haven't spoken to her since before her fall."

Naomi nodded. "I'll let her know and I'll ask Melinda to assist her down the stairs. Go through to the parlor. We'll give you two your privacy there. But, Fletcher, keep in mind she's been through a lot. She's very sensitive right now."

"I won't say anything to upset her," he promised.

As troubled as he was by Anna's last communication to him, Fletcher's primary concern at the moment was her well-being. Naomi had a tendency for excessive fretfulness; perhaps she was exaggerating the extent of Anna's memory loss? Pacing back and forth across the braided rug in front of the sofa, Fletcher wiped his palms on his trousers and bit his lower lip. The past few days without seeing Anna awake had seemed unbearably long, but this delay felt even more difficult to endure.

Someone cleared her throat behind him. He turned as Anna made her way down the hall. Her honey-blond tresses, customarily combed into a neat bun, were loosely arranged at the nape of her neck, her fair skin was a shade paler than it normally was and she clutched a drab shawl to her shoulders, but she took his breath away all the same. Rendered both speechless and immobile with conflicting emotions, he choked back a gasp.

Her eyes were downcast, carefully watching her footing as she tentatively stepped into the room. He studied her heart-shaped lips and oval face, her slender nose and the tiny beauty mark on her left cheekbone. But it was the vast depth of her eyes, accentuated with a curl of lashes and gently arched brows, he yearned to behold. Fletcher and Anna had often conveyed a world of feeling with a single glance, and, in spite of everything, he hoped one glimpse into her eyes would convince him of her abiding love.

"Anna," he stated, moving to offer her his arm to help steady her gait.

She looked up and locked her eyes with his. Even in the dim glow cast by the oil lamp, he could appreciate their magnificent emerald green hue. She seemed to be searching his features, reading his expression, taking in his presence. He waited for what felt like an eternity, but his gaze was met by an impassive blankness.

"I've been told you're my fiancé, Fletcher," she finally said, although it sounded more like a question than a statement. His last wisp of hopefulness dissipated when she shook his outstretched hand, as if they were strangers meeting for the first time.

As Fletcher's expectant countenance crumbled into one of stark disappointment, Anna immediately regretted her gesture. What was she thinking, to shake his hand like the *Englisch* would? She wasn't working in the shop, introducing herself to a customer. She didn't understand why everything seemed so jumbled in her mind.

"I'm sorry, but I need to sit," she said and settled into a straight-backed chair, which made Fletcher frown all the more.

He perched on the edge of the sofa nearest her, leaning forward on his knees. His large, sky blue eyes, coupled with an unruly shock of dark hair, gave him a boyish appearance, but his straight nose and prominent brow and jawline were the marks of a more mature masculinity. She wondered how she could have forgotten knowing such a physically distinctive young man.

"I've been very concerned about you," he stated. "How are you feeling?"

"*Denki*, I'm doing better," she said, although she had a dull headache. "Oh! But where are my manners? I should offer you something to drink. Would you like a cup of—"

She rose too quickly from her chair and the room wobbled. Fletcher again offered her his help, which she accepted this time, grasping his muscular forearm until the dizziness passed. Then he assisted her back into her seat.

"I didn't *kumme* here to drink *kaffi*, Anna," he said, crouching before her, still holding her hand. "I came here to see *you*."

Flustered by his scrutiny and the tenderness of his touch, she pulled her arm away and apologized. "I'm sorry I look so unkempt, but combing my hair makes my head ache."

He shook his head, insisting, "I wouldn't care if your hair were standing on end like a porcupine's quills, as long as I know you're alright."

Although she sensed his sentiment was earnest, her eyes smarted. Couldn't he see that she wasn't alright? And didn't he understand his nearness felt intrusive, given that she had absolutely no memory of him? He seemed so intense that she didn't want to offend him, but she wished he'd back away.

As if reading her thoughts, Fletcher retreated to his cushion on the sofa and said, "It's okay if you don't remember me yet, Anna. The doctor said this could happen. They told us your memories might return in bits and pieces."

Anna nodded and relaxed her shoulders. She hadn't realized how uptight she'd felt. She noticed his voice had a soothing quality. It was deep and warm, like her dad's was.

"Melinda told me a bit about you, but I have so many questions, I don't know where to start," she confessed.

"Why don't I give you the basics and if there's anything else you want to know, you can ask?" Fletcher questioned. When Anna nodded in agreement, he said, "Let's see—my name is Fletcher Josiah Chupp and I'm twenty-four. My *daed* was a carpenter. He and my *mamm* passed away by the time I was fifteen. I have three older sisters, all married, and sixteen nieces and nephews. I moved to Willow Creek, Pennsylvania, from Green Lake, Ohio, in September. My *onkel* Isaiah had been in dire need of another carpenter on his crew for some time."

"Because my *daed* died?"

Fletcher glanced down at his fingers, which he pressed into a steeple. "*Jah.* Your *daed* worked for Isaiah and he had a reputation among the *Englisch* of being an excellent carpenter. He left a big gap in my *onkel*'s business. No one could ever fill his shoes."

"No one could ever replace him as a *daed*, either," Anna murmured. After a pause, she asked, "So then, you live with your *ant* and *onkel*, and with Aaron and his sisters?"

"*Neh.* There wasn't room enough for me there. I live in my *groosdaaddi*'s home."

"Elmer! Your *groossdaadi* is Elmer Chupp! I remember him," Anna exclaimed. Then she realized aloud, "But of course I would, wouldn't I? I've known him for years. He was my *daed*'s first employer, before Isaiah took over their family business. You must greet him for me."

Fletcher rubbed his forehead. "I don't want to distress you, Anna, but my *groossdaadi* died in late December from pneumonia."

"*Neh!* Oh, *neh!*" Anna's bottom lip began to quiver.

"His passing was peaceful and it's a blessing to know he's not suffering the pain he endured toward the end," Fletcher said. "He always appreciated the soups and meals you made for him. And you were very consoling to me while I mourned."

"Dear Elmer Chupp." Anna clucked sorrowfully. "Didn't you say you lived with him?"

"*Jah*, I moved in with him when I first arrived in Pennsylvania," Fletcher clarified. "Now I live there alone. After you and I became betrothed, I discovered *Groossdaadi* willed his house to me, as his first grandson to tell the family of my intention to marry. For some reason, *Groossdaadi* chose not to follow the traditional Amish practice of bequeathing it to his youngest son, my *onkel* Isaiah. In any case, there were property taxes due, which you and I paid from my construction salary and your savings from working at Schrock's Shop, so the house is as *gut* as ours."

Anna's mind was reeling. She and Fletcher owned a house? On one hand, getting married and setting up her own household was a desire she'd harbored for years. On the other hand, with every new piece of information revealed to her, she was becoming increasingly uneasy at how seriously her life was intertwined with the life of a man who seemed like a virtual stranger, albeit, an appealingly thoughtful and stalwart one.

Pinching the bridge of her nose, she admitted, "I'm confused about the timing. In Willow Creek, it's customary for most Amish couples to keep their courtships as private as they can. They wait until July or August to tell their immediate families that they intend to marry. Their wedding intentions aren't published in church until October, and wedding season follows in November and December, after harvest. Yet Melinda says it's now March. Why did we already tell our families we intend to marry next fall?"

"We actually intend to marry next month," Fletcher responded. "You don't recall, but last October, Willow

Creek was struck by a tornado. So many houses were damaged that Bishop Amos allowed those betrothed couples who needed to help their families rebuild to postpone their weddings until April. Of course, you and I were just getting to know each other last October, so we weren't yet engaged, but by January, we were certain we wanted to get married. We decided to take advantage of the bishop's special provision allowing for spring weddings this year."

"We only met in September and we're getting married in April?" Anna asked, unable to keep her voice from sounding incredulous. Six months was a brief courting period for any couple, and it seemed especially out of character for her. She had walked out with Aaron for over two years. As fondly as she dreamed of becoming a wife and a mother, lingering qualms had kept her from saying yes to Aaron's proposals, no matter how many times he asked. How was it she'd decided so quickly to marry Fletcher?

"Jah," he stated definitively. "As we confirmed to the deacon, we fully and unequivocally believe the Lord has provided us for each other."

Anna understood the implications. Prior to making their engagements public, Amish couples underwent a series of meetings with the deacon during which time the couple received counseling on the seriousness of entering into a marriage relationship. Although Anna had no recollection of those meetings, she knew if she and Fletcher completed the series and announced their intentions, it meant they were resolute about getting married.

"Have the wedding intentions been published in church?"

"They were announced on Sunday," Fletcher replied. "We'll be wed on Tuesday, April 7, five days before Easter and a week before Melinda and Aaron get married."

Anna inhaled sharply. "Melinda and Aaron are getting married?"

"Uh-oh," Fletcher said, smacking his forehead with his palm. "I assumed Melinda already told you."

"She probably didn't want to upset me."

Fletcher cocked his head. "Why would Melinda marrying Aaron upset you?"

"I d-don't know," Anna stammered. "I have no idea why I said that."

She was far more concerned about her own wedding than Melinda's. *I might as well be marrying the prince of England as this man, for as foreign as he is to me*, Anna thought, deeply disturbed. *Perhaps I should consider canceling our upcoming nuptials?*

"You were so excited after the intentions were published that you mailed the invitational letters to all of our out-of-town friends and family members first thing on Monday morning," Fletcher said. "Of course, the *leit* at church were invited and I extended several personal invitations on Monday evening, as well."

Upon hearing just how far their plans had progressed, Anna felt as overwhelmed by the prospect of calling off the wedding as she was by the prospect of carrying through with it. She silently prayed, *Please, Lord, if I really do know and love Fletcher Chupp and*

believe he's Your intended for me, help me to remember
soon. If he isn't, please make me certain of that, too.

Fletcher noticed Anna's face blanched at his words
and he worried she might cry—or faint. "This must be
a lot to take in," he said, trying to reassure himself as
well as to console her. "The doctor said your physical
well-being is the priority, and if you get enough rest
your memories should take care of themselves."

Fletcher could always tell when Anna's smile was genuine because she had a small dimple in her right cheek.
He saw no sign of it as she responded, "I can't imagine
there will be much time for me to rest, with two weddings planned. I wonder how Naomi has been faring."

From his discussions with her, Fletcher knew how
concerned Anna had been about her stepmother ever
since Anna's father died. Naomi, who periodically
suffered from immobilizing depression, was so grief
stricken in the months following Conrad's death that
Anna had almost single-handedly managed their household, with sporadic help from Melinda. In addition to
caring for Eli and Evan, comforting Naomi and tending to the cooking, cleaning, laundering and gardening, Anna also worked at a shop in town so she could
contribute to the household expenses. Her cheerful diligence was one of the qualities Fletcher most admired
about her.

"I know you can't remember this," Fletcher said, "but
Naomi began to regain some of her…her energy in Jan-
uary when you confided our decision to marry to her.
You told me she embraced the distraction of planning

for a wedding. She said it gave her something hopeful instead of dreadful to think about, and rather than wringing her hands, she could put them to *gut* use preparing for our guests."

"That sounds like the old Naomi, alright," Anna remarked and for the first time, her dimple puckered her cheek. But her smile faded almost as quickly as it appeared. "So then, if she is doing better, did I return to working at the shop full-time?"

During Naomi's period of bereavement, Anna reduced her working schedule from full time to part-time, much to the dismay of the shopkeeper, who valued Anna's skills. But as efficient as she was at assisting customers, Anna told Fletcher she drew more satisfaction from meeting her family's needs at home. She worked in the store only as much as was necessary to contribute to their living expenses.

"*Neh*, you're still only working there part-time."

A frown etched its way across Anna's forehead. "If I helped pay the property taxes for the house with my savings, and I've still only been working part-time, how has my family been managing financially? Furthermore, what will Naomi do when I move? Raymond's salary as an apprentice won't be enough to cover their expenses."

"*Jah*, you're right. That's why I asked my *onkel* to promote Raymond to a full-fledged crew member and to allow me to apprentice Roy. Raymond had already been satisfactorily apprenticed by your *daed* and there have been plenty of projects in the aftermath of the tornado, so Isaiah readily agreed. The arrangement has worked well for them and you've been happy that instead of needing to work full-time, you've been able to continue helping Naomi, er, recover, especially as you prepare the house for the weddings."

Averting her eyes toward the window, Anna responded in a faraway voice, "It sounds as if we've thoroughly addressed all of the essential details, then."

That's what I thought, too—until I received your message. Fletcher agonized, chewing the inside of his cheek to keep his emotions in check. He knew this wasn't the time to broach the subject, no matter how desperately he wanted Anna to allay his suspicions about her note.

"Supper's ready," Melinda announced from the doorway. "*Ant* Naomi says you're *wilkom* to join us, Fletcher."

"*Denki*, it smells *wunderbaar*, but I need to be on my way," he replied. As little as he'd eaten lately, Fletcher felt as if there were a cement block in his stomach and he doubted he could swallow even a morsel of bread.

As it was, Anna said she felt queasy and she wanted to go lie down.

"May I visit you tomorrow?" Fletcher asked before they parted.

"*Jah,*" she replied simply. Her voice sounded strained when she added, "*Denki* for coming by tonight," thus ending their visit on as formal of a note as it began.

Shaken by how drastically his relationship with Anna had changed within the span of a few days, Fletcher numbly ushered the horse along the winding roads leading to his home. Once there, he collected the mail from the box and entered the chilly house. He turned on the gas lamp hanging above the kitchen table to read his sister's familiar penmanship.

Dear Fletcher,
We were so joyful to receive word of the official date for your upcoming wedding that we got together to write you the very moment the letter arrived from Anna!

As your older sisters, permit us to say we knew how disappointed you were when Joyce Beiler abruptly called off your engagement, even though you tried to disguise the tremendous toll the breakup took on you. Ever since then, we have been faithfully praying that the Lord would heal your hurt and help your heart to love and trust another young woman again. We are grateful He answered our prayers for you so quickly in Willow Creek. It still puzzles us that Joyce chose to marry Frederick Wittmer, but we are grateful you have found a woman who truly recognizes what an honorable, responsible, Godly man you are.

Although our interaction with Anna was brief and we weren't yet aware you were courting, we were fond of her the moment we met her in Willow Creek in December. Even during such a somber time as Grandfather's funeral, she demonstrated a warmth and graciousness that lightened our burden. It is no wonder you are as committed to her as she is to you. Surely, your marriage will be blessed.
With love from your sisters,
Esther, Leah and Rebekah (& families)

Sighing heavily, Fletcher folded the letter and slid it back into its envelope. He understood the sentiments were well-intentioned. But under the circumstances, they opened old wounds of the nearly unbearable heartache and humiliation he suffered when Joyce canceled their wedding.

A single tear rolled down his cheek when he lamented how wrong his sisters were. Anna didn't even recognize his face, much less his character. While he didn't doubt her memory would return eventually, he was far less certain about her commitment to him. His sisters were right: the breakup with Joyce had nearly cost him his physical health and emotional well-being. He didn't think he could endure it if another fiancée called off their wedding.

He knew the message Anna had sent him by heart, but he picked up her note from the table where he'd left it that morning and held it to the light. *I have a serious concern regarding A. that I must discuss privately with you before the wedding preparations go any further.*

There was only one person she could have been referring to when she wrote "A."—Aaron, her former suitor. Fletcher shook his head at the thought. Even though his cousin had become romantically involved with Melinda, Fletcher long sensed Aaron was still in love with Anna. But once when Fletcher expressed his concern to Anna, she dismissed it out of hand.

"That's ridiculous. He broke up with me to court Melinda. She's the one he loves now," she argued. "Besides, you should know from all of our conversations that *I* haven't any feelings for *him* anymore. And whatever feelings I once had pale in comparison with how I feel about you. I may have liked Aaron, but I love—I'm *in* love with you, Fletcher Josiah Chupp."

On the surface, her response reminded him of the many conversations he'd had with Joyce, whom he suspected had developed a romantic affection for her brother-in-law's visiting cousin, Frederick. Joyce vehemently and consistently denied it, until four days before she and Fletcher were scheduled to wed, when she finally admitted the truth. But there was something fundamentally different about Anna, and as she declared her love for Fletcher, she stared into his eyes with such devotion that all of his worries melted away.

Fletcher remembered how, a few weeks after he and Anna confided their marriage intentions to their families, Melinda and Aaron announced they'd begun meeting with the deacon and they also planned to wed in the spring. Because Melinda seemed especially immature, their decision surprised Fletcher, but he was relieved to confirm Anna was right: Aaron was wholly committed to Melinda. Or so he'd thought at the time. But Anna's recent note shook his confidence to the core.

What in the world could have transpired concerning Aaron to make Anna hesitant to carry on with preparations to marry me? Burying his head in his hands, Fletcher shuddered to imagine. He knew from experience that people changed their minds. Engagements could be broken, even days before a wedding. There was still time. Was he was about to be forsaken by his fiancée for another man again? The possibility of having to withstand that kind of rejection a second time made Fletcher's skin bead with sweat. The only way he'd know for certain was to talk to Anna about her note. But first, she'd have to remember what she meant when she'd penned it.

Chapter Two

As the sun began to light the room, Anna peered at her cousin asleep in the twin bed across from her. She rose to make the boys' breakfast, but when her feet touched the chilly floor, she pulled them back into bed, deciding to snuggle beneath the blankets just a little longer.

The tiny room on the third floor of the house was actually a part of the attic her father had sectioned off especially for her. More than once she'd knocked her head against the sloping ceiling and the room tended to be hotter in the summer and colder in the winter than the rest of the house, but she had always relished the privacy it afforded her from the four boys.

She'd had the room all to herself until Melinda's father sent Melinda to live with Anna's family a year ago in January because he wanted her to have better influences than he could provide. Naomi's sister had died twelve years earlier and her brother-in-law never remarried, so Melinda had grown up without any females in her home. It was said by many that she was capricious, or perhaps undisciplined. Some went so far as to call her lazy, a quality condemned by the Amish. Anna observed that the girl was generally willing to perform almost any chore, but she often became distracted in the middle of it and moved on to another endeavor.

"Half-done is far from done," was the Amish proverb Anna most often quoted to Melinda the first year of her residence with Anna's family. Serving as Melinda's role model had been a frustrating effort, yet Anna mused that if Melinda had committed herself to following God and had been baptized into the church, then her living with them had been worthwhile. It meant Melinda had put her wild *Rumspringa* years behind her; surely if she'd made that change, there was hope for other areas of her behavior, as well.

Melinda's eyes opened. *"Guder mariye."* She yawned. "I'm Melinda, your cousin."

Anna giggled. *"Jah,* I know. Are you going to introduce yourself to me every time I wake?"

Melinda laughed, too. "You were staring at me. I thought you didn't know who I was."

"I was marveling that such a young woman has decided upon marriage already."

Melinda sat straight up. "You remembered Aaron and I are getting married!"

"Neh, Fletcher mentioned it. He thought I already knew."

"Oh. Well, I'm not that young—I'm eighteen now. You're only four years older than I am," Melinda reasoned. "Besides, I've known Aaron over twice as long as you've known Fletcher. I think that makes us far better prepared to spend our lives together."

"Hmm," Anna hummed noncommittally. Melinda may have been eighteen, but at times she acted fourteen. Yet Anna couldn't deny she made a valid point about the brevity of Anna's relationship with Fletcher. Then she raised her hands to her cheeks as her cousin's words sank in—she herself was older than she remembered.

"That's right, I must be twenty-two now since my birthday was in September! Time flies when you have amnesia."

Melinda giggled and the two of them made their beds, got dressed and followed the smell of frying bacon down the stairs. When everyone was seated around the table, Raymond said grace, thanking the Lord especially for Anna's recovery. She was so hungry that she devoured as large a serving of food as her brothers did.

"If it's Saturday, that must mean you're working a half day today, right?" she asked Raymond and Roy, who both nodded since their mouths were full. "I can drop you off on my way to the shop. Joseph Schrock will be relieved to have me back."

"Neh," Naomi answered. "The doctor said you couldn't return to work until after your follow-up appointment. In fact, he said you should limit activities of exertion and anything that requires close concentration, such as sewing or reading, until he sees you again."

"Nonsense," Anna argued. "I'm as healthy as a horse—physically, anyway. There's no reason I can't ring up purchases and help *Englisch* customers decide which quilt to purchase or whether their grandchildren might prefer rocking horses or wooden trains. Besides, we need the income and Joseph needs the help."

Naomi began twisting her hands. "You have a doctor's appointment on Wednesday. Please, won't you wait until you receive his approval before returning to the shop?"

Not wishing to cause Naomi any undue anxiety, Anna conceded. "Alright, I'll wait. But you must at least allow me to help with the housework. How about if I prepare an easy dinner?"

"That sounds *gut*," Melinda interjected. "If I drop the boys off at the work site before I go to the market, I'm certain Fletcher or Aaron will give them a ride home. Perhaps we can invite them for dinner, since Fletcher wanted to check in on Anna again today anyway?"

Anna caught Naomi's eye and gave a slight shrug. Melinda's habit of finagling a way out of chores in order to spend time with Aaron predated Anna's accident and she remembered her cousin's tactics well.

"*Jah*," Naomi permitted. "They're both *wilkom* to eat dinner with us. But I'll drop the boys off and go to the market myself. You may begin the housework and assist Anna in the kitchen if she requires it. Evan and Eli have yard and stable chores to complete."

Although Anna made a simple green bean and ham casserole for lunch, with apple dumplings for dessert, it took her twice as long as usual and she was grateful when Naomi suggested that she rest before everyone arrived. She felt as if her head had barely touched the pillow when Melinda wiggled her arm to wake her again. She disappeared before Anna could ask for help fixing her hair, because it still pained her head when she attempted to fasten her tresses into a bun. She winced as she pulled her hair back the best she could and pinned on her *kapp*.

"*Guder nammidaag*, Anna," Fletcher said when he crossed the threshold to the parlor. Warmth flickered along her spine as she took in his athletic, lanky build and shiny dark mane, but she wasn't flooded with the rush of additional memories she'd been praying to experience at the sight of him. "How are you feeling today?" he asked.

"I'm fine, *denki*," she answered. Standing rigidly before him, trying to think of something to say that didn't sound so punctilious, she impulsively jested, "You're Aaron, right?"

Fletcher looked as if a horse had stepped on his foot. *"Neh!"* he exclaimed. "I'm Fletcher. Fletcher Chupp, your fiancé. Aaron is my cousin."

"I'm teasing!" she assured him, instantly regretting her joke. "I know who you are."

"You do?" he asked, raising his brows. "Your memory has returned?"

"Oh dear, *neh*," she replied. "I mean, I remember you from last night. I know that you're my fiancé. But *neh*, I don't remember anything other than that."

For a second time, he grimaced as if in pain, and Anna ruefully fidgeted with her *kapp* strings, wary of saying anything more for fear of disheartening him further.

"Naomi and Melinda are putting dinner on the table," someone said from the doorway.

When Fletcher moved aside, Anna spotted the familiar brunette hair, ruddy complexion and puckish grin. Although the young man bore a slight family resemblance to Fletcher, he was shorter, with a burly physique.

"Aaron!" she squealed, delighted to have recognized another person from the past, even if it was someone who'd brought her considerable heartache.

"I'm happy to see you, too, Anna," he replied before leading them into the kitchen.

Because there were two extra people, everyone had to squeeze together to fit around the table and Anna kept her elbows tightly to her side to avoid knocking into Fletcher, whose stature was greater than the other young men's.

"You made my favorite dish," Aaron declared appreciatively after grace had been said and everyone was served.

"Did I?" She didn't remember Aaron liking this casserole in particular.

"Don't pay any attention to him," Melinda piped up. "He says every dish is his favorite so the hostess will serve him the biggest helping."

Anna thought that sounded more like the jokester Aaron she remembered.

"Don't scare me like that," she scolded. "I panicked my memory loss was getting worse."

"Sorry, I didn't mean to," Aaron apologized. "But honestly, this casserole is Fletcher's favorite dish. Right, cousin?"

Without warning, Fletcher spat the mouthful of noodles he'd been chewing onto his plate and guzzled down his water. Scarlet splotches dotted his face and neck.

"Does this have mushrooms in it?" he sputtered.

"Cream of mushroom soup, *jah*," Anna answered, appalled by his lack of manners. "I didn't realize you don't like them."

"I'm *allergic* to them!" Fletcher wheezed.

"Quick, bring me the antihistamine we use for Evan's bee sting allergy," Anna directed Melinda, who darted to the cupboard and produced the bottle.

Anna poured a spoonful of syrupy pink liquid, which she thrust toward Fletcher's lips. After he swallowed it, she gave him a second dose.

"Perhaps Raymond should run to the phone shanty and dial 9-1-1," Naomi suggested.

"*Neh*, the redness is starting to fade," Anna observed.

Indeed, Fletcher's breathing was beginning to normalize and within a few more minutes, his heart rate slowed to a more regular pace. Anna, Melinda and Naomi encircled his chair while the boys remained motionless in their seats, too stunned to move. Aaron nervously jabbed at his noodles with a fork, but didn't lift them to his mouth.

Fletcher coughed. "I feel quite a bit better now. Please, sit back down and eat your meal, if you still can after my unappetizing display. I'm sorry about that."

"I'm the one who is sorry, Fletcher." Anna's voice warbled and her eyes teared up. "I didn't know you were allergic. I could have killed you!"

"That's one way to get out of marrying him," Aaron gibed, reaching for the pepper.

"Aaron Chupp, what a horrible thing to say! Anna didn't do it on purpose," Melinda admonished, swatting at him with a pot holder in mock consternation as Anna fled the room.

"It was only a joke," he objected contritely. "No need to be so sensitive."

Fletcher pushed back his chair. "If you'll excuse me, a little fresh air always helps me feel as if I can breathe better after one of these episodes."

He stalked across the backyard, stopping beneath the maple tree. Inhaling deeply, he took a mental inventory of his grievances. First, Anna pretended she thought he was Aaron and then when Aaron actually entered the room, she seemed more delighted to see him than she'd been to see Fletcher. Second, he felt slighted by how carefully Anna avoided his touch. Of course, spitting his food out at the table—even if it was necessary—wasn't likely going to cause her to draw nearer to him anytime soon. But most irksome of all was Aaron's jape, *That's one way to get out of marrying him*. Was that just another one of his cousin's goofy attempts at humor, or did the joke have a more weighty meaning?

Fletcher picked up a stone and threw it as hard as he could in the direction of a wheelbarrow across the yard. With all of his might, he pitched another and another.

"*Gut* aim," Naomi said after each rock had clattered against the metal and he was empty-handed again.

"I didn't know you were behind me," he answered, embarrassed she'd seen his temperamental behavior.

"I wanted to be certain you were okay. Whenever Evan gets stung, the effects of the adrenaline linger for him, too. He says he has the most irritable thoughts, claiming it's as if the bees are buzzing around in his brain as well as under his skin."

"I don't know if I can blame my thoughts on adrenaline," Fletcher replied.

"Sometimes, we're not quite ourselves when we're ill or upset. Not Evan. Not you. Not me. Not Anna," Naomi said pointedly. "You have to give it time. Things will work out."

Naomi Weaver's gentle way of imparting wisdom reminded him of his own mother. *"Jah,"* he answered. "I understand."

"Gut. Now *kumme* inside for dessert."

Melinda was placing fresh bowls on the table, where the boys sat in silence. Anna had returned to the kitchen and was preparing dessert at the counter with her back to the others.

"Since I didn't eat any dinner, I should be allowed two helpings of dessert, don't you think?" Fletcher questioned Evan, tousling the boy's hair to break the tension in the room.

"How do you know if you'll like it, when you don't know what it is?" Evan asked.

"Well," Fletcher said, winking at him as Anna turned with a tray, "I've got high hopes it's molasses and mushroom pie."

Anna paused before pushing her features into an expression of exaggerated dismay. "Oh, dear! I've made the wrong thing—I thought mushroom *dumplings* were your favorite."

Fletcher clutched his sides, laughing. Now *this* was more like the kind of interactions he and Anna usually shared. Hilarity filled the room and when it quieted, Anna announced, "I am truly sorry for my mistake, Fletcher. I meant you no harm."

"There's no need to apologize—I'm the one who should have reminded you."

"Do you have any other allergies I should know about?"

"Just mushrooms," he stated.

"Gut." Then she addressed everyone. "What else has happened around here since early September? *Gut* or bad, I want to know. I *need* to know. It may help my memory *kumme* back. Also, I'd prefer that no one outside of this room, with the exception of the Chupp family, finds out I have my amnesia. In order to ensure that, I'll need to be made aware of what's been going on in Willow Creek."

"Grace Zook had a *bobbel*—a girl named Serenity—in January," Naomi told her.

"How *wunderbaar*!" Anna's fondness of babies was reflected in her tone.

Melinda added, "Doris Hooley married John Plank last fall, shortly after the tornado."

"Was anyone from Willow Creek hurt in the storm?" Anna asked.

"Neh, not seriously, although many houses and offices needed repair," Naomi said.

"Jah, the tornado was *gut* for business. For a while,

we couldn't keep up with the demand. So I took over as foreman for my *daed*'s Willow Creek clients in May," Aaron stated. "He's handling the Highland Springs clients. They were hard hit, too."

Anna raised her brows and Fletcher wondered whether her expression indicated she was dubious or impressed to hear about Aaron's promotion to foreman. She extended her congratulations.

"We lost a beloved family member," Evan reported, his lower lip protruding. "Timothy."

Anna gasped. "Who is Timothy?"

"He was my turtle. I found him at the creek in October. His foot was injured from a fishing hook and I was caring for him until he was well again."

"That's very sad he died," Anna said, her mouth pulling at the corners.

"He didn't die," Evan clarified. "We lost him. *You* lost him. You were supposed to be watching him in the yard after church when it was our Sunday to host, but he crawled off. How could that happen? Turtles are naturally slow on land—and he was injured."

It happened because she wasn't watching the turtle, Fletcher reminisced as wistfulness twisted in his chest. *She was with me behind the maple tree and we were sharing our first kiss.*

"I'm sorry but I don't remember anything about that," Anna said and it took Fletcher a moment to realize she was speaking to Evan, not him. "How about if you, Fletcher, Eli and I take a walk to the creek to see if he has returned for the spring? Just let me do the dishes first."

"I'll do the dishes," Naomi insisted. "You ought not to touch any mushroom leftovers, lest your hands *kumme* into contact with Fletcher and he suffers another allergic reaction."

But there was little danger of that. Despite the temporary connection he'd just shared with Anna, Fletcher noticed she stayed closer to Eli and Evan than she did to him as they strolled down the hill, through the field and along the creek. Fletcher knew Anna's amnesia prevented her from recalling they rarely walked anywhere together without interlocking their fingers, but he felt too tentative about their relationship now to take her hand.

This early in March, they failed to spot any turtles, with or without injured feet. Once they returned home, Anna thanked Fletcher for his visit. Before leaving, he arranged to call on her the next day after dinner.

"Perhaps by then I'll be able to remember what your favorite dessert really is," she jested. "Although I suppose once my memory returns, we'll have more serious concerns to discuss."

"No doubt," Fletcher agreed as anxiety surged within him at the mention of "serious concerns," the same phrase she'd used in her note. Speaking to himself as much as to her, he added, "I guess we'll just have to wait and see what tomorrow brings."

"You look a little peaked," Naomi said when Anna entered the parlor where she was sewing. She folded the material into a square and stowed it in her basket.

"The glare of the sun bothered my eyes," Anna admitted. "And I feel a bit nauseated."

"Uh-oh, the doctor told us to let him know if you became sick to your stomach."

"I wasn't sick, just nauseated. But I don't think it's from my head injury," Anna rationalized. "It's probably because I ate too much too soon after going without."

"Kumme." Naomi extended her hand. "Take a little nap in my room. That way, you needn't climb the stairs."

"But I've been so lazy. I've hardly helped with a thing today."

"And well you shouldn't—I keep telling you that. Now go lie down on my bed and I'll fix us a cup of ginger tea. That should settle your stomach."

Anna removed her shoes and reclined on the side of the bed her *daed* had always slept on. His dog-eared Bible still lay on the nightstand. She picked it up and tried to read the print in German, but she felt too woozy to focus. Squeezing her eyes, she imagined her father poring over Scripture whenever he had a free moment toward the end of the day. She lifted the Bible to her nose, hoping to smell the honey and oatmeal scent of the salve he used on his cracked, calloused hands in winter, but she couldn't.

"I used to keep your *daed*'s sweatiest shirt hidden in my drawer so I could smell it whenever I missed him," Naomi said when she came in and saw Anna sniffing the Bible.

"Used to?"

"After a while, it stopped smelling like him and just smelled musty," Naomi reflected. "And I was ready to let the shirt go, because my memories of him are more tangible and comforting to me now. As the saying goes, 'A happy memory never wears out.'"

Bursting into tears, Anna placed her cup on the nightstand so she wouldn't spill her tea.

"Oh, Anna." Naomi sighed. "I'm so thoughtless. I shouldn't have mentioned my memories when you're struggling so hard to recall your own."

"*Neh*, it's fine, truly. I'm relieved to know you've been doing a bit better, Naomi. I wanted to ask, I just didn't know how to talk about…about your grief."

"Your faithful prayers and your quiet strength, along with all of your hard work, have kept our household going, Anna. I'm grateful for all you've done, even if it seemed I was too sorrowful to notice." Naomi squeezed her hand. "You remind me so much of your *daed*. I'll miss having you here every day, but I'm grateful *Gott* provided you such a *gut* man as Fletcher."

"Is he such a *gut* man?" Anna wondered aloud. "How do you know?"

Naomi blew on her tea before responding. "I suppose I don't know for certain. You and Fletcher were very secretive about your courtship—even more than most Amish couples customarily are. But I have observed how sincerely considerate he is of me and how helpful he has been to Raymond and Roy at work. Beyond that, I trust your judgment. I know there must have been very sound reasons you decided to marry him."

"I want to believe that," Anna said. "But I honestly don't remember what they are."

"Give it time, it will *kumme*."

"But there's hardly any time left! Aaron courted me for two and a half years and I still wasn't sure whether to marry him. How was it I was certain I should marry Fletcher after knowing him for less than half a year? What if the reasons don't return to me within this next month?"

"We'll build that bridge when we *kumme* to the creek," Naomi responded with Anna's father's carpenter variation on the old saying, "We'll cross that bridge when we come to it."

The two of them shared a chuckle before Naomi continued, "Even if it takes a while longer for your memory to fully return, I'd suggest you wait to make any changes to your wedding plans until the last possible moment. After all, if you postpone the wedding now and your memory suddenly *kummes* back, you'll have to wait until autumn's wedding season to get married. That delay can seem like forever to a young couple in love! Plus, you've already invited all of your guests. And, if you and Fletcher don't marry in the spring, it's my understanding the house could possibly go to Aaron and Melinda, which hardly seems fair since the two of you have already paid the back taxes. But you needn't think about any of that today. Right now, rest is the best thing for you."

Feeling reassured, Anna dropped into a deep slumber until she woke to someone rapping at her door. It was Melinda, declaring, "*Guder mariye.* Time to get up, *schlofkopp.*"

Noting her surroundings, Anna suddenly understood

why her cousin referred to her as a sleepyhead. "I slept here all night? Where did Naomi sleep?"

"Upstairs, in your bed," grumbled Melinda. "When I came in after curfew, she lectured me about how I must guard my reputation, even though I'm soon to be wed. By the time she finished her spiel, I hardly got a wink of sleep, but she let you sleep in, since it's an off-Sunday."

Although she felt completely refreshed, Anna was just as happy that church wouldn't meet again until the following Sunday—she didn't feel prepared to field questions about her injury from the well-meaning *leit* of her district. After breakfast, the family read Scripture and prayed together. They followed their worship with a time of writing letters, individual Bible reading and doing jigsaw puzzles, but since Anna was prohibited from activities that required using close vision, Evan and Eli took turns reading aloud to her. Then, after a light dinner, the boys were permitted to engage in quiet outdoor leisure and games.

"What will you and Fletcher do when he visits today?" Melinda asked her.

Anna shrugged. "I have no idea what kinds of things we enjoy doing together. I suppose we'll take a walk and talk." She secretly just hoped to get to know him better.

"That sounds rather boring. Why don't you *kumme* out with Aaron and me?" Melinda suggested. "We're going for a ride to the location where Aaron plans to build our house later in the spring. It will be a tight squeeze in his buggy, but we can fit."

"Are you sure you won't mind if we accompany you?"

"Of course not. After all, think of how many times you and Aaron let me tag along on your outings," Melinda said.

Anna remembered. She'd intended to demonstrate how a young Amish woman ought to behave in social settings and she naively believed Aaron was being forbearing in allowing Melinda to join them: she didn't realize he was interested in Melinda romantically.

"Besides," Melinda chattered blithely, "Naomi won't fret about my reputation if I'm out with you."

Anna sighed. So that was the reason she was being invited. Still, it seemed she and Fletcher had an easier time conversing when there were more people around. "I'd like that," she said. "As long as Fletcher doesn't mind."

Because they'd been so discreet about their relationship, Anna and Fletcher usually favored spending any free time they had with each other instead of attending social events within their district, such as Sunday evening singings. They'd certainly never accompanied another couple on an outing before, so Fletcher was startled when Anna asked if he'd like to join Aaron and Melinda on a ride to see the property Aaron intended to buy. But, realizing Anna wouldn't have remembered their dislike of double dating, Fletcher deferred to her request. Besides, he was heartened by the fact Aaron was considering buying property—perhaps it meant he was as dedicated as ever to marrying Melinda, and Fletcher's concerns about him and Anna were for naught.

The afternoon was unseasonably sunny and warm, and the tips of the trees were beginning to show dots of green and red buds. As the two couples sped up and down the hills in Aaron's buggy, Anna kept marveling at the changes in the landscape. She noticed nearly every tree that was missing and each fence post that had been replaced after the October tornado. She seemed especially aghast to discover the schoolhouse was one of the buildings that had suffered the worst damage, but she was relieved to learn none of the children had been harmed.

"Now that you've had more rest and you've seen the destruction, surely you must remember the storm," Aaron suggested. "It was so violent that I couldn't forget it if I tried."

Anna shrugged. "I still have absolutely no recollection of anything that happened in the past six months, whether big or small, positive or negative."

"I guess that's *gut* news for you, huh, Fletcher? Anna can't remember any of your faults," Aaron needled his cousin. "On the other hand, she probably can't remember why she agreed to marry you, either."

Fletcher's mouth burned with a sour taste but before he could respond, Anna abruptly shifted the subject, asking Melinda, "Where will the two of you live until Aaron has time to build a house?"

"With Naomi and the boys," she replied, clutching Aaron's arm as he rounded a corner. "It will be crowded but I'm trying to convince Naomi to temporarily move into the room in the attic so we can have her room downstairs."

From the corner of his eye, Fletcher caught Anna frowning. He usually felt as if he could read her expression as easily as the pages in a book, but today he couldn't tell if she was scowling because of Aaron's rambunctious driving, Melinda's gall in asking Naomi to take the attic room, or some other reason altogether. The uncertainty caused his mouth to sag, too.

"Here we are," Aaron announced as he swiftly brought the horse to a standstill. He made a sweeping motion with his hand to indicate the field to their right.

"The old Lantz homestead?" Fletcher asked.

The modest square of land on the corner of the Zooks' farm used to belong to Albert Lantz, who resided with his granddaughter, Hannah. After their home was flattened by the tornado, they chose not to rebuild because Hannah married a visiting cabinetmaker from Blue Hill, Ohio, and thus moved out of state. Her grandfather accompanied her, but first he sold his property back to the youngest generation of the Zook family, who now lived on the farm.

"Their old homestead and then some," Aaron boasted. "The Lantz plot was barely as big as a postage stamp. I'm in negotiations with Oliver Zook to purchase the acreage running all the way down the hill to the stream."

"Isn't it *wunderbaar*?" sang Melinda, spreading her arms and twirling across the grass.

"*Jah*, it's lovely," Anna answered, but Fletcher noticed how taut her neck and jaw muscles appeared. Was she jealous? Was she imagining herself, instead of Melinda, owning a house with Aaron in such a picturesque location? Fletcher stubbed his shoe on a root as the tumultuous thoughts rattled his concentration.

"*Kumme*, have a look at my stream," Aaron beckoned.

"I believe the stream belongs to *Gott*, although He's generous enough to allow it to run through your property—or actually, through Oliver Zook's property," Fletcher stated wryly.

"Lighten up. Worship services are over for the day," Aaron countered. "Or if you're going to preach at me, how about remembering the commandment, *Thou shalt not covet*?"

"Stop bickering," Melinda called. "This is a happy occasion, remember? Hooray!"

She picked up a handful of old, dried leaves and tossed them into the air and then tried to catch them as they fluttered around her. Then she and Aaron cavorted down the hill like schoolchildren, racing to tag each other's shadows until they disappeared into the woods, while Fletcher and Anna followed at a slower pace, neither one speaking.

When they reached the stream, Anna closed her eyes and inhaled deeply. "Mmm, it smells like spring," she said, and then raised her lids to view the bubbling current, the gently sloping embankment and the thick stand of trees. "What a beautiful place."

"I have to agree, it's a fine fishing spot," Fletcher responded. Thinking aloud, he added, "But Aaron's too impatient to fish and even if he weren't, Melinda's such a chatterbox, she'd frighten the fish away."

Anna narrowed her brows. "That may be true of

them now," she said, "but people change. They grow. With *Gott*'s help, we all do."

Fletcher hadn't intended to be insulting. He simply meant the location seemed better suited to his and Anna's preferences than to Aaron and Melinda's, since he enjoyed fishing and Anna appreciated solitude, so he was surprised by how quickly Anna seemed to defend them. And what did her comment about people changing and growing mean, anyway? Was she indicating that she had changed? Was she implying she thought Aaron had grown? Fletcher's brooding was interrupted when Melinda capered up the embankment.

"Help!" she squealed. "Aaron's trying to splash me and that water's freezing!"

Aaron reappeared and the four of them ascended the hill. At the top, they were greeted by Oliver Zook. "*Guder nammidaag.* Grace sent me to invite our prospective new neighbors and their future in-laws for cookies and cider."

"That sounds *wunderbaar*," Melinda said, accepting the invitation for all of them.

The fragrance of hot cider and freshly baked cookies wafted from the kitchen when Grace ushered everyone inside. As they situated themselves in the parlor, where Doris and John Plank were also visiting, the Zooks' baby began wailing in the next room.

"I'll get her while you prepare the refreshments," Oliver said, squeezing his wife's shoulder.

"Wait till you see how much she's grown since the last time you saw her, Anna," Grace remarked before leaving the room, understandably ignorant of Anna's amnesia.

When Oliver returned, jostling the fussy baby, Aaron suggested, "You should let Anna take her. She has such a soothing, maternal touch. She was always able to comfort my eldest sister's son when he was a newborn."

"*Jah*, I remember," Anna said, smiling as she lifted Serenity from Oliver's arms. "Your nephew had colic and your poor sister was exhausted because he gave her no rest."

Although he knew it wasn't Anna's fault, Fletcher felt a slight twinge of sadness that she could remember everything that happened during her courtship with Aaron, but not a thing that happened during her courtship with him. And who was Aaron to openly flatter Anna, as if he were still her suitor? Of course, Aaron's compliment was well deserved: within a few moments of cooing and swaying, the *bobbel* had fallen asleep in Anna's arms. She sat back down and accepted a cup of cider from Grace with her free hand.

"See that, Fletcher? The *bobbel* in one hand, a cup in the other." Oliver laughed. "Anna will have no problem keeping your household in order."

Anna demurely glanced at Fletcher from beneath her lashes and a tickle of exhilaration caused his nerves to tingle. He momentarily forgot all about her note as a glimpse of their future *bobblin* flashed across his mind's eye.

"You're a fortunate man, indeed," Doris Plank interjected. "But I have to say, you could have knocked me over with a feather when the intentions were announced.

For the longest time, I suspected Aaron was betrothed to Anna. Even after it was rumored he'd begun walking out with you, Melinda, I always assumed he'd eventually wind up with Anna again, don't ask me why. But then, I never expected I'd marry John, either, so I guess it's a *gut* thing I'm not a matchmaker!"

As Doris gleefully tittered at her own humor, Fletcher's ears burned and his jaw dropped. Doris had a reputation for making bold remarks, but he'd personally never been on the receiving end of one and he didn't know how to respond without sounding rude himself.

"*Jah*, life is full of *wunderbaar* surprises for everyone, isn't it?" Grace diplomatically cut in. She passed the tray to Anna. "Here, Anna, you haven't had a cookie."

"*Denki*, but *neh*," Anna declined. "I… I…"

"She has to watch her figure," Melinda finished for her. "But I don't, so I'll take some."

"Ah, you must have finished sewing your wedding dress then, Anna?" Grace's eyes lit up. "You don't want to have to make any last-minute alterations, is that it? If you're anything like I was, you're counting down the days!"

Blushing, Anna gave a pinched smile and a slight shrug but didn't answer.

"You're fortunate your intended is so calm, Fletcher," Oliver remarked, as he patted his wife's hand. "As soon as our intentions were published, the wedding preparations were all Grace talked about to anyone who would listen. And even to some people who wouldn't!"

As everyone else laughed, Fletcher did his best not to frown, acutely aware that Anna's last communication about their wedding preparations had been anything but enthusiastic.

Suddenly, Melinda sniffed exaggeratedly and declared, "Oopsie! I think Serenity needs a diaper change."

All three couples soon made their way out the door. As they departed the farm and headed back toward Anna's house, Fletcher thought, *The* schtinke *of a dirty diaper makes a fitting end to this afternoon.* Disappointed that he and Anna hadn't exchanged a private word between them, and feeling even less certain about their future today than he'd felt all week, Fletcher decided the next time he went out with Anna, they were going out alone.

Chapter Three

The Sabbath was supposed to be a day of rest, but Anna felt utterly exhausted by the time she said her prayers and slipped into bed. Yet as achy and tired as her body was, her brain was wide-awake, reliving the afternoon's unpleasant events.

First, the buggy lurched about so much, she'd become increasingly nauseated as they journeyed toward their destination. Second, she was nettled by Aaron's wisecrack about her continued inability to remember Fletcher—and judging from Fletcher's expression, he was equally peeved. Third, Melinda's prancing and twirling caused Anna's head to spin. Then, Fletcher and Aaron squabbled like two boys on a playground. Finally, when she tried to focus her attention on something positive by commenting on the beauty of the scenery, Fletcher pulled a face. His remarks about Aaron's and Melinda's personalities may have been true, but they weren't especially generous, which made her wonder if he was characteristically judgmental.

Not that Aaron or Melinda took much care to measure their own words about others: Melinda's pronounced insinuation that Anna needed to watch her weight would have been humiliating, had it been true. In reality, she'd been far too nauseated to eat any cookies, but she didn't want to draw attention to herself by saying so.

Of course, all eyes had been on her when Grace questioned Anna about whether she'd sewn her wedding dress or not. Making her dress was one of the wedding preparations an Amish bride reveled in most, but Anna couldn't even recall if she'd bought her fabric yet. Nor did she know if she'd selected her *newehockers*, also known as sidesitters or wedding attendants, and given them the fabric for their dresses, which would match hers. Had she made Fletcher's wedding suit for him, as was the tradition?

If she hadn't begun sewing yet, should she bother starting now, given that her memory might not return in time to carry through with the wedding? On the other hand, if she delayed making the garments until her memory returned, it was likely she'd have to rush to finish them, since there were only a few weeks until the wedding as it was.

Of course, her dilemma about their wedding clothes wasn't nearly as disconcerting as her growing concern about whether or not they should get married at all. Anna hesitated to bring up the subject with Fletcher, who demonstrated no signs of hesitation about carrying through with their plans. Considering all they'd apparently invested in their relationship, their house and their wedding, how could she tell him she had doubts about their future together? Once her misgivings were voiced, there'd be no taking them back. Even if her concerns were legitimate under the circumstances, Anna was aware of how deeply they might hurt Fletcher. Completely exasperated, she cried herself to sleep, stirring only once when Melinda's footsteps creaked on the stairs.

By morning, she resolved to exercise more patience as she waited upon the Lord to guide her about what to do next in regard to the wedding. After praying once again for her memory to return—and for a sense of peace in the meantime—she managed to comb her hair into a loose likeness of a bun. She had breakfast on the stove before Naomi could forbid her to help. She knew her stepmother was only concerned for her health, but Anna was growing increasingly restless from being told she couldn't do her share of work around the house.

Naomi chided her anyway. "The doctor said for you to take it easy. Where is Melinda hiding this morning?"

"Here I am," Melinda answered, skittering into the room.

"*Gut.* Since you and Anna need the buggy to go into town today, I'll drop Raymond and Roy off at work," Naomi suggested. "While I'm gone, I'd like you to clean the breakfast dishes and wring and hang the laundry, please. And remember, Anna isn't to help with any housework until she's seen the doctor again."

The ride to the mercantile was much smoother than it had been in Aaron's buggy, and on the way, Anna asked Melinda about their shopping list. She assumed they were picking up grocery staples for the week and she thought dividing the list would make the task easier.

"Oopsie, you must have forgotten our plan, since we arranged today's outing prior to your accident," Melinda replied. "We're not buying groceries. I'm buying organdy for my wedding apron. I also need to check to see whether the fabric has arrived for my dress and my *newehockers*' dresses. Aaron's mother is sewing his wedding suit, so I needn't concern myself with that. What do you intend to purchase today?"

Anna swiveled toward her and cocked her head, racking her brain. If only Melinda had reminded her they were going fabric shopping, she might have had an opportunity to discuss the matter with Naomi, whose practical and Godly advice she valued.

"I don't know that I'll purchase anything," she finally responded. "After Grace's question yesterday, I checked my sewing basket and the closet this morning and I didn't find evidence I've been working on my wedding dress, but I didn't have a chance to ask Naomi if I might have hung it somewhere else. Nor do I know if I've finished Fletcher's suit. I don't even know whether I've chosen my *newehockers* or who they might be."

Melinda clicked her tongue. "That's the trouble with being so secretive. To be honest, it hurt my feelings a bit that you never confided in me about your relationship with Fletcher. Perhaps if you'd told me more, I'd be able to help determine your sewing needs now. But, as Aaron and I agree, it makes sense that you and Fletcher hid your courtship from everyone, especially from us."

Anna silently counted backward from ten before responding. "Plenty of Amish couples still practice discretion about sharing their courtship—the custom isn't intended to insult anyone, so I'm sorry if you felt that way," she said. Taking a deep breath, she asked, "But what do you mean it made sense we'd keep our courtship hidden, especially from you?"

"Oh, you know," Melinda prattled on obliviously, working the reins. "I imagine you might have worried if you brought Fletcher around socially, he would have been drawn to me, the way Aaron was. Not that I'd ever be interested in Fletcher, of course, but you must have some lingering worries. It's only natural. Also, Aaron said the two of you never kept your courtship such a secret. He thinks that you and Fletcher didn't let anyone know you were courting because you were worried Aaron might tell Fletcher that he was your second choice."

"Oh really?" Anna asked drily. What hogwash! She was the one who begged her father and Naomi not to send Melinda back to Ohio after she discovered her shenanigans with Aaron! And she was the one who insisted she was glad Melinda had found an Amish boyfriend instead of an *Englischer* because maybe he'd be a good influence on her! As for Aaron, she'd gotten over their breakup within a couple of weeks. Some of his ideas were so preposterous Anna wondered why she'd ever accepted him as her suitor.

They continued in silence until they reached the designated horse and buggy lot on the far end of Main Street. After they'd secured the animal at the hitching post, Anna said, "I'm going to Schrock's while you're at the mercantile. I expect you back within half an hour, please."

The bells jingled when she pushed open the door of Schrock's Shop, and Anna's agitation was replaced with a sense of nostalgia. She took special pleasure in the resourcefulness and creativity of the Amish *leit* from her district, who consigned their handiwork in the large store. Today the gallery bustled with tourists in search of specialty Amish items such as quilts, toys, furniture, dried flower wreaths and naturally scented candles. She knew Joseph Schrock must have been pleased so many people were making purchases, although he looked overwhelmed by the line stretching from the register to the door. It seemed such a shame Anna couldn't work that afternoon, but she decided not to add to Joseph's burden by interrupting him with small talk.

She browsed the aisles, noting the price and location of the inventory. *I don't recall any of these items being stacked here*, she thought. She took a square of paper and a pencil from her purse and jotted down the contents on the shelves so she could study them before returning to work. When she finished, she turned to leave, nearly bumping into another young Amish woman whose arms were loaded with bars of homemade soap.

"Excuse me," she apologized, bending to retrieve the bars that had spilled from the woman's grasp.

"Anna!" the woman declared. "It's so *gut* to see you—I wasn't sure if you'd be stopping in today. We've been praying for you since we heard about your head injury. How do you feel?"

Anna surveyed the woman's olive complexion, pronounced cheekbones and deep-set eyes. She couldn't register who she was, although she deduced the woman also worked in the store.

"I'm much better," she said slowly. "*Denki* for your prayers."

"Of course," the woman replied. "As you can see, there's a long line now, but if you give me fifteen minutes, I'll be able to take my break and we'll catch up on everything."

"Actually, I was just popping in for a moment. Will you kindly tell Joseph I'll return to work on Thursday if the doctor approves? I'm sorry, but I have someone waiting and I can't stay." Anna backed away before it became apparent she couldn't recall the woman's name.

On the way home, Melinda jabbered nonstop about how irritated she was because the particular shade of purple fabric she'd ordered for her wedding dress hadn't arrived yet. Anna didn't get a word in edgewise until they sat down for tea at home, where she told Melinda and Naomi about her puzzling interaction with the unfamiliar woman.

"She's clearly new to Willow Creek. She's about my height and has dark hair and a ready smile," Anna commented.

"It must have been Tessa, one of the Fisher sisters," Melinda guessed. "Was she a homely woman with a big nose?"

"Melinda!" Naomi snapped.

"What?" Melinda chafed. "I'm only giving an honest description of what she looks like. Doesn't *Gott* require us to be honest?"

"First, beauty is in the eye of the beholder, and second, *Gott* requires us to be kind," replied Naomi. "And in this house, so do I."

Anna seldom heard Naomi raise her voice like that and Melinda looked as surprised as Anna felt. The young woman snatched her coat from the hook and stomped outside.

After the door banged shut behind Melinda, Naomi confessed, "Even though she's my dear departed sister's *kind*, there are times when her churlish behavior tries my last nerve and I fear I don't have any patience left."

"She's young and she doesn't always weigh her words," Anna acknowledged, consoling herself as much as Naomi. "I suppose that's the result of not having a *mamm* or sister in her home for so many years and then running around with the *Englisch* as often as she did."

Naomi sighed. "'Tis true, I suppose. In any case, Tessa Fisher and her older sister, Katie, moved to Willow Creek together in the fall. They rent Turner King's *daadi haus*. Katie took Doris's teaching position when Doris got married. Tessa works at Schrock's. The three of you became fast friends—you've spent many sister days and Sunday visits at their house."

"No wonder she looked so perplexed," Anna said. "She must have thought me terribly rude not to even greet her by name."

"I'm certain she'll understand once you explain the reason. But even without having all the facts, a *gut* friend will always give another the benefit of the doubt."

"*Jah*, that's true," Anna agreed, sipping her tea. As she reflected on Naomi's words, Anna decided that although she didn't have all of the facts about Fletcher, she was going to try to be more open about giving him every benefit of the doubt, too. As her fiancé, he deserved that much.

"I'll take Roy and Raymond home," Aaron offered at the end of their workday.

"*Neh*, I gave Naomi my word I'd do it when I saw her this morning," Fletcher countered. He had also been asked to stay for supper.

Aaron shrugged. "Suit yourself, but I'm going that way anyhow, since I'm picking up Melinda. She and my *mamm* and sisters are working on the wedding clothes together."

Fletcher was relieved Aaron and Melinda wouldn't be at the house. While he didn't expect to be able to spend much time alone with Anna, he was already on tenterhooks about his relationship with her; he didn't want to be harried by Aaron's snide remarks or Melinda's animated mannerisms. Besides, his appetite was beginning to return and he looked forward to eating another home-cooked meal instead of the soup and sandwich supper he usually prepared for himself.

After supper, he turned to Anna. "It's a clear night. Would you like to take a drive in the buggy or a stroll down to the creek?" he asked. "I'll bring a flashlight."

She hesitated. "How about if we sit on the porch instead? I'm afraid my energy is lagging. Would you like a cup of hot tea?"

"*Jah*, please," Fletcher answered.

They carried their steaming mugs out to the porch and peered over the railing, up at the starry sky, standing so close that Fletcher could hear the soft puff of Anna's breath as she pursed her lips to blow on her tea. A week ago, he would have draped his arm around her shoulders and nestled her to his chest, but tonight he had no assurance the gesture would be welcome, so he stepped away so as not to bump her with his elbow when he lifted his own mug to drink.

"I think spring might be coming early this year. Listen, you can hear the peepers," he said, indicating the chirping call of nearby frogs.

"Speaking of peepers, don't turn around," Anna instructed, glancing sidelong. "Evan is doing something he's expressly been forbidden to do—he's eavesdropping at the window. Ignore him. He can't hear us anyway."

Despite her admonishment not to look at him, Fletcher wheeled around and made a monstrous face to send Evan scampering, which sent Anna into a fit of giggles.

"Let's sit," she suggested, but no sooner had they settled into the swing next to one another than Anna got up and moved to the bench.

"Do I smell bad or is something else wrong?" he asked, suddenly fearful she'd remembered the misgiving that caused her to write the note the day of her accident.

"*Neh!* Of course not. I'm sorry, I should have explained… I've been so nauseated that even the rocking of the swing causes my stomach to flip. I haven't wanted to say anything because I didn't want to alarm anyone."

"Oh, I see," Fletcher said and his muscles immediately relaxed. So that was all it was. "Are you sure you shouldn't call the doctor?"

"*Neh*, I'm not sick," she assured him. "They told me I might temporarily have motion intolerance and I think I'm still recovering from Aaron's handling of the buggy yesterday. It seems lately I've been sensitive to certain smells and sights, too. And even though Melinda was the one twirling in circles yesterday, I felt as if I was the one becoming dizzy just from watching her."

"Is there anything I can do to help?" Fletcher asked.

"Don't twirl in circles," Anna quipped.

Fletcher chuckled heartily; Anna always could make him laugh. "I hope the bouts of nausea pass soon."

"*Denki,*" Anna replied. "To be on the safe side, I'll mention it to the doctor when I see him on Wednesday, although I'm more interested in knowing when he thinks my memory will fully return. Meanwhile, it would be helpful if I could ask you a few questions."

"Of course," Fletcher agreed.

"Well, right now, my immediate concerns are actually about the wedding preparations."

Fletcher's hand trembled so noticeably he had to set down his mug of tea. Squaring his shoulders as if to brace himself for whatever Anna was about to disclose, he could only utter, "*Jah?*"

"For starters, I don't know if I've made your suit yet. Do you?"

There was a pause while her question sank in and

when it did, Fletcher was nearly woozy with relief. *"Jah,"* he answered, half coughing and half choking on the word. *"Jah*, you've already made my suit and I feel pretty dapper in it if I do say so myself."

"Oh, *gut*." Anna's teeth shone in the moonlight. "How about my wedding dress? Have I mentioned anything about that?"

"Only that you might plan a sister day to work on it, along with your *newehockers*."

"Have I told you who they are?"

"Katie and Tessa Fisher."

Anna exhaled. "It's so *gut* to know these things. Now I can get back to working on the preparations before too much time elapses and I fall behind with the things that need to be done. I mean, obviously, there's so much I want to remember about you and about our relationship, too, but I've been praying fervently that my memory will return any moment now and all will *kumme* clear in that regard."

"Jah, any moment now, all will *kumme* clear," Fletcher repeated. But what would happen once it did? A shiver made his shoulders twitch.

"Oh, you're cold," Anna observed. "We should go inside."

"Actually, it's getting late and I ought to head home." Fletcher felt drained from the gamut of emotions he'd just experienced. "Unless you have any other urgent questions for me?"

"Only one. Actually, it's more of a favor. As I mentioned, I have a doctor's appointment on Wednesday. It's all the way in Highland Springs and it's at three o'clock, the middle of your workday. But I'm not supposed to take the buggy out until I've gotten the all-clear from the doctor and you know how nervous Naomi gets. I'd ask Melinda, but she isn't too careful on the major *Englisch* roadways... More important, I'd like you to be able to ask the doctor any questions you might have, too."

"Of course I'll take you," Fletcher agreed, although he very much doubted the doctor was the person who could give him the answers he most needed to know.

When Anna told Naomi about the plan for Fletcher to bring her to the medical center, Naomi seemed relieved not to have to take the buggy through city traffic.

"You promise you'll ask the doctor whether or not you're able to return to work?" she prodded.

"Of course I will," Anna reassured her. "What I'm more concerned about is helping you with preparations for the weddings."

"Don't worry about that," Naomi said, cupping Anna's face in her hands. "Having to prepare for the weddings was the best thing that could have happened to me. Without the deadline of your wedding dates, who knows how long I might have lolled about in misery?"

"I'm glad you're feeling more energetic, but I still intend to help. There's so much cooking, cleaning and organizing to do. And wherever will our guests stay?"

"I'll *wilkom* your help if the doctor allows, and for what it's worth, I intend to put Melinda to work, too. As for our guests, some of them will stay here and those who are related to the Chupps will stay with Aaron's family. We'll make do. I'm just pleased to hear you're more certain about going through with your wedding now."

Anna hardly felt certain, but Naomi was so upbeat that Anna didn't want to discourage her by rationalizing that even if she canceled her wedding to Fletcher, their household preparations wouldn't be in vain, since Melinda's wedding was only a week later. Instead, she replied, "As you've said, there's still time to decide. And I'm hopeful the doctor will have something promising to say about when I can expect my memories will return."

The medical center was on the opposite end of Highland Springs and although Fletcher worked the horse into a fast clip, he took care to ensure the carriage remained steady. They arrived in plenty of time for Anna to check in and he dropped her off in front of the building so he could take the buggy around the corner to the designated lot. Aaron had rarely been heedful of her comfort, so Anna was pleasantly surprised by Fletcher's chivalry, especially in light of her anxiety about the appointment.

"Would you like me to *kumme* into the examining room with you?" Fletcher asked when he reunited with her in the waiting area.

"*Jah*, I think the doctor is only going to look into my eyes and talk to me about my progress. And this way, you can ask him your questions, too," she suggested. The truth was Fletcher's presence had a calming effect on her, and she needed that right now.

The doctor was a rotund bald man, who shook hands with both of them. "I'm Dr. Donovan," he said. "I've met you and your family in the hospital, Anna, but you may not remember me. Many patients don't after they've had a head injury. Sometimes it's because of their concussions and sometimes it's because of the medication we give them."

Anna squinted at the doctor and then apologized. "I'm sorry, I don't."

"That's okay, I've been told I have a forgettable face, although my wife likes it," the doctor jested. "How have you been feeling?"

"Fine," Anna answered, clasping her hands on her lap.

"*Fine* as in you don't want to complain in front of your fiancé, or *fine* as in you haven't had any nausea, fatigue, headaches or blurred vision at all? Most patients do, you know," the doctor stated, settling into a chair.

"Well, my head feels a bit heavy but I wouldn't say it aches, and I suppose my energy isn't what it usually is," she admitted. "The other day I had a pretty severe bout of nausea, too."

"Has that happened often?" the doctor asked.

"Only once." Anna dipped her head and scraped at her thumbnail. "But it was because my friend handles his buggy like a madman."

"I see. Well, that's understandable. And how about your moods, how are they?"

Anna bit her lip. "With the grace of *Gott*, I try to be *gut*-natured, but I'm afraid I don't always succeed."

"I'm sure you do your best, Anna," Dr. Donovan said and his eyes twinkled. "But what I mean is, are there times when you experience extreme mood swings?

Times when you've felt exceedingly angry or despondent, or even elated? Anything like that?"

She hesitated, wondering if her ambiguous feelings about the wedding qualified as mood swings, before shaking her head.

"It's not extreme, but I have noticed Anna is weepier than she was before the accident," Fletcher offered. "She seems on the verge of tears more often than not."

"Does she—" Dr. Donovan began to ask Fletcher, but then rephrased the question and directed it toward Anna instead. "Do you suffer any prolonged periods of crying? Times when you just can't stop? Or any other unprovoked outbursts of emotion?"

"*Neh*, nothing like that," she stated.

The doctor smiled. "I suppose with four brothers at home, there's plenty to provoke an outburst now and then, isn't there?"

The three of them chuckled before Dr. Donovan continued, this time asking Fletcher, "Have you noticed any other differences in Anna's temperament?"

Fletcher replied carefully, "She's, er, less relaxed than she used to be. Not as easygoing."

Heat rose in Anna's cheeks. She realized she'd felt tearful and tense lately, but she regretted it was so obvious to others. Was her behavior off-putting to Fletcher?

Dr. Donovan must have caught her expression because he winked at her and joshed, "When your fiancé suffers a traumatic brain injury, we'll see how relaxed he feels, right?"

"I didn't mean to sound critical," Fletcher said, and

it was his turn to blush. "I only meant to point out a difference."

"It was good you did," the doctor replied. "I asked about it because it's important for me to be informed immediately if Anna experiences any extreme mood changes, like those I mentioned. That said, many head and brain injury patients are generally out of sorts following their accidents. Some of that is due to residual pain, some of it's a medication side effect and some of it is because they're quite literally not themselves. At least, not until their brains are fully recovered. It takes patience. Which may be very frustrating and even frightening for them as well as for the people who care about them. But it's all part of the healing process."

Anna leaned back in her chair, reassured by the doctor's assertion that what she was experiencing was both normal and temporary.

"How is your memory, Anna?" he asked. "Do you recall what happened the day before the accident? How about the week before? The month?"

With each question, Anna shook her head. They discussed what she did recall—confirming her latest pre-accident memories were of late August—and then the doctor performed a brief examination, looking into her eyes and checking her neurological reflexes.

"Overall, I'm pleased with your progress," he said when he completed the exam. "Your scans look good—great, in fact. I think the nausea you described will subside in time, especially now that you're not taking any medication."

"I'm glad to hear that," Anna responded politely. "But what about my memory loss?"

"You do have a longer period of amnesia than most," Dr. Donovan admitted. "It's called retrograde amnesia—meaning, you can't recall things that happened before the accident. Most people lose a few minutes, a couple of hours or even a day or two. You've lost about five or six months of memory. Now, before you get too worried, I'll tell you I've had patients who have lost up to three years!"

This fact was little consolation to her and judging from the wrinkles across Fletcher's forehead, he wasn't finding it to be reassuring, either.

"Your memories could return like that," Dr. Donovan said and snapped his fingers. "Or, more likely, they could come over time. Sometimes, patients will experience random memories we call *islands of memory*, because they might recall certain details of an event, but not the surrounding circumstances."

Anna bent toward him, her hands folded as if in prayer. "But isn't there anything I can do to hasten my memories to return?" she asked.

Fletcher heard the note of desperation in Anna's voice and it echoed his own feelings.

"I've had patients' families and friends try to recreate lost memories for them. Others surround themselves with familiar scents. Some people insist sage tea helped their memories return. I've even known people to try hypnotism," answered Dr. Donovan. "What I recommend is getting plenty of rest."

"I've been resting all week," Anna asserted. "But I have a job. I'm a clerk at a shop in town and I think I'm ready to return to work now."

Dr. Donovan crossed his arms. "I'd highly recommend you don't. In fact, you shouldn't do any more than what you've done at home this week, both mentally and physically. It will sound funny, but you need to avoid thinking too much. I'd also advise minimal reading and problem solving. Nothing involving lengthy periods of close concentration, such as sewing. And no strenuous activities. No pitching hay, no floor scrubbing, nothing more vigorous than collecting eggs from the henhouse. I'd suggest limiting your exertion to a slow, daily stroll in the fresh air."

"But I have to help prepare the house for the wedding," Anna protested and her eyes welled.

Dr. Donovan raised his brows at Fletcher. "I'm certain your fiancé would rather have his bride healthy than anything else, right?"

Whether Anna actually became his bride or not, Fletcher agreed her health was paramount. "Anna, if rest is what it takes for you to recover and your memory to return, I'm sure Naomi will take over until you're better," he reasoned.

Dr. Donovan held up his hand. "I want to caution you both that while rest *may* be helpful in restoring Anna's memory, there's no guarantee. But the benefits of rest—for both body and mind—greatly outweigh the risks of overexertion at this point. Further, the more pressure Anna is under, the less likely she is to get the memory results you both want. So, take each day as it comes and keep your expectations in check. And remember, it's crucial that Anna doesn't experience a lot of stress or become too upset."

Fletcher and Anna both nodded without replying.

"Why such long faces?" the doctor inquired. "Anna is recovering well, whether or not her memory returns. There's a good chance it will, but if it doesn't, it's a loss but it's not the end of the world. You have your entire lives together to make new memories, right?"

Fletcher cleared his throat and spoke deliberately. "Anna and I only met in September. She has no recollection of me and we're scheduled to be wed in about a month. We have certain…certain concerns."

Dr. Donovan blew the air out of his cheeks and took off his glasses to rub his eyes. "Ah, I understand now," he said, before readjusting his frames behind his ears. Slanting forward, he said, "I see how that could be problematic. But it also might be one of the best blessings a couple could ever receive. There's no thrill like falling in love with each other for the first time. It sounds as if you two have the opportunity to experience that joy twice!"

From the corner of his eye, Fletcher could see Anna's cheeks blossom with pink. Amish couples didn't usually speak of such intimate matters to anyone, much less to *Englisch* acquaintances, but Dr. Donovan didn't seem to notice their embarrassment.

He rolled his chair back, saying, "Alright, then, I'd like to see you back here in two weeks unless any of your symptoms worsen instead of improve. Meanwhile, have a little fun getting to know each other again. Falling in love is a gift. It's something to celebrate."

Fletcher realized the kind man meant his words to be encouraging, but as he shook the doctor's hand goodbye, he thought this felt nothing like a time of celebration. Indeed, while they journeyed back toward Willow Creek, Anna seemed somber, as well. He wasn't ready to discuss what the doctor said about her memory returning or how they might spend the next couple of weeks, so Fletcher was relieved when she didn't broach those topics, either. But she remained quiet for so long he finally asked if the journey was nauseating her.

"*Neh*, not at all. This has been a very smooth ride," she replied. "I was just thinking how disappointed Joseph will be to learn I can't yet return to the shop."

"Are *you* disappointed?" Fletcher asked.

Anna giggled. "To be honest, *neh*, not really. I'd much rather help Naomi manage the household. And I'll admit that it's been necessary for me to rest in between tasks recently, which I couldn't do at the shop. I worry I wouldn't be efficient there, even if I were allowed to return. But I feel bad leaving Joseph shorthanded. The store was packed with customers when I stopped by the other morning."

Fletcher pulled on the rein and the horse turned toward the right, exiting the main roadway. "Would it be possible for Melinda to temporarily take your place?"

"*Jah!*" Anna practically hopped up from the seat. "What a great idea, Fletcher! I'm sure she'll prefer working in town, and I dare say Naomi will appreciate having her out of her hair for a while."

Fletcher grinned, pleased he could provide Anna with a satisfactory solution to at least one of the problems she was facing. Her praise always made his chest swell and today, it gave him hope that they might be able to work out whatever other concerns she had, too. But first, he'd have to help her remember them, of course. So, before dropping her off for the evening, he said, "I'll have to work late tomorrow and Friday night because I left early today, but I'd like to take you out alone on Saturday, if I may?"

"*Denki*, I'd like that." Her cheek dimpled as she replied.

Fletcher felt so encouraged that when he returned home, he took out his toolbox for the first time since receiving Anna's note and began working on his wedding gift for her: he was resectioning one area of the parlor into an alcove so she could have privacy for reading and writing in her journal. As he was sanding a length of board, he began thinking about ways in which he could help jog Anna's memory without pressuring her. By the time he put away his tools for the night, he was so eager for the date he'd planned that he almost hoped her memory wouldn't come back before he had a chance to see her again.

Chapter Four

Upon waking on Saturday morning, Anna kept her eyes closed, hoping her memory had been restored overnight. Once again, she was disappointed that nothing from the past six months came to mind. She blinked to see Melinda rummaging through a drawer. Usually Anna was awake long before her cousin, who required considerable rousing to get out of bed, especially after she'd been out with Aaron the previous night. Anna figured Melinda must be excited about beginning her first day of work at Schrock's Shop.

"Guder mariye," Melinda sang out. "Do you suppose I might borrow a few hair clips?"

Anna yawned as she pushed herself onto her elbows. "I gave you my hair clips earlier in the week. Did you misplace them?"

"Neh, you never gave them to me," Melinda replied. "Perhaps you gave some to Naomi, but not to me."

"I'm certain I gave them to you," Anna insisted. "In fact, I was running low myself but I let you use them because it hurt my head to gather my hair tightly. Don't you remember?"

Melinda shrugged. "*Neh*, but that's okay. Naomi probably has extras."

Anna didn't mind about the hair clips in particular as much as she minded the fact Melinda denied Anna gave her the accessories in the first place. How could Melinda be that inattentive? Before Anna could think of a kind way to point out her carelessness, the young woman hurried from the room.

Anna dressed quickly and scurried into the kitchen, too. Fletcher had already picked up Roy and Raymond for their half day of work, and he'd bring them home at dinnertime, too, since he was taking Anna on an outing. Meanwhile, she decided to offer to transport Melinda into town. Whether unintentionally or not, the doctor hadn't expressly prohibited Anna from handling the horse and buggy, and she was feeling cooped up. Besides, she wanted to purchase more hairpins so she could tidy her appearance before going out with Fletcher.

When Anna suggested to Naomi that she wanted to take Melinda to Schrock's, her stepmother replied, "*Denki*, but I have to go to town anyway to buy baking supplies."

"Why don't you let me pick them up?" Anna asked, knowing the heavy Saturday traffic would be unsettling to Naomi, who was easily flustered by the *Englisch* trucks and tour buses.

"*Neh*, I need to buy in bulk, in preparation for our wedding guests," she countered. "The items will be too heavy for you to carry. The doctor's list prohibits heavy lifting, remember?"

"I'll take Eli and Evan with me. They're strong—they can carry the packages. If they're especially helpful, we might even stop at Yoder's Bakery for a treat afterward," Anna bargained. "I'll be fine."

"*Jah*, we'll help Anna. Please can we go, *Mamm*?" pleaded Evan.

"It will keep us out from underfoot," Eli reasoned, using one of his *mamm*'s expressions for effect, "instead of muddying your freshly scrubbed floors."

"*Jah*, alright, but you'll still have to complete your chores when you return," Naomi warned the boys as they shot out the door ahead of Anna and Melinda.

On the way, as Eli and Evan were distracted in the back seat with dividing the shopping list between them, Anna again brought up the topic of the hair clips. "I can replace the pins, Melinda," she said. "But it troubled me to hear you say I never gave them to you. You need to be more focused. If a customer at Schrock's gives you a large bill and you aren't paying attention, you may neglect to give them their correct change. That will create problems for everyone."

"I'm quite certain that won't happen," Melinda said breezily. "After all, I'm not the one with amnesia."

Anna's ears were ringing, but she responded calmly. "What do you mean by that?"

"Only that I don't recall you ever giving me your hairpins, so I have to believe you're mistaken. It's not your fault, necessarily. You're probably just remembering it wrong."

Anna squeezed her eyes shut and inhaled through her nose and then blew the air out through her mouth. She opened her eyes and moderated her voice to state, "Melinda, I gave you the hairpins after my accident and after I ceased taking any medication. I remember everything from the past week perfectly."

Melinda wrinkled her nose. "Why are you getting so prickly about such a trivial matter?" But before Anna responded, Melinda shrieked, "Oh, take the reins, will you? I can jump out at this stop sign instead of walking to Schrock's from the horse and buggy lot. See you later!"

As Melinda bounced down from the buggy and tore through traffic, Eli exclaimed, "Everyone knows you're not supposed to do that! Doesn't she have any common sense?"

Shaking her head, Anna wondered the same thing herself. In the pause it took for traffic to start moving again, Melinda scudded across the street and pulled open the door to Schrock's. Watching her, Anna feared her cousin might not even last a week in the shop before Joseph would have to let her go. He'd be short staffed again and Anna would feel obligated to return, since she was the one who recommended Melinda for the temporary position. *In that case, I better make hay while the sun shines*, she thought. *Or at least make my dress while I have a chance.* Although the doctor had prohibited prolonged periods of sewing, Anna figured she could stitch it together a bit at a time, but first she'd need to purchase her wedding dress fabric.

After all of the groceries had been secured in the

buggy, Anna shepherded the boys into Yoder's Bakery, where she treated them to a cup of cocoa each and allowed them to split one of Faith Yoder's renowned apple fry pies.

"How are you?" Faith asked with a look of concern. "We heard you took a bad fall."

"*Denki*, I feel fine now." Anna deliberately kept her answer vague; she didn't want to lie, nor did she wish to tell anyone else about her memory problems, lest they question her about her wedding plans, as well. "How about you? Is your business thriving in its new location?"

"*Jah*. It's made such a difference to have a shop on Main Street instead of working out of the kitchen at home," Faith said. "I'm already up to my eyeballs in Easter orders for my *Englisch* customers' celebrations. Oh! That reminds me, are you planning to order a wedding cake?"

Although many of the desserts at Amish weddings were homemade by the bride's family and friends, it was common for the bride to order at least one special-made cake from a professional baker, as well, and Anna didn't know quite how to reply. She figured it was one thing to buy fabric for a wedding dress at this point, but it was entirely another to order a wedding cake.

Despite experiencing the first sweet stirrings of infatuation for Fletcher, Anna realized that if her memory didn't return in full, there was still the possibility they wouldn't marry. If the wedding was called off, she could always wear her dress to church, since it would be in the same pattern as the rest of her clothes. But if she placed an order for a cake, Faith might turn down future business so that she would have time to fill Anna's order. Anna didn't want to inconvenience Faith and affect her business like that.

"Er," she hedged. "I'm not quite certain."

Faith's creamy complexion splotched with pink. "Of course, that's fine. I only asked because your wedding date is so close to Easter, I wanted to be sure to reserve time to make your cake if you wanted one. I wasn't trying to pressure you into ordering anything from me—"

"*Neh*, I didn't think you were." Anna stammered, "It's just that I... I haven't made up my mind yet."

"Better you should wait, then." Faith chuckled. "Your cousin Melinda ordered hers last week and she's already changed her mind three times. I'm not going to stock up on any specialty ingredients for hers until the week before the wedding, when I give her a final deadline."

"*Gut* idea." Anna laughed. "I'll be sure to place my order as soon as I've given it more thought. Meanwhile, would you mind if I leave Eli and Evan here to finish their cocoa? I need to make a last-minute purchase from the mercantile. They'll behave themselves, won't you, boys?"

"With six brothers, I know how to keep these two out of mischief," Faith jested.

Anna was glad for the opportunity to shop for the fabric without the boys around. The two of them had eyes and ears for everything, and she was concerned they might report her purchase back to Naomi, who would fret endlessly about Anna sewing, no matter how many breaks she took. Anna swiftly backtracked down Main Street to the mercantile, but selecting the color took more time than she'd anticipated. Brides in her district tended to choose a traditional blue for their wedding dresses, although some, like Melinda, favored brighter variations, such as shades of purple. Anna liked both colors, but neither particularly appealed to her over the other.

She was fingering a swatch of navy blue cotton when she caught sight of a bolt in a deep green hue. It reminded her of the shade of the grass beneath a willow tree. She'd be pleased to have a new dress in that color, regardless of whether it ended up being her wedding dress or not. And somehow, just the act of selecting the fabric made her feel more confident about the future. She bought enough for herself and her two *newehockers* and hustled back to the bakery, knowing Naomi would begin to worry if she and the boys didn't return home soon. A young Amish woman was exiting Yoder's with a stack of cardboard boxes full of treats in her arms and two bags of doughnuts swinging from her hand as Anna was entering.

"Excuse me," Anna apologized, peering around the large package of fabric she carried.

The woman held the door open for her with her elbow as she balanced her own packages.

"*Denki*, but I don't think there's room for me to squeeze by. I'm just here to summon my brothers anyway." Anna smiled, calling, "Eli, Evan, *kumme* please."

The woman made a discontented huffing noise as the boys passed her.

When they were out of earshot, Anna instructed,

"Boys, it's only proper to hold the door for someone who has packages in her hands, even when she's being very polite and holding it for you. I think you offended that lady."

"I'm sorry, Anna. We'll remember that next time," Evan promised.

"*Jah,*" agreed Eli. "I didn't want to get my handprints on the door handle. But we'll apologize to Katie Fisher at church on Sunday."

"That was my friend Katie Fisher, Tessa's sister?" Anna asked abashedly.

Suddenly she understood why Katie had acted so crabby: it must have seemed as if Anna was snubbing her, just as she'd apparently snubbed her sister, Tessa. Anna pressed her lips together, silently praying for her memory to return before she hurt anyone else's feelings or had to tell another person about her amnesia.

Fletcher pried the lid off a paint can. Painting was no one's favorite part of the job, but it was a necessary one. He wanted to be certain Raymond and Roy took as much care performing the mundane aspects of their responsibilities as they did the more challenging tasks.

"We'll have to move up our completion date on this site," Aaron announced. "I accepted another project that begins next week."

Fletcher voiced his surprise. "This office suite is going to require hanging more than the usual amount of trim, which we don't even have on hand yet."

"*Jah*, that's why I'm heading to the lumber store now."

"Now?" Fletcher repeated. If Aaron left, they'd fall behind on the painting.

"It's not as if I can call them on my cell phone, is it?" Aaron cracked. "If I don't talk to them today, I won't know if they have what we need in stock."

Fletcher hesitated. "The boys and I could stop on our way to their house after work today," he suggested.

"*Neh*, I'll go now," Aaron insisted.

To Fletcher, it seemed a waste of time and manpower for Aaron to run errands during the workday when Fletcher offered to do it off the clock, but he knew that was Aaron's decision to make, not his, since Aaron was the foreman. After giving it more thought, Fletcher concluded he'd prefer to arrive at Anna's sooner rather than later anyway, so he could finally spend an afternoon alone with her, helping her to recall the past. As he painted he silently asked God to bless their time together, and before Fletcher knew it, Roy signaled that it was nearly dinnertime.

At Anna's house, Evan and Eli zipped pell-mell across the yard to greet them.

"Fletcher!" Eli shouted. "*Mamm* says you're joining us for dinner. We made certain to taste test your food for mushrooms—just like Nehemiah did for King Artaxerxes in the Bible."

"Really?" asked Fletcher. "I didn't realize King Artaxerxes was allergic to mushrooms, too."

"Not mushrooms but anything poisonous," Eli explained solemnly.

Fletcher nodded seriously and clapped Eli's shoulder in return. "I appreciate that."

When Fletcher entered the kitchen, Naomi was slic-
ing bread. Anna had just slid a pan from the oven and
her cheeks were glowing. She gave him a little half wave
with the oversize oven mitts she wore on her hands and
then giggled at herself. He hadn't realized how much
he'd missed her spontaneous sense of humor and he
suddenly felt unnerved by her charm.

"Hello, Naomi. Hello, Anna," he said. "You smell
appenditlich."

He'd meant to say the *food* smelled delicious, but
before he could correct his mistake, Evan hooted,
"Fletcher said, 'you smell *appenditlich*' instead of 'the
food smells *appenditlich*'!"

"Beheef dich," Anna shushed Evan with the com-
mand to behave himself before giving him a playful
swat with the oven mitt. "Go wash your hands, please."

"I'd better wash my hands, too." Fletcher quickly
ducked into the washroom until his ears lost their crim-
son flush.

After the meal, he informed Anna she might want to
wear a heavier shawl, as they'd be spending time near
the creek, where the air was especially cool.

"You're going to the creek?" Eli asked. "Can we
kumme, too? We finished all of our chores."

"Jah. We can look for Timothy again," Evan begged.
"Please?"

For a split second, Fletcher feared Anna would allow
Eli and Evan to accompany them, but then she glanced
in Fletcher's direction and gave him a wink.

"I think the turtles are still in brumation," she said.

"Besides, you boys already went on an outing with me today. Now it's Fletcher's turn."

Satisfied, Fletcher uncrossed his arms, but there was still a delay before he set out with Anna: she insisted on washing and drying the dishes, despite Naomi's protests. When they were finally seated in the buggy and traveling down the lane, he glanced sideways to see Anna smiling broadly.

"Look!" she exclaimed, pointing to a robin in the field. "I guess that means winter is officially over, although our winter was so mild this year, it was as if it hardly happened."

"You remembered our mild winter?" Fletcher asked, unable to keep the tension from his voice.

"*Neh*, Naomi told me," Anna confessed. "I'm sorry if I got your hopes up. I assure you, as soon I remember anything from the past six months, I'll let you know."

"Of course you will." Fletcher hadn't meant to sound as if he were pressuring her. He loosened his grip on the reins and lightened his tone. "We did have a white *Grischtdaag*, though. The landscape was blanketed in pristine perfection."

"So then, white must be your favorite color?" Anna asked him cheekily. "And winter must be your favorite season?"

"*Neh*, spring is my favorite season—same as yours. And green is my favorite color," he answered, thinking in particular of the green radiance of Anna's eyes.

"Oh, that's interesting to know," Anna replied. "Because today I purchased green fabric for my wedding dress."

Fletcher again felt a surge of apprehension. She was making her dress, which was another significant step in the wedding preparations. Although that was a good sign, he had to remind himself that once Anna's memories returned, it was possible she'd cancel the wedding to him in favor of a renewed courtship with Aaron. Even so, Fletcher allowed himself a small measure of optimism.

They rode in silence until they came to the public park that hosted the stony path running adjacent to the creek. Following the trail, they eventually arrived at the same spot Anna and her brothers frequented by cutting down the hill and through the meadow directly behind their house.

"We could have walked straight to the creek from my house," Anna noted. "I'm not as fragile as everyone seems to think I am."

"*Jah*, but the creek isn't the only stop on our itinerary," Fletcher replied as he pulled a blanket and thermos from the back of his buggy. "We'll need the buggy to travel to the other place we'll visit today."

"As long as our next destination isn't Tessa and Katie Fisher's house," she remarked. "I'm afraid I've managed to slight them both on separate occasions. I had no idea who they were and I feel awful I don't remember them." Anna sighed.

"You'll remember them yet," Fletcher encouraged her.

When they reached the water's edge, Fletcher spread the blanket he'd been carrying beneath a barely budding willow tree and motioned for Anna to have a seat.

Then he poured fragrant hot liquid from the thermos into a cup and presented it to her.

"What's this?" she questioned.

"It's sage tea," he replied, filling a cup for himself. "Remember? Dr. Donovan said he had patients who claimed it helped their memories return."

Anna pursed her lips to blow on the steaming drink. "He also said some of his patients practiced hypnotism. You're not going to try to hypnotize me, too, are you?"

Fletcher could tell by the way her cheek dimpled that she was pleased rather than annoyed. "*Neh.* But he did say it was important to get rest—which is why we're going to relax here for a while."

"Oh, I see," Anna said with a lilt in her voice. "We're not merely whiling away a Saturday afternoon. We're actually following doctor's orders?"

"Doctor's orders," Fletcher reiterated, enjoying their flirtation. "Actually, we're following his orders and his patients' suggestions. He mentioned some of their families and friends tried to recreate memories in order to jog the patients' recollection. There's no pressure, but I hope these surroundings might prompt memories of our early days together. You see, I hadn't been in town for more than a week when I first met you fishing down at the bend in the creek."

"I was fishing?" Anna was surprised. "But I've never liked handling grubs."

Fletcher gave a hearty laugh, exposing nearly perfectly aligned teeth, except for one at the top left corner, which was slightly crooked, as if it didn't quite fit among the others.

"Neh," he said. "I meant *I* was fishing. You were leaning against a willow on the embankment."

"Just loitering there?" That didn't sound like something she would have done, either.

"Actually, you were weeping," Fletcher admitted.

Anna's cheeks went hot when she heard Fletcher had first encountered her in such a vulnerable state. "I'm afraid I did a lot of crying in the months following my *daed*'s death."

"Perhaps, but when I made a dumb joke about suddenly understanding why the tree was called a *weeping* willow, you were gracious enough to laugh."

"You don't expect me to start weeping under this willow again now, do you?" Anna bantered.

"Neh," Fletcher replied. "If there's one thing I hate, it's seeing you in tears."

Fletcher's response was so earnest it warmed Anna to the tips of her toes. She looked around and noted, "I've always appreciated what a peaceful place this is."

Fletcher guffawed. "That's the very thing we first argued about."

"We did?" Anna's curiosity was piqued. "Why?"

"Well, after I met you here the first time and you were crying—you hadn't yet confided the reasons behind your tears—I made that dumb joke, but then I contrived an excuse to leave, so you'd have your privacy."

"That was kind of you," Anna commented.

"Not really," Fletcher admitted. "I was agitated because I believed our voices had scared away the fish.

See, I'd specifically chosen this spot instead of the location upstream where everyone else was fishing because it seemed more peaceful here. So, when you showed up the next evening, we got into a bit of an argument about who had more of a right to be here."

"You were a newcomer to our community," Anna said. "I'm sorry I wasn't friendlier. That was rude of me."

"*Neh*, what's rude is what I did on the third evening."

Listening to Fletcher talk about their first encounter was like reading a very good book: Anna wanted to hear all of it at once yet she didn't want the story to come to an end.

"What did you do on the third evening?" she asked.

"I presented you with a pen and a journal and suggested you might benefit from writing about your heartache instead of reflecting on it here at the stream," Fletcher said, cringing at himself. "What a heel."

"You weren't a heel. I can be a bit territorial—my *daed* always said it came from living as an only child for so long and not having to share my space. I was being selfish."

"*Neh*," Fletcher countered. "*What a heel* is what you wrote about me on the first page of the diary I'd given you. You scribbled, *This journal was given to me by Fletcher Chupp, what a heel*. And then you thrust the diary under my nose to show me what it said."

"I did?" Anna was mortified. "That was childish."

"It was *true*. I was being a heel. I cared more about fishing than about your feelings. And I tried to disguise my self-centeredness with a gift."

"How did we ever end up courting after introductions like ours?" she asked.

"It's simple—we got to know each other. I kept coming here to fish and you kept coming here to be alone with your thoughts. Neither of us had the privacy we needed to accomplish our purpose, but we were both too stubborn to budge, so we began talking to each other instead. Soon, there was nothing we didn't tell each other. Nothing," Fletcher said.

When he looked at her, his eyes were dark as the midnight sky and his voice was husky with ardor. A subtle yet familiar emotion stirred inside of Anna and she shivered.

"What is it?" Fletcher asked, sitting up straight. "Did you remember something just then?"

"Almost," she said, sorry to disappoint him. "But it was more of a feeling than a memory."

"A happy feeling?"

"Decidedly so." She smiled, holding his gaze.

"Gut." He stood and took her empty cup. "There's another important stop along our stroll down memory lane, so we ought to get going now."

As they were returning to the buggy, Anna suddenly uttered, "The journal you gave me! Surely I must have recorded my memories in there."

"I hadn't even thought of that, but you're right," Fletcher agreed. "When was the last time you wrote in it?"

"Wrote in it? I didn't even know it existed! Where do I keep it?"

"I don't know. You told me you wrote in it all the

time but you had to squirrel it away in a secret place because you didn't want the boys happening upon it."

"Really?" Anna was deflated. "Well, what did it look like?"

"It was about this big," Fletcher answered, squaring his hands, "and it had a brown leather jacket with a little gold lock attached at the side."

"I'll search for it as soon as I get home," Anna said enthusiastically as Fletcher supported her into the buggy. "It must hold a storehouse of memories."

Fletcher's palms grew sweaty as he contemplated what Anna might find written in her journal. He'd gotten so caught up in the nostalgia of first meeting her that he'd momentarily lost sight of the fact his ultimate intention for the outing was to help her recall her hesitation about marrying him, so he could address it. He removed his hat and swept his hand through his hair, as if to brush away the troublesome thoughts.

"Someone's been painting today, I see," Anna noticed. "You've got flecks of white in your hair."

"If you think my hair is bad, you ought to see Roy's and Raymond's," he replied. "Their saving grace is that they're blond, rather than dark like me, so it doesn't show up as much."

"*Denki* for mentoring them, Fletcher. I don't know what Naomi would do without a man around to train them in a vocation."

"It's a privilege," Fletcher said soberly. "Now, as you know, to the right is Turner King's *daadi haus*, but we won't drop in there until you resolve your misunderstanding with Katie and Tessa. A little farther along the lane is our house."

Anna hesitated when Fletcher turned in the driveway. "I'm not sure it's appropriate for the two of us to spend time together unchaperoned here. I wouldn't want people to see us and think—"

"Of course not. Neither would I," Fletcher said. He shared Anna's commitment to modesty and decorum. "I only want to show you something. Wait here and I'll be right out with it."

He scooted into the house and emerged carrying a black suit on a hanger.

"I don't suppose you recall making this?" he asked.

"Hmm, I don't know." Anna scrunched her brows together and teased, "That stitching doesn't look like mine. Are you sure *you* didn't make the suit?"

"These hands can work a hammer, but not a sewing needle," Fletcher argued.

"*Jah*, that would explain why the side seam appears crooked."

"It's not crooked, you're looking at it askance."

Anna giggled. "One thing is certain—you will look very dapper in that, indeed. Now please go put it away. I'm freezing," she said.

Despite his best efforts to guard his emotions, Fletcher felt his knees go weak and his hopes grow strong because of Anna's compliment. He whistled as he brought the suit inside and quickly returned to take Anna home. He idled at the end of the lane as another buggy sailed past. Even if he hadn't recognized the familiar style of the carriage, he knew only one person who worked his horse that hard.

"That was Aaron," Anna said, as if reading his thoughts. "He probably picked Melinda up after her first day at the shop. Look at him go! I'm queasy just watching him."

Anna's remark cast doubt on Fletcher's concern about her affection for Aaron, and he chuckled zealously. As they rode, she peppered him with questions about his work as a carpenter, his sisters and their families, his likes and dislikes, and other important aspects of his life.

Finally, he teased, "There isn't going to be a quiz about this, Anna."

"*Neh*, but I want to learn as much about you as I can as quickly as I can, Fletcher Chupp."

Fletcher drew the horse to an abrupt halt and shifted to study her face in the waning light. "Why did you say that?" he asked, his voice throaty.

She tipped her head. "I said it because I meant it."

"That's exactly what you said—and I do mean word for word—when I first began walking out with you," he explained. "I thought maybe you'd remembered saying it."

"*Neh*, but it's still true," she responded. "Rather, it's true again."

As he clicked to the horse, Fletcher's stomach turned somersaults. Dr. Donovan was right: there was nothing more exhilarating than falling in love, and he was on the brink of falling for Anna a second time.

"Whoa, steady," he commanded the horse, directing it down the lane to Anna's house. He might as well have been talking to his own heart, which seemed in danger of rearing wildly and galloping away with him. He couldn't allow himself to forget Anna's note, even if she had.

"Look, Aaron has hitched his horse," Anna pointed out. "That must mean he's staying for supper. You're *wilkom* to join us, too."

"*Denki*, but I have work to do at home," Fletcher said. He needed to clear his head. Besides, he didn't want to take advantage of Naomi's hospitality, even if his cousin was staying, so he walked Anna to the porch, but before he could say goodbye, the door swung open. The tantalizing aroma of pork chops filled Fletcher's nostrils and when Naomi insisted he stay for supper, he couldn't refuse. This time when everyone joined hands for grace, Anna gave his palm a quick squeeze before letting go, and when he accidentally knocked his knee into hers, she didn't flinch or move her chair.

"How was your first day at the shop?" Anna asked Melinda as they were eating dessert.

"Easy as pie," Melinda replied. "No wonder you prefer working there to helping us at home."

"Anna's reputation for industriousness is what afforded you a temporary position at Schrock's Shop," Naomi diplomatically reminded her niece. "But because you've had such an easy day there, Melinda, you may clear the table and wash and dry the dishes, as well. I'm sure Aaron has chores to get to at home and will be leaving straightaway, too. As it is, I've got mending to do and the boys need to take a bath. *Kumme*, Evan and Eli, say *gut nacht* to everyone. Roy and Raymond, the wood bin is running low."

"I'll walk outside with you," Fletcher suggested to Aaron after Naomi and the boys left the room, fearing his cousin wouldn't take the hint that it was time to leave.

"Okay," he agreed amiably. "But first I have something to give Anna. It's in my buggy."

Anna stopped rinsing the pan in her hands long enough to shrug her shoulders and cast a puzzled look at Melinda. Fletcher stood by the door of the mudroom until Aaron returned with a pot of pale blue flowers.

"For you," he said, extending it to Anna.

She looked confused. *"Denki,"* she said, accepting the pot. "How thoughtful."

Melinda clapped her hands and tittered. "They're forget-me-nots, get it? You know, because you have amnesia. I was telling Aaron about the hair clips as we drove by the nursery in town and he was suddenly inspired. He said the flowers would make the perfect get-well gift for you!"

"I get it. *Denki*," Anna repeated, red-faced, before abruptly saying good-night to everyone and excusing herself from the room.

Fletcher strode to his buggy without waiting for Aaron to stop laughing with Melinda. Filling his lungs with the night air, he tried not to rush to conclusions about the name of the flower Aaron had chosen for Anna. He was familiar enough with Aaron's sense of humor to know that his cousin's jokes were often misplaced. It was entirely possible there was no hidden message—other than the obvious pun in reference to amnesia—intended by his choice of flowers. As for Anna leaving the room so quickly, perhaps she merely felt nauseated or tired.

Yet as the horse pulled his buggy toward home, Fletcher noticed the optimism he'd felt earlier in the day was replaced by a gnawing insecurity that he couldn't seem to shake. *Dear Lord*, he began to pray, but then he stopped. Unsure of what to ask for, he kept his request simple: *please help*.

Chapter Five

After retreating to the washroom to splash water on her face, Anna patted her cheeks dry with a towel. Over the course of her relationship with Aaron, she'd grown accustomed to overlooking his jokes and pranks, and once again she reminded herself that his intention was to make her laugh, not to mock her condition. Recalling that Dr. Donovan said it was normal for head injury patients to be hypersensitive during their recoveries, she decided rather than to waste any more time feeling irritated, she'd turn her attention to searching her bedroom for the journal Fletcher had given her.

When she didn't find it, she searched again a second time, patting beneath her mattress, opening every drawer and examining the shelf in her closet. Like most Amish homes, theirs was furnished simply and contained little clutter, so finding lost items was usually only a matter of retracing one's steps. Unfortunately, Anna's amnesia kept her from being able to do that.

She shone the flashlight into the other half of the

attic, which was completely empty except for the package containing the wedding dress fabric she'd stashed there that afternoon because she was afraid Naomi might reproach her for sewing if she happened upon it in Anna's closet. Although Anna knew it would be unlikely for her to keep a personal item like a journal elsewhere in the house, she checked each room and asked each family member if they might have known where she'd put it.

"You're always writing in it, so you'd better find it soon," Melinda answered as she furiously scoured a pan. "It would be a shame if someone discovered your secrets."

To Anna's ears, that almost sounded like a taunt. Did Melinda know something she wasn't saying about the journal? Had she read it? Almost immediately, Anna was filled with shame. Assuming ill of another person was not the Amish way. Besides, Fletcher said the diary had a lock, so when Anna found the key on a string inside her drawer, she immediately looped it around her neck.

"I'm not concerned about someone discovering my secrets," she replied affably, picking up a towel to dry the dishes stacking up next to the sink. "But the diary could go a long way in helping me regain my memory, so please keep your eye out for it. Now, how about if you tell me more about your first day at the shop?"

Melinda was pleased to regale Anna with descriptions of the *Englischers* who came into the shop, recounting their questions and comments, and detailing their purchases. Listening to Melinda's exuberance about the experience, Anna was glad her cousin had the opportunity to work outside their home. Perhaps by representing the Amish community's wares to *Englisch* customers, Melinda might take better care to reflect Amish values, too.

By the time they finished cleaning the dishes, any tension Anna experienced concerning Aaron's gift had been washed away, as well. But her head felt as heavy as an anvil and she retired to her bedroom early. She searched her drawers and under the bed one last time, wishing she could find her journal. Not only did she want to read what she'd already written there, but she wanted to record her current feelings about Fletcher, in order to make sense of them. She found him to be thoughtful, respectful and fun, as well as strong, handsome and Godly. It was no wonder she'd been smitten with him from the start.

Yet, as she leaned against her bed to unlace her shoes, she ruminated that being infatuated wasn't reason enough to marry someone. She didn't doubt she professed to the deacon after their meetings concluded that she believed Fletcher was the husband the Lord provided for her. But despite her growing affection for Fletcher, Anna just didn't know if she could honestly make that same vow again when the bishop asked her to affirm it during the wedding ceremony in church.

Anna slipped into a kneeling position on the floor and folded her hands, beseeching, *Please, Lord, return my memory to me soon. And if it's Your will, help me find my diary, as well*.

"Oh, *gut*, you're still up," Melinda said when she

burst through the door. "Do you want to see the material for my wedding dress? It arrived at the mercantile today and I picked it up after work."

"Sure." Anna straightened into a standing position.

Melinda unwrapped a layer of brown paper from a large package.

"It's beautiful," Anna gushed about the violet fabric, fingering it along the edge. "This will look lovely with your brunette hair and big brown eyes."

"That's what Aaron said, too," Melinda commented as she secured the string around the bundle again.

As they donned their nightclothes, Anna realized perhaps Melinda simply didn't realize how she came across when she repeated Aaron's remarks, whether kind or far-fetched. She extinguished the lamp.

"Melinda?" Anna asked into the darkness. "Remember how you were talking about secrets and wishing I'd confide in you more often? I have a secret I'd like to share with you."

Anna could hear Melinda scramble into an attentive position. "What is it?"

"I bought my wedding dress material today, too. It's forest green. I'm not supposed to concentrate on sewing for long periods of time, but I figure I can work on it now and again, provided Naomi doesn't catch me and start to fret."

"I promise not to tell," Melinda said and flopped back down against her pillow, sighing. "I don't know where I'm going to find time to make mine now that I'm working at the shop."

"I'll tell you what," Anna offered. "The light in our

room isn't the best, but perhaps we can spend a few evenings a week sewing up here together. And I'm happy to help sew yours if you find it becomes unmanageable while you're working at the shop."

"*Denki*, Anna." Melinda yawned. "I'd really appreciate that."

After a few minutes of silence, Anna was on the brink of sleep when Melinda mumbled, "I'm so happy you decided to buy your material even though you can't remember your groom. Aaron told me today that he didn't think Fletcher could handle another fiancée calling off the wedding. The first time nearly crushed him."

"What?" Anna whispered. When there was no reply, she asked again, "What did you just say?" but Melinda's breathing rose and fell in the steady pattern of sleep.

Anna listened to it all throughout the night as she tried to drum up a satisfactory reason for why Fletcher neglected to mention his previous fiancée. Instead, she just came up with additional questions, each one more alarming than the last: Why did Fletcher's first fiancée call their wedding off? If Anna had known the reason, would she still have agreed to marry him so quickly? Was there anything else he was keeping from her? If so, how would she know?

She was relieved when daylight filled the windows and she could rise and ready herself for church. The family squeezed into the buggy, three seated in the front and three seated in the back, with Evan balanced against Naomi's knees. This Sunday, they traveled to James and Amelia Hooley's home on the other end of town. Their basement was used as the gathering room for the worship service; afterward, the men flipped the benches, fashioning them into makeshift tables for lunch. Anna was eager to speak to the Fisher sisters and she figured she'd find them in the kitchen, helping serve and clean up.

"Look who's here!" Tessa exclaimed, nudging her sister.

"I'm Ka-tie," her other friend greeted her, pronouncing her name very slowly.

"And *I'm* sorry," Anna apologized. "I'm afraid you both must think me terribly rude—"

"It. Is. Okay," Katie enunciated loudly. "Why. Don't. You. Sit. Down?"

Anna didn't know what to make of Katie's manner of speaking. Did she always talk like that? She squinted at her.

Tessa explained in equally deliberate speech. "Please don't cry. We aren't angry with you. We know about your brain injury."

"Is that why you're talking like that?" Anna inquired, suddenly realizing their strange intonations were supposed to be for her benefit. "*Jah*, I had a traumatic brain injury, which is another name for a concussion, and I'm experiencing something called retrograde amnesia, but there's nothing wrong with my hearing, I'm not about to cry and I don't need to sit down."

Tessa threw her hands in the air. "Ach! Melinda told everyone at the shop your faculties haven't been the same since your fall. Oh dear, Anna, now *we're* the ones who are sorry!"

Katie covered her face with the dishtowel. "I'm so embarrassed I could cry!"

Anna should have known Melinda was at the heart of the misunderstanding—she was such a *bobblemoul*, as Evan would say! Nevertheless, she sympathized with her friends. "That's exactly how I felt when I learned I'd accidentally slighted each of you."

"It wasn't like you at all," admitted Tessa. "I couldn't understand why you were standing me up—we'd made a date to walk over to the mercantile during my break to look at material. I thought perhaps you'd changed your mind about asking me to be a *newehocker*."

"*Jah*, and when you made a remark about not being able to get past me at the door of the bakery, I took it as a judgment on my weight," Katie confessed. "Especially since I was carrying a load of goodies. Which, by the way, I was purchasing to bring here for dessert—it was my turn but I'd had a cold and I didn't want to spread germs by baking for everyone."

"*Neh*, not at all!" Anna assured them. "I simply couldn't—I *can't* remember any part of my life after August. The doctor says those memories may return soon and I hope they do because by all counts, I've heard we've had many *gut* times together."

"We still can," Katie suggested. "And nothing makes for a *gut* time like a treat from Faith Yoder's bakery. Follow me and I'll show you where I'm keeping a secret stash!"

Fletcher scanned the yard for Anna, wondering if she'd stepped outside for a breath of air. They had a long-standing practice of "bumping into each other" under the tallest tree in the church hosts' yards after he helped put the benches into the bench wagon and she participated in dish cleanup. He wondered if there was any chance she'd remember and meet him there that day. But beneath the Hooleys' oak, he happened upon his uncle instead of Anna.

"My knee acts up when I sit that long so I have to get out and move around," Isaiah explained to his nephew. "Especially when the weather is damp and dreary like it is today."

"It must run in the family," Fletcher replied. "My *daed* suffered from arthritis, too."

"*Jah*, I remember. Speaking of suffering, how is Anna?"

"She's not in much physical pain anymore, but her memory still hasn't returned."

"It will, son." His uncle's confidence was comforting. Isaiah continued, "She's young. It's not like when you get to be my age. The memory just goes. The other day I climbed down a ladder to get a tool and couldn't remember what I was looking for. I climbed back up, remembered, climbed back down and forgot again by the time I reached the landing."

"No wonder your knee hurts, with all that ladder climbing." Fletcher chuckled. Then he confided, "I wish it were just a single item Anna couldn't remember. But she doesn't remember events, she doesn't remember people… She doesn't remember me."

"*Mamm* sent me to round you up, *Daed*," Aaron interrupted, suddenly present at Fletcher's side. "One of the girls has a headache and needs to get home."

"*Jah*, alright. But speaking of headaches, if you need to take Anna to her doctor appointments, you go right ahead, Fletcher, you hear?" Isaiah ordered.

"I'm glad you mentioned that, because she has a follow-up appointment on Tuesday afternoon in Highland Springs. It's possible Naomi or Ray—"

"*Neh*, it's better if you're the one who brings Anna to Highland Springs," Isaiah interjected. "I trust you to manage your workload. As for Anna not remembering you, she will. Just wait a little longer, pray a little harder and keep spending every spare moment you can with her. Either way, the more she's with you, the more she'll know you. And as they say, to know you is to love you."

"*Denki*, *Onkel*, that's *gut* advice," Fletcher said as Isaiah clapped him on his shoulder before meandering away. He was heartened by his uncle's perspective.

"Like *Daed* said, it's okay if you leave early Tuesday afternoon, but you'll need to clear it with me in the future if you change your schedule," Aaron remarked. "You can't just leave the site without notifying anyone where you're going or when you'll be back."

"Of course," Fletcher agreed, even though he was thinking that Aaron was the one who left the work site without telling anyone where he was going. Upon waking that morning, Fletcher had asked the Lord to forgive him for his annoyance about Aaron's get-well gift, so he didn't want to slip back into a resentful attitude. He also prayed that while he waited for Anna's memory to return, he'd be able to maintain a more positive outlook about their future. "Have you seen Anna around?"

"She and the Fisher sisters were eating doughnuts on the side porch a few minutes ago."

Approaching the house, Fletcher heard the trio's laughter before he saw them. "That's the sound of old friends," he said as he hopped up the porch steps.

"Who are you calling old?" Katie teased him.

"I meant to say it's the sound of *gut* friends," Fletcher clarified. "*Gut* friends and *gut* women."

"For that, you may have the last doughnut." Tessa passed him a cream-filled pastry.

As Fletcher chewed, he noticed how reserved Anna seemed. She had dark circles under her eyes and he hoped he hadn't exhausted her with yesterday's activities. Or was there another reason she appeared fatigued? What happened after he left the previous evening? Did she remember something? Was it about Aaron? Determined not to let his dread get the best of him, he wiped his lips with the back of his hand and stood up.

"May I take you home, Anna?" he asked. "I know your family must have had a full buggy this morning."

"*Jah, denki*, Fletcher," she answered formally. "*Mach's. Gut.* Ka-tie. And. Tes-sa," she said slowly, and for some reason, this elicited peals of laughter from the Fisher sisters.

"Why did you use a funny voice when you said goodbye to Katie and Tessa?" Fletcher asked conversationally as they rode away.

"It was a private joke," was Anna's terse reply.

"Oh, I understand," Fletcher said, although usually Anna enjoyed sharing her funny stories with him.

"*Jah*, I figured you might, since you like to keep certain matters private yourself," she replied stiffly.

Now Fletcher knew something was wrong. He jerked the reins, causing the horse to detour down a gravelly side road overlooking a meadow where stubbles of crocuses, tulips and wildflowers were beginning to poke through the rich soil.

When they stopped, he said, "If there's something troubling you, Anna, I wish you'd tell me outright."

"Ha!" she declared. "You're one to talk, considering what you haven't told me!"

"I honestly have no idea what you're referring to."

"I'm referring to the one very important, very personal thing you neglected to tell me!" Anna harrumphed, crossing her arms over her chest.

Fletcher was utterly baffled. Was the issue that was upsetting Anna now the same issue that caused her to write the note? "I'm sorry, but I still don't know what you're talking about."

"I'm talking about your first fiancée," she said, staring straight ahead.

Fletcher noticed he'd curled his fingers into a fist. The mention of Joyce always caused him to tense up. He loosely shook his hands and then rested them on his knees. "What about her?"

"Then you don't deny you were engaged to someone else before me?"

Fletcher snickered. "Of course I don't deny it. I told you all about her shortly after we first met."

Anna wasn't satisfied. "Perhaps, but why didn't you tell me about her after my accident?" she pressed. "You knew I wouldn't have remembered hearing about her."

Fletcher's temper flared, imagining how Anna might have learned about his first engagement. "Who has been telling you about these things from my past anyway? Was it Aaron? Melinda?" he guessed. "Or did you find your diary and read something there?"

"The question isn't who told me about your past, Fletcher. The question is why didn't *you* tell me about it?"

"It didn't seem important," he stated.

"Not important?" she challenged. "How can you say being engaged isn't important?"

She was sobbing into her hands now, and Fletcher recalled Dr. Donovan's concern about unprovoked emotional outbursts. He was worried that this might qualify. Then he realized that if it did, he also probably needed to consult a doctor because he felt disproportionately emotional, too. He had to calm down himself if he was going to be a comfort to Anna.

"Anna," he said, nudging her shoulder with his. "I didn't tell you about my allergy to mushrooms, either. Now *that* was important, but I didn't bring it up because at the time, it didn't seem relevant. That's the phrase I should have used. My first engagement didn't seem relevant."

Anna's giggle reassured Fletcher there was no need to seek medical attention: her tears had nothing to do with her concussion. His mind eased, he offered her a handkerchief, and soon her sniffing had quieted and she'd dabbed her cheeks dry.

"I'm sorry," she apologized and carefully folded the handkerchief into a triangle, ashamed to face him. "I didn't sleep a wink last night, but even so, that wasn't a very mature way for me to approach this topic."

"I should be more understanding," Fletcher acknowledged. "I can't imagine what it feels like to lose your memory."

"It feels like the sky looks," Anna said, pointing to the white, overcast expanse. "It feels vast and empty and colorless. I want to remember, but when I try, there's nothing there."

"Then it's up to me to do a better job of filling in the blanks," Fletcher stated firmly. "Joyce Beiler was the name of my first fiancée. We courted for a year and although in hindsight I wouldn't say we were in love, I did care deeply for her and believed she felt the same way about me. Anyway, the summer before we decided to get married, Joyce's brother-in-law's cousin, Frederick, came to live with him and Joyce's sister, to help with growing and harvest seasons. I thought it was only natural that Joyce spent a lot of time with Frederick, since she was responsible for helping her sister and brother-in-law at the farm, too."

Noticing Fletcher's voice drop, Anna said softly, "It's okay, you needn't explain. I think I understand what happened."

But Fletcher cleared his throat and continued talking. "Eventually, I had a conversation—I had *several* conversations—with Joyce about my concerns, but she assured me she felt nothing but a sisterly type of fondness for Frederick. She and I completed our meetings with the deacon and announced our wedding intentions to our families and to the *leit* in church. Four days before the wedding, she told me she couldn't go through with it—she was in love with Frederick."

Anna gasped and touched Fletcher's forearm. "Oh! That must have been so painful for you."

"It was." He grimaced and hung his head. "At the time it felt personally excruciating and publicly disgraceful. I have to admit, I was relieved to leave Green Lake."

Anna understood only too well; Aaron's betrayal had wounded her deeply, too. But her relationship with Aaron hadn't progressed nearly as far as Fletcher's relationship had with Joyce, nor was the reason behind Anna's breakup public knowledge. She winced to imagine the extent of disbelief, disappointment and dejection—not to mention, embarrassment—Fletcher must have had to overcome, and her admiration for him burgeoned.

The air was silent except for the sound of the horse occasionally swishing his tail or shuffling his hooves, and after a few moments, Anna apologized. "I wish I hadn't made you relive that memory."

"It was necessary in order for me to clear it up with you," he replied. "I have nothing to hide so I don't want you to feel as if I'm keeping anything from you. I don't want you to feel as if there's something you need to keep from me, either. No matter what it is."

"Of course," Anna pledged pensively, noting the edge in Fletcher's tone. Did he think she was keeping something from him? If so, what? There was no other man in her life. The only person she'd ever walked out with was Aaron, and they'd broken up more than six months before Fletcher arrived in town. Since Fletcher was Anna's intended, she assumed she must have confided her intimate secrets to him, just as he'd confided his to her. That meant she must have told him what happened with Aaron and Melinda, didn't it? But, maybe she hadn't. Without asking, she couldn't be certain.

"What have I told you about my past?" Anna questioned.

Fletcher looked taken aback. "What do you mean?"

"I must have told you things about my life, but I can't remember what they are. What do you know about me?"

Fletcher wiped his upper lip. "Well, you told me about your *mamm* dying when you were a *bobbel* and how your *daed* and you lived with your *groossmammi* until she passed, too. I know that your *daed* married Naomi when you were sixteen, and it was a big adjustment for you to suddenly have four brothers around. You felt as if they were forever underfoot or spying on you."

Anna giggled. "Sometimes, I still feel that way about Eli and Evan."

"*Jah*, but you also said that helping Naomi care for them as young *kinner* made you eager to have *bobblin* of your own one day."

"What did I tell you about Melinda?"

Fletcher tilted his head from side to side, as if to work a kink out of his neck, before he said, "You said her *daed* sent her to stay with you because she was getting into trouble during her running-around period. He thought you might be a *gut* influence on her, since her *mamm* died long ago and she hadn't any female relatives living nearby."

"Go on," she prompted him.

"You tried to set a *gut* example and invited her to attend social events with you and Aaron, whom you'd been walking out with for about two and a half years. But then last February, you discovered Melinda and Aaron, um…"

Anna concluded his sentence for him, "Kissing behind the stable."

"Jah," Fletcher acknowledged.

"Did I tell you how I felt about that?"

"How you felt?" he repeated hesitantly. "Anna, are you sure you want to relive this?"

"I have no need to relive it—I already distinctly remember that part of my life. It happened long before my accident. What I want is to know what I told you about it. As your betrothed, I must have confided my innermost secrets in you. What did I tell you?" she challenged.

"You told me you were devastated at first, of course. But you said you soon realized it wasn't that Aaron had broken your heart as much as he'd broken your trust that pained you. Compared with losing your *daed*, you said ending your courtship with Aaron was easy. That's how you knew you hadn't truly been in love with him—because losing Aaron didn't split your heart in half."

"That's right." Anna nodded, contented to confirm

Fletcher knew exactly how she felt. "What else did I tell you about the months following the breakup and my *daed*'s death?"

Fletcher's voice was gentle with compassion. "You told me spring was a blur. That everyone said how strong you were in the wake of your *daed*'s passing, caring for Naomi and the boys and putting up with Melinda's antics besides. You told me your secret was that you made yourself numb and kept as busy as you could. You said the only thing you looked forward to was the half hour you allowed yourself each day to weep in private—in the hayloft during the spring, and then beneath the willow by the creek in the warmer summer months. Which, as I've indicated, is where we first met."

Anna's eyes smarted. *I must have trusted him whole-heartedly to confide those emotions in him*, she realized.

Aloud, she said in a raspy voice, "*Denki* for telling me all that. It helps me to know we've both shared our feelings and experiences so openly."

"Of course," Fletcher replied. Although time would tell if she'd come to remember she hadn't quite been open about sharing *all* of her feelings, he was grateful for the sense of calm that seemed to have settled over Anna. He wouldn't have forgiven himself if she'd gotten so upset they needed to call Dr. Donovan.

"Melinda told me I've seemed prickly since my accident," Anna said, interrupting his thoughts. "I don't mean to be that way, but it's frustrating trying to make sense of things. So I'll probably continue to ask you a lot of questions."

"Please do. As I said, we spent our early courting days down by the creek, just talking. We told each other all about our dreams and disappointments, our triumphs and our failures. We used to spend hours talking about our faith and our families, and we shared other details from our lives, too. For example, I even know that when you were a girl, you believed lightning bugs were actually made out of lightning."

"You mean they're not?" Anna laughed before requesting, "Now tell me some little thing I know about you that I don't know I know about you."

Relieved to engage in a little levity after such an intense discussion, Fletcher pushed up his coat sleeve and lifted his arm. "See this scar? You know that I got it hurtling over a fence."

"Who was chasing you?"

"It wasn't a *who*, it was a *what*. It was Thistle, the neighbor's goat, to be precise."

"Ach! The mischievous animal!"

"Actually, I was the one who was mischievous. I was taking a shortcut, which amounted to trespassing. My first and last time."

"How old were you?"

"Oh, around twenty-two," Fletcher said.

"*Neh!*" Anna exclaimed. "Really?"

"*Neh,*" he admitted. "Not really. I was about eight or nine. Definitely old enough to know better."

Laughing, Anna asked, "Did I confess any of my wayward escapades to you?"

"Only that you once burned your finger snatching an

oatmeal cookie from your *groossmammi*'s oven. And that you used to climb trees to hide on your brothers."

"I still do that sometimes."

"Really?" Fletcher questioned.

"*Neh*, not really," Anna echoed impishly. "I'd like to think my behavior is a little more mature than that now. Although I haven't forgotten how to climb so I still could if I wanted to."

"Perhaps in warmer weather, you'll teach me, then," Fletcher suggested, caught up in their whimsical banter. "That's one skill I never mastered. I have a slight fear of heights, which isn't one of the best qualities in a carpenter, so please don't tell Melinda. I don't want Aaron finding out about it and giving me a hard time. On the job, I do whatever needs to be done, including roofing—but how I feel about doing it is our little secret."

"I won't tell a soul, especially not Melinda," Anna agreed conspiratorially. "I don't think she intends any harm, but she has a habit of blurting things out before she's really thought them through."

"I've noticed that, too," Fletcher said. "Not only does she seem to share things she shouldn't, but half the time her perspective isn't exactly reliable."

"Is that why we were so discreet about our relationship, because we didn't want her to tell everyone and share her thoughts on the matter?" Anna wondered aloud.

"That was one of the reasons, I suppose," Fletcher confirmed. "I had similar misgivings about Aaron finding out. It was also that you wanted to be respectful of

Naomi's mourning period. I think you felt a little guilty for being so happy when…"

"When my *daed* had recently died?"

"*Jah.* But there were a few people who knew we were courting early on, before we officially told our families."

"Who?"

"Well, Tessa and Katie. And my *groossdaadi.* Mind you, I never told him myself. He just knew. After you'd visit, he'd say, 'Fletcher, your Anna makes the best beef barley soup I've tasted since your *groossmammi* was alive.' Or, 'Your Anna's eyes were sure sparkling today, weren't they, Fletcher?' It was always 'your Anna,' not just 'Anna.' We never discussed it, but I think that was his way of letting me know he knew we were courting and he approved."

"I'm glad—on both counts," Anna said, rubbing her hands together.

The tip of her nose was pink and Fletcher's heartbeat quickened as he regarded the brightness of her lips, recalling how silky they used to feel against his own.

Her voice cut through his thoughts. "I'm afraid I'm getting a little chilly."

"Me, too," he said reluctantly. He picked up the reins and directed the horse back onto the roadway so he could drop Anna off and head toward his own house. The rhythmic cadence of the horse's clopping along the road made his eyelids droop and he decided that when he got home, he'd lie down for a much needed nap. After stabling the horse, he realized he'd had such a full day with Anna on Saturday that he'd neglected to collect the mail that evening. Checking the box, he found an envelope addressed in penmanship he didn't immediately recognize. He quickly read its contents.

Fletcher,
We've received the invitation to your wedding from Anna, along with the note from you asking us to be your *newehockers*. We already have our suits from the last time you almost got married, so how could we say no?

In all sincerity, we're both glad you found a good woman and we look forward to meeting her and celebrating your marriage.

We expect to arrive on Monday, the sixth of April.
Your friends,
Chandler Schlabach & Gabriel Ropp.

In the turmoil following Anna's accident, Fletcher had forgotten he'd asked Chandler and Gabriel to be his *newehockers*. Recalling how supportive they'd been after his wedding debacle with Joyce, he knew their reference to it was intended lightly, and he was grateful he had friends who'd gladly make such a long journey on his behalf. Still, the remark touched upon his concerns that this wedding might not happen, either.

Yet as his head sunk into the pillow, he was cautiously upbeat as he reflected on the discussion he'd just had with Anna. Simply repeating what she'd told him about her breakup with Aaron made Fletcher feel more confident. Nothing about Anna's comments or behavior, past or present, indicated she held any enduring affection for his cousin. Fletcher still didn't know what to make of Anna's note, but maybe it was time for him to stop worrying about it. Perhaps the note only represented a single moment of hesitation, compared to an entire courtship of certainty. Could it be that today's conversation with Anna was further proof that there was nothing the two of them couldn't work out together if they talked it through? As Isaiah suggested, the best course of action might be to spend as much time with Anna as he could. *To know me is to love me*, he thought drowsily.

His mind made up, Fletcher felt more relaxed than he had since Anna's accident and he drifted into a languorous snooze.

Chapter Six

The house appeared to be deserted when Anna entered it, but she knew from experience that even if Melinda and the boys were out, it was likely Naomi was resting in her room. Tiptoeing down the hall, Anna hoped her stepmother wasn't relapsing into a period of depression and fatigue. If Naomi was sleeping, she didn't wish to rouse her, but if she was awake, Anna hoped she could be of some comfort.

"Are you asleep?" she asked quietly as she paused outside the closed bedroom door.

"I'll be right there," her stepmother called and Anna heard the patter of footsteps followed by what sounded like a drawer closing. When Naomi opened the door, her face was flushed. "Oh, *gut*, it's you, Anna."

"I'm sorry to disturb you. I wanted to see if you were alright and if there's anything I can do for you."

"Anna, dear, you're always so considerate of me, but I'm fine," Naomi said. She stepped aside and motioned Anna into the bedroom. "Actually, I was in here looking for some fabric. Mind you, I wasn't sewing on the Sabbath—I was only looking to assess what I might have left over. I wanted to make new trousers for Raymond, as I've let down the hems in his church pants as far as they'll go and today I noticed they're still too short. I remembered starting a pair for your *daed* that I never finished. I'd tucked the material away until I could face seeing it again. While I was searching for it today, I found this. I'd forgotten all about it..."

She opened the bottom drawer of her bureau and removed a thick, neatly folded bundle of eggplant-colored fabric.

"Oh! That would be such a becoming color on you, Naomi," Anna replied, fingering the material. "Are you going to make yourself a new dress?"

Naomi's eyes shimmered. "I haven't sewn a dress for myself in so long, I've forgotten my measurements!"

"Then it's past time for you to have one."

Naomi laughed. "That's exactly the kind of remark your *daed* would have made, Anna."

"Well, he would have been right. Anyway, now that you've found the material, it would be wasteful to allow it to continue to sit in the drawer."

"You know what?" Naomi asked, patting the fabric. "I think I *will* make a new dress for myself. A wedding is such a special occasion and I'll wear the dress again to church for years."

Naomi's exuberance delighted Anna. In the past when her stepmother mentioned Anna's *daed*, she sounded so forlorn but today she conveyed only a sense of mirth and anticipation for the future, and her hopefulness felt contagious. Naomi set the material atop her sewing basket and the two women ambled into the kitchen for a cup of tea.

"Where are the boys this afternoon?" Anna asked.

"The four of them loped off to the creek. Roy and Raymond wanted to practice their casting and Eli and Evan tagged along for the fun of it. They were all hoping Fletcher might *kumme* down and join them for a while, too."

"He would have enjoyed that, but he left after he dropped me off."

Naomi narrowed her eyes. "Is something the matter? I assumed he'd stay for supper. We're only having leftovers because it's the Sabbath, but I figure our leftovers are tastier than whatever he might make on his own."

"*Neh*, nothing's wrong," Anna assured her. "I think he didn't want to wear out his *wilkom*, that's all."

"Ach! That's because I was so cranky the other night, isn't it? I didn't mean to be inhospitable, but I was short-tempered because of Melinda's comments. The truth is, both she and Aaron seem to be lacking in diligence. I think if they spent less time frolicking and more time tending to their responsibilities at home, instead of just those at their paid jobs, they'd have a better idea of what it means to manage a household. But it wasn't charitable of me to chase Aaron away as I did and I certainly wasn't hinting that Fletcher should go, too."

"I doubt Fletcher thought twice about leaving when he did," Anna replied. "As it was, I think he was surprised to be invited for supper since he'd already had dinner with us. He wouldn't take advantage of your generosity—he's very considerate in general."

"*Jah*, but I want you both to know he has an open invitation to join us for dinner or supper whenever he pleases. I know how important it is for the two of you to…to get to know each other again."

"*Denki*, Naomi, I'll tell him that," Anna said as she lifted the whistling kettle from the front burner of the gas stove. "I have my follow-up doctor's appointment Tuesday afternoon, which he intends to take me to. It would be convenient if he could eat with us that evening, since we'll be returning home around five thirty or six o'clock."

"Of course," Naomi agreed, arranging several thimble cookies on a plate. "So, have you learned anything else about him other than that he's 'very considerate in general'?"

Anna carried the teacups to the table. Although she and Naomi shared an unusual closeness, most Amish couples in their district seldom discussed their romantic relationships.

"Well," she said, hesitating. Then her face broke into a huge grin. "I think the most important thing I've discovered is the more I know him, the more I like him."

"Look at you blush," Naomi gushed. "That's *wunderbaar*. Then do you still plan to marry him even if your memories don't fully return by your wedding date?"

"Oh, I haven't given up hope that my memories will *kumme* back!"

"That's what I'm praying will happen, too, and I

have faith *Gott* will answer our prayers in His time and in His way."

Anna pensively bit into a cookie. After she swallowed, she said, "I guess at this point—without having my memories restored—I'd say I might not be ready to marry Fletcher yet, but I can clearly see he has the qualities I'd want in a husband." She was referring to his fortitude and candor, and to how respectful, protective and understanding he'd shown himself to be.

"And are you drawn to him?"

"Drawn to him?" Anna repeated, drizzling honey into her tea.

"A number of men might have the qualities you'd desire in a husband, but they don't set your heart aflutter," Naomi stated candidly.

Anna thought of how her heart melted within—like honey in tea—whenever Fletcher's eyes met hers. *"Jah,"* she said, "I'm drawn to him."

"Then it sounds as if you just need a little more time," Naomi suggested.

"Or for my memories to return," Anna replied, frowning. "Although I'd settle for finding my journal. As fond as I'm growing of Fletcher, I'm still surprised I made the decision to marry him so quickly."

"It's wise to know someone well before committing to marriage, but knowing someone well doesn't necessarily mean having a long courtship," Naomi reasoned. "I only knew your *daed* for four months before I married him. I had a solid sense of his character from the first day I met him and that never changed. I loved your *daed* early on and I knew he loved me. We were meant for each other. There was no other way to explain it and no other explanation needed."

Anna kissed Naomi's forehead as she stood to bring the empty teacups to the sink. "I'm so blessed you and my *daed* got married, Naomi. I'm sorry for how cross I acted that first year because I had to give up my bedroom to Raymond and Roy."

Naomi laughed. "You've more than made up for it by sharing your room with Melinda so graciously." Then, in a serious tone, she said, "I must admit I hoped— even prayed—Melinda and Aaron might have second thoughts about getting married. I think they both could benefit from maturing a little individually before they begin a life together as husband and wife."

"Well, as you've been reminding me, there's still time…"

Anna's comments were disrupted by the sound of footsteps on the porch as the four boys burst through the mudroom into the kitchen.

"Don't worry, *Mamm*, Evan's fine, he's just wet," Raymond immediately announced as he placed his soggy brother down on the floor.

"And cold," Evan said, shivering.

"Haven't we had enough accidents in this family? Didn't I warn you to keep a close eye on him?" Naomi upbraided Raymond and Roy as she rushed Evan to the washroom for a hot bath.

As Anna pulled plates from the cupboard to set the table for supper, she couldn't help but think that if Fletcher had gone fishing with the boys, he would have snatched Evan out of the creek before the boy had a chance to get wet. Because not only did Fletcher have the most striking eyes she'd ever gazed into, but Anna noticed he had particularly strong arms, too.

On Monday morning, Raymond delivered a note to Fletcher from Anna. *Fletcher,* it said, *would you like to join us for supper? I'm making meat loaf and brown-butter mashed potatoes, with butterscotch cream pie for dessert. Naomi wanted to be sure you know you are* wilkom *to join us. —Anna.*

Fletcher's mouth watered at the thought of Anna's cooking, but he had to decline. He had to work late in order to make up for the time he'd miss the next day when he left early to take Anna to Highland Springs. As it was, he, Aaron, Raymond and Roy would have to struggle to keep up with their contracts. The trim Aaron ordered for the first site wasn't delivered that morning, so Aaron suggested they temporarily abandon the location to begin working on the new project at a second site. Fletcher was concerned the first customer would be upset by the delay in the completion of the assignment, but Aaron shrugged it off.

"It's unfortunate, *jah*, but when I explain to the customer that our supplier hasn't delivered the trim yet, he'll understand," Aaron said. "The *Englisch* crews are usually much farther behind their deadlines than we are, so the customer won't think twice about it."

Fletcher had gritted his teeth. Aaron was a good carpenter, but he lacked the kind of drive and the organizational skills his father possessed. If Isaiah had been managing this project, he would have seen to it the supplies were ordered ahead of time.

"Perhaps, but our purpose is to honor our word and bring glory to *Gott*, not merely to do better than our *Englisch* competitors," he reminded his cousin.

"If you're so worried about it, tonight you can stop at the lumber store after you're done making up your time and ask the clerk to expedite the order. I've also made a list of supplies we need for our next job. Most of it is small enough to load into your buggy. The rest they can deliver with the trim."

"How will I pay for it?" Fletcher asked.

"Here, take the card. Just sign the receipt 'Chupp,' like you usually do."

Fletcher knew he was the only crew member Aaron entrusted with this task, but it wasn't a job Fletcher appreciated being assigned. The purchasing of supplies was usually the foreman's responsibility. Fletcher was only willing to do it because it would expedite progress on their customers' projects. It wasn't until later in the evening, when he was alone, wolfing down a cheese and bologna sandwich, that it dawned on Fletcher what the real reason was Aaron tasked him with visiting the lumber store that evening: Aaron didn't want go himself because he feared he'd miss the opportunity to be invited to Melinda's house for supper. In fact, he was probably devouring a thick slice of Anna's meat loaf at that very moment.

Fletcher relished Anna's cooking, knowing the satisfaction she took in providing healthful, tasty meals for her family, her friends or *leit* in the church who happened to be visiting or ailing. Yet he realized even she needed a break from her responsibilities from time to time, and he decided he'd like to treat her to supper out after her doctor's appointment. It would be a surprise—a good one, for once.

The very thought carried him through his work that evening and the following day, and before he knew it, he was knocking at her door. Knowing Naomi would fret if he and Anna were late returning from the medical center, but anticipating he might not be able to speak to Naomi in private, Fletcher carried a folded note. *Naomi,* it read, *I'd like to surprise Anna by taking her out for dinner after her appointment. We may not be returning until later in the evening. Is that okay with you? —Fletcher.*

When Anna went to retrieve her shawl, Fletcher slipped Naomi the note and gestured for her to read it. She quickly scanned the slip of paper and crumpled it in her fist just as Anna came back into the room. With a wink at Fletcher, Naomi bid them goodbye. They were about to board the buggy when she called from the porch, "Be careful and have an *appenditlich* time, you two!"

Waving back at her, Anna asked Fletcher, "What do you think she meant by that?"

Fletcher recalled the time he told Anna she smelled *appenditlich* and his cheeks burned. Avoiding her question as he assisted her into the buggy, he advised, "Watch your step."

The sunlight played off the trees, which waved their branches in a light breeze, and the landscape was beginning to blossom with azaleas, crocuses and daffodils. As Fletcher and Anna passed them, he recognized how much more buoyant he was during this trip than he'd been the last time he'd taken Anna to Highland Springs, and he hummed a few measures of the hymn they'd sung in church on Sunday.

"How are you feeling, Anna?" Dr. Donovan asked when he entered the exam room.

"Wunderbaar," Anna answered in Pennsylvania Dutch. She quickly clarified, for the doctor's benefit, "I mean, wonderful."

Dr. Donovan's round cheeks grew even rounder when he chuckled. "Even if I hadn't known what you meant by the word *wunderbaar*, I could have guessed by the color in your cheeks and the glint in your eye. *Wunderbaar* is a big improvement from *fine*, isn't it?"

"It is," Anna agreed.

After questioning her about any ongoing nausea or headaches, he told her to hop onto the examining table, where he looked into her eyes and quickly tested her reflexes before telling her to take a seat in the chair next to Fletcher again.

"Physically, you're in great shape," the doctor reported. "I'm glad to hear the nausea has subsided. The dull headaches you mentioned are probably a sign you're doing a bit more focused concentrating than you ought to be doing. Have you been heeding my advice not to do too much sewing or reading?"

"Oh, I haven't been reading at all," Anna stated with a wide-eyed innocent look.

"Aha!" Dr. Donovan pointed his finger in mock accusation, grinning. "You'll need to cut back on sewing, then. I'd advise that you don't return to your job at the shop yet, either. Now, how about your memories, have they returned yet?"

Anna shook her head. "Not yet."

"Hmm," the doctor murmured thoughtfully. "Well, they still might. Although, as I said before, there's no guarantee. But something tells me the two of you may have gotten reacquainted, perhaps rediscovered some of the qualities in each other that made you fall in love in the first place. Am I right?"

Anna modestly dipped her head so Fletcher answered for them both, saying, "We've enjoyed spending time together recently, *jah*."

"Wunderbaar!" Dr. Donovan exclaimed, smacking his desktop, and Anna and Fletcher both laughed. "Have faith and keep heading forward and things will turn out alright, one way or the other."

While Anna was scheduling an appointment to return in four weeks, Fletcher went to retrieve the buggy from the lot. After picking her up, he skillfully maneuvered the horse through the heavy traffic along the main road. Oddly feeling as skittish as he did the first time he formally asked to court her, he didn't speak until they turned down a side street.

"If you're hungry, I'd like to take you to supper," he said.

"Denki, that's a very nice invitation," Anna replied slowly, as if considering the offer, "but Naomi will grow concerned if we're not back by six or six thirty."

"It's okay, I cleared it with her first," Fletcher confessed.

"Really? You're so thoughtful!" Anna said, clasping her hands and shuffling her feet. "Is there a special place we've frequented?"

"*Neh.* We've never actually eaten out together, but I think it's time to do something new to both of us, not just new to you. Don't you agree?"

"I'd like that," Anna said and Fletcher stared into her eyes so long a driver from behind tapped on his horn to indicate the signal light had turned green.

They chose to dine at a pizza place Anna had heard some *Englisch* customers rave about in Schrock's Shop, and the food lived up to the recommendation. Together Anna and Fletcher polished off a medium Hawaiian pizza as well as a pitcher of root beer, which gave Anna hiccups that lasted all the way home.

"*Gut nacht*, Fletcher," she said when he walked her to her door. "I *hic*—had an absolutely *scrumptious* time. *Hic.*"

By the time he turned in for the night, Fletcher's jaw ached from grinning but he still couldn't stop smiling. Their evening out seemed to underscore what Dr. Donovan suggested: Anna and Fletcher needed to move forward, not backward. They needed to have faith and to focus on the future, not on the past. As the doctor said, there was no guarantee Anna's memory would ever return. If not, she wouldn't ever be able to tell him what she'd meant when she sent her note the day of her accident. But since nothing about her actions or attitude indicated any special affinity for Aaron, Fletcher decided it was time to put the note behind him for good. He turned off the lamp and floated into sleep.

On Wednesday, Anna woke to the thrumming of rain on the rooftop and the low rumble of distant thunder, which struck her as odd. It seemed early in the season for thunder. The last storm they had was in October, on Fletcher's birthday. She lay there thinking about how upset she'd been when the cloudburst ruined her carefully planned picnic beneath the willow at the creek. Making a dash for Fletcher's buggy, she'd tripped on a tree root, stumbling face-first toward the ground. When Fletcher lunged to catch her, he'd dropped the basket he'd been carrying, upending its contents beside her. They both ended up splattered with cake and mud. She wondered how she ever explained her appearance to her family that day.

Then she sat bolt upright in bed: she had remembered something from the last six months!

She tucked her hair into her prayer *kapp* and knelt by her bed. "Dear Lord, *denki* for restoring my memory. *Denki, denki, denki!*"

"Shh," Melinda groaned. "I can't take a nap in the middle of the day like you can and I still need to sleep."

"But I remembered! I remembered!" Anna said, shaking her cousin's shoulders. When she elicited no further response, she dressed and hopped down the stairs and into the kitchen.

"I remembered something!" she announced, hugging Naomi, who was standing at the stove scrambling eggs.

"*Gott* is *gut*," Naomi proclaimed, dropping her

wooden spoon to take Anna's face in her hands. "See? It just took time."

"Why are you two crying?" Raymond asked when he entered the room.

Anna leaped to hug him. "Because *Gott* is *gut*!"

"What's all the noise? Is there a party going on in here?" Roy asked a few seconds later.

"Not yet, but there will be tonight, if your *mamm* allows it," Anna said. "We'll invite Fletcher, Aaron, Katie and Tessa for supper and a cake. I'll buy the ingredients and do all of the work myself, I promise."

"Anna, you know what the doctor said about overexertion—"

"He only warned me about up close activities. Besides, it won't be any different than preparing a meal for our family—it will just be a bigger meal. If I truly need help, Katie and Tessa will pitch in," Anna countered. "I had a great sleep last night and I'm obviously getting better or else I wouldn't have experienced one of my memories returning."

Eli rubbed his eyes as he took his seat. "Your memory came back?"

"Now maybe you'll remember what happened to Timothy!" Evan added, picking up a fork.

"It was only a single memory and it wasn't about your turtle, Evan, but it's still a cause for celebration."

"*Jah*, okay," Naomi agreed. "As long as you don't overdo it."

"*Denki,*" Anna said. "I'll drop Melinda off, so I can go to the market. She can invite Tessa and Katie when she sees Tessa at work. They'll probably give her a ride home, too. Raymond, I'll give you a note to give to Fletcher. But whatever anyone does, you mustn't let him know I started to remember again—even after he arrives here. I have an idea for how I want to surprise him with the news. So, mum's the word, right, Eli and Evan?"

"Right," said Evan, pretending to seal his lips shut. Then out of one corner of his mouth, he squeaked, "I won't say a word."

"You'd better not," Eli warned. "Terrible things happen when you spy or share other people's secrets."

"I don't know if that's true," Anna commented as she searched a drawer for a piece of paper. She and Naomi were concerned about Melinda's influence on the younger boys, so they'd been trying to teach Eli and Evan the value of discretion, but Anna wondered if they'd been too strict on the subject. "I would just appreciate it if we kept this a secret. This way, we'll all have the pleasure of seeing the surprised look on Fletcher's face!"

Dearest Fletcher, she wrote on a piece of paper. *Please come to supper tonight at six. You will like what I am making. —Your Anna.* Sealing the note with a piece of tape, she instructed Raymond to give it to Fletcher as soon as he got to the work site.

"And please tell Aaron he's invited, too," she added, knowing that when Melinda finally dragged herself from bed, she'd be as pleased about her fiancé joining them for supper as Anna was about hers.

Fletcher began whistling the moment after reading Anna's message. It wasn't just that he was happy he'd get to see her again this evening; it was that she used not one but *two* terms of endearment in her note. Even before her accident, she was careful about what she expressed to him in writing. She said she trusted Raymond not to read her messages, but she wasn't as certain she always trusted him to remember to deliver the notes and she didn't want her "sweet nothings" ending up in someone else's hands by accident.

He was still whistling when he, Raymond and Roy packed up their tools for the day. Despite the fact that Aaron had left early to go to the lumber store again, they were managing to keep on schedule with their new project. Anna's *daed* had trained the boys well. They were hard workers and applied whatever techniques he taught them. Raymond was already nearly as handy of a carpenter as Aaron was, and what he lacked in skill, he made up for in perseverance.

"It's rainy, getting dark and there's a lot of traffic. Roy, you need more practice," Fletcher instructed, handing the boy the reins.

Roy gladly accepted the responsibility and soon they were situating Fletcher's buggy next to Tessa and Katie's at the Weavers' house. As Fletcher was hitching the horse to the post, Aaron arrived.

"Looks like quite a gathering," Fletcher remarked, pulling a carrot from a sack he kept for the animal. "It should be a pleasant evening."

"*Jah*, provided Anna doesn't sicken anyone with her cooking tonight." Aaron laughed. "Although Katie Fisher probably eats the most, so she's in the greatest danger."

Fletcher didn't know whether Aaron's remarks were

intended to be as derisive as they sounded or if they were only another misguided attempt at humor. "I wish you wouldn't talk about Anna or her friends like that. Or anyone else, for that matter," he said. "Some of your remarks aren't funny. They're unkind."

"If I'm so unkind and unfunny, why did Anna date me for almost three years?" Aaron asked as water dripped off the brim of his hat. Then he answered his own question. "She dated me because she liked me."

Surprised but undaunted by his cousin's bluster, Fletcher lifted his chin and straightened his posture. "And yet, she's marrying *me*," he said defiantly.

"Only because I chose to walk out with Melinda instead," Aaron challenged. He patted his horse on the flank before adding, "And whether or not Anna marries you is yet to be seen." Then he strode toward the house.

Fletcher removed his hat and looked toward the sky, allowing the rain to cool both his skin and his temper before he joined the others inside. *Please, Lord, forgive me my anger. Give me patience and bless our fellowship tonight.*

"*Denki*, Naomi, for having me over again," he said after he'd removed his muddy boots and was standing in the kitchen.

"This is all Anna's doing," Naomi explained, "but you're always *wilkom*, Fletcher."

As Anna glided into the room, he noticed her eyes were luminous and her creamy complexion was tinged with pink. He sensed something about her had changed. Rather, something was very much the same as it used to be. He didn't know exactly what it was, but the width of her smile was accentuated by the sincerity of her tone when she said, "Hello, Fletcher. I'm very glad to see you again."

After they were seated, said grace and filled their plates with creamed chicken, noodles and chow chow, Katie complimented Anna. "This chicken is so yummy. You've done something different with the recipe, haven't you?"

To Fletcher's consternation, Aaron butted in, spouting, "*Jah*, she left all of the poisonous ingredients out this time."

Before Fletcher could defend Anna, she was gripped with paroxysms of laughter and then Eli and Evan were, too. Their laughter was so infectious it wasn't long before Katie and Tessa were clutching their sides, although they had no idea why, so Anna recounted the incident, with the younger boys performing an exaggerated re-enactment that included Fletcher's eyes bulging before he fainted to the floor, gasping for air.

Whether Anna realized it or not, her ability to turn something that was intended as a barb into a source of amusement was one of her former qualities he deeply appreciated, and Fletcher chuckled in spite of himself. The rest of the meal was also accentuated by spirited conversation and peals of laughter. Afterward, Katie and Tessa cleared the dishes from the table while Anna prepared the dessert.

"Okay, now, Evan," she said to her youngest brother, who dimmed the lamp.

Fletcher didn't understand why until Anna turned from the counter balancing a large cake aglow with candles. *She looks so pretty*, he thought. *But I wonder whose birthday it is.*

"Happy birthday to you," Katie started to sing.

Although he didn't know who they were singing to, Fletcher joined the others. He was surprised when Anna hovered near his shoulder and everyone sang, "Happy birthday, dear Fletcher, happy birthday to you."

"Denki," he said hesitantly when she placed the cake in front of him. He didn't want to embarrass her in front of everyone by telling her it wasn't his birthday.

"Make a wish and then blow them out," she instructed merrily.

As soon as he extinguished the candles, everyone burst into applause. When Naomi turned up the lamp again, he noticed the cake Anna had prepared was his favorite: turtle cake, a gooey, melt-in-your-mouth chocolate cake that included pecans, chocolate chips and caramel.

"This is a *wunderbaar* celebration!" he said, "I haven't had turtle cake since—"

"Since I made one for your actual birthday in October and you were carrying it and you tripped. We both ended up wearing it instead of eating it," Anna said, her eyes gleaming.

"That's right. You were so—" Fletcher began to speak but his mouth dropped open midsentence. "Anna! You remembered?"

She nodded and his heart palpitated. He was torn between feelings of absolute jubilance that Anna might begin to remember their courtship and utter despondency that she might also recall her hesitance to marry him.

"Stop catching flies," Aaron ribbed him. "Don't you have anything to say?"

"You remembered?" he asked again, quieter this time, staring into Anna's eyes.

"I remembered," she confirmed. "I still can't recall anything else from the past six months, but I definitely remember your last birthday."

"Are we going to get a piece of cake before his *next* birthday?" Roy interrupted and the others all laughed.

While they were devouring their cake, Fletcher's mind reeled. He could hardly concentrate on the anecdote Anna was sharing about his birthday picnic mishap, which kept everyone in stitches, especially when she got to the part about trying to salvage the cake from the puddle it landed in.

"I guess that's why they call it *turtle* cake," Evan punned.

"They're going to call *you* a turtle at school tomorrow if you stay up much later," Naomi said. "*Kumme*, it's time for you and Eli to get ready for bed."

Since Anna refused Tessa's and Katie's help with the remaining dishes, they bid their goodbyes. To Fletcher's surprise, Aaron gamely offered to walk them to their buggy.

"I'll *kumme*, too, since I have a flashlight," Melinda chimed in and followed them out the door.

As Fletcher was lacing his boots in the mudroom, Anna brought him the remainder of the turtle cake, which she had secured in waxed paper for him to take home.

"*Denki*, I will savor this," he said, although eating was the last thing on his mind.

"There's something else." She handed him a small package wrapped in bright green cellophane. "What's a birthday party without a present?"

He untied the silver bow and pulled out a round jar with a black top. "Honey and oatmeal salve," he read. "This is something I definitely need."

"It's the kind my *daed* always used. I noticed your hands are a bit dry, too. *Daed* often said if the floors he installed cracked as badly as his skin, he'd be out of work," she quoted. "Here, try it."

She unscrewed the lid and dipped her finger into the salve. After applying it to the back of his hand, she began caressing it into his skin in gentle circles. "Doesn't that feel better?" she asked, reaching for the jar again.

Agitated by her news and fearful she'd notice his hand shaking, Fletcher pulled away, saying, "*Denki*, but it's getting late. I should go."

"Oh, okay," she said, quickly wiping her fingers on her apron.

The pained, perplexed look that crossed Anna's face rivaled Fletcher's aching inner turmoil. In bed that night, he shifted his body from side to side as his mind leaped from one thought to another. How long before Anna recalled what she meant by her note? Should he tell her about it before she remembered, or would that only upset her? And what about him? Could he really bear to know the truth, now that the past was no longer past?

Chapter Seven

On Thursday morning, Anna lay in bed, thinking about the previous evening. As euphoric as she was that her memories were starting to return, she simultaneously felt let down by Fletcher's subdued reaction. In response to her news, she had imagined a scenario in which he would have picked her up, twirled her around and declared there was no better "birthday" gift he could have received than having her memory come back. Instead, he hardly uttered a word about it and he noticeably flinched when she later took his hand in hers to soften it with salve.

Wasn't he a physically demonstrative person? Try as she did to recall, she couldn't summon any recollection of the two of them holding hands or embracing before her accident. After her accident, he'd occasionally offered his hand or arm to steady her, but not as a spontaneous gesture of affection. Perhaps his reticence was simply part of his personality. Or was he upset by something else? Had she done something to perturb him? Was he taken aback that she shared the story of his original birthday party with everyone else?

There was only one way to find out: talk to him. He'd indicated he wanted them to be open with each other, didn't he? That was her desire, too. Anna quickly rose, donned her *kapp* and thanked the Lord for the memory He'd restored and for those yet to come. Then she finished dressing, made her bed and tiptoed out of the room in order not to wake Melinda.

After making oatmeal with raisins for her brothers, she scribbled a quick note for Raymond to deliver to Fletcher. *My dear Fletcher,* she began, but then she feared he might think it sounded too coquettish. She ripped up the paper and started again. *Fletcher, will you join us for supper at six o'clock? There's something I'd like to discuss with you. —Anna.*

Aaron had arranged to pick Roy and Raymond up that morning, and as soon as his buggy departed the lane, Eli and Evan entered the kitchen.

"Eggs, oatmeal, or cinnamon raisin French toast, boys?" she asked them.

"French toast, please!" they chorused.

"How did I know?" Anna chuckled as she sliced the loaf of bread Naomi made the day before.

The boys sat quietly at the table, rubbing their eyes and chatting with Anna she made their breakfast. She was glad her stepmother was catching a few extra minutes of sleep; she always relished spending time alone with Eli and Evan. When they were younger, she used to pretend they were her children, not Naomi's, and she suddenly realized how quickly they were growing and how much she'd miss their familiar childish expressions and antics.

"Have you remembered anything else, Anna?" Evan asked, stifling a yawn.

"*Neh*, not yet. But I trust it won't be long until everything returns to me, so if you've done anything naughty in the past six months that I never found out about, don't think you've gotten away with it!" she joked, kissing the tops of their blond heads as she reached over them to set the platter of French toast on the table.

"Don't worry," Evan said, shaking his head vigorously. "*Mamm* already reprimanded me for anything I did that I shouldn't have done!"

Anna had to pinch the skin on her wrist to keep from laughing so she could say grace. After she lifted her head, she picked up the serving fork and asked, "How many slices would you like, Eli?"

"I'm… I'm not hungry," Eli whimpered. "My stomach hurts."

"Your stomach hurts?" Naomi sounded alarmed as she entered the kitchen. Placing a hand on Eli's head, she said, "He doesn't seem hot to me. What do you think, Anna?"

Anna felt his forehead and then slid her hand down to his cheek. "*Neh*, he's not warm. But if you think he should stay home from school, I could—"

"I don't want to stay home from school," Eli insisted. "I'm just not hungry. May I be excused from the table?"

"Of course," Anna said. "Why don't you go lie down on the sofa and I'll fill a hot water bottle for your tummy? Evan and I will do your morning chores for you before school starts—how's that?"

"*Gut,*" the boy replied, shuffling out of the room.

"If he's too sick to eat, may I have his pieces of French toast?" Evan asked.

"*Neh*, we don't want you getting a tummy ache, too," Anna replied. "But you may have *one* additional piece, since you'll need extra energy to help me with his chores."

"*Denki*, Anna!" Evan said, leaning over his plate.

"Why are you smiling like that?" Anna whispered to Naomi above Evan's head. "Is it because of his appetite?"

"*Neh*, it's because of your aptitude. You're going to make a *wunderbaar mamm.*"

Anna couldn't keep the bliss from her voice when she replied, "That's because I had you as my example."

"Some example I am—I almost slept as late as Melinda did today!" Naomi pointed to the window. "It's cloudy, but it's supposed to be warm again. I think I'll take advantage of the weather and begin some gardening today."

"While you're doing that, I'll wash the windows," Anna suggested.

"I don't know if that's wise. Did Dr. Donovan say it's okay to resume strenuous activities?"

"It's hardly strenuous. In fact, it gives my brain time to wander and that's when the memories seem likely to return."

Naomi reluctantly approved. "Well, the windows do need cleaning. I suppose if you take breaks, it might be alright. It will also give me time to work on preparing bedding arrangements for our guests' *kinner*. I'm thinking of putting all the boys on the second floor. Do you think it's warm enough for the girls to sleep in the attic room next to yours?"

"It will be if they're all tucked in side by side," Anna said.

Naomi's question reminded Anna that she needed to retrieve her new material from the other side of the attic and store it in her closet. She'd been helping Melinda with her dress so frequently that she hadn't taken her own fabric out of its wrapping, except to discreetly give Katie and Tessa their share of the material the evening before. Because she didn't want Naomi to hear her talk about sewing, Anna hadn't had the chance to ask her friends if they wanted to schedule a sister day to work on their dresses. Worried about whether they'd finish them on time, Anna thought, *Katie's a terrible procrastinator. A day before* Grischtdaag, *she still didn't even know what gifts she was going to give to her* mamm *and* daed.

It took a moment for Anna to realize she'd recalled another memory, and when she did, she was nearly as ecstatic as when it happened the first time. Throughout the day, additional remnants of the previous six months flitted through her mind. Her recollections were random and relatively minor—she recalled quilting with other women from the church, wading with the boys at the creek and the day an *Englisch* customer inquired about purchasing a dozen *kapps* in the shop. Many of the memories were fragmented and some were hazier than others, but there was no doubt her recollections were authentic, since no one had given her any hint about the events she recalled. She was so invigorated that she breezed through washing all of the windows in the house.

She was wringing out her rag after wiping the final pane when Evan and Eli returned from school and Melinda from the shop. Shortly afterward, as Anna was peeling potatoes for supper, she heard a buggy in the lane and had to restrain herself from throwing open the door to greet Fletcher. But it was Aaron who walked in with Roy. A minute later, Raymond followed, bearing a return message for her.

Anna, Fletcher wrote at the bottom of her own note to him, *I have to work late tonight and again tomorrow installing trim. Perhaps I can see you on Saturday? —Fletcher.*

Her eyes stung as she reread the note. Fletcher had told her how eager he was to complete the remaining trim for their first customer, so she understood why he needed to work late, but she was disappointed his message didn't contain so much as a jot of endearment or tittle of appreciation for the invitation. She supposed he could have simply been in a rush when he replied, but again she wondered if he was displeased with her. Or could it be he was tiring of eating at Naomi's with Anna's entire family?

Not knowing what to think, Anna penned a simple response under Fletcher's signature: *I'll be doing housework and gardening, so I should be home if you stop by on Saturday.* There wasn't room left on the page for her full name, so she merely scrawled her first initial.

There, she thought. *That doesn't sound the least bit cloying, so he shouldn't feel obligated to visit.* But deep down, she hoped by Saturday afternoon Fletcher would be as eager to see her as she was to see him.

Fletcher couldn't shake his apprehension that any second now, Anna would recall whatever it was that had caused her to write the note on the day of her accident. He felt as if his temples were being compressed by a vise, and his persistent nausea was exacerbated by the messages Raymond delivered. The first one, which read, *there's something I'd like to discuss with you*, was reminiscent of her preaccident note, *I have a serious concern regarding A. that I must discuss privately with you.* The chilly tone of her second inscription further heightened his jitters.

He was actually relieved to have a valid excuse for turning down her supper invitation: the trim had finally been delivered for the first project and he wanted to hang it as soon as possible. Aaron wouldn't release him from the second customer's site during the day, claiming the trim could wait another week. As a matter of providing good service, however, Fletcher assured the first customer he'd hang the trim after hours, completing it by Friday evening.

By Saturday morning, however, Fletcher was so sleep-deprived, miserable and beside himself with agitation, he could hardly wait to talk to Anna about the topic he'd been dreading for so long. As devastating as he anticipated their discussion would be, he knew it was better to face the truth than to suffer the agony of waiting for the issue to come to light.

Bleary-eyed, he whacked his thumb with his hammer, a carelessness even Roy hadn't demonstrated after his first month on the job.

"Ouch!" he yelled and flung the hammer to the floor.

"You need ice?" Raymond asked.

"I need air," Fletcher responded, heading out the door.

In the parking lot, he paced in circles, trying to shake off the pain. When it didn't subside, he took a short jaunt to the corner store to purchase three cups of coffee and what passed for glazed doughnuts in the *Englisch* community. Upon returning, he crossed paths with Aaron, who had just arrived to work and was hitching his horse.

"Where have you been?" Aaron asked.

Fletcher held up the tray of coffee to indicate his response. "Where have you been?" he asked in return.

"Not that I have to answer to you, but I was assessing another project," Aaron said. "I told you once before, if you're going to change your schedule, you need to let me know. You shouldn't leave Roy and Raymond unsupervised at the work site."

"I didn't change my schedule," Fletcher explained, thrown off by Aaron's tone. "I was gone all of five minutes."

"Don't let it happen again," Aaron warned before helping himself to a cup of coffee from the tray and strutting away.

Fletcher kicked at the dirt. The throbbing in his thumb was nothing compared to the pounding in his head. *Please* Gott, *give me grace*, he prayed. *The grace to deal with Aaron's attitude and the grace to accept whatever Anna has to say this afternoon.*

His morning progressed without further injury and Fletcher was pleasantly surprised when Isaiah arrived midmorning and took him aside to thank him for finishing the trim at the other customer's site. After his shift ended, Fletcher stopped at home to change his shirt before traveling to Anna's house. The closer he drew, the drier his mouth grew and by the time he pulled into the yard, he felt as if his tongue were made of wool.

"Fletcher!" Evan beckoned from behind a tree near where Fletcher hitched his horse. "Don't tell Anna you saw me—we're playing hide-and-seek."

"Too late, Evan," Anna said, creeping up from behind and tagging him on the shoulder. "You're it!"

"Aww, alright," Evan moaned. "Fletcher can play, too."

"*Neh*, Fletcher and I are going to take a walk to the creek, aren't we, Fletcher?"

"*Jah,*" was all he could say.

Before ambling away, Anna instructed Evan, "After you find Eli, I'd like both of you to take that basket of laundry inside the house and wash your hands for dinner. Then ask your *mamm* if there's anything you can do to help her."

As she and Fletcher traipsed down the hilly field, they chatted about the spring birds they spotted, Fletcher's new project at work and Isaiah's visit to the site.

Fletcher assumed Anna was stalling until they arrived at the creek before discussing her note, and with each step he felt as if he wore cinder blocks strapped to his feet.

When they reached the embankment, he viewed the rushing water and remembered a saying his sister Leah often quoted, "If the river had no rocks, it would not have a song."

"What?" Anna questioned.

Fletcher didn't realize he'd spoken aloud. "Oh, that's a proverb my sister often says. I think it means you can't have something beautiful without also having some rocky, difficult patches."

"That's true," Anna said, thoughtfully furrowing her brow.

Unable to endure the suspense any longer, Fletcher blurted out, "You mentioned there was something you wanted to speak with me about. What is it?"

Anna shuffled backward. "Let's sit," she said and they positioned themselves next to each other on a large boulder overlooking the water. "It's…it's uncomfortable to discuss this."

Fletcher licked his lips and forged ahead. "Whatever it is, it's better that we're open with each other about it."

"I guess I… I was disappointed by your reaction the other night when I told you my memory had begun to return. I thought you would have been happier," Anna confessed. "I thought you would have been thrilled, actually. When you weren't, I wondered why not. I wondered if I'd done something to upset you."

Fletcher closed his eyes as he absorbed the realization that Anna still didn't recall writing her original note. For a split second, he considered not telling her about his concern, but he knew he'd only be prolonging the inevitable. Besides, it had become too big of a burden for him to bear even a second longer.

"You're right, Anna. I probably didn't seem as excited as I should have been," he intoned. "That's because there's something about the past I've wanted to discuss with you, but I couldn't because Dr. Donovan warned us it would be detrimental to your health if you became too upset or if you felt too pressured to recall your memories before your brain had a chance to heal. But it's been weighing heavily on my mind and I can't keep it to myself any longer, especially since it affects our wedding."

Anna gasped and pressed a hand to her mouth before asking, "What is it?"

"It's this," he said, removing the slip of paper from his coat and shoving it into her hand.

She unfolded the note and read it aloud. "'Fletcher, I have a serious concern regarding A. that I must discuss privately with you before the wedding preparations go any further. Please visit me tonight after work. —Anna.'"

Then she read it again to herself. Finally, she said, "It's sloppier than usual, but it's definitely my handwriting. When did I give you this?"

"You sent it with Raymond the morning of your accident."

"Really? I'm sorry, but I have no recollection of what I wanted to talk to you about."

"I believe the A. stands for Aaron."

"Aaron? What does he have to do with our wedding preparations? He hasn't lifted a finger to help as far as I can tell, has he?"

"Neh." Fletcher grimaced. It was clear he was going to have to spell it out for Anna and his stomach lurched as he formed the words. "I believe you meant... You meant you had second thoughts about how you felt about him, so you had second thoughts about marrying me."

Anna hooted, "That's absurd!" She leaped up and twirled to face him with her hands on her hips. "How could you believe such a thing, especially after all the conversations we've had?"

"I don't want to believe it, but it's possible something happened immediately before the accident that caused you to change your mind about how you felt about Aaron and you just can't remember it."

"I might not remember all of what *happened* in the past six months, but I remember how I *felt* ever since breaking up with Aaron," Anna insisted, smacking the back of one hand against the palm of the other. "My *feelings* haven't changed! My *preferences* haven't changed. It's like... It's like lima beans. I didn't like them before my accident and I still don't like them after my accident. I tolerate them because it's rude not to when they're served as part of my family's meal, but do I suddenly like them? Have I changed my mind about loving them? *Neh*, never."

Put in those terms, Fletcher's worries about Aaron suddenly seemed absolutely ridiculous and he felt like the biggest *dummkopf* who ever lived. Yet he still couldn't quite dismiss Anna's note.

* * *

"Then how do you explain what you meant by having 'a serious concern regarding A.'?" Fletcher pressed.

Anna sat down beside him again. "Well, I could have meant any number of things," she said, counting on her fingers. "A. could stand for Amos, as in Bishop Amos. Or maybe it was short for April? Perhaps I wanted to change the date from April to March. Or possibly it stood for attendance—the list of people invited. Could I have meant arrangements? Naomi has been fretting over where the *kinner* will sleep. Perhaps I thought—"

"Okay, okay, you can stop now!" Fletcher laughed, holding up his hands. A blush crept over his face as he looked into her eyes. "I clearly let my imagination get the best of me. I don't know what to say except I'm very sorry."

Anna understood: given his history with Joyce, it wasn't any wonder he'd jumped to the wrong conclusions about the context of her note. "You're forgiven," she promised. "I'm just relieved I didn't do anything at the party to offend you."

In response, Fletcher slid his fingers between Anna's as if into a glove, sending a tingle up her arm and dispelling her concern that he wasn't a physically affectionate person.

"Somebody has been using the salve I gave him," she noticed.

"*Jah*. It's working well and it smells *gut*, too."

"You hurt yourself though," she said, indicating his thumbnail. "Poor aim?"

"Poor concentration. I was thinking about a certain *maedel*."

"I've been thinking about you a lot, too, Fletcher. As difficult as it was, I'm glad we had this discussion."

"If the river had no rocks, it would not have a song," he quoted as he picked up a stone and tossed it into the creek.

She crumpled the note into a ball and cast it into the current, as well. "For the birds to make a nest," she said and tugged at his fingers. "Now *kumme*, let's go have dinner before my brothers eat it all."

They dropped hands before entering the kitchen, where Naomi had set a place for Fletcher.

"You're just in time for grace," she remarked warmly.

After thanking the Lord for their food and other blessings, Fletcher said to Naomi, "I hope I'm just in time to help Roy and Raymond with any house repair or yard projects you'd like finished before the wedding, too."

Anna's pulse skittered at his reference to their upcoming wedding. Although she still wasn't positive their pending nuptials would occur as scheduled, with every interaction they shared, she was growing more confident he was the husband God had provided for her.

"*Denki*, that would be appreciated," Naomi said. "There's a fence post in the yard Roy and Raymond are having trouble setting and I'd like your opinion on the window in the attic. It feels drafty up there and I don't want our guests' *kinner* to catch a chill."

"I noticed a loose floorboard in the mudroom, too,"

Fletcher commented. "The boys and I may also have to take a look at the porch stairs."

The three young men clomped into the mudroom. Eli and Evan were tasked with helping Naomi till the soil for her gardens while Anna focused on scrubbing the floors. In deference to Dr. Donovan's advice, she stopped short of beating the rugs herself, instead hanging them so Melinda could complete the task later that afternoon. The day took on a festive air and by the time the group stopped for supper, they'd accomplished more than they'd set out to.

"If it's alright with you, Anna, I'd like to take you for a ride after supper," Fletcher said over dessert.

"Not so fast." Naomi waved a finger at him, "You still need to address the draft in the attic."

"Of course," Fletcher agreed. "I meant after that."

"Why the disappointed expression? You're being let off easy," his future mother-in-law teased. She turned to her sons. "When your *daed* was keen on me, he volunteered to help your *groossdaadi* build an entire house just for the chance to say hello to me when I came out with a pitcher of water."

Anna fidgeted in her chair and glanced at Fletcher, who was studiously focused on scraping the ice cream from his bowl. Nothing escaped Naomi's notice.

"There's no need to be embarrassed, you two. It would serve most couples well to remember after they're married how eager they were to spend time in each other's company before they wed." Naomi sighed, wiping the corner of her eye. "Time spent with those we love is one of *Gott*'s most precious gifts. We ought to value it more dearly because it passes so quickly."

"Mamm," Evan whined, "the last time Melinda and Aaron mentioned mushy grown-up love talk at the table, you said my ears were too young to hear that kind of thing."

The others joined Naomi in laughter. "That's right," she said, patting his head. "How about if we talk about turtles instead?"

By the time Anna finished washing and putting away the dishes and Fletcher and the boys installed insulation and repaired the window in the attic, it was dusk.

"Why don't we have a cup of tea on the porch instead of going for a ride?" Anna suggested.

They sat side by side on the swing, gently swaying as they chatted. The rhythmic motion lulled Anna into a deep sense of relaxation, and she rested her head against Fletcher's shoulder. Lowering her lids, she imagined the two of them spending evenings like this on the porch of their own house. She could picture their children romping on the front lawn and in her imagination they all had Fletcher's lustrous wavy hair and intense blue eyes.

"Are you tired?" he asked.

"Neh, I'm peaceful," she replied. "In fact, I haven't felt this peaceful in a long time."

"That's too bad," Fletcher said. "Because there's something I want to show you, but you'll have to get up and *kumme* with me."

He took her by the hand, caressing her icy fingers to warm them as they made their way to the expansive maple in the backyard. Its branches appeared black against the ebbing light of the sky, which was beginning to glisten with early stars.

Anna tittered when they stopped beneath its mighty boughs. "Did we argue under this tree, too, as we did when we first met beneath the willow?"

"Hardly," Fletcher replied and his voice sounded gravelly. "You really don't remember what happened here?"

Noticing his impassioned tone, she paused, wishing she could claim every second of their courtship was etched indelibly across her heart. "I'm sorry, Fletcher," she admitted, "but I don't."

Fletcher reached for Anna's shoulders, gently positioning her against the trunk. "Well, you were standing like this. And I was leaning with my hand here, above you. Your hair was dappled with bits of light and your eyes mirrored the greenery all around us."

Fletcher gently touched Anna's cheek with the back of his hand, remembering.

"What happened next?" she whispered.

"May I show you?"

"You may."

He leaned toward her for a soft kiss.

After a quiet pause, he had to know if she experienced the same depth of emotion he felt. "Now do you remember?" he asked.

"I may not remember the first time," Anna spoke slowly, "but I won't forget this time."

Fletcher's heart pranced. It wasn't exactly the answer he'd hoped to hear, but it was the next best thing.

"Evan would be disappointed to hear you couldn't remember the first time," he joked, leading her back toward the house.

"Evan?"

"*Jah*. You and I were sharing our first kiss when you were supposed to be watching Timothy the Turtle. That's how he wandered away."

Anna's laughter rang out through the darkness. "That's terrible!"

Terrible for Timothy, but wunderbaar *for me*, Fletcher thought as he ambled up the steps to accompany Anna to the door. "I suppose it's time to say *gut nacht*."

"Could you please help me find the teacups, first?" Anna requested. "It's gotten dark and I'm not sure I'll be able to see where we set them."

As they cautiously advanced toward the front of the porch, Fletcher abruptly stopped, realizing there was someone sitting in the swing.

"I don't know what Naomi's so upset about," Melinda was saying. "I was only an hour or two late. She's such a worrywart. Besides, if we had arrived in time for supper, she wouldn't have asked you to stay, even though Fletcher was invited."

Fletcher coughed to signal Melinda he could hear her, while from behind, Anna loudly cut her short with, "Is that you, Melinda?"

"*Jah*, and I'm with her," Aaron answered. "Where did the two of you *kumme* from?"

"We were taking a stroll. Enjoying the evening air," Anna responded curtly as she and Fletcher approached the other couple. They were still holding hands and if

Fletcher wasn't mistaken, Anna tightened her grasp as she spoke.

"See what I mean?" Melinda continued, unabashed to have been caught complaining about them. "Naomi gives you and Fletcher her blessing to do whatever you want whenever you want. It's not fair."

"*Neh*, what's not fair, Melinda," Anna rebutted, "is that everyone in this household, including Fletcher, has been working all afternoon on house and yard projects that need to be completed before the weddings. Yet you didn't arrive home until after seven o'clock, even though your shift at Schrock's ended at four. If you want Aaron to be included at mealtime, the two of you ought to consider pitching in."

Melinda shifted in her seat and began to protest, but Anna wasn't finished speaking.

"As for Naomi being a worrywart, it's true," she said. "Naomi often frets when the people she *cares* about aren't home when they should be. In part that's because the last time someone other than you didn't return home on time was when I had my accident, and the time before that was when my *daed* died. So you—and Aaron—should think about what goes through Naomi's mind when you decide to amble home several hours after you're expected!"

Anna dropped Fletcher's hand as she stooped to pick up a teacup and saucer near the side of the swing. Fletcher retrieved the other cup and saucer from where Anna left it balanced on the railing and wordlessly followed her to the side door. When she turned to say goodnight, Anna's hand was shaking so furiously that the cup rattled against the saucer. Fletcher took the china from her and stacked it with his on the bench beside them. He gingerly ran a finger beneath her chin, tilting her face upward. It was too dark to read the expression in her eyes, but he felt the wetness of a tear moisten his skin.

"Anna," he whispered. "This evening has been too special to allow anything to spoil it."

"I know it has and it still is." She sniffed. "But there are still many memories about our courtship I hope will return to me, so I don't want Melinda's rude comments about your presence here to keep you from visiting me as often as possible in the next two and a half weeks before the wedding."

"Are you joking? Wild horses couldn't keep me away!"

"Do you promise?" Anna asked.

"I promise and I'll even seal it with a kiss," Fletcher pledged, bending to brush his lips against hers.

On the way home, he marveled over the amount of time he'd spent anguishing over Anna's note, when he could have spoken to her about it earlier and alleviated his fears. Even if she still couldn't say for certain what she meant by her message, her guesses seemed more likely than the assumption he'd made. He belatedly reckoned his experience with Joyce had colored his perception, but he wasn't going to allow it to cast a shadow on his relationship with Anna any longer. No, after their conversation—and their kisses—this evening, Fletcher was thoroughly convinced she carried a torch for him and him alone.

"*Denki*, Lord!" he prayed aloud as his horse trotted

through the night. "*Denki* for Your grace and goodness toward Anna and me, by providing us for each other and by keeping my foolishness from destroying our relationship."

In light of his conversation with Anna, any misgivings he'd felt toward his cousin dissolved completely and soon he was asking God to bless Aaron's marriage to Melinda, too. *The two of them seem to need all the prayer and help they can get before becoming husband and wife*, he mused.

But by the time Fletcher stretched out on his bed, Melinda and Aaron were far from his mind. His only thoughts were of Anna: Anna beneath the willow and Anna under the maple; Anna in sunlight and Anna in starlight; Anna then and Anna now. *Anna, Anna, Anna*, he mumbled drowsily before dozing off. *My bride-to-be*.

Chapter Eight

On Sunday morning, Anna sat bolt upright in bed, unsure whether the vision that just raced through her mind was a memory or a dream. In it, Fletcher had just kissed her and she was filled with repulsion. The images were fuzzy, but the way they made her feel was undeniably clear and Anna shuddered violently.

"What's wrong with you?" Melinda muttered, squinting one eye at her.

"I had a nightmare, that's all," Anna replied.

Melinda rolled over and pulled the quilt up to her ears, but Anna got up, made her bed and dressed and then padded downstairs to begin making breakfast before the family held their home church services. She was cubing potatoes for breakfast when the image of kissing Fletcher crossed her mind again, except this time she recalled his hands gripping her shoulders as well as the breeze lifting his dark, wavy hair when he pulled her toward him for an emphatic kiss.

Disconcerted that the dream played itself out in her

waking moments, Anna sat down at the table and covered her eyes with her hand. *I must be overly tired*, she thought. *My mind is playing tricks on me.*

"Are you okay?" Eli cheeped, startling her.

She jumped up and said, "*Guder mariye*, Eli. *Jah*, I'm fine. I was just resting my eyes before I started making breakfast casserole. Look, I'm going to use bacon instead of sausage, the way you like it. I notice you haven't been eating a lot lately."

The boy's eyes brightened. "*Denki*, Anna. I'll go get the eggs from the henhouse."

Naomi was the next person awake. "That smells *gut* already, Anna. But you should allow me to make breakfast. I'll have to get used to cooking all our meals again once you move out."

"Mmm," Anna said noncommittally.

Naomi immediately panicked. "Uh-oh. Is something wrong? Did you and Fletcher decide not to carry through with your wedding? You were getting on so well yesterday."

Anna chuckled. "All I said was 'mmm.'"

"*Jah*, but it was the way you said it," insisted Naomi.

Eli burst into the kitchen with his basket of eggs. "*Guder mariye, Mamm*," he greeted Naomi. "Anna's putting bacon in the casserole instead of sausage."

"Just the way somebody in this family likes it, but I can't remember who," Naomi teased.

"Me!" Eli cheered.

"I guess your sister has a better memory than I do," Naomi said. "She must have decided to make it specially tailored for you, because you're the first one up. Now please go wake everyone else—without shouting."

After Eli dashed out of the room, Anna replied to her stepmother's earlier question. "Nothing went wrong between Fletcher and me. In fact, yesterday was one of the best days we've had together yet."

"But?" Naomi asked, setting the plates around the table.

Anna sighed; Naomi was so perceptive. "But I guess I'd still like to remember more about our courtship and I'd still like to find my journal," she admitted. "I think that would allay any lingering qualms I might have."

Especially after this morning's nightmare, she thought.

"I can't make your memories return, although I'll continue to pray about that," Naomi offered. "As for your journal, we've practically turned the house inside out with our spring cleaning, so it seems we would have found it by now. Is it possible you stashed it in the stable?"

"I doubt it," Anna said, "although it's worth a look."

"Guder mariye," Roy, Raymond and Evan greeted the women before taking their seats.

"I couldn't get Melinda to wake up," Eli reported, wiggling onto a chair.

"She's probably tired because she was out on the porch late last night with Aaron," Evan commented knowingly.

"Evan, what did *Mamm* tell us about eavesdropping?" Eli chastised his younger brother.

"I wasn't eavesdropping," he insisted innocently. "The window was stuck open."

"Oh! I'm sorry," Anna quickly apologized. "I couldn't get it down again after I washed it. I hope you boys weren't too cold last night. Roy or Raymond, you should take a look at how it sits in the frame."

"See? That wasn't my fault so it doesn't count as eavesdropping," Evan retorted to Eli. "Besides, I didn't even repeat that I heard Melinda asking Aaron if he was jellies because Fletcher is marrying Anna, not him. And Aaron said if he was jellies, would he do this, then she said to stop that because it tickles and then she kept laughing."

"Melinda didn't ask Aaron if he was jellies, Evan," Eli hotly refuted. "She asked him if he was *jealous*, but you still repeated gossip because you just told everyone."

"Boys!" Naomi squawked, clapping her hands sharply together once. That's all the reprimand they needed to stop talking.

No one else said a word, either, until Melinda sidled into the room. "It's so quiet in here, I thought maybe it wasn't an off-Sunday and you'd all left for church without me," she joked as she heaped casserole onto her plate.

After everyone had eaten their fill, Anna cleared the table, contemplating Evan's disclosure about the conversation he'd overheard. She knew Melinda had come up with some ludicrous theories in her time, but this one took the cake. If Aaron was envious of Fletcher, it was because of Fletcher's inherent character and his superior abilities—it had nothing to do with Fletcher marrying

Anna. Still, Anna hoped Melinda and Aaron had resolved the issue; the last thing she wanted was more tension between her and her cousin. Anna felt bad enough about her strong words from the previous night as it was.

Once they finished worshipping together, Evan asked if Anna would accompany him and Eli to the stream.

"Why not?" she asked, eager to lighten the mood after their morning squabble.

"Watch yourselves around the rocks," Naomi cautioned, waving goodbye.

The trio spritely marched through the dewy grass, down the hill and across the meadow. Once they arrived at the creek, Anna alighted on the boulder nearest the willow. Due to the spring rains, the creek's current was moving swiftly and she kept a close eye on the boys as they attempted to chuck stones across to the opposite bank. She was thinking about how the willow's lengthy fringe dancing in the breeze reminded her of a woman's long hair, when she was struck with another memory like the one that had afflicted her earlier that morning.

In the recollection, Fletcher stood not five feet from where Evan was now pitching a rock into the rushing water. He had just kissed her and she was trying to secure her prayer *kapp* over her hair, which had become mussed when she jerked away from him. She recalled that they had argued and she was crying. As the scant details manifested in her mind's eye, Anna's knees trembled and she began to pant, trying to catch her breath.

"Boys," she weakly summoned them. "It's time to go. *Kumme*, take my hands, please. I'm not feeling quite right."

They steadied her up the hill and delivered her into Naomi's care.

"You're as pale as a sheet and shaking like a leaf," Naomi fretted. "I never should have permitted you to do so much last week. I'm sending Raymond to the phone shanty to call Dr. Donovan."

"*Neh*, please don't," Anna argued feebly as her teeth chattered. "I j-just need to get warm. It was nippy near the creek. Dr. Donovan's office is probably closed for the weekend anyway."

Naomi scrutinized Anna's face. Finally, she allowed, "I'll put on a pot of tea and Melinda will draw you a bath. We'll see how you're doing after that. But if I suspect so much as a hint of a fever, I'll have Raymond bring us to the hospital straightaway."

Although she couldn't stomach the tea and toast Naomi prepared for her, Anna stopped shaking after taking a bath. At her stepmother's insistence, she nestled into Naomi's bed, where Naomi swaddled her in quilts and set a bell at her side to ring if she needed assistance. But Anna only wanted to be alone, and once she was, she wept into her arms, wishing she could forget the very memories she'd been praying so fervently to recall.

When Fletcher arrived at Anna's house on Sunday afternoon, Naomi greeted him at the door. Her skin was wan and her eyes were bloodshot. "*Guder nammidaag*, Fletcher. I'm afraid I can't invite you in. Anna has taken ill and Eli is sick, too. I don't want you to catch whatever is plaguing our household."

Fletcher's heart raced. Anna was ill? But at least it

couldn't have been related to her concussion, since Eli was also sick, right? "Is there something I can do to help?" he asked.

"*Neh*. Neither one of them has a fever. And although Eli's had terrible stomach pains, they seem to have subsided. Right now I think rest is the best thing for both of them."

"May I call on Anna this evening?" Fletcher asked.

"*Neh,*" Naomi responded sharply before softening her tone. "I'm sorry, Fletcher, but I fear it was my fault she overdid it last week, which is why she's sick now, so I have to put my foot down. I'll be sure to tell her you asked after her and wanted to see her, but I wouldn't allow it."

"But—"

"If you don't want her to risk having to return to the hospital, you'll support her recovery by allowing her to rest," Naomi reiterated firmly.

Fletcher couldn't argue with Naomi's logic, so he reluctantly returned home. Once there, he found himself at a loss for things to do. He'd already spent the morning in worship with his uncle's family, and usually Anna and her brothers were the only people he visited during off-Sundays. Since moving to Willow Creek, he'd been befriended by a few of the older men in the district, but he didn't feel comfortable dropping in on them and their families uninvited.

Since it was the Sabbath, all but the most essential work was prohibited. As it was, he'd already completed everything except painting the alcove he'd created for Anna, and he routinely kept up the stable and yard. In regard to the house's interior, it was tidy, but he realized it definitely needed a woman's touch. *Soon enough*, he thought as he sat down in the parlor.

He read Scripture for an hour and then enjoyed a long nap. When he awoke, he decided to write his sisters, as he was long overdue in replying to their letter.

Dear Esther, Leah, Rebekah & Families,
I hope this note finds everyone healthy. Thank you for your good wishes and faithful prayers, as expressed in your last letter. I am sorry for my delay in responding. I'm afraid I've been distracted because Anna recently suffered a head injury that resulted in substantial memory loss. Rest assured, she is recovering well. Physically, she no longer suffers from the headaches or nausea she endured immediately following her fall, and her recollections are also returning to her. Still, I covet your prayers for her complete healing.

I look forward to hearing all about what has been happening in your lives when we talk in person at the wedding, if not by letter before then.

Until then, may the Lord bless you.
—Fletcher.

After he affixed a stamp to the envelope, Fletcher carried the letter to the mailbox for the carrier to pick up the following day. When he unlatched the door to the box, a flurry of envelopes fluttered to the ground and he snorted to realize it must be been days since he'd retrieved the mail; clearly he valued the notes

Raymond delivered much more than those the carrier brought. Most of the spilled items were advertisements and bills, but one was a personal letter written in a hand he didn't immediately recognize. Tearing it open as he walked, he read:

Fletcher,
I've heard the news that you are soon to be wed and I hope you will accept my sincere congratulations. I also hope you will permit me this belated apology for the anguish I caused. Whether you believe me or not, I didn't deliberately intend to deceive you. I honestly didn't know my own heart. That is, I honestly didn't fully comprehend how I felt about Frederick until it was almost too late.
   For both of our sakes, I'm grateful you and I didn't marry and I trust you are even more grateful than I. In any case, I pray for you all of the love and happiness you so richly deserve. May the Lord bless your marriage abundantly.
Joyce Wittmer.

Fletcher stopped in his tracks and reread the note. On one hand, he was appalled that Joyce had the nerve to write him—especially because she said how grateful she was they hadn't gotten married! On the other hand, she was right: he was even more grateful than she was. If it hadn't been for Joyce calling off their wedding, Fletcher never would have discovered what true love was, because he wouldn't have moved to Willow Creek and met Anna. As for forgiving Joyce, he'd done that long ago, even if he occasionally battled leftover feelings related to their breakup. But Fletcher accepted her apology for what it was: an earnest expression of contrition.

When he got inside, he crumpled up the note and threw it in the woodstove. It was a reminder of old hurts that belonged to the past. He was looking ahead now, to his future with Anna. As he stirred a pot of canned soup for supper, he thought about the tender kisses they'd shared the day before, and he imagined those they'd exchange in the future; perhaps even as soon as tomorrow. He ate quickly and, despite having taken a nap, he turned in to bed early, hoping to hasten the arrival of a new day.

Instead, he slept fitfully and the night seemed to stretch on twice as long as usual. As he listlessly twisted this way and that, a single unbidden thought came to mind: *What if* Anna *doesn't know her own heart, either?* He dismissed the idea almost the second he thought it, chalking it up to his thwarted longing to see her again. But his restlessness kept him awake for hours, until he finally decided to dress and go to work, arriving well before the break of dawn.

He was surprised when Roy and Raymond walked in carrying a battery-powered nail gun and drill less than a half an hour after sunrise.

"Guder mariye," Fletcher said. He barely waited for a reply before asking, "How's Anna?"

"I think she's alright," Roy replied. "*Mamm* took her some broth last night and she finished it all."

"But there's no note for you," Raymond said, anticipating Fletcher's question. "She was still sleeping when we left."

Although his hope was deflated, Fletcher responded, "That's okay. I'm sure I'll speak to her tonight. Do you two need a hand carrying in more tools?"

"*Neh*, there's only one more load. We've got it," Raymond replied as the brothers exited and Aaron entered.

He looked startled to see Fletcher. "What time did you get here?"

"An hour and a half ago," Fletcher replied.

"Why are you always doing that?" Aaron challenged him, setting down the portable table saw with a loud clatter.

"Doing what?" Fletcher had no idea what the problem was.

"You've always got to show me up. Staying later, coming in earlier. What are you trying to prove?"

"Aaron, I'm *helping* you, not *competing* with you," Fletcher argued.

"Well, don't think just because you came in early you're going to leave early. The entire reason I'm here now is because we've got to finish up this floor today. I took another contract that starts tomorrow morning."

Fletcher resisted the urge to ask Aaron why he accepted another simultaneous project when they clearly weren't finished with this one. He could tell his cousin was tense enough as it was, so instead, Fletcher channeled his frustration into performing his work, motivating himself with the fact that the sooner they finished, the sooner he'd get to see Anna again.

On Monday, Anna lingered in bed. After Sunday's long nap and a good night's rest, her quivering had stopped, but she kept her eyes closed, trying to convince herself that yesterday's recurrent unpleasant memory of kissing Fletcher was only a dream. Yet deep down she knew sooner or later, she'd have to ask for Fletcher's help in making sense of the awful image that kept coming to mind. He'd told her he didn't want her to hide anything from him, didn't he? But what would she say? How could she tell him, "I have a vague recollection of kissing you at the creek and being wholly repulsed"? After his vulnerable confession the other day, she didn't want to shake his confidence about her feelings for him.

"Are you still asleep or are you just pretending so you won't have to make breakfast?" Melinda whispered.

"Neither," Anna said, raising her lids. "I'm awake but I'm not deliberately trying to get out of helping with breakfast. That would be irresponsible."

"Oh," Melinda said, seemingly deaf to Anna's reproach. "I was wondering, how far have you progressed with your wedding dress?"

"I've got considerable work to do," Anna responded vaguely, sitting up. Although she was certain she hadn't moved her wedding dress fabric from the other side of the attic, it was no longer there. For fear of being teased about her forgetfulness by her cousin, Anna didn't want to inquire if Melinda had moved it. "Why do you ask?"

"Well, since Naomi will likely confine you to our room today anyway, do you suppose you'd mind making some adjustments to the sleeves and hem on mine? Joseph has asked me to work extra hours at the shop and I don't see how I'll finish my dress unless you help me."

Anna felt like suggesting Melinda might try staying

in instead of running around with Aaron every night. But since she knew her suggestion was futile, she reluctantly agreed. "Alright, try it on and let me see what needs to be done."

As her cousin was changing into the violet dress and she was making her bed, Anna asked, "So, Joseph wants you to work extra hours at the shop?"

"*Jah*, he even mentioned keeping me on after you return. Sales are up since I started working there," Melinda boasted as she climbed onto a stool so Anna could examine the hem.

Anna held pins pressed between her lips and she didn't reply.

"I think it's because I have a way with *Englisch* customers," Melinda babbled. "Tessa Fisher barely utters two words to them, so I think they appreciate having a chatty, comely Amish girl like me to approach— Ouch! You pricked me with that pin!"

"Did I?" Anna asked innocently. "Turn toward me, please."

"How do I look?" Melinda hinted.

"Crooked." Anna frowned, smoothing the hem.

"Not the dress—*me*," Melinda emphasized.

Anna took a step backward and tipped her head upward for a better look at the full dress. The color accentuated Melinda's dark hair and eyes, gathering modestly over the curves of her girlish figure. She would make a beautiful bride.

Anna answered honestly, "You look lovely, absolutely lovely." Which was exactly how Anna wanted to feel in her own wedding dress.

It's not fair, she thought in an instant of self-pity. *Why should Melinda get to experience such excitement about her wedding, when I've experienced little but anxiety about mine?*

"*Denki*," Melinda said, hopping down from the stool and twirling in a circle before giving Anna a hug. "*Denki* for everything, Anna. If it weren't for you, I wouldn't be getting married and I wouldn't have a job at the shop. In a way, it's almost a blessing you had a concussion."

Annoyed by Melinda's complete lack of sensitivity, Anna tugged her cousin's arms from around her neck. "Stop that," she snapped. "You're hurting me." *And I've been in pain for long enough as it is.*

After dressing, she made her way into the kitchen where she said good morning to Naomi and then asked, "Are Raymond and Roy out milking?"

"*Neh*, Aaron picked the boys up very early this morning. How do you feel today?"

"As strong as an ox," Anna claimed. She supposed it was just as well the boys had left before she could send a note with Raymond, since she wasn't sure what to write to Fletcher anyway. She figured he'd come for supper and by then she would have collected her thoughts.

"Oh, am I ever relieved to hear that!" Naomi exclaimed. Then she said, "This morning, I'll be taking Evan to school and dropping Melinda off in town, and then I'm stopping at the phone shanty to make an appointment for Eli at the clinic in Highland Springs."

"The clinic in Highland Springs?" Anna repeated. The *Englisch*-run clinic offered pediatric care exclusively to members of the Amish community. "What's wrong with Eli?"

"He was sick to his stomach shortly after you returned from the creek. His cramps came and went all night, but he doesn't have a fever. I recall his stomach hurting him the other day, too, so I want to be sure there's nothing seriously wrong."

"That's a *gut* idea," Anna agreed. "I'll stay here with him now and then accompany you to his appointment when you get back."

As it turned out, Naomi couldn't schedule an appointment until four o'clock. She sat next to Anna in the front seat, while Eli curled up with a hot water bottle in the back. Once they arrived at the clinic, Naomi was softly reading aloud to her son when the disturbing image again troubled Anna's mind.

"I'm going to stretch my legs," she announced before ambling down the long corridor.

She was examining a colorful mural of barnyard animals when a voice behind her resounded, "Anna! What brings you to the children's clinic?"

She recognized his voice before she angled around to greet him. "Hello, Dr. Donovan." She couldn't help but smile when speaking to the kind man. "My brother has a stomachache."

"Ah, we get a lot of those around here. I mean, our patients do. I volunteer here once a month," he explained. "Usually, the stomachaches are nothing serious. But what about you, how are you feeling?"

"I'm fine," Anna said, but to her dismay, her eyes unexpectedly spouted fat tears.

Dr. Donovan clasped her elbow, ushering her into an empty office, where he motioned for her to sit. Then he passed a box of tissues across the desk and clasped his hands over his belly while she blew her nose. "I take it your memories haven't returned then, eh?" he asked.

"Actually, they have. Not too many of Fletcher or our courtship, but plenty of other people and events."

"That's a good sign, yet you're not happy?"

"I'm… I'm frustrated. And confused," she confessed. "At first, my recollection of the past six months seemed as blank as a field of snow. Now when the memories come back, some of them remind me of scuffling along a winding path covered with fallen leaves. They're turned every which way and I can't make sense of them. I don't know what's a memory and what's a dream."

Dr. Donovan bobbed his head vigorously. "Those are excellent metaphors for what it feels like to have your memories return. I've never heard a patient describe the process quite like that, but it's very common for them to tell me their recollections are fuzzy, foggy or dreamlike."

"It's common?" Anna raised her eyebrows. "Then how do your patients know what really happened and what didn't?"

"As I've said before, it takes time for the brain to heal. I'd suggest you hold on to your recollections loosely for the time being, because things aren't always as they seem to be. Meanwhile, trust this," Dr. Donovan advised, placing his hand over his heart. "Not this," he added, pointing to his head.

Her mind eased, Anna gushed, "Thank you, Dr. Donovan! Thank you!" as his phone buzzed.

She closed the door behind her and stepped into the hall to find Naomi approaching. Eli was holding her hand and sucking on a lollipop. It occurred to Anna he looked healthier and more energetic than his *mamm* did. After Naomi confirmed the doctor said there was nothing wrong with Eli that two more days of a restricted diet wouldn't cure, they walked to the buggy.

By the time Anna steered them through an especially grueling rush hour traffic jam and up the lane to their house, it was six o'clock. Naomi said she had a blinding headache, so Anna advised her to lie down, even though by then her own head was beginning to pound. Figuring she was probably only peckish, Anna anticipated a good hot meal would revive her and she swiftly stabled the horse before entering the house, where it was clear Melinda hadn't started supper. When she found her cousin in the sitting room with her *kapp* askew and her arms draped around Aaron's neck, Anna clenched her teeth. Couldn't Melinda ever be counted on to perform the most basic tasks without being prompted? Anna's knees felt wobbly and she steadied herself against the doorframe.

"Are you alright, Anna?" Aaron asked and his voice was so sympathetic, for a moment he sounded just like Fletcher. But then he added, "You look as if you've been wrestling a greased pig."

"And she lost," Melinda added, crowing uproariously.

"I'm fine, *denki* for asking," Anna replied in her politest voice to show they hadn't ruffled her feathers. But suddenly, she changed her mind and said. "Actually, Melinda, *you're* the one who looks as if she's been wrestling a greased pig—and he's sitting right there beside you!"

Then she spun around, leaving them to stare at each other in shocked silence.

Fletcher was exhausted. It was nine o'clock and he wasn't nearly finished laying the customer's floor. As he headed for home, he mentally reviewed the dispute he'd had with Aaron earlier that afternoon.

"You know what Anna said about how worried their *mamm* gets when they arrive home later than expected," Aaron argued after announcing he was leaving work at four o'clock and taking Roy and Raymond with him.

"*Jah*, but I can't finish this project on my own. Why don't you just take Roy and leave Raymond here with me? I'll bring him home when we've finished."

"*Jah*," Raymond said. "I'll stay here."

"I can stay, too," Roy volunteered. "I need to learn all the steps of installing flooring. Since you said you arranged to pick up Melinda in town anyway, you can just ask her to relay the message to *Mamm* that we'll be late."

"See what you've done?" Aaron asked Fletcher. "You've trained the apprentice to think his preferences override the foreman's decision."

Fletcher saw the sense in what Raymond and Roy were suggesting and he appreciated their dedication. But, from his recent heated interaction with Aaron, he also recognized his cousin probably felt his authority was being challenged, so Fletcher tried to show his support.

"They respect the fact that you're in charge," he said. "They were only trying to be helpful."

"If they want to be helpful, fine, they can be helpful, but it will have to be on a volunteer basis. They've been here for over eight hours already today and we've got a busy week in front of us. I can't pay them to stay after hours."

Fletcher again tried to reason with his cousin. "Look at that section there—it hasn't even been stapled yet. Then we've got to take care of the baseboards, the gaps, the puttying—"

"I know the order of layering a floor," Aaron jeered. "Listen, we tried our best to finish it today, but it just wasn't possible. If you feel obligated to keep working on it, that's up to you, but I've made my plans for the evening clear and I'm not changing them."

Fletcher was so frustrated he couldn't speak. He couldn't understand why Aaron didn't pride himself on his work ethic, the way virtually all Amish people did. Yet even as the thought entered his mind, he realized he was guilty of judging another person. Running his hand over his face, he silently prayed, *Dear* Gott*, please forgive me for judging my cousin and enable me to be a help, not a hindrance, to my* onkel*'s business.*

"Fletcher," Raymond suggested, "maybe you should take a break. *Kumme* have supper with us and then we'll all return to put in a few more hours—how's that?"

"Speak for yourself!" Aaron chortled.

"*Neh*, you go ahead," Fletcher told Raymond. "But let me give you a note for Anna."

After finding a scrap of paper, he removed the pencil he kept tucked behind his ear. *Dear Anna*, he wrote. *I hope you are feeling better. I have to work late tonight, but I will see you tomorrow. I haven't forgotten my promise.*

While he paused, deliberating whether to sign the note "your Fletcher," or just plain "Fletcher," Aaron ribbed him, "Hurry up, will you? I'm hungry!" So he simply signed the note "F."

Now, some five hours later, Fletcher decided he'd better let Aaron know he was unable to complete the project and they'd need to return in the early morning. He made a detour toward his uncle's house. There was still a lamp lit in the kitchen, so he gave a quick rap on the door before entering the house, where he found Isaiah sitting at the table, drinking something that appeared to be lemonade.

"It's apple cider vinegar, lemon juice, ginger, honey and everything else except the kitchen sink," his uncle joked, raising the mason jar. "It's supposed to help my arthritis. Want some?"

Fletcher laughed. "*Denki*, but I'll pass. I stopped by to talk to Aaron. Is he still up?"

"Up? He's not home yet," Isaiah said. "I'm waiting for him myself. Is there a message you want me to pass along to him?"

"Well…" Fletcher hesitated. He was concerned he might get Aaron in trouble with his father if Isaiah found out they hadn't completed a project before taking on a new one again.

Isaiah prompted him, "At this time of night, there must be a *gut* reason you came here."

"*Jah*, if you could tell him I'll be installing the floor early tomorrow morning, I'd appreciate it."

"Will do," Isaiah confirmed.

Fletcher was about to board his buggy when he heard

the familiar plodding of a horse's hooves, so he waited until his cousin pulled into the yard and explained the situation to him.

Uncharacteristically amenable, Aaron said, "That's fine. I'll join you, if I can pull myself from bed that early. I didn't mean to stay out so late, but you know how it is when you're having fun—you lose track of time. You should have been there. After Anna made supper, we all played Dutch Blitz for hours."

"Anna doesn't like to play Dutch Blitz," Fletcher argued. "She says it makes her head swim."

"That goes to show how well you really know your fiancée," Aaron responded. "She not only suggested the game, she beat us all!"

How could that be? Fletcher wondered, long into the night. *She told me her preferences hadn't changed.* His old worry about what else she might feel differently about plagued his thoughts almost until the sun came up, and by then it was time for him to rise, too.

Chapter Nine

The next morning Anna got up early to fix a tray of coffee, eggs and toast for Naomi before making breakfast for the rest of the family.

"Are you awake, Naomi?" she asked as she slowly pushed open the door to her stepmother's room.

"Oh, *guder mariye*, Anna," Naomi replied, lifting her head from the pillow. "This looks *wunderbaar*, but I feel much better now. I can get up."

"Please don't," Anna pleaded. "I've already checked on Eli and he's sleeping peacefully, so I thought I'd sit here with you and drink my *kaffi* before the boys *kumme* in from milking. I stayed up too late last night."

Naomi held a forkful of eggs midair. "You weren't ill again, were you?"

"*Neh*, I played several games of Dutch Blitz with Melinda, Aaron and the boys. It was nearly nine o'clock when we stopped and then I had to do the dishes."

"But I thought you loathe playing Dutch Blitz?"

"I do...but I was trying to make peace with Melinda

and Aaron. Lately I've made a few comments to them I wish I hadn't."

"Whatever you said, I have a hunch they deserved it."

"You wouldn't be saying that if you'd heard the remark I made to them yesterday," Anna hinted before detailing her exchange with them.

"Oh dear," was all Naomi said when Anna was finished.

"I told you it was bad!" Anna lamented. "What I need to do is apologize. Do you suppose I could make a special dinner tonight and invite Aaron, by way of smoothing things over?"

"But you've been ill—"

"I'm all better now," Anna asserted. "In fact, at the clinic yesterday I bumped into Dr. Donovan and we discussed what was ailing me and he said everything I'm experiencing is perfectly normal." Anna didn't clarify that what was ailing her was emotional, not physical.

"Really?" Naomi questioned. "I'm so glad to hear it! In that case, *jah*, we can serve a special dinner tonight. I was invited to Ruth Graber's for supper this evening, but I'll stay home to help you instead—"

"Neh!" Anna butted in. "You deserve a night out with your friends. Please go!"

Naomi hesitated before surrendering. "I'll go under one condition," she stated seriously, holding up her finger for effect. "Whatever you do, don't make ham or pork chops for dinner. Otherwise, Melinda and Aaron might question how sincere you are about apologizing for calling anyone's behavior piggish!"

They burst into laughter as the door swung open. It

was Eli, declaring he was starving. While Naomi went to fix breakfast, Anna returned to her room to tell Melinda about the special supper, but her cousin had a pillow covering her head and was snoring softly.

Anna took out a notepad and wrote, *Dear Fletcher, I hope you will be able to come to supper tonight.* Without thinking twice, she signed it, *Your Anna.* Then, she scribbled an invitation to Aaron, too. *Aaron, you're invited to join us for supper tonight. —Anna.*

For their meal, Anna made beef stew and corn bread, with sugar cream pie for dessert, since it was Melinda's and Aaron's favorite treat. After Naomi had left for the evening and the four boys were finishing their evening chores in the stable, Anna approached Melinda and Aaron in the sitting room to apologize before Fletcher arrived.

"I want to apologize to you both for the remark I made the other day," she said, glad the room was dim so they couldn't see the heat rising in her cheeks. "I hope you'll forgive me."

Melinda stuck out her lower lip. "If you must know, I've grown accustomed to your surly disposition since the accident and I've learned to overlook it, but Aaron isn't used to your attitude. He was upset for a long part of the evening, weren't you, Aaron?"

Anna linked her fingers behind her back, squeezing them together as tightly as she could as a reminder to hold her tongue, even though she was thinking that Aaron wasn't so upset he couldn't play several games of cards.

"Jah," he admitted. "I never expected you to make such a churlish remark, Anna."

Please, Lord, she silently prayed, *give me grace*. "I understand how surprising that must have been for you," was as close as she could come to expressing further regret. "I assure you it won't happen again. Now *kumme*, supper is ready."

"Wait!" Aaron leaped to his feet, positioning himself directly in front of Anna and boring into her eyes with his. "I'm sorry, too. I could sense you were in pain or upset and I… I tried joking to make you laugh. I always used to be able to make you feel better, but lately, it's as if… I don't know, as if we're enemies or something."

Anna's feet seemed nailed to the floor and her mouth fell open. She hadn't heard Aaron sound so contrite since before Melinda came to live there. Perhaps she'd been judging him too harshly?

"We're not enemies at all," she said, smiling graciously to prove her point. "In fact, we're about to become family."

"Now there's the dimple I've missed seeing!" Aaron declared, taking a step closer.

"Am I too late?" Fletcher asked from behind Anna.

She twirled, eager to see his toothy grin once more, but she was met with a somber frown. *"Neh,"* she consoled him. "That's the *gut* thing about stew. It can simmer on the stove until we're ready to eat it, which we are! *Kumme*."

"Stew?" Aaron sounded pleased. "Did you make corn bread, too?"

"Jah," Anna replied distractedly, leading them to the table.

"I haven't had your stew and corn bread for ages," he commented. "No one makes it quite the way you do."

During their meal, Eli and Evan recounted the fiasco they'd witnessed that day in school when one of the oldest scholars got wedged between the rungs of the porch stairs during lunch hour and couldn't get free. Then, the men summarized their newest project at work, and afterward, Melinda described her activities assisting customers at the shop.

"It's always so busy there," she remarked to Anna. "I enjoy it, but sometimes I long for the days when I was home and I could have a cup of tea or take a little nap whenever I wanted."

"I'm sure you do," Anna replied, getting up to bring the pie to the table.

"Is that sugar cream pie?" Aaron asked. "My favorite!"

"It's one of Melinda's favorites, too," Anna said. "That's why I made it."

"Will we need forks to eat it or are you going to serve it in cups?" Aaron questioned.

For a split second Anna didn't understand what he was referring to, but then she exclaimed, "Oh! I almost forgot about that! The first time I invited Aaron over for Saturday night supper with *Daed* and Naomi, I made this pie—do you remember, Roy and Raymond? I was so nervous I forgot to put in cornstarch and I doubled the cream. No matter how much I beat it, the mixture wouldn't thicken, but I put it in the oven and hoped for the best."

"It was runnier than that gravy!" Ray chortled, pointing to Evan's half-eaten bowl of stew.

Anna giggled into her napkin. "*Jah*, but if I recall correctly, that didn't stop Aaron from eating his entire serving! He said he wanted a spoon so he could get every last drop."

"I was trying to make a *gut* impression on your *daed* and Naomi," he confessed.

"I have to give you credit for that, especially because of the stomachache you endured for two days afterward," Anna said, catching her breath.

She remembered how her father's eyes had twinkled when he'd come home from work and confided to her and Naomi that Aaron spent the better part of the following Monday morning locked inside the men's washroom. Picturing her father's amusement as she conveyed the anecdote made Anna smile from ear to ear.

"You've become a much better cook since then," Aaron said through a mouthful of pie.

"Denki," Anna said. "At least, I haven't poisoned anyone lately, have I, Fletcher?"

She reached for his hand beneath the table but he pushed back his chair and dropped his napkin on his plate. "I need some fresh air," he said. "Eli and Evan, do you want to go turtle hunting down at the creek with me?"

The three of them were out the door before Anna had time to put the leftovers away.

Fletcher took such long strides the boys had to run to keep up. He could hear Anna calling him from a distance, but he didn't stop until Evan said, "Fletcher, I think Anna wants to *kumme*, too. We're supposed to wait whenever she calls us."

He stopped abruptly but didn't turn around to watch her approach. When he heard footsteps and the rustle of her skirt behind him, he resumed walking.

She instructed the boys, "I'm going to walk with Fletcher and I'd like the two of you to give us our privacy. You may run up ahead of us, but what's the rule at the creek?"

"We have to stay ten steps back from the edge unless an adult is present," they droned, before sprinting down the hill.

"Are you trying to stay ten steps away from *me*?" she breathlessly called to Fletcher, who slowed his pace slightly.

"Do you want me to?" he asked.

"Of course not! Why would I want that?"

Fletcher didn't mince words. "You seemed to be standing very close to Aaron when I came in. I thought perhaps your *preferences* had changed."

Anna grabbed his wrist, pulling him to a complete stop. Her brows formed a severe line across her forehead as she glowered at him. "Whatever are you talking about, Fletcher?"

"I'm talking about the fact you spent the evening playing cards with him yesterday. You sent him a personal invitation this morning. You were practically standing nose-to-nose with him when I walked in this evening. You made his favorite dessert for supper. And you spent the entire meal reliving your courtship. *That's* what I'm talking about!" he ranted.

Anna didn't so much drop his wrist as flung it at him before she wordlessly tromped down the hill.

"Is that your response?" Fletcher shouted after her. "You have nothing to say?"

Twirling around, she glared at him and shouted back, "Believe me, you wouldn't want to hear the things I might say if I didn't hold my tongue at this moment. Besides, I've lost sight of the boys and I need to make sure they're okay."

Although he was seething, Fletcher followed her at a distance, also concerned about the boys' safety. After cutting through the woods, he spotted them overturning rocks along the upper embankment. Anna was watching from her roost on the boulder. Fletcher picked up a handful of pebbles and tarried midway between Anna and the boys, aimlessly chucking the stones one by one into the water.

"I think if there are any turtles here, they've gone in for the night," Eli hollered.

"*Jah*, probably," Fletcher called back. "They like warm sunshine, not cool evening air. But the frogs might be out. See if you can sneak up on one of them."

While the boys dropped to their knees in the grass, Fletcher ambled over to where Anna was sitting and leaned against the far edge of the same boulder. Her profile was set like concrete as she gazed across the creek and spoke in a controlled monotone.

"The card game, the invitation, the special dinner—it was all because I referred to Aaron as a pig yesterday.

I was trying to make amends. When you entered the parlor before dinner, I'd just finished apologizing. You can ask Melinda and Aaron if you don't believe me."

Feeling like a fool, Fletcher said, "That won't be necessary, Anna. I believe you."

"Really?" Her nostrils flared as she faced him. "Because I've told you repeatedly I don't have feelings for Aaron, yet you keep accusing me of—"

"It's not an accusation, Anna," Fletcher interrupted. His throat burned as he admitted, "It's… I don't know. I guess it's some kind of nagging concern on my part."

"But I keep telling you there's no reason for such concern."

Fletcher hesitated. He knew he was in dangerous territory but if he didn't voice his complaint now, it would resurface in his thoughts and affect his relationship with Anna until he did. "But you really did seem to cherish recalling your courtship with Aaron tonight."

Anna threw her hands into the air and then slapped them against her lap. "What I cherished recalling was a happy memory of my *daed*, not of Aaron!"

Just then one of the boys let out a tremendous shriek. Anna and Fletcher sprang from the boulder and whipped around: the noise had come from behind them.

"He yanked my hand really, really hard!" Evan wailed, purple-faced and sobbing.

"He wouldn't *kumme* when I told him to," Eli tattled.

Anna crouched to examine the mark on the back of Evan's hand where Eli had grabbed it and then she lifted it to her lips and blew on it before giving his skin a kiss. "I know it hurts," she said. "But you'll survive.

Why don't you go search that patch of grass over there to see what kinds of creatures you can find?"

Then she took Eli by the shoulders and looked into his eyes. "What has your *mamm* taught you about using your voice instead of your hands to express yourself?"

"But he was spying on you and Fletcher and you said you wanted privacy!" Eli blubbered. "Terrible things happen when you spy and I didn't want you to get hurt again!"

As Anna pulled the sobbing child to her chest and patted his back, she sent Fletcher a quizzical look and he shrugged in return, their own argument momentarily suspended. When Eli was quieted again, Anna took his hands in hers and asked, "What do you mean, you don't want me to get hurt again?"

Eli shook his head. "I can't tell you."

Anna lifted Eli's hands and gave them a small shake for emphasis. "I promise you, no matter what you say, you won't be punished for telling the truth. Do you know something about my accident? Is that what you meant about me getting hurt again?"

The boy nodded and a few more tears bounced off his round cheeks.

"Eli, it's very important you tell me."

Eli sucked his bottom lip in and out as he confessed, "I was spying on you and Aaron at the creek the night before your accident. People can get hurt when other people eavesdrop or repeat gossip, that's what *Mamm* and you always tell me, but I did it anyway and then the next day you got injured. I'm sorry, Anna. I'm really, really sorry."

Fletcher felt as if he'd been walloped in the abdomen with a fifty-pound sack of feed. The night before Anna's accident was a Monday; he remembered because he was personally extending wedding invitations to people outside their church, as was the Amish custom in their district. What were Anna and Aaron doing at the creek together?

"Shh, shh, shh," Anna shushed Eli, enfolding him in her arms. "You were very brave to tell me the truth, but I promise you, Eli, it wasn't your fault I hurt my head."

"Neh," Fletcher confirmed, peeling Eli out of Anna's grasp. "It wasn't your fault at all and this one time, it's okay to repeat what you heard when you were eavesdropping. So I want you to think hard, Eli. What were Anna and Aaron talking about at the creek?"

Anna straightened into a standing position. "Why are you asking him that? He's a *kind.* I'm sure he can't remember what two adults were talking about, much less understand the context—"

"Do you?" Fletcher was squatting on the balls of his feet next to Eli as he stared into the child's eyes. "Do you remember what Anna and Aaron were talking about?"

"Neh." Eli shook his head. "I wasn't close enough to hear. I only saw them kissing and then *Mamm* called me home from up the hill."

The boy's reply staggered Fletcher and he landed on his backside, too stunned to speak or move.

"It's getting dark." Anna felt light-headed and her voice trembled. "Eli and Evan, I'd like you boys to go directly into the house and tell Melinda or Raymond or Roy that Anna said one of them is to draw a bath for you. Fletcher and I will follow you from a distance."

After the boys scurried into the woods, Anna extended her hand to Fletcher, but he pushed it out of his way. He stood up of his own volition and smacked the dirt from the back of his trousers before striding after the boys.

"Fletcher!" Anna called. Her legs felt as if they were made of pudding and she struggled to keep up. "I don't know what Eli thought he saw, but you can't possibly take it seriously. He's a *kind*. He doesn't know what he's talking about."

Fletcher pivoted and marched back toward her, his eyes ablaze. "You're right, Eli is a *kind*, so I can't trust his interpretation of events. And you have amnesia, so I can't trust yours, either, can I? However, there is *one* person who knows for certain what happened that Monday night and although I've never found him to be entirely reliable, this time I'll have to take him at his word!"

"Neh!" Anna pleaded, tugging on his arm. "You can't ask Aaron that."

"Why not, Anna? Because you don't want me to find out the truth—is that it?"

"Neh, because it's so false as to be *narrish*!" Anna negated the notion, referring to it as crazy. "Besides, you'll upset the *kinner* if you go tearing into the house like a rabid dog! Eli has been bearing the guilt of my accident for weeks. That's probably why he's had such terrible stomachaches. Do you want to upset him fur-

ther? You know how that will affect Naomi! And what about Melinda? How will she feel if you accuse her fiancé of kissing me?"

Fletcher shook Anna's hand from his forearm. "She'll feel devastated, the same way I feel now—but it's better if she knows the truth before she marries Aaron."

Anna charged up ahead of Fletcher so she could angle to face him as he approached. "It doesn't have to be that way, Fletcher. You don't have to feel devastated and neither does Melinda. The only reason you feel that way is because you've already decided I'm guilty. You're not giving me the benefit of the doubt!"

"I've been giving you the benefit of the doubt since the moment I received the note from you, Anna. I've been hoping and praying and believing it didn't mean what I thought it meant. I convinced myself—*you* convinced me—that there had to be some kind of logical explanation. It had to be some kind of mistake," he sputtered.

For a moment Anna thought he was going to cry, but instead he stopped talking. When he spoke again, his volume was subdued. "I want to believe Eli is mistaken more than I've ever wanted anything in my life. But until we talk to Aaron about it, I'll always have a doubt in my mind."

"Okay, fine," she conceded. "We'll talk to him—but outside, just the three of us. Not where the *kinner* or Melinda can hear."

When they got within sight of the house, they noticed Roy heading indoors with the milk pail, so they asked him to send Aaron outside to the barn. While they were waiting, Anna lifted her apron to wipe her face, and then smoothed the fabric back into place, unable to look Fletcher in the eye. A second later, she heard the house door slamming, followed by the patter of footfall.

"I have a direct question for you and I expect the absolute truth," Fletcher said frankly when Aaron stood before them near the side of the barn. "Did you and Anna kiss the day before her accident?"

Aaron jerked his head backward and then a bemused smirk snaked across his lips. "You remembered?" he asked Anna, and immediately Fletcher kicked the side of the barn so forcefully the cows inside lowed.

Overcome with disbelief, Anna closed her eyes until the spinning sensation stopped. By the time she opened them, Fletcher had left. Her fists clenched, she snarled at Aaron, "Get out of my way." When he stepped aside, she rushed across the yard to where Fletcher was unhitching his horse from the post.

"Perhaps the kiss didn't mean what you think it means," she said. She was nearly on her knees, pleading for him to consider other possibilities. "Things aren't always as they appear to be—"

"Stop!" Fletcher directed, holding up his hand. "Enough is enough! The kiss means exactly what I think it means and so does your note. I can accept the truth, but now it's time—it's *past* time—for you to admit it."

"And what truth is that?"

Fletcher glanced toward the back door of the house, waiting until Aaron went inside again. "You still love Aaron," he hissed.

Anna's mouth twisted as she cried openly. "But I

don't. I'm telling you, Fletcher, I don't love him. May the Lord forgive me, but most of the time I don't even *like* him."

"The facts say otherwise."

"They aren't facts. They're perceptions. Erroneous perceptions," she sobbed. "I don't know how to explain what happened the day before my accident, but I do know what it feels like to be betrayed and I would never, ever do that to anyone, especially you."

"Perhaps not willingly, not consciously, but you don't know your own heart, Joyce."

The slip of his tongue wasn't lost on Anna. "I do, too, know my own heart. I know it far better than you do," she contradicted, "and my name is Anna, not Joyce."

"*Jah*, but you're sure acting a lot like she did."

Anna shook her head sadly, slowly backing away. She choked out the words, "I can't marry a man who doesn't trust me."

"And I can't marry a woman I can't trust," Fletcher retorted as he climbed into his buggy.

Clasping her hands over her mouth, Anna fled to the house. When she got inside, she sailed past the dirty dishes still on the table, avoided the sitting room where Aaron and the older boys were taking out the cards for a game of Dutch Blitz and ignored Melinda's request for assistance above the sound of sloshing water in the washroom. As far as Anna was concerned, the entire household could collapse around her. She was tired of helping them: at this moment, she was the one who needed help. In her bedroom, she threw herself to her knees beside her bed, but found she couldn't say a word to the Lord. Instead, she poured out her heart in the form of rasping sobs, knowing He'd understand.

It was a good thing the horse often traveled the route between Anna's house and his, because Fletcher was so angry he couldn't see straight, and the animal was guided more by habit than by Fletcher's hand. He hardly recalled stabling the horse and walking into the house, but once inside, he paced from room to room, attempting to make sense of the events that had just unfolded. No matter how desperately he tried to allow for the possibility that all was not lost, he kept circling back to the same conclusion: Anna loved Aaron. Or, at the very least, she felt conflicted enough to kiss him only one day after publicly announcing her engagement to Fletcher. In either case, the wedding was off. Their *marriage* was off. Their bond was broken.

Asking himself how this situation could possibly be happening again, he reflected on his early days with Anna. After what he'd been through with Joyce Beiler, he could scarcely believe it when God blessed him with the type of relationship he shared with Anna. She had been trusting, open, good-humored and gracious beyond measure. Until he met her, he hadn't really known what love was—and not just the love he had for her, but the love she reciprocated toward him. The connection they shared grew stronger every day until he was certain it wouldn't just endure throughout their lifetime; it would flourish. But he'd been wrong.

Raking his hand through his hair, he spotted his wedding suit carefully arranged on a hanger that was hooked to a peg on the wall of the parlor. He'd put it there the day after kissing Anna for the first time since her accident. It was meant to remind him to focus on the future. But now the suit's form seemed to mock how lifeless he felt internally and he lunged toward it, swiping it from the peg and hurling it to the floor, where it lay in a crumpled heap like the rest of his dreams.

He kicked it aside and smacked the heel of his hand against the outer wall of the alcove. Then he did the same with the opposite hand. The force of his blows left two cracked dents in the plasterboard, but he was so embittered he swung his foot, putting a third hole in the wall before dropping backward onto the sofa. The damaged wall looked like two eyes and a serious mouth staring disapprovingly at him, so he quickly jumped to his feet and stormed out of the house.

Unaware of where he was going, Fletcher only knew he couldn't sit still. He trekked long into the night, ruminating about what would come next. Unfortunately, he knew from experience that he and Anna would need to meet with the deacon before announcing publicly that they'd called the wedding off. As for the humiliation that would follow, he supposed some might think he'd be better equipped to handle it the second time around, since he knew what to expect. But instead, he felt doubly mortified. Not only would he have to bear the disgrace of his broken engagement in Willow Creek, but word would travel to Green Lake, where he imagined he'd become something of a laughingstock.

Sniggering bitterly, he realized he was running out of places to go to escape the humiliation of being jilted.

Nevertheless, he'd have to find somewhere else to live and work. He'd finish up the project they were working on now and give Isaiah and Aaron time to find another crew member to replace him, but then he was going to move on. There was no way he could continue to work for his cousin: it was only by the grace of God he hadn't verbally unleashed his fury on Aaron back at the barn. He knew what the Bible said about forgiveness and anger, yet he also knew what it said about fleeing temptation. Given the option, Fletcher thought it was wise to make himself scarce as soon as possible.

As he ambled up the lane to his own yard again, he realized he'd probably have to forfeit the house to Aaron and Melinda. Or worse, to Aaron and Anna. Crossing the grass, Fletcher tried to convince himself that the tears in his eyes were due to spring allergies and he wiped his face with the back of his sleeve. Still too distraught to sleep, he took out his tools and supplies and began repairing the holes he'd made in the wall. By the time he was finished, the sun was just peeking over the horizon and he was finally exhausted. He laid down on his bed fully dressed and was asleep before he had a chance to remove his shoes.

He woke to a loud banging on the door. Although he had no idea what time it was, he guessed from the sunlight flooding the room that it was after ten or eleven o'clock. *That better not be Aaron coming to lecture me for being late to work*, he thought.

When he tugged open the door, he was surprised to see his uncle. Had Aaron told him about what happened the previous night? Was that why he was here?

"*Onkel* Isaiah, *kumme* in," Fletcher said. "I... I wasn't feeling my best last night so I decided to sleep in. I'm late for work."

"*Jah*, I can see that," he noted. "I'll put on a pot of *kaffi* while you wash up."

After shaving, Fletcher emerged from the washroom. His uncle was in the alcove, examining the built-in bookshelf and opening and closing the built-in drawers on the interior wall. Extending a mug to Fletcher, Isaiah made a sweeping motion with his hand and said, "This is the finest design and craftsmanship I've ever seen from someone your age—your *daed* trained you well. Anna must be delighted."

Fletcher swallowed. So, Aaron hadn't told his father about last evening's debacle after all. Then why was Isaiah calling on him? "She hasn't seen it yet," he replied. "It's supposed to be a surprise."

"How is she doing?" Isaiah inquired cordially.

"She's healing slowly but surely," Fletcher answered. Until Anna and Fletcher met with the deacon, he decided he'd keep the news of the breakup to himself.

"That's *gut*," Isaiah continued. "You've probably been under a lot of financial pressure, what with her injury and medical bills and the work of preparing the house for her to move into it, including making these renovations?"

Fletcher was puzzled by what his uncle was getting at. "*Jah*, I was," he answered without elaborating.

"That must be costly," Isaiah commented, appearing to read Fletcher's reaction.

Fletcher wondered if his uncle had come to discuss

his wages. "I try to be a *gut* steward with my resources," he said. "*Gott* always provides."

Isaiah didn't seem to hear him. His uncle's posture was so stiff and his skin so ashen, Fletcher wondered if he was ill. But he reasoned Isaiah would have gone directly home from work if he was sick. Besides, how did his uncle even know he could find Fletcher here instead of at the job site? Had Aaron or Roy or Raymond told him?

Isaiah pulled at his beard, finally stating gravely, "There is no easy way to approach this subject, so I will be direct. I have been looking over our accounts and there are some discrepancies."

"Discrepancies?" Fletcher echoed, confused. "What kind of discrepancies?"

"We have an unexplained deficit of nearly two thousand dollars," his uncle explained.

Fletcher whistled. "That's a lot. Could there be a mistake?"

"I have repeatedly tried to reconcile it myself."

"I see. I'm very sorry to hear that and I'd like to help you, *Onkel*, but aside from using a measuring tape, math and numbers have never been strengths of mine."

"*Neh*, son, I don't want you to look over the account," Isaiah said, his ears purpling. "I—I want to know if you know anything about this matter."

Suddenly the real concern behind Isaiah's comments about medical bills and the expense of making renovations to the house came clear. Fletcher felt as if his uncle had clocked him over the head with a wrench.

"While it's true I've occasionally signed off on the

company account—under Aaron's direction—or used the bank card to purchase supplies or withdraw cash for our work projects, I've always provided him the receipts," Fletcher declared. "I don't know anything about this matter."

His uncle took him by the shoulders and looked him in the eye. "I believe you, Fletcher, but it was only fair and right for me to ask. Now drink your *kaffi* and then make yourself some eggs. You look like you could use a little nourishment."

But after the door clicked shut behind Isaiah, Fletcher was too nauseated to eat. He hadn't thought it was possible to feel more betrayed than he'd felt when he confirmed Anna kissed Aaron, but once again, he was wrong. Having his own uncle accuse him of thievery was an indignity greater than he could bear. Setting his hat on his head, he decided then and there that he'd return to work alright—but only long enough to tell Aaron he quit. Then he was packing up his things and leaving immediately. He couldn't get away from Willow Creek fast enough.

Chapter Ten

After her *daed* died, Anna discovered one of the horrible truths about grieving: no matter how many tears she shed, her eyes never ran dry. It was as if her body had an unlimited capacity to mourn. She found this truth returning to her as she soaked her pillow with sadness the morning after her argument with Fletcher, just as she'd done the previous night.

There was a tap on the door and Anna sat up. Her eyelids were so swollen she practically had to pry them open with her fingertips, but since the shades were drawn she hoped her stepmother wouldn't notice she'd been crying. *"Guder mariye,"* she said as Naomi entered with a tray of tea, cheese and fruit.

"You mean *guder nammidaag*," Naomi replied. "How are you feeling?"

"Groggy, but otherwise alright. I'm sorry. I really overslept."

"*Neh*, I don't mean how are you feeling physically, Anna dear. Clearly something is troubling you and I'd like to help."

Anna was moved by Naomi's expression of compassion. Knowing she could disclose even her deepest heartaches to her stepmother, Anna confided what transpired the evening before and the decision she and Fletcher had made. She managed to get through most of the details without weeping, but when she started to sniff, Naomi moved to wrap an arm around her shoulders.

When Anna finished speaking, Naomi exhaled heavily. "I'm disappointed," she said. "Very, very disappointed."

"I know, Naomi. You've put so much work into preparing the house and—"

"Neh!" She clarified, "I'm not disappointed for my sake. I'm disappointed for yours. Quite frankly, I'm disappointed in Fletcher. I thought he was more mature than that."

Anna was surprised to hear herself defending him. "But, Naomi, as difficult as it is for me to believe it myself, there's very little question that I kissed Aaron. It's no wonder Fletcher is upset."

"Upset, *jah*. But Fletcher knows your character, just as I know your character, and I sense a piece of this puzzle is still missing—especially because Aaron is involved."

Anna took a napkin from the tray and blew her nose with it. "It hardly matters anymore. Fletcher and I have made up our minds. I suppose we'll have to talk to the deacon before we tell the *leit* from church that the wedding is off. We'll want to notify our out-of-state guests as soon as possible, too. I guess we'll call them from the phone shanty, so they can cancel their travel plans. But I don't know how or what I'm going to tell Melinda. I don't think she has any clue about what happened last night."

Naomi patted Anna's shoulder. "You shouldn't concern yourself with those matters right now. Melinda's wedding is still almost three weeks away. You needn't tell her anything right now. Today, you need all the rest you can get. Your head will be clearer tomorrow."

"*Jah*, since I don't have to keep up with my own wedding preparation schedule anymore, I'll take a leisurely walk down to the creek."

"That sounds like a *gut* idea," Naomi replied as she stood to leave. "It's a beautiful spring day. Just be careful not to slip on any rocks."

By the time Anna finished picking at the plate of food Naomi had brought her, got dressed and journeyed to the creek, she felt so fatigued she wished she were back in bed. Her lethargy was more emotional than physical: every thought she had was of her breakup with Fletcher. Closing her eyes, she reclined on the boulder and tried to concentrate on the warmth of the sun on her skin, the smell of damp earth and the sound of water cascading over the stones. But it was no use: she kept envisioning the shocked look on Fletcher's face when Eli announced he'd seen her and Aaron kissing.

Hearing a rustle coming from the direction of the park, she snapped her eyelids open and pushed herself upright. At first, she could only spy a dark head of hair through an opening of the trees and her breath quickened: it was Fletcher! But then the figure rounded the bend and she realized her mistake. The man's build was stocky and short, not lanky and tall.

"What are you doing here?" she demanded to know.

"*Guder nammidaag* to you, too," Aaron replied. "I've *kumme* to talk to you about what happened when we kissed. I wanted to tell you that you mustn't blame yourself."

Anna shielded her face with her hands to hide her humiliation. Her stomach was turning upside down and she wished Aaron would just vanish, but it sounded as if he was about to apologize and the least she could do was hear him out.

Instead, he patted her shoulder and said, "I know you can't remember it now, but initially you were taken in by Fletcher because you were grieving and he provided a shoulder to cry on."

Anna shook her head. "*Neh*, that's not true," she contradicted.

Aaron persisted, "When he offered to walk out with you, you accepted in order to get back at me for dating Melinda. I confess, I was only feigning interest in her to hasten you to marry me because you'd been putting off the decision for so long. The entire situation had gotten completely out of hand, like a prank that had gone too far. But by the time we came to our senses, you had already agreed to marry Fletcher and I had proposed to Melinda."

"*Neh*." She panted, rising from the rock and spinning to face him. "*Neh*, it wasn't like that. My relationship with Fletcher had nothing to do with you."

"You don't remember, but it did. You as much as told

me so yourself, when we discussed the matter under this very tree the day before your accident, the day we kissed," Aaron murmured, inching closer. "You said the charade had gone on long enough. Even though I was conflicted about breaking Melinda's heart, you insisted that I tell her how I really felt. I have to believe that was because you wanted me back."

"Neh," Anna repeated, although some small part of what he was saying struck a chord deep in her memory. Her eyes began to spill and she swiped her cheek against her shoulder. "That's not right. It can't be."

"Jah, it is. But the next morning, you suffered your concussion and since then, you've never been able to recall what we discussed here, have you?"

"I've forgotten, but—"

"After a few weeks, it was clear to me your memory of our conversation would never return, even though I dropped as many hints about how we still felt about each other as I could. Since you were intent on marrying Fletcher, it seemed wrong for me to interfere, especially because Melinda and I had pressed forward with our own wedding plans."

Anna covered her ears to block out Aaron's words but he pulled her hands away and gripped them in his own.

"The other night, playing cards, we had such a *wunderbaar* evening together, like old times. You can't deny it," he insisted. "And now, Fletcher finally knows the truth… I think *Gott* may have brought us back together, Anna. I think it's time we acknowledge we've been His intended for each other all along."

"It was you, not Fletcher!" Anna squawked, suddenly

understanding the memory she had of a man kissing her beneath the willow there at the creek. So *that* was why the feelings associated with it were so disturbing to her!

"Exactly, it was me you loved, not Fletcher," Aaron cooed, wrapping his arms around her trembling shoulders and whispering into her ear. "Now you've got it."

"Neh," she threatened. "Now *you're* going to get it if you don't let go of me this instant and get out of my sight."

Aaron stepped back and his mouth dropped open as if he was about to retort, but Anna screwed her face into the most menacing look she could muster and he left without uttering another syllable. Then, she picked up a stone and lobbed it into the current. *I knew I wouldn't have voluntarily kissed Aaron!* she thought. *I knew it!* But her discovery was of little satisfaction: even if she set the record straight by telling Fletcher what happened, he already admitted he didn't trust her. *If he really knew and loved me, he would have trusted me no matter what Aaron had said*, she thought.

She stumbled back to the boulder, where she lay covering her face with her hands and crying until her head began to ache, and she knew if she didn't stop she'd wind up in Dr. Donovan's office again. Squinting, she thought she saw something glinting overhead between the trunk and an arm of the willow. She circled the tree, craning her neck: there was definitely something up there. Like a flash of lightning, the phrase "squirrel it away in a secret place" occurred to her. That's what she'd told Fletcher she did with her journal!

She leaped up and grabbed hold of the bottom

branch. However depleted she felt physically, she made up for it in sheer determination, hoisting herself over the limb in a burst of vigor. Once upright, she was an avid climber, ascending the branches as easily as a ladder. She wrenched the tin from its storage place and scampered back to the ground. Scraped raw, her fingers trembled as she pried the rusted tin open.

She removed the journal and pressed the cold leather to her cheek. Using the key from the string she'd worn around her neck ever since she'd learned the journal was missing, she could feel her heart thudding as she unclasped the lock and opened the diary to the first page. *This journal was given to me by Fletcher Chupp, what a heel*, it said.

Her tears were bittersweet as she ran up the hill to the house, clutching all that remained of her relationship with Fletcher to her heart.

When Fletcher arrived at the work site after lunch, he found Roy and Raymond working unsupervised. He didn't want them to hear what he had come to say to his cousin, so he planned to conduct his conversation outdoors. "Where's Aaron?" he asked.

"He was already here this morning when Melinda dropped us off," Roy reported. "But after he talked to her, he left again. It was too early for Melinda to go to the shop—the two of them probably sneaked off for *kaffi* and doughnuts somewhere."

Raymond rolled his eyes over Roy's head. "He also mentioned he had to run an errand," Raymond elaborated. "I wonder if he went with his *daed* to the lumber store to talk about the problem with the accounts."

"What do you know about the problem with the accounts?" Fletcher's ears perked up.

"Nothing," Raymond replied. "Only that Isaiah came here this morning and questioned Roy and me about a discrepancy."

"I told him I didn't know anything about it, either," Roy chimed in.

"We aren't even allowed to sign for anything," Raymond stated. "But Isaiah said as a matter of fairness he was asking each of us on the crew. He said he intended no offense, but he needed to check with us before making a major decision that would affect the responsible party."

"Jah," Roy agreed. "It sounds as if we may be taking our business to another lumber store soon. Either that, or Aaron's really going to get an earful. It all depends on whose fault it was, I guess."

Ach, Fletcher realized, *Onkel wasn't singling me out!* Fletcher was absolutely dumbfounded. He had completely misread the situation. He'd been so indignant about what he deemed was Isaiah's unwarranted insinuation that he'd been ready to quit his job and abandon his family on the spot over the offense. But come to find out, Fletcher was the one in the wrong: Isaiah didn't mean what Fletcher thought he meant. "Things aren't always as they appear to be," Anna said the night before and Fletcher had scoffed at her for it.

Isaiah's words, "I believe you, Fletcher, but it was only fair and right for me to ask," echoed in his mind.

Isaiah simply asked the question and accepted Fletcher's response immediately, regardless of how incriminating his financial circumstances may have appeared.

But had Fletcher demonstrated the same level of trust in Anna, the woman he claimed to love? No. On the contrary, he'd badgered her with repeated inquiries and then dismissed her answers anyway. He'd as much as said she was ignorant, if not lying, about her deepest feelings. The realization of how he'd failed her caused his heart to spasm with a searing pain. He had to apologize. He had to beg her forgiveness and keep begging it until she accepted his apology.

"Are you alright?" Raymond asked.

"*Neh*, I'm not," Fletcher answered. "I have to leave immediately. If Aaron returns, tell him…tell him I'm not coming in for the rest of the day."

Before he could see Anna, there was a present Fletcher wanted to buy, something he'd seen in the gift shop at the medical center in Highland Springs. He wasted no time journeying there, and when he arrived he hastily hitched the horse in the adjoining lot and hustled toward the building. He made his purchase inside and was about to exit when a familiar form breezed through the door.

"Fletcher!" Dr. Donovan's voice reverberated. "You're not here visiting anyone, are you?"

"*Neh*. Just taking care of a personal matter. Getting a gift for Anna, actually."

"Glad to hear it. After what the two of you have been through, I wouldn't want any more challenges coming your way before the big day." He thrust his arm forward to shake hands with Fletcher. "Congratulations, son—and give that bride of yours my best wishes, too."

"Thank you, I will," Fletcher said. *Provided she's still talking to me.*

Realizing he hadn't changed his clothes since the morning before, Fletcher stopped at home to put on a fresh shirt and pants before calling on Anna. He brushed his teeth and hair and was locking the door behind him when he noticed his uncle sitting on a bench on the porch.

"My knee aches—it must be going to rain tomorrow," Isaiah said by way of greeting.

Clearly his uncle had come back to discuss something more important than the weather, and Fletcher wished he'd let him know what it was because he needed to be on his way to Anna's house.

"I'm getting too old for the kind of work we do," Isaiah confided. "I'm definitely too old to have a son who behaves so irresponsibly. I had hoped by working with you every day, he'd pick up on some of your values and habits, but instead, he's only taken advantage of your scrupulous work ethic."

Fletcher couldn't deny the truth of what Isaiah was saying but neither did he think it prudent to confirm it, so he remained silent.

"What's more, he's made a mess of our orders and our accounts. His sloppiness nearly cost us our relationship with our supplier in the process. But I believe he can improve his abilities if he receives additional training under my tutelage," his uncle proposed. "I'd like him to work with me on our projects in the Highland Springs community."

Fletcher nodded, relieved that Isaiah seemed to have reconciled the deficit in the account. Although he imagined the demotion was disgruntling to his cousin, Fletcher marveled at Isaiah's forbearance toward Aaron. Anna's words, "People change. They grow. With *Gott*'s help, we all do," ran through Fletcher's mind as he realized his uncle still carried that kind of loving hope for his son. Fletcher prayed Anna would see Fletcher's own potential for change and growth, too.

Isaiah continued, "What this means, however, is I'll need a reliable, knowledgeable foreman to handle our *Englisch* clients and to supervise the crew. Raymond is too inexperienced to be a foreman, although he'll get a pay raise. Eventually Roy will, too, if he keeps progressing like he is… Anyway, what do you say? Will you accept the position of foreman?"

Denki, Lord, Fletcher prayed.

"The promotion would mean a raise for you, too, of course," Isaiah offered, prompting Fletcher to his senses.

"*Jah*, of course I will accept the position," he confirmed. "*Denki, Onkel* Isaiah, *denki*!"

"You're the one I should be thanking," Isaiah stated. "You're unfailingly dependable, just like your *daed* always was. But that doesn't mean you don't need a hand yourself. I've been worried about the emotional and financial burden you've been carrying ever since Anna's injury. I understand there were back taxes to pay on the house, too. If you need help, that's what family is for, Fletcher. Just ask."

Fletcher further understood that when his uncle was questioning him about his expenses, it wasn't because Isaiah was accusing him; it was because Isaiah was *concerned* about him.

"*Denki*, I will," Fletcher replied.

Before doddering down the steps, his uncle handed him an envelope. "This is from your *groossdaadi*. I don't know what it says, but he asked me to give it to you in the event your wedding was published in church this spring. Because of the chaos following Anna's accident, I'm sorry to say I forgot all about it until now."

Fletcher waited until he'd embarked his buggy to tear open the envelope. The note read:

To Fletcher J. Chupp,
If you are reading this, it means the lovely Anna Weaver has agreed to become your wife—an answer to my prayers. Although the two of you may have thought you were keeping your courtship a secret, nothing could have been more obvious to me than your mutual fondness, respect and loyalty. It was a delight to spend the last part of my life witnessing the kind of young love that reminded me of my own courtship with your grandmother so many years ago.

Although you both suffered painful betrayals, I'm glad you've decided not to allow past hurts to rob you of future hopes and present happiness. As I've discovered this last year in particular, time passes too quickly, so be sure to keep your heart open to love.

May you, Anna and your family experience God's grace and blessings in your new home.
From Elmer J. Chupp.

Fletcher folded the letter and tucked it beneath the seat. Emboldened by its message, he flicked the reins, working the horse into a rapid gallop. He didn't have a minute to spare.

Anna could hear the distant clatter of pots and pans as Melinda fixed dinner, and she was glad for once she didn't have to participate in the meal preparation. As soon as she returned from the creek, Anna had secured Naomi's promise that her stepmother wouldn't allow anyone to disturb her, and she sequestered herself in her attic room, perusing her diary page by page.

As she read, she rediscovered many of the events Fletcher had already described to her, but many more she had no idea had ever happened. Whether she'd written about a picnic by Wheeler's Pond, reuniting with Fletcher after the tornado struck, or even a small argument over what time they arranged to meet after church, one theme consistently ran throughout the entries: she was in love.

Placing the open book on her stomach as she reclined in bed, Anna realized she didn't need her journal to tell her that. She knew she'd fallen in love with Fletcher all over again because breaking up with him didn't merely split her heart in two; it smashed it into a million bits. A

few tears trickled down her temples before she picked
up the journal and turned the page. A folded sheet of
paper fell to her chest.

The entry in the journal where the letter was tucked
was dated January 12 and it said, *Today Naomi gave
me the enclosed letter, which she only just discovered
hidden in Dad's Bible on his lamp stand. Although it's
nearly a year old, I'm so glad to have received it now.
I'll treasure it always.*

Unfolding the paper, Anna gasped at the sight of her
father's lopsided penmanship. His letter was dated February 18 of the previous year.

My darling Daughter,
Tonight I stood at the bottom of the attic stairs,
as I have every evening this week, listening to
you weeping in your room where you thought no
one could hear you. I am torn between wanting to
comfort you and respecting your privacy (which
you have always fiercely guarded, much to your
brothers' chagrin!).

As difficult as it is to know you're suffering,
I don't believe Aaron is the Lord's intended for
you. He has his admirable qualities to be sure,
but he lacks the sense of responsibility, selfless-
ness and genuine kindness you deserve. If Aaron
possessed those qualities, you would have married him long ago.

Instead, I believe you've continued to allow
him to court you in an effort to model the char-
acteristics he ought to have developed by now. I

see you exhibiting the same gentle patience with Melinda that you've always shown to Aaron. But ultimately, such growth has to come from inside them, through the grace of God, as it does for all of us.

I wish I could take away your heartache, but I trust God will use it for your good. It is my prayer He will provide you a husband who brings you joy instead of grief—perhaps even joy in the midst of grief. When you meet a man like that, you can be certain he is God's intended for you.

Your loving Father.

Anna's heart palpitated as she replaced the letter and turned the page of her journal to the next entry, dated January 19. It read: *Fletcher asked me to marry him and I eagerly accepted. He was willing to wait until wedding season next autumn, but I want to become his wife as soon as possible, so we will take advantage of the bishop's special spring wedding provision and marry on the first available date in April. Nothing would make me more grateful than having him as my husband by Easter.*

There it was, in black and white, the explanation she'd been seeking for why she had been certain after such a brief courtship that Fletcher was God's intended for her. It was what her father wrote about finding a man who brought her joy in the midst of grief that must have helped her to be sure... *But it does me no gut now,* she lamented.

She knew she could show Fletcher the journal. She

could flip to the last entry, as she'd already done and
insist that he read her words, dated Monday, March 2:
*Tonight, Aaron told me he never loved Melinda—he
was only courting her to try to make me jealous. Then
he kissed me and I was so angry, I would have liked
to push him into the creek, may the Lord forgive me! I
pleaded with him to confess the charade to Melinda before the wedding preparations went any further, but he
refused. I don't know what to do, except to tell Fletcher.
He'll know how best to handle it.*

But even if Fletcher saw the error in his thinking
this time, Anna knew that at some point in the future,
an issue or circumstance would arise in which Fletcher
would doubt her and she would feel burdened to prove
herself again. She meant what she said; she couldn't
marry a man who didn't trust her, no matter how much
she loved him. The tears flowed freely and she rolled
onto her side and burrowed her face into her pillow.

She had nearly cried herself to sleep when she heard
a tap at the window. At first she thought it must be the
maple tree's branches blowing in the wind, but when
suddenly it scraped the pane again, she wondered if it
was a bird or a squirrel. She heard it scratch the glass
a third time, louder now, as if it were deliberately trying to enter the house. She crossed the room and slid
the window open, peering into the maple, which was
leafy with new growth.

"Scat," she rebuked the concealed animal. "Go away.
Get!"

"Anna, is that you?" a man's voice called softly.

"Who's there?" she questioned, although she realized

it had to be Aaron. He hadn't been permitted to visit Melinda at suppertime, so he must have been sneaking to speak with her now.

"It's me, Fletcher," he answered.

"Fletcher?" She was completely bewildered. "What in the world are you doing up here?"

"I'm… I'm going out on a limb for you, Anna," Fletcher chuckled awkwardly. "I've *kumme* to apologize."

Anna laughed. In the midst of her grief, Fletcher was bringing her joy. "But you're afraid of heights," she said.

"Naomi wouldn't let me inside to see you," he explained. "But, uh, I would like to get down now. Would you *kumme* outside?"

"I'll be right there," she agreed. She was so glad to see him that she made it downstairs and outside quicker than he descended the tree's branches, but she stopped short of embracing him when he dropped to the ground. She needed to hear his apology first.

"Hello again, Anna," he said, wiping his hands on the sides of his trousers.

"Hello again, Fletcher," she replied. She started to suggest they go sit on the porch swing, but he gently placed a finger to her lips to silence her.

"Please, what I have to say can't wait another instant," Fletcher insisted. He dropped his hand and continued, "I don't know how to explain the note you sent me, or the kiss you and Aaron shared—"

"But I do," Anna interrupted. "It's all in my journal and I can show—"

"Neh!" Fletcher declared urgently. His eyes brimmed

and his voice quavered as he explained, "What I wanted to say was I don't know how to explain those things, but I don't have to explain them, because I know *you*. You've always been truthful and trustworthy about your thoughts and feelings, and having amnesia doesn't change that. So when you told me those things didn't mean what I thought they meant, I should have believed you the first time. The fact that I doubted you is a reflection of my character, not yours. My lack of trust— my insecurity—is a weakness I hope *Gott* will change and you will forgive, because I'm very, very sorry."

Upon her hearing the depth of Fletcher's remorse and the intensity of his belief in her trustworthiness, Anna's wounded feelings evaporated and she was consumed by the yearning to be reconciled with him. She hurtled herself into his arms with such force she nearly knocked him over. "Of course I forgive you!" she exclaimed.

After they'd nearly hugged the breath right out of each other, Anna dropped her arms and said, "I need to ask you to forgive me, too. Your suspicion that Aaron still had feelings for me was correct. But because I didn't reciprocate even an ounce of that affection, I was completely blind to his behaviors and I dismissed your concerns. I'm sorry. Perhaps if I had been more aware—"

"I'm not eavesdropping," Evan announced loudly from where he stood by the side of the house. "*Mamm* sent me out here to see if you want any supper before they put the leftovers away, Anna."

Anna laughed. "*Jah*, please. I'll be in in a few minutes and Fletcher would like to join me, as well."

"Alright, if you want to," the boy said to Fletcher, ruefully shaking his head. "But Melinda made ground beef and cabbage skillet and it tastes even worse than it smells. Eli called it ground beef and *skunk cabbage* skillet!"

"Evan!" Anna scolded, but the child had already darted off.

"Are you sure it's okay if I *kumme* in for supper?" Fletcher asked. "Naomi didn't seem too happy to see me earlier."

"She'll be delighted now," Anna insisted. "So will Evan and Eli, since it will mean fewer of Melinda's leftovers for them tomorrow!"

Oh, how Fletcher had missed this kind of easygoing repartee the past few days. "Okay, but just don't tell Naomi I climbed the tree outside your window. She'll lecture me to no end."

"Well, I can't blame her for that—you could have slipped and gotten a concussion," Anna joked. "And I would have been devastated if you didn't remember me."

No sooner had she spoken the words than she clapped her hand over her mouth.

"That's how I injured myself!" she exclaimed. "I fell as I was letting myself down from the tree."

"You climbed the maple tree, too?" Fletcher wondered.

"*Neh*, the willow," Anna expounded. "I was letting myself down from the last branch, but my feet couldn't quite touch the ground. When I released my grip, I sort of floundered and then toppled backward. I remember bouncing onto my backside and thinking 'that wasn't so bad,' and then total darkness."

"You must have hit your head on a rock as you tumbled. But why were you climbing the tree in the first place? You weren't hiding, were you?"

"*Neh*, I wasn't hiding. Rather, I wasn't hiding myself. I was hiding my journal, which contained a terrible secret. You see, the day after our wedding intentions were published, Aaron came to me at the creek and confessed he never really loved Melinda. He'd only been trying to make me jealous, which didn't work, of course. I captured it all in my journal, even the part where he kissed me…" Anna shivered, making an awful face.

Fletcher felt his jaw harden and his temples pulsate, but he silently prayed, *Forgive us our trespasses as we forgive those who trespass against us*. If Anna could forgive Aaron for kissing her, he could, too.

She continued, "So actually, you were partially right when you thought the 'A.' in my note referred to Aaron. I did have serious concerns about him I needed to discuss with you before the wedding preparations went any further. But the wedding preparations I was referring to were Aaron and Melinda's, not ours!"

"Oh, Anna, I'm so sorry," Fletcher said.

"You've already apologized, Fletcher, and it's understandable why you might have thought what you thought, at least initially, so please say no more," Anna replied. "The important thing now is that Melinda needs to know the truth."

"*Jah*, but Aaron is the one who needs to tell her, not us. I'll have a word with him. Something tells me he won't want to risk getting in any more hot water with his *daed*. He'll own up, don't worry. Meanwhile—" Fletcher bent to retrieve the gift bag from where he'd left it propped against the tree "—this is for you."

"*Denki*," Anna said. She gingerly removed the colorful bouquet of tissue paper to retrieve the bag's contents: a leather-bound journal with a silver lock on the side and a willow tree embossed on the front cover. "It's beautiful!"

"But now that you've found yours, I guess you don't really need a second one."

"But I do!" she protested. "My old journal is nearly full. I can use this to record the next chapter of our lives together."

Fletcher lightly ran his knuckle beneath Anna's chin, tilting her face toward his. "I just hope the next chapter isn't as rocky as the past few weeks have been."

"Oh, but all *gut* love stories have a few rocky patches. That's how they get their beauty," Anna said. "I wouldn't change our story for anything in the world."

"Neither would I," Fletcher agreed as he searched her eyes. They had never appeared so dazzling.

"What is it?" she asked. "Why are you staring at me that way?"

"I haven't seen that look in your eyes for a long, long time," he whispered.

"It's a look of recognition," she whispered back, causing his heart to throb. "I know who you are. No matter what I may remember or forget about the past, I know who you are."

"Who am I?" he asked playfully.

"You're Fletcher Josiah Chupp—*Gott*'s intended for me."

"And you, Anna Catherine Weaver, are *Gott*'s intended for me," Fletcher pledged, pressing his forehead to hers.

"I love you," she murmured.

"And I love you," he echoed.

He could have stayed like that for hours, but when a breeze rustled the leaves overhead, Anna backed away. She smiled, revealing her dimple, and then linked her fingers with his. "*Kumme*, let's go inside. I can't wait to tell Naomi her faithful prayers have been answered!"

Epilogue

Anna expected tears or even an outburst from Melinda the evening Aaron called off their wedding, but instead, the young woman almost seemed relieved.

"I enjoy working in the shop more than anything I've ever done," she told Anna, taking off her prayer *kapp* in preparation for bed. "But I'd have to quit working if I had a *bobbel* after I got married. Besides, once you move out, I'll have this entire room to myself. It will be a little bit like having a home of my own, without all of the work of a house."

"But aren't you sad about…about Aaron?" Anna carefully inquired.

"Why should I be sad? It's not his fault his salary was cut because he's no longer the foreman. His *daed* needs his personal help with their Highland Springs customers—it would be selfish of him to put marrying and building a costly house for me above his obligation to his *daed*." Melinda lowered her voice as if to reveal a great secret. "Isaiah's getting older, you know. He has *arthritis*."

"That's why Aaron told you he wanted to call off the wedding?" Anna asked, thoroughly astounded by his ability to concoct a tale that actually bore some semblance, however slight, to the truth. She found herself wondering if he ever truly intended to be so disingenuous, or if he simply was so optimistically self-deceived he didn't realize how distorted his perspective was. No matter: as Fletcher reminded her, it wasn't her place to set Aaron's record straight.

"Jah," Melinda said as she ran a brush through her hair. "I told him I understood, but that I didn't know if I wanted to continue to walk out with him."

"Really?" Anna's eyebrows shot up.

"Jah." She leaned forward and whispered. "Don't tell anyone I said this, but I heard that Joseph Schrock's nephew Jesse is coming to visit for the summer. He's about my age and by all counts, he's supposedly very charming."

Even after a year of living with Melinda, Anna still never knew what was going to come out of the young woman's mouth next, but she supposed in this instance, it was a good thing Melinda had such a fickle attention span: it seemed to have saved her from a world of hurt.

Anna slid her feet under her quilt. Soon, it would be too warm for such a heavy bed covering. "By the way, have you seen the fabric for my dress?" she asked. "I left it in the other side of the attic but it's missing and there's only about a week and a half until the wedding."

"*Neh*. But I thought you were supposed to be cured of amnesia." Melinda yawned.

"I *am* cured. Mostly, anyway. But there's a difference between the fabric being missing and forgetting where I put it. I'm telling you, it's not where I left it!"

"What's not where you left it?" Naomi asked. She'd crept up the stairs without Anna hearing her and she was standing in the doorway with her arms behind her back.

"My wedding dress fabric. I can't find it and I hardly have any time to sew my dress."

"That's because you spent too much time working on Melinda's dress, even though Dr. Donovan warned you to restrict your sewing activities."

Anna felt her face go warm as Melinda giggled. "I think that's the first time I've ever heard Naomi scold you, Anna!"

Anna playfully tossed a pillow at her cousin. "At least I'm being scolded for doing too much work instead of too little," she responded.

"Now, girls, do I have to separate you two?" Naomi teased, joining their laughter. She entered the room, displaying a deep green dress across one arm, and a dark purple dress on the other. "One for you, one for me, and Melinda's dress makes three."

Melinda and Anna both jumped out of their beds. Melinda darted to the closet while Anna approached Naomi and accepted her dress.

Holding it to her shoulders so it draped along the front of her figure, she looked down admiringly and said, "Oh, *denki*, Naomi. It's beautiful. Look—I can't even see the stitches they're so tiny!"

"Let's try them on, all three of us at once!" Melinda cried, sliding her own dress off its hanger.

"Melinda, you know that vanity is sinful," Naomi chastised.

"*Jah*, but we need to make sure they fit," Anna wheedled. "Please?"

"Not you, too, Anna!" Naomi clucked before agreeing it made sense that they should be certain no alterations were needed.

As soon as Melinda had changed, she twirled in a circle and asked her aunt, "What do you think?"

"It's a perfect fit," Naomi said carefully. "Anna did a very nice job sewing it for you."

Melinda's shoulders slumped and her lip jutted out. "But what do you think of how I look?"

Naomi blinked rapidly and wiped away a tear. "I think you look more and more like your lovely *mamm*—my sister—each day."

Melinda pranced to the mirror to view her reflection and Naomi turned toward Anna. In the soft glow of the lamp's light, Naomi appeared youthful and elegant, the lines of worry seemingly erased from her skin.

"I knew that color would be striking on you," Anna whispered. "I wish *Daed* could see you now."

"I wish he could see *you*," Naomi responded. "But when Fletcher gets a glimpse, you're going to set his heart aflutter!"

Anna threw her arms around Naomi, half crying, half laughing. "*Denki*, Naomi. *Denki* for sewing my dress and for your encouragement and for your prayers. *Denki* for everything!"

"There, there, we don't want to wrinkle our dresses," Naomi said, but instead of letting go, she squeezed Anna even tighter.

The wedding ceremony was everything Fletcher prayed it would be: he'd never been as certain of anything as he was when he answered "yes" to the bishop's four traditional wedding questions, especially the one about whether Fletcher was confident that the Lord had provided Anna as a marriage partner for him. Anna's voice rang out with an equally clear affirmation when the same question was posed to her about Fletcher.

The dinner following the three-hour sermon was especially bountiful, thanks to Naomi and also to his aunt and cousins, who generously shared their supply of celery for the traditional Amish wedding dishes, as well as other ingredients and foods they'd already begun preparing for Aaron's wedding. Tessa and Katie Fisher spent several days baking an excess of pies, cookies and other goodies. And, despite the short notice, Faith Yoder managed to deliver the most unusual wedding cake she said any bride—including Melinda—had ever requested: turtle cake.

To her credit, Melinda was a huge help on the day of the wedding. After the ceremony, she was in high spirits, flitting about the house in her violet dress and engaging the guests in conversation as if she were the bride herself. Although Aaron appeared forlorn at first, Fletcher later noticed him laughing with the young

Emma Lamp in the parlor. As afternoon gave way to evening, Naomi and his aunt and cousins spread the tables with supper and more desserts, and the last local guests stayed until after ten o'clock.

Shortly after that, Fletcher readied his own buggy while Anna was inside saying her final goodbyes to Naomi and the rest of the overnight visitors. He'd just provided his faithful horse a carrot when the door swung open and his three sisters, Esther, Leah and Rebekah, emerged.

"You look disappointed. You must have been expecting Anna instead of us," Leah needled him. "She'll be right out."

"Are you getting impatient?" Esther asked.

"Neh," he answered. "I'll wait for Anna as long as it takes."

"Spoken like a man in love," Rebekah noted. "But you don't have to wait any longer, here *kummes* your bride now."

As Anna stepped outside, the light from the kitchen illuminated her silhouette. Although it was too dark to see her face, he could hear the smile in her voice when she said, *"Gut nacht,* everyone, and *denki.* See you tomorrow."

"Are you certain you don't want to spend the night at Naomi's house?" Fletcher asked when she was seated beside him. That was the customary Amish expectation of the bride and groom, because it enabled them to assist with the cleanup first thing in the morning.

"Just this once, I think we ought to do something irresponsible," Anna answered. Then she corrected herself. "Well, not irresponsible, since we'll *kumme* back to help bright and early, but something—"

"Out of character?" he asked.

"*Jah.* Besides, the house is bursting at the seams with out-of-state guests."

"That's true," Fletcher said. His pulse pounded louder and louder in his ears the closer they got to home. He couldn't wait to show Anna the alcove he'd created for her.

But when he brought the horse to a halt, she said, "Wait, before we step down, I have a gift for you. There wasn't really any way I could wrap it, so you have to take a look at it now. It's in the back seat, under the tarp."

"When did you have a chance to sneak a present back there?"

"I didn't," Anna replied, giggling. "Your *newehockers*, Chandler and Gabriel, put it in the buggy for me while I distracted you. Go ahead—see what it is."

Using the flashlight he kept secured to a hook in the front of his buggy to supply him with light, Fletcher twisted in the seat and lifted the tarp.

"A fishing rod!" he exclaimed. "*Denki*, Anna, it's a really nice one."

"Roy and Raymond told me that yours snapped the other day and I know how you enjoy fishing," she said. "You should be able to bring in a *gut* catch down at the creek using that rod."

"*Denki,*" Fletcher repeated. "But *you're* my best catch, Anna."

Her laughter made light work of stabling the horse

and soon Fletcher was accompanying her to the house. He kissed her once on the cheek before he unlocked the kitchen door and led her down the hall in the dark.

Before illuminating the room in the alcove, he confessed, "I realize I said I didn't want either of us to feel as if we were hiding anything from each other, but there is one thing I admit I've been keeping a secret."

After Fletcher turned up the gas lamp, Anna blinked several times. Rendered completely speechless, she ran her hands over the shelves and opened each of the drawers before perching on the window seat.

"Fletcher, I don't know what to say," she cried. "I can't believe how beautiful this room is."

"I made it exclusively for you," he said. "So you'll have the space and privacy you need to read or write. There is one condition, however."

"Anything," she said.

"You can't use the room to write, *Fletcher Chupp, what a heel*, in your diary," he said softly into her ear.

"I accept the terms of the agreement," she pledged.

"Not *gut* enough," he replied. "You have to seal your promise with a kiss."

Leaning in, he gave her a firm, meaningful kiss. When he pulled away, he stared into her eyes, which were exquisitely enhanced by the green tint of her dress.

Suddenly, Anna clapped her hands against her cheeks as her eyes widened and her mouth dropped open. "Oh *neh*!" she exclaimed.

"What is it?"

"I think I may be suffering a relapse of amnesia. I can't recall what happened just now between us."

Fletcher threw back his head to laugh. "Don't worry," he consoled her. "I know how to jog your memory."

"With sage tea?" she flirted.

"Neh," he answered. "With this."

He feathered his lips across hers once, twice, three times before asking, "Is what happened coming back to you now?"

"Not quite," she teased. "It's still a bit hazy. But that's alright. As Dr. Donovan said, you and I have a lifetime to make memories together…"

Fletcher chuckled and wrapped his arms around her. A warm breeze wafted through the window: spring was definitely here, a season of hope, a season of renewal, a season of love. He and Anna were married at last.

* * * * *

WE HOPE YOU
ENJOYED THIS
LOVE
INSPIRED®
BOOK.

If you were **inspired** by this

uplifting, **heartwarming** romance,

be sure to look for all six Love

Inspired® books every month.

Love Inspired®

Save $1.00

on the purchase of ANY

Love Inspired® or

Love Inspired® Suspense book.

Available wherever books are sold,
including most bookstores, supermarkets,
drugstores and discount stores.

✂

Save $1.00

on the purchase of ANY Love Inspired® or Love Inspired® Suspense book.

Coupon valid until August 30, 2019.
Redeemable at participating retail outlets in the U.S. and Canada only.
Limit one coupon per customer.

52616381

Canadian Retailers: Harlequin Enterprises Limited will pay the face value of this coupon plus 10.25¢ if submitted by customer for this product only. Any other use constitutes fraud. Coupon is nonassignable. Void if taxed, prohibited or restricted by law. Consumer must pay any government taxes. Void if copied. Inmar Promotional Services ("IPS") customers submit coupons and proof of sales to Harlequin Enterprises Limited, P.O. Box 31000, Scarborough, ON M1R 0E7, Canada. Non-IPS retailer—for reimbursement submit coupons and proof of sales directly to Harlequin Enterprises Limited, Retail Marketing Department, Bay Adelaide Centre, East Tower, 22 Adelaide Street West, 40th Floor, Toronto, Ontario M5H 4E3, Canada.

U.S. Retailers: Harlequin Enterprises Limited will pay the face value of this coupon plus 8¢ if submitted by customer for this product only. Any other use constitutes fraud. Coupon is nonassignable. Void if taxed, prohibited or restricted by law. Consumer must pay any government taxes. Void if copied. For reimbursement submit coupons and proof of sales directly to Harlequin Enterprises, Ltd 482, NCH Marketing Services, P.O. Box 880001, El Paso, TX 88588-0001, U.S.A. Cash value 1/100 cents.

5 65373 00076 2 (8100)0 12422

LICOUP47010

*When a young Amish man needs help finding a wife, his
beautiful matchmaker agrees to give him dating lessons…*

Read on for a sneak preview of
A Perfect Amish Match *by Vannetta Chapman,
available May 2019 from Love Inspired!*

"Dating is so complicated."

"People are complicated, Noah. Every single person you meet
is dealing with something."

He asked, "How did you get so wise?"

"Never said I was."

"I'm being serious. How did you learn to navigate so seamlessly
through these kinds of interactions, and why aren't you married?"

Olivia Mae thought her eyes were going to pop out of her head.
"Did you really just ask me that?"

"I did."

"A little intrusive."

"Meaning you don't want to answer?"

"Meaning it's none of your business."

"Fair enough, though it's like asking a horse salesman why he
doesn't own a horse."

"My family situation is…unique."

"You mean with your grandparents?"

She nodded instead of answering.

"I've got it." Noah resettled his hat, looking quite pleased with
himself.

"Got what?"

"The solution to my dating disasters."

He leaned forward, close enough that she could smell the
shampoo he'd used that morning.

"You need to give me dating lessons."

"What do you mean?"

"You and me. We'll go on a few dates…say, three. You can learn how to do anything if you do it three times."

"That's a ridiculous suggestion."

"Why? I learn better from doing."

"Do you?"

"I've already learned not to take a girl to a gas station, but who knows how many more dating traps are waiting for me."

"So this would be…a learning experience."

"It's a perfect solution." He tugged on her *kapp* string, something no one had done to her since she'd been a young teen.

"I can tell by the shock on your face that I've made you uncomfortable. It's a *gut* idea, though. We'd keep it businesslike— nothing personal."

Olivia Mae had no idea why the thought of sitting through three dates with Noah Graber made her stomach twirl like she'd been on a merry-go-round. Maybe she was catching a stomach bug.

"Wait a minute. Are you trying to get out of your third date? Because you promised your *mamm* that you would give this thing three solid attempts."

"And I'll keep my word on that," Noah assured her. "After you've tutored me, you can throw another poor unsuspecting girl my way."

Olivia Mae stood, brushed off the back of her dress and pointed a finger at Noah, who still sat in the grass as if he didn't have a care in the world.

"All right. I'll do it."

Don't miss
A Perfect Amish Match *by Vannetta Chapman,*
available May 2019 wherever
Love Inspired® books and ebooks are sold.

www.LoveInspired.com

Looking for inspiration in tales
of hope, faith and heartfelt romance?

Check out **Love Inspired**® and
Love Inspired® **Suspense** books!

New books available every month!

CONNECT WITH US AT:

Facebook.com/groups/HarlequinConnection

 Facebook.com/HarlequinBooks

 Twitter.com/HarlequinBooks

 Instagram.com/HarlequinBooks

Pinterest.com/HarlequinBooks

ReaderService.com

LIGENRE2018R2